Chain Reaction

The Agency

Volume One

Chain Reaction

K.P. Merriweather

Majestik Multimedia · St. Louis

Chain Reaction
The Agency: Volume 1
Published by Majestik Multimedia
A subsidiary of Create Space Independent Publishing Platform
Copyright © 2009 Kimberly Merriweather

First Edition

This book is set in Georgia Type Text, with some portions in Imperial BT.

Printed in the United States of America
First Edition: November 2013
First Printing: November 2013
Second Printing: October 2014
Third Printing: December 2015

ISBN-13: 978-0692309988

ISBN-10: 0692309985

For more awesomeness, visit *Majestik Multimedia*!

www.majestikmultimedia.com

PART ONE

Insight Out

ONE

Fade away into the light that shines, seeing what darkness lies here before you...

A message, sent from another place, another time, just off the border...

Separated without form, in the realm of memory...

Worlds apart of your waking mind...

There lies another, who has your face, through the mirror...

In the space without days, without nights as you tread the halls of sanity...

From the darkness into the light, so fragile the threads, how they disappear...

There is a message from another time...

Go beyond the pain from the light into the darkness...

***

Erik Hart awakened with a gasp, chilled as cold sweat stung his eyes and ran down his face and neck. The shadows from the realm of dreaming slowly parted and his eyes adjusted to dawning sunshine filtering through his bedroom window, with weak rays of morning sun cutting into the pale white tiled walls.

The intense glow of fluorescence from buzzing plate lights beamed harshly down shifted into warm yellow wallpaper that had faint fluffy, cotton-candy clouds on a blue-sky background.

The sensation of hard leather straps holding down his wrists fell away to twisted bed sheets and the medicated smell gave way to the odor of bacon wafting from the kitchen downstairs.

His initial sensation of fear also dissipated into the realization that he was safely and comfortably in his own bed and not strapped onto some foreign restraining table. Yet, the coppery scent of blood never seemed to fully go away...

"Why do I keep having terrible dreams like this?" Erik thought, groaning as he pulled the bedspread over his head, knowing he would not be able to take much pleasure in rest any longer.

"Erik, it's time to get up," a faint female voice called.

"Not yet..." Erik moaned and turned onto his face, burying his head into the pillow.

"Come on, Son," called a cheerful male voice. "Rise and shine!"

"It's a nice day today," said a female Erik barely recognized. "Let's go out and enjoy it..."

Erik blew a heavy sigh in return. *"They just won't let up,"* he mused, hearing his bedroom door open. "Alright, I'm getting up!" he grumbled.

Reaching out, Erik paused when his hand touched cold steel. Before his mind could figure what his fingers grasped, Erik froze, hearing that all-too familiar metallic click.

"Die," a dark voice hissed.

Erik quickly sat up and stumbled out of bed, landing on the floor with a hard thud. His head crashed against his nightstand and he clutched it, reeling in pain as his ears rang loudly.

Erik panted weakly for breath, trying to focus on his surroundings and make sense of where he was. Grasping a hand to his chest, he took in a shallow breath and let it out slowly, concentrating on keeping in his banging heart threatening to jump out the confines of his ribs.

Erik blew a shaky sigh and he rubbed at his eyes, trying to adjust to his surroundings, relieved when he found no one standing before him wielding any weapons to do him some grievous bodily harm. He moaned and hunched forward, wiping a hand over his face drenched with cold sweat, struggling to recall where he had been.

Annoyed that his head felt stuffed with cotton, he cursed at himself when no matter how hard he tried, his memory produced no results. Erik looked around the room, only to find that once his vision finally cleared, he stared at the blank beige walls of his apartment.

"I need to stop eating strange things so late," Erik muttered, kicking off the tangled sheets trapping his ankles. Yawning loudly once he got to his feet and stretched, he padded down the short flight of stairs into the kitchen and switched on the electric percolator.

Turning on the small television he had stationed on the nearby counter, Erik let the morning news filter in as he headed back to the bathroom to get ready for the day.

Washing his face, Erik looked back into the mirror and stared back at a porcelain-skinned young man with fiery red hair and sleepy deep-set emerald green eyes who had slight freckles dotted across his narrow nose and highly defined cheeks. He smiled, displaying straight white teeth.

"Looking good," he said brightly at his reflection and finished washing in the face bowl. Returning to his bedroom, Erik stepped into a pair of pajama pants, then glanced out to the busy street below as he tied the ties around his narrow waist.

Approaching the glass doors, he opened them wide and stepped out onto the small balcony, taking in the sights of the morning rush while watching cars going to their various destinations, choking the air with their exhaust.

On the horizon, looming high above the rest of the buildings, was the famous hundred-storey Farmless Tower at the edge of the city. The crystal-like structure held numerous offices and machinery that controlled the city's power grid, only accessible by underground elevators.

It seemed to hover above ground with no wires with a single steel support beam running through its center that also served as its antenna. Surrounded by many panels coated with shiny, almost iridescent blue material that soaked in the sun's rays to keep the electricity it harbored flowing, it was not only the city's monument, but also the city's singular power source.

The testament to the former farm and mining town's tower ran a newly discovered energy source, a substance called Corite. The diamond-like mineral burned like coal, though very slowly and it provided billions of hours of energy in addition to heat for millions of homes in the area. The strange mineral was also claimed to save the planet.

Shaking his head to clear the vague memories almost reaching the surface of his mind, Erik experienced slight illness in the pit of his stomach as he left the window and returned to the parlor.

He opened the drapes and the room became washed in morning light. Erik perched on the edge of his simple dark beige leather couch, enjoying the view of the bustling city in which he lived, also admiring the people who went about their day.

The telephone's shrill ring interrupted Erik's thoughts and he slipped off the couch, fetching the receiver from the end table close to the kitchen.

Picking it up, all he heard was a dial tone. Staring back at the receiver, he noted it was a blue-green princess model from a telephone company he could not quite call to mind. Erik shut his eyes, clutching the receiver as another faint memory surfaced. He grew tense, unable to suppress the ill feelings it caused.

"Erik," the faint female voice called to him, "who was that?"

"They didn't say, Mother," Erik called back.

"Maybe they realized they dialed the wrong number..."

"Maybe you're right."

Erik opened his eyes and cried out in alarm when he found he held a pink princess model. Dropping it as if it were hot, he watched the receiver hang by its cord and swing from the end table's ledge.

Turning away, Erik slowly counted to five and peered over his shoulder, finding the blue-green telephone back in its place with the receiver resting on the cradle. Blowing a disconcerted sigh, Erik returned to the kitchen. The scent of coffee permeated the air and he drew a cup to drink while watching the newscast.

Erik sat curled at the kitchen table, sipping plain black coffee from a mug while he half-listened to the droning reporter read out reports. He choked at the sight of his picture on the small screen with the caption underneath stating 'wanted for questioning'. The mug crashed to the floor as Erik came closer, turning up the volume.

"That can't be...!" he murmured and touched the glass surface as he peered at the screen more closely. "But it *is* me..."

At a loss when unable to remember the night before, Erik madly searched his mind for clues to where he had been. The ring of the telephone startled him and Erik left the kitchen, immediately picking up the line.

"You have twenty minutes," said a cold female voice.

Erik stared at the receiver in dismay while the dial tone flooded his end of the line. He slammed the receiver back in the cradle and bolted for the bedroom.

"... Considered a prime suspect wanted for questioning about the murder of a federal official," said the voice of the reporter as Erik sifted frantically through his closet.

He paused once finding a suitcase with a note taped on its side: 'for when you need it', then opened it, revealing a change of clothing and a smaller case taped with a note: 'for emergency use only'.

Opening the smaller case, he found a thin translucent blue pen with a silvery-blue cap resting inside and several cartridges. His fingers tingled slightly as he took out the pen and removed the cap, revealing a crystal nib.

"What a strange fountain pen," Erik muttered, unable to decipher its meaning. He tucked the pen behind his ear and strained to hear the continuing newscast in the next room as he changed into jeans, T-shirt and slip-on sneakers.

"Menoka City public security officers and Montana State troopers are on guard;" continued the reporter, "as Federal and other law enforcement officials are citing caution, for this individual may be armed and highly dangerous..."

The telephone rang again, and Erik quickly snapped shut the case, taking it with him as he hurried downstairs. Nervous as he slowly approached the phone, Erik picked up the receiver once more with shaking hands.

"Go to where the stars shine brightly," said the mysterious female voice. Erik cringed, startled at the sound of a sudden bang outside his door. "Oh, and by the way, they're directly outside." The click followed and he dropped the receiver.

Rushing for the balcony, Erik let go of the case and threw open the glass doors. Before he could leap out onto the sidewalk below, sudden electricity surged through him. Erik howled in pain and involuntarily sank to his knees, stunned and unable to move.

Suddenly charged as the sensation immediately passed, Erik scampered to his feet, picking up the case along with him. He swung it at one uniformed guard who dodged the attack.

The guard, wearing a dark cap and glasses, rushed for Erik and Erik knocked him back with force from one more swing. The guard tumbled backwards into another who came directly behind him. The third jumped on Erik's back, wrestling him down to the ground. Erik cried out, dropping the case and it struck the floor with a dull thump.

Erik ground his teeth as his arms were tied back with an orange ring. The guard tightened the restraining device around his wrists, applying enough pressure to cut off his hands.

Erik screamed when another jolt of electricity blasted through him, sending him forward on his knees. Panting hard for breath, he tensed when heavy footsteps stormed up to him from his side. A fourth officer grabbed his hair with a heavy hand, yanking back his head.

Forced to look up, Erik faced a uniformed officer wearing a dark helmet with a smoky visor that concealed his eyes. Erik spat at the officer and his head whipped to the side from a heavy backhand.

"We expected more of a fight outta you, boy," sneered the guard.

Erik noted their uniforms were similar, though the one who held his head had three gold buttons on the collar of the suit, while the three others had one silver button.

"*He must be the leader*," Erik thought, wincing when violently shaken. "*Why does his voice sound familiar...?*"

"Anything to say, boy?"

"What do you want with me?" Erik grumbled.

The uniformed guardsman withdrew a small silver pen from his pocket, flipped a switch on its side and shone a blue light into Erik's eyes. Erik yowled in pain and shied away.

"You ain't goin' nowhere, boy."

"It seems I have no choice."

Erik yowled when the guard increased his grip.

"Now tell me what you know," demanded the sentry.

"I don't remember anything," Erik spat and groaned when his head propelled back from another hard slap.

He wheezed for breath through gritted teeth as his nose bled and stiffened when he saw himself kneeling over a bloodstained body wearing a suit and carried a silver attaché case riddled with bullets.

"We saw the aftermath of your little show," snapped the guard.

"But...!" Erik yelped when struck again. He shook his head, trying to clear the grisly image of himself pulling the dead body out into a deserted alley and hoisting it with apparent ease into a large refuse bin.

"Who sent you?" demanded the guard.

"Nobody!" Erik protested.

"What we want is an answer: yes or no."

"I don't understand -- for what?"

The lead guardsman let out a short laugh, and the three others chimed in with nervous guffaws. "Hear that, men?" he crowed, "He wants to know 'for what'!" The guard grabbed Erik by the throat and yanked him up, holding him dangling several inches from the floor. "Don't play stupid with me, boy."

"I don't remember," rasped Erik, "honest!"

"Do you think he got wiped before returning here, Sir?" asked the guard behind Erik. "The attaché case that held the schematics was never recovered..."

"My scanner picks up that he hadn't uploaded any programs to the system," said the one behind the head officer, holding a small chirping monitoring device.

"He's clean, Sir," murmured the guard on the lead officer's other side.

"Check that case of his," barked the senior warden. "The one you fools didn't recover is most likely in plain sight!"

"On it," one junior guard replied.

Erik kicked back at the officer's chest and the guard let go, dropping him as a heap on the floor. Erik flipped to his feet and paused, hearing a high whine and facing a sleek black pistol at his forehead.

"I suggest you stop struggling, boy," the high-ranked officer sneered. Erik slackened; watching listlessly at the two guardsmen closest to the senior officer opened the case and sweep it with small hand-held scanners.

"Just an ordinary change of clothes and a fountain pen set, Sir," said one guard. "No blueprints."

"Do you think it's the *other* one?"

"Either way, kill him."

Erik broke out in cold sweat when the three remaining officers withdrew their pistols, pointing at him.

"*This can't be the end!*" Erik thought and screamed when all four shot at him at once. The immediate plain blinded him and he hit the floor on his side.

Suddenly Erik heard his heart beating in his ears and he gasped after realizing he wasn't dead. His eyes snapped open and dark cyan electricity surrounded his body. Sitting up, he shook his head, getting rid of the initial stun.

"Stop him!"

Erik rolled out of the way, dodging four more beams of high-powered shots before standing unsteadily to his feet. His hands grew eerily warm and the orange ties restraining him shattered, freeing his wrists. Sensing stinging pain at his ear, Erik reached up, locating the slender pen still tucked behind his ear.

"Don't you dare, boy!" snarled the head guardsman as he turned the dials on the side of his pistol.

"What?" Erik spat back and waved the pen at them. "It's a damn pen!" he shouted. "What are you getting freaked out over?"

The officer readjusted the settings on his gun and Erik drew in a sharp breath in shock, watching in awe when the pen began glowing in faint green light. Bright white light suddenly flashed and the pen transformed into a blue steel long sword.

"Get out of here!" Erik shouted, waving intensely cackling sword in their general direction. "Don't make me use this -- whatever this is!"

He turned, slashing at one officer who approached from behind, felling him in a wing of silver light that cut his torso in half. Blood splashed over him and the hardwood floor and stained the wall behind him. Erik backed away, shuddering in fright as the two remaining junior guards stepped away, clearly disturbed.

"Sir..." murmured one, "what do you think...?"

"Well, I think..." the second one interjected.

"It doesn't matter what you think!" roared the head guard and fired at Erik. Erik seethed and staggered back, clutching his wounded shoulder that bled blue blood.

"*What's going on here?*" Erik wondered, heaving for breath. "*What should I do now?*"

"You're just lucky, boy," snapped the lead officer. "Look, let's get this over with and let us kill you -- let it be quick and painless."

"Not this time!" Erik shrilled.

"Yeah, I know there's probably nothing in the world that can hurt you, but that doesn't mean you're gonna stop me from finishing my job, boy."

"You're down by one!"

The head guard turned away, cupping an ear with his gloved hand. "Second team, take him out," he ordered. "He's a little hostile..."

Erik turned around as several more helmeted guardsmen burst through the front door of the apartment. He turned for the balcony and ducked, then kicked away the first guard.

"*This is insane,*" thought Erik as he sliced through one on his left and one from behind.

Another guard attempted to force him to drop the blade by grabbing his arm. Erik slammed his back into the wall, struggling to loosen the fighter's tight grip. He hurled the guard toward the balcony's window, sending him crashing through the glass.

Erik ran on automatic, decimating his highly equipped opponents with a long sword that hummed as he swung it through the air, effortlessly cutting through flesh as if it were a hot knife through butter.

Only the senior warden remained in the limb-strewn bloodstained parlor floor, standing across from Erik as he panted heavily for breath. The guard had few gashes in his uniform and a cracked helmet.

"If I can't get what I said through to you," wheezed the guard, "then I've got other means…"

"Obviously you don't seem to understand that you're outmatched," spat Erik. "Now get out of here!"

"Not when we have a fail-safe," a familiar voice said from behind. Erik turned and took a step back, facing a golden handgun pointed at his head held by a smiling young man, a stranger to Erik who happened to have his face.

"Who are you?" Erik asked and swallowed hard when the pistol shone brightly in dark vermilion light.

"Well, well," the young man said, "it's a shame that you woke up too late…"

"…What?" A blast of gunfire blinded Erik and his ears rang. Seeing nothing but red, he lost his grip on the sword and staggered backward, then tripped over the edge.

In the nanosecond as he plunged, Erik realized with absurd clarity what a beautiful and perfectly still day it was, with no wind and few clouds. He looked up in mute horror after it dawned on him that he was free-falling. He stared up at a stranger who had his face who grinned madly at the sight of his impending end.

As gravity took hold and Erik started the rocket ride ever swiftly down, he entertained ideas of seeing himself crashing barely a quarter-mile onto the ground below, where his body would become nothing more than a soft, wet, smashed beef slab and his skull disintegrating into fine powder.

Erik prayed to any deity who would listen to die of shock before the harsh reality of death's painful onslaught overtook him.

TWO

Erik's eyes snapped open and he realized he faced a plain white ceiling and not a blood-tinged sky. Glancing cautiously to his side, he found the familiar yellow wallpaper and waited for his swiftly-beating heart to still.

Why is it happening again...?

"I'm probably only nervous since I'm starting a new high school today," Erik murmured once the familiar sights and smells did not change.

He carefully sat up, gripping the sheets and slowly counted back from twenty under his breath until he could hear again. The smell of frying bacon returned to titillate his nose and the sweet voice he always liked to hear drifted upstairs and he knew things were back to where they should be.

You will never truly cleanse yourself of this...

"*And what's that?*" Erik thought. Hearing no answer, he hurried out of bed and across the hall, showered quickly and returned to his room to rummage through his chest of drawers, looking for something decent to wear.

Knocking over several frames of various photographs in his rush, Erik quickly righted them and gave pause to one portrait of a young woman. Erik frowned, studying the woman with bright indigo eyes wearing her raven hair pinned up in a loose chignon. She smiled brightly at the camera before a pale ocean blue background and he frowned when nothing occurred to him about her.

Turning the frame around, Erik found the back loosened and pulled it apart to readjust. He spotted a faint inscription written in an elegant hand in the upper right-hand corner on the back: *let your spirit prevail at any given cost.*

"*What a strange thing to write,*" Erik mused. "*I look at it and nothing ever comes to mind...*" At a loss when unable to recollect who she was and wondering why he had a photograph of her on his dresser, Erik set it back, overwhelmed by mixed emotions and faint guilt biting at him when he placed the photograph before all others. He swallowed hard. "*It's like I should know who she is, yet, it's like I'm not allowed to...*"

Erik threw on briefs, undershirt then hopped around, pulling on his socks and later grabbed his already-pressed clothes folded neatly in the drawer - a yellow button-down flannel shirt and jeans.

Grabbing a braided leather belt from his closet and tossing all three items on the bed, Erik returned to his mirror on the back of the door, staring at his likeness shining back at him from the reflection of the sunlight.

These dreams mean something else...

"This is a new day for me," Erik said to the mirror as he pulled on his jeans, "and I'm going to give this school year my best shot!"

It must mean something sinister...

"I'm with this nice family," Erik continued, grabbing the button-down shirt from the bed and pulled into it. "I hope the

Greenfields won't be too clingy once I start freshman year. I've been catching up on my work in between hanging out with Raider and his friends..."

There are dark secrets they do not want you to know about...

"Sometimes I wonder why I'm here in the first place," Erik muttered, fiddling with the buttons. "I've always had this feeling that I don't *belong* here, that nobody really *cares* about me." His body suddenly turned numb and his face flushed in response as he cuffed his jeans. Grabbing the belt, he put it through the loops and buckled it tightly. Erik looked up, facing the reflection of a saddened sixteen-year-old staring back at him with intense blue eyes and slight freckles across the cheeks. "Still, I'm happy the Greenfields care about me. Without them, I'd probably be..." Sudden pain coursed through Erik's head and he grunted, staggering back as everything flashed in red.

You'd like to, wouldn't you? Given the chance, if it ever should happen...

"John," called a lighthearted voice from downstairs. "Check to see if he's awake."

"I'm on it, Jane," John Greenfield's voice called back. "Son," he called from outside Erik's bedroom door. "Are you ready?"

"I'm almost dressed, Father," Erik called back, falling onto his bed. He shook the fog from his head and flipped over, grabbing his tennis shoes from underneath the bed. Pulling into them, Erik winced from the sharp pain behind his eyes once he stood and gave his reflection another look.

With questions like these, who would answer them?

"Well, I'm dressed and ready to go," Erik murmured, running a hand through his cropped blond hair. "I have to get going... I'll do my heavy thinking later."

Erik moved his backpack off the bedpost, ignoring the noise in his head and grabbed his lucky cap from underneath. Opening the door, he hurried out into the hall and made his way down the stairs. Erik paused in the middle of the corridor when John Greenfield called for him.

"Are you heading out early?" John Greenfield asked. "You've got another hour; why don't you eat something first?"

"I'm heading over to Raider's place," Erik replied, turning around.

"Oh?" John Greenfield answered, standing in the master bedroom's doorway and combed back his brown hair styled into a pompadour.

John Greenfield wore navy slacks and trouser socks, lavender dress shirt, and an untied dark periwinkle tie hung loosely around his neck. Erik shifted anxiously on his feet, wanting meet Jane Greenfield downstairs and his breakfast.

"My friends are going to give me a ride to school today," Erik said. "I want to get there early so I won't make them wait."

"I'm sure you have time to eat. Besides, your mother just prepared a nice meal for you!" John Greenfield smiled brightly at Erik. "Stay for a moment and at least taste it. You don't want to pass out before lunch at school." He chuckled and Erik flushed slightly in response.

"What's special about eggs and toast?" Erik replied.

John Greenfield chortled. "You'll see."

Erik hurried down the rest of the stairs and entered the main hall. Turning left for the parlor, Erik approached the large sunny kitchen. His usual awe overcame him whenever he saw the morning sunshine brightening the modest whitewashed pane windows every time he came downstairs.

It's so unreal, and yet...

"Sit, Erik," Jane Greenfield said warmly to him as she headed to the old white refrigerator with the chrome accents. She wore a crisp white spotless apron over one of her usual beige dresses. "I have something special for you."

Erik paused, trying to sort out his emotions between fear and eager curiosity.

How many times have I heard that...?

Erik approached the kitchen table and placed his cap on the oak chair's post. "What did you get me?" he asked tentatively and dropped into his seat, sitting on his hands to keep from drumming the table's edge.

Erik's mind drifted, as if he were watching some other blond-haired blue-eyed teenager watching the woman silently as she pulled out a carton of milk and tended to the stove, pouring some of the contents into a pot.

What is wrong with you?

"*I'm fine,*" Erik told himself. "*Everything will be okay.*" He took in a shallow breath and shook his head, trying to clear his uncertain symptoms.

Will you be able to stand it much longer...?

"*What is it I'm on guard for...?*"

Pleased instead at Jane Greenfield, Erik let out a content sigh and put a hand under his chin, noting how her usual pale skin now had some flesh tone from contrasting against the bright red lipstick she always wore. He mused over the fact that he enjoyed the sound of her pearl bracelets that always clattered softly as she cooked.

How old are you now...?

Erik glanced behind him, trying to find the source of the voice. He cleared his throat as cold sweat broke out on the back of his neck.

"*If I mention it, they'll think I'm crazy,*" Erik mused.

Waiting patiently, he let his gaze fall on Jane Greenfield who continued working behind the stove and tried keeping his attention away from his idle thoughts. After several moments, she turned to Erik and gave him a plate of differently shaped food from all the other times she cooked him breakfast.

It still feels somehow wrong...

"Do you think you'll enjoy it?" Jane Greenfield asked, smiling lovingly down at Erik.

Erik winced, gazing at his plate holding a heart-shaped pancake, a fried egg with two sausage links for eyes and a slice of bacon for a mouth. "I wonder if it tastes as good as it looks?" Erik quipped and Jane Greenfield laughed lightly, blushing. He relished the sound; likening it to her glass wind chimes she had hanging over the carport.

She's faking and you know it!

Erik smiled warmly in return, trying to mask his general unease as he took up his fork.

"Do you know why I made it like this?" Jane Greenfield asked, breaking his thoughts. Erik shook his head, unable to formulate an answer. "For one, I love you very much. Secondly,

I think it's a wonderful surname for a wonderful young man!"
She kissed Erik on the cheek and he flushed, touching his
cheek, half-expecting for the lipstick to rub off.

"Er, thank you Mother," Erik replied, looking down at his
fingers in awe and noticed the stain did not rub off. *"What a
strange new invention,"* he mused. *"So modern..."*

What year is this...?

Erik glanced up at Jane Greenfield who grinned down at
him in return. "So eat up, honey," she said gaily. "You've got a
lot of work today!" Erik nodded and started the task of applying
the condiments as she left to tend to her stove.

Hopefully the work won't kill you this time around...

"This time...?" Erik wondered. While he was eating quickly
through the pancake, the bacon, sausage and eggs, Jane
Greenfield handed him another plate of toast and a bowl of
farina, along with a glass of orange juice and another of milk.
After eating those as well, he belched and excused himself.
*"Mother Greenfield will only cook such a large breakfast if
there's a special reason... I'm the special reason today!"*

But why exactly...?

After stacking the dirty dishes, Jane Greenfield scolded
Erik before he stepped out, and he reluctantly returned to help
wash and put the dishes away. Glancing at the clock, he realized
he only had five minutes to visit his friends.

"I hate to eat and run, Mother," Erik said apologetically,
kissing her on the cheek again.

He lingered a bit, secretly enjoying the scent of Jane
Greenfield's favorite perfume, a brand called 'Earth Magic' that
she wore to work daily. Hoping she would never switch to

another brand and the manufacturer would keep producing it, he thought the perfume reminded him of watered-down sugar and musk and something *else* he couldn't quite place...

Don't gag on the fumes, you idiot!

The ticking clock reminded Erik of the time and he pulled away, grabbing for his lucky cap.

"See you, Mother," Erik called and hurried through the parlor. He waved to John Greenfield descending the staircase and adjusting the cuffs of his crisp navy blazer.

"Take care, Son," John Greenfield chirped.

"See you later, Father!" Erik called and bolted out the front door.

THREE

Racing through the farm fields across the street from his house, many thoughts swirled through Erik's mind.

Why did the local farmers continue to complain about the Greenfields' two-storey ranch-style home being out of place from the other residences in farmland Montana?

Why did the Greenfields move from the larger city of Keely to the small town of Aynslea when they made a decent living at AMASTCOMS's office complex?

Why did a shadowy organization have so much interest in building mines in Keely and nearby Aynslea after work stopped in Menoka?

Why did City Hall clear so much land only to not use it and neither confirm nor deny any claims that it was used for secret government testing?

Giving the matter no further thought, Erik mulled about John Greenfield who seemed to enjoy being away from the nearby busy city of Keely.

John Greenfield admitted to laughing at his co-workers who constantly chided him, claiming he and his wife were half-baked to move out into such a rural area, forcing them to get up earlier to drive to the office in downtown Keely. Erik recalled the several days he had to prepare for school and talking to John Greenfield about it.

"Well, I personally don't mind this nice alternative," John Greenfield declared to Erik. "I like it here. It's nice and quiet and there are no gangs or drugs here." Erik shook his head as his adoptive father chuckled. "They hate it, knowing I'm always quick to point out how everyone else is mad to continue living in the city and yet has the audacity to complain about it."

"Why *did* you want to move out here?" Erik asked.

"I know moving to the outskirts of Aynslea after being in Keely for as long as you can remember doesn't seem like the brightest of ideas. Now don't tell anyone else, but I didn't want you to attend a school where there might be guns present, or our house vandalized into because of the reasonable sum of money we worked so hard for." John Greenfield tousled Erik's hair gently. "I also dislike the idea of hearing about students fighting each other after they've been stepped on by accident and the school system ignores this."

"But they haven't issued uniforms yet."

"Just be careful."

Erik secretly agreed with John Greenfield's thoughts and he personally disliked the idea of being bullied over the fact he would unintentionally ruin another pair of white hundred-dollar or more name-brand sneakers. Though he did not care all too much for uniforms, he felt if it cut down on the fighting, he'd put up with it, despite the flak he was bound to catch from his friends.

He was pleased the Greenfields enjoyed the quiet atmosphere, not having to be bothered by nosy neighbors. The farmers they sometimes met in passing were generally nice and friendly when spoken to, sometimes offering to help with various projects John Greenfield worked on around the house. Though sometimes the unsettling emotions he couldn't quite place burdened him.

They're hiding something... why else move into some backwater town away from everything and everyone?

"Hey, there he is!" a voice yelled, scattering Erik's current thoughts to the wind.

Erik looked up, catching sight of a large pickup truck coming toward him, throwing dust behind as it ground through the loose gravel road.

Forcing himself to slow his run so his feet would not leave the ground, Erik came down to a jog, then walked the rest of the way.

The truck idled for a moment and Erik placed his cap on his head then held a hand to his chest, still surprised at himself for not panting hard as other people usually did after running, especially at the speed he raced.

Unnerved that he wasn't tired or out of breath from the run, Erik wiped a hand on the back of his neck, finding no perspiration as he walked toward the rambling truck. The truck's engine revved and rumbled away, with the voice calling for him again.

You know the real reason... Draw that kind of attention to yourself and you know what would happen if they really examined you closely...

"Yo, Erik, hop on!"

Erik snapped to attention and raced ahead, jumping on the back on the pickup. Strong arms grabbed Erik by the wrist and upper body, pulling him in. He took a seat near the edge of the truck bed with the frame at his back and grinned.

"Thanks!" Erik said brightly.

He watched the cheaply-built one-storey wall-to-wall town homes the townspeople called apartments grow smaller in the distance. Erik always wondered about the people who lived there, especially the men and women in suits who were always coming and going. Why they lived in such a small town away from the city, he could not comprehend.

"So excited you ain't talkin', huh?"

Erik broke his gaze, glancing at his good friend Raider who sat across from him, grinning. Raider stood out among the group, wearing a black T-shirt underneath his distressed brown leather bomber jacket with a pair of oversized denim jeans with flared leg, along with motorcycle boots.

"*Raider is so cool,*" Erik thought wistfully, staring at Raider's ever-stylish feathered black hair thrown about from the breeze yet still maintained its form. "*How does he do it?*"

Erik chortled at the memory of Raider's comments about his hair had been cut to appear as if it were blown away by 'unseen winds'.

Though seemingly relatively easy to care for, Raider made it look nearly too easy. He was also known to be notoriously vain about his hair, so much at any given moment; Erik could spot him preening at it.

"What's with the weird look, man?" Raider asked, giving Erik a wary glance.

"I'm so vanilla compared to him." Erik looked skyward, blowing a short sigh. *"Why did he bother becoming friends with a dorky geek like me?"*

Raider nudged Erik's chest with his elbow and Erik chuckled as he adjusted the cap on his head before the wind blew it away.

"You alright, man?" Raider inquired.

Erik quickly cheered up, pushing him back playfully. "How's everyone doing?" he asked instead.

One of the girls of the group, Francisca Stewart, sat next to Raider. She wore her usual black slacks, a white dress shirt with quarter-length sleeves, and calf-high leather boots. Around her wrists were handcrafted glass beaded bracelets adorned with small conch shells she bought from a metaphysical store in the city.

Francisca threw back her long single-braid of sandy hair draping over her shoulder and Erik clenched his hands, trying to resist touching her hair that met the back of her knees. He always wondered what it felt like, beset by the attractiveness of her long hair.

She looks like someone familiar…

"I'm ready to punch something," answered Francisca. "Namely *you* if you keep staring at me!"

"I'm sorry," Erik answered sheepishly as his face burned red. "But your hair…"

Francisca shook her fist at him in return. "Are you turned on by long hair or something?"

"I don't know…"

"Then stop creeping me out, or I'm knocking your face in!"

Erik giggled. "That attitude of yours is cute when you're like that." His head whipped back from her hard slap and Erik held his cheek, grinning. "I love you too!"

Raider guffawed. "In a bad mood again 'cause of yer daddy, huh?" he cracked, breaking the tension.

Erik laughed when Francisca delivered a swift punch into Raider's chest and Raider grunted, doubling over.

"For your big fat information, yes, Collin pissed me off this morning!" Francisca yelled. "That son of a bitch wanted me to cook before I left! He acts like it's so damn difficult to put some stupid heat-and-eat sausage biscuit in the microwave!"

"You ain't hurt me that bad!" Raider wheezed, sitting up.

"Raider, you need to quit," Erik teased. "She's just as bad as you are!"

"Yeah, we can double team fools no problem."

Erik smiled, enjoying Francisca's headstrong nature and her attitude about using her talents outright. When Erik asked why she always found her way into another brawl, Francisca admitted there wasn't anyone difficult to come to blows against, considering everyone had their share of weaknesses and she always joined fights with whomever and wherever alongside Raider.

"I only fight those that strike me first," Francisca said. "I leave it up to Raider to start first. Anyways, I don't care what happens to me; just remember that *you* fight only in self-defense!"

Erik nodded and touched the bridge of his slightly crooked nose. A blank spot entered his mind how it came to be.

You had the point stressed to you the hard way...

"I don't understand why your father is so mean to you," Erik said softly, touching her arm. "You're so nice…" Francisca smiled tersely in response and pried his fingers off.

When she wants to be!

"I'm just tired, man," Raider muttered as he crossed his arms across his chest and leaned forward, shutting his eyes. "This school thing… it ain't me, dig it?"

"I am doing fine as always," replied the other girl in Erik's circle of friends, Hanalei Kahananui, who sat across from Francisca and next to Erik, "like a spring wind over calm waters."

Erik sighed, smiling pleasantly at Hanalei, while taking in her beautiful appearance. She wore a tailored red dress cut narrow at the waist with a thin yellow belt framing her slim figure and matching red dress shoes with a flat heel, covering her slender feet like slippers.

"You're cute today, Hana," Erik complemented.

Hanalei blushed as she tucked her bobbed black hair behind her ears, revealing her clipped earrings of red and yellow flowers. "Stop staring!" she snapped and thumped Erik upside the head.

Erik giggled, rubbing his temple. "That's great, Hana," he replied. "I can't help it… I've always admired your beauty and taste in clothing." Hanalei waved her fist at Erik, smiling slightly. "I just want to enjoy your company some more!"

"Stop drooling over her, Doofus," Francisca said to Erik, waving a hand in his face to gain his attention. "She's too good for you and you know it!"

"I can always try," Erik murmured, feeling his face flush darker scarlet in embarrassment. Hanalei glanced at him and looked away, shying slightly behind the books she carried.

"So you're finally starting school with us," Raider cut in.

"About time, Doofus." Francisca nudged Erik, smiling wryly. "Say, I'm in your History class."

"I'm in your Foreign Language class," Hanalei replied, smiling gently at Erik, "as well as Geometry."

Erik beamed back as her eyes disappeared into crescent lines on her face. "Please keep smiling, Hana," he said. "Your good mood and pretty smile is always so rare!"

"Do you hear anything at all?" Hanalei snapped and threw a book at him. Erik caught it as Raider broke out laughing. "Now you're being weird!"

"You're always either yelling at us or so serious," Erik protested, handing the book back to her. "Francisca's a bad influence on you; you sneer at the world too much... I can't figure you out at all!"

"Yeah," Raider retorted, "Hana's pickin' up Franny's bad habits, the way she's always punching at ya or stompin' on ya or cussin' your fool ass out, man."

"Don't call me Franny!" Francisca snapped and punched Raider again on the chest. He coughed as he doubled over in agony.

"Keep that up," Raider wheezed, "and you gonna kill me!"

"Learn your place!"

"Cool it, dig? I'm yer friend here!"

"Whatever!"

"Maybe I ought to start liking girls that aren't so quick to deliver a boot to the crotch or a smack to the head," Erik murmured. "Abusive women are hazardous to my health!"

"Then don't be so insulting," Hanalei replied.

"I'll try not to," Erik promised.

"Man, check this," Raider muttered. "Women are like the stars. You can study, look at, and ask questions 'bout them stars, but you can never reach or touch those stars. Dig it?"

"Right," Francisca declared. "Look but don't touch, or we'll burn you!"

Hanalei giggled and Erik blew a raspberry. "Horrible, the both of you!" he complained.

"Hey man, stick with me and I'll tell ya err'thing ya wanna know 'bout them hip ladies," Raider said as he sat up and leaned over, draping an arm around Erik's shoulders. "I'm personally popular with 'em; they can't resist my sexy good looks."

"Oh, come off it," Francisca said and scoffed.

"You can't be serious," Hanalei said and put a hand to her mouth, trying to suppress her giggles.

"I mean it, man," Raider protested. "They misunderstand how cool I am, always callin' me stupid or dumb in the head or treating me like some badass hood. I act suave not to cover up my lack of brains, it's because I am, damn it!"

"Don't worry, Raider," Erik said, nudging him with his elbow. "I know the truth about you; you're quite smart and almost everything always comes easily to you!"

"Right, especially when it comes to dealing with people," Francisca drawled and Erik laughed when Raider's face turned red. "He makes it seem so effortless!"

Raider withdrew from Erik and folded his arms across his chest, pouting.

"His fists always put people and everything else into easier perspective," Hanalei interjected, "so they can understand clearly how awesome he is."

Francisca, inundated by the hilarity of it all, laughed along with Erik as Raider's face burned beet red.

"Can it, the both of yas!" Raider snapped, shaking his fist at them both, only to make Erik and Francisca laugh even harder.

"Don't worry, you badass hood you," Erik needled and draped an arm around Raider's shoulders, giving a firm squeeze. "Don't ever change for whatever reason." Erik poked Raider in the chest. "I like you just the way you are!"

"Yeah," Raider huffed and shoved Erik off. "Some friends y'all are, crackin' at my expense!"

"Oh, lighten up!" Francisca said and razzed him. "You're being too serious!"

"You know it's true," Erik insisted.

"The hell you mean?" Raider squawked and Erik and Francisca fell into another round of giggles. Raider grunted and shook his head. "Damn haters," he muttered. "Y'all crazy!"

"Sure, we're crazy about you!" Erik acknowledged and he and Francisca doubled over in cachinnation while Raider pouted and his face burned hotly.

Hanalei grinned and pet Raider on the head and Francisca hooted at them. Erik fell over, guffawing.

"Yeah, go on and get it outta yer system," Raider grumbled. "Think I'm some clown, huh? Y'all ain't gonna be laughing no more once I kick y'all's asses!"

"Then you'll only be proving their point," Hanalei warned.

Raider let out a yell in frustration and punched both Francisca and Erik in their arms. They continued with their gales of laughter anyway, until tears ran down and they could no longer breathe.

FOUR

After a mile of traveling down gravel road, the truck entered paved streets and after another mile, narrow sidewalks appeared as they reached the major city of Keely.

The truck headed toward the large local high school known formally as Number 367, which the locals called Wyndham High. When the truck driver idled behind the buses lined up in front of the school, Erik nudged Hanalei.

"Why didn't the bus come out to where we live and pick us up?" he asked. "We're not that far from the route, are we?"

"Hush up," Hanalei ordered.

"But, why?"

Francisca leaned toward Erik, speaking into his ear. "He's the only ride for Raider," she muttered, "and Raider had to really convince him to let us come with, so don't mess it up!"

Erik nodded and turned, looking through the pickup's rear window at the driver who wore a black baseball cap, darkly tinted glasses and a dark navy windbreaker.

The driver glanced at the rear mirror and stiffened as Erik continued to stare. The driver's face and hands twitched slightly before he turned his eyes back to the road. Overcome by a sensation of recognition, though not quite able to pinpoint where he knew him from, Erik felt uncomfortable and chose to stay quiet about the matter.

"Right," Raider grumbled, poking Erik's side firmly with his elbow and Erik turned to face him. "Check this Erik; if he ain't hassling us, then we ain't gonna hassle him, dig it?"

Erik nodded. "You didn't say what classes you had with me," he said, changing the subject.

Raider blew a disgruntled sigh and rolled his eyes. "'Course I ain't said nothin'!" he spat. "I got your lunch hour and Home Room which ain't nothin' but a fucking total waste of my energy, man!"

"Well, it's not all bad," said Erik brightly. "We all see each other, right?" They all said their forms of 'yes', with Raider giving Erik a sour glare. "I'm just being positive!" he protested. "Besides, you'll live longer!"

Raider jabbed Erik's chest with his elbow and Francisca pounced on him, putting Erik in a half-nelson while running her knuckles over his head. Erik laughed, batting her away.

Hanalei leaned forward and tickled Erik's side until he pushed them all away, gasping for breath after a fit of laughter. Erik gave Hanalei a goofy grin and she returned with a bright smile.

The truck finally moved forward and stopped in front of Wyndham High. Erik and the others jumped out from the flatbed and he blew a sigh of relief after finding his lucky cap had not blown away, but stayed on his head.

Taking it off, Erik gave it a quick check, noticing it dusty from the ride. He slapped it against his jeans and placed it back on his head then hurried after his friends who followed Raider up the stairs. Erik paused in step once he took in the building's sheer size.

"Wow!" he exclaimed. "I can't believe that this is a school!"

"It's approximately one thousand, seven-hundred and sixty-three kids that come here... well, give or take," Francisca replied when she spotted the amazed expression on Erik's face. "It takes in all the kids from nine different schools."

"It is almost filled to capacity," Hanalei interjected. "The building itself holds two-thousand students."

"Keely's a big town," Raider said. "You can get lost easy out here!" He glanced to Erik and concern masked his face. "Breathe, okay?" Raider snapped, slapping Erik across the shoulder blades and jostling him out of his initial astonished impression. "I ain't kissin' a toad just to revive ya!" He smirked and Erik gave him a wary glance. "Besides, I'm the pretty one."

Erik chortled as Raider stomped ahead. "I hope it'll be a great day," he said and followed his friends up the stairs. "I can't wait to find what's in store for me!"

"It ain't nothin' to get excited about," Raider spat. "It's just school man, so cool yer jets!"

They passed through one of the several double doors and into the large foyer. Erik noticed four hallways going ahead and the two stairways on his right and his left.

"Where do I go from here?" he asked.

"Come on, Erik," Raider called as he waved his hand at Erik to follow. "Hurry up!"

Erik said quick goodbyes to Francisca and Hanalei and followed Raider through the congested hallway full of other students.

Flustered when he kept being shoved into and his feet stepped on, Erik felt no pain as he continued to say 'pardon' to those that bumped into him, only to receive strange looks in return, apparently standing out somehow.

Erik stumbled over his steps, slightly envious at Raider who marched on with an air of confidence, his body never touching anyone else in the crowded corridors; even those around them seemed to step aside for Raider.

Erik's mind wandered, losing attention to where he headed. Someone pressed into him and Erik turned, thinking Raider had been the one, only to hear 'yoink', and his cap suddenly left his head.

"Hey!" he cried and whirled around, spotting the thief bobbing and weaving through the crowd smoothly with his hat on their head, not apparently bothered by the fact that they took what belonged to him. Erik reached out, pushing past the other students, only to get knocked down.

"Watch where you're going, idiot," a student snapped as they and others walked around him. Erik seethed when his hands were stepped on and tried to get up, only to get pushed down again.

"Watch it, loser," another student spat and guffawed.

Overcome by anger rather than pain, Erik finally sprung to his feet, realizing the person with his cap had escaped.

"Not today!" he growled, clenching his hands. "There's no chance I'm going find that thief in a building built for over one-thousand people," he moaned in despair, running his hands through his hair. With the school seemingly filled to capacity, Erik now hated that very number of students that existed: one thousand, seven-hundred and sixty-three.

Hearing a commanding shout, the mob of students parted as if a wedge magically shoved itself through. Erik stood on one end of the hall, suddenly nervous and small compared to Raider who stood at the easternmost staircase's edge, confident and controlled.

Erik chafed under Raider's annoyed glare as he stomped down to face him. Erik clenched his teeth and stepped back, picking at his nails as Raider closed in.

"Ay, you comin' or what?" Raider grumbled, shooting him an irritated look. He snapped his fingers at Erik to hurry before he had a chance to answer. "I got people to meet. It ain't my thing to wait."

"But...!" Erik started.

Raider raised a hand as he turned on his heel. "You comin' with me, whether you like it or not!"

Erik let out a defeated sigh and stopped his picking to hurry after him. "Alright, I'm coming!" he grumbled, following in step.

"And you ain't even breathin' heavy," Raider drawled.

"Okay, what?"

Raider chuckled, shaking his head. "You don't wanna know, man."

Once they approached the staircase, the mob closed behind them, resuming whatever it did before. Raider and Erik made their way up the stairs and entered a long corridor before entering a room on the end with a brass plate with black text: Room 230.

The other students in the classroom were hanging around, doing whatever they wanted to do to pass the time and making general noise. Raider clenched his hands and held them at his sides as he stood in the doorway. He nodded to Erik and entered after him.

"Ay!" Raider shouted, his voice cutting into the air. The atmosphere suddenly changed into dead silence as everyone immediately stopped what they did and turned to him.

"'Sup?" called a student from the classroom's rear, breaking the tension.

Raider gave a quick nod to the other student's general direction and pointed a thumb in Erik's direction. "You: Erik Hart," he said, and then switched hands to point his other thumb to a group of students clustered nearby. "Them: Bonita, Jeromeo, Spardek, Arnice..."

Erik gave a halfhearted wave to the people Raider named. "Hi," he said shyly and the students returned with nods, grunts, and other forms of greeting.

"Antony Gregg, Hartlan, Sharif, Special Kaye, Two-tone Tony, Rotobot. Them three break dance, if you know what I'm sayin'..." Raider rambled on. "Finne, Sharla, Rhetta, Heinrich and Gottfried, though better known 'round here as Henry and Jeffery but I didn't tell you that. Anyway, they're brothers on the wrestling team and," Raider snapped his fingers, "your protection."

Erik waved at the two burly brothers with red hair and gray eyes who seemed distant and removed from the group. "Nice to meet you," he said nervously.

"Do you wrestle?" one of the brothers asked.

"Gosh, no!" Erik put up his hands, breaking out in a cold sweat as self-consciousness dwarfed him when he made a mental comparison of himself to them. "You two would break me like a twig!"

Why do they seem so familiar...?

"You're a lot stronger than you look," said the other brother.

"Well, I'm built for speed," Erik replied and let out a nervous laugh as he ran his hands through his hair. "That's the best I can say." The brothers gave him a wary look and Erik awkwardly shoved his hands in his pockets.

As Raider continued to name the students and Erik waved to show he had seen them and put their faces to their names, Raider suddenly had a goofy grin creep up on his face after he finished pointing to everyone else.

"...Ronzell, Janeczka, Mackleford, Lanzky, Jones, Washington and the talented Miss Fyne." Erik turned to face Raider's direction as he said this with a lopsided grin on his face. Everyone else scattered to their seats to pretend that they were busy reading or catching up on something of importance.

In entered a slim coffee-colored woman with short dark brown hair wearing a gray pantsuit and a dark blue overcoat with silver buttons. Erik's skin flushed as he noticed how her name fit her well, given her beauty.

"Caelan, please sit," she said, placing notebooks and binders on her desk, then came out of her overcoat, setting it on the back of her chair.

"What?" Erik inquired in shock and turned to Raider. "Is Caelan really your name?"

"To *you*, it's Raider," Raider said smugly, "but I *let* her call me that." The teacher looked up, giving him a wary glance. Raider firmly jabbed Erik's chest with his fingers. "She likes calling me that, but it's Raider 'round here. Call me Caelan, just even once, and you lose yer privileges."

"Okay, alright," Erik said nervously, putting up his hands in surrender.

"Erik," Fyne called, "you can sit in that empty seat between Antony Gregg and Henry."

Erik headed to the empty desk between one the large wrestler who wore a red tracksuit with the school's mascot in yellow, and a thin dark student who sat with his head in his arms as Raider left his side and stomped for the rear of the room.

Antony Gregg wore an oversized sweater, jogging pants along with loosely laced high-top sneakers and a floppy denim hat perched slightly slanted on his head. Erik caught his foot tapping, indicating he had not fallen asleep.

Slipping into his assigned seat, he slumped forward, his tall frame resting uncomfortably in the chair. Erik tried another position and sat back, having his long legs stick out, appearing as if he were about to ooze out of his seat. He sat upright and then found a slightly comfortable position, folding his hands atop the worn wood.

Raider yawned loudly as he propped his foot against a nearby desk, buckling his boot, then retreated to a desk in the classroom's rear corner, dropping into it. He slouched forward and folded his arms across his chest. After shifting a bit in his seat to turn sideways, Raider put up his feet and dropped his head back, shutting his eyes and let out a long sigh, apparently ready for a Home Room snooze.

"Is he allowed to do that?" Erik murmured as the teacher called for an attendance check, ignoring Raider's actions. Figuring he did this often since she paid him no attention, Erik focused on the teacher as she called names from her list.

When she came to the 'H's' he paid close attention and called 'present' when his surname was called. The teacher glanced up over her reading glasses and Erik stiffened.

"You're the only one who actually said anything," she said. "Well, other than the monotonic 'here', a 'yo', or a grunt," She straightened up her stance, looking over the rims of her glasses to concentrate on an object in the back of the room.

"Did I do something wrong, Miss Fyne?" Erik asked.

She turned her attention back to him, smiling faintly. "No, no you didn't."

"So, no one says 'Present' anymore?"

"I think they've stopped penalizing students for not calling 'Present' years ago." The teacher smiled warmly. "The only one who does say 'present' is you, but I must give credit to those who need it, as in Zeadeas's case, who gives a snore!"

Saying it loud enough for Raider to hear, he opened one eye, closed it then fell back asleep. The other students laughed.

"Is he always this tired?" Erik asked and more laughter followed him than he cared to hear.

"I heard he's always fighting every night at the club downtown," Antony Gregg grumbled from his folded position on his desk. "He gets in late then he's gotta get up early."

"Really now?" Erik replied.

"Yeah, that's what I heard, but hey, what the hell do I know?"

Miss Fyne resumed her attendance check and Erik hunched forward in his seat, still trying to find a comfortable position.

Surprised in learning that Raider's name was in fact Caelan Zeadeas, Erik held his chin in his hand, wondering if Raider always acted cool wherever he went. He then thought about the possibility of Raider making up a fresh name to become popular in the school.

"*As long as I've known him, he wanted me to address him as Raider,*" Erik mused and glanced at Raider who snored softly. "*I never questioned his nickname either...*" He blew a sigh and turned away. "*Why didn't he want me to know his name? It's not like it's lame or anything...*" Erik gave it no more of his consideration and concentrated on the other students around him.

FIVE

Already dreading his experience in Wyndham High, Erik clenched his teeth, concentrating on what to do to the student who stole his cap.

"I'd probably do more serious harm than Francisca usually does when she fights," he thought.

The debate got underway and Erik tried to add his opinion, hardly getting in any words at all. He waited on Miss Fyne to call on him, only to be ignored as she went around the room. Once the subject changed from government to religion, Erik found it interesting.

Erik's face flushed in embarrassment as the other students wanted to hear what he felt about the subject.

"What do you mean," Antony Gregg asked, turning to him, "you don't believe in a god?"

"I'm not sure," Erik murmured. "I mean, my parents aren't overly religious. We don't go to a church or a temple or some shrine or anything like that. My father always advocated research and I read a lot." He shrugged his shoulders. "I guess I never gave it much thought."

"Who are you accountable to?"

"Hey, I'm accountable for my own actions." Erik snorted. "What kind of crazy question is that?"

"So what are you, atheist or something?"

"I didn't say that; I just said I'm not sure if I can believe in something I don't know that exists."

"So how do you explain how we were created?"

"Well, science says…"

"Never mind what those scientists say," Antony Gregg snapped. "Even they're not so sure."

"So if a creator goddess or god created us, then who created them?"

"Aliens," Raider interjected in a muffled tone from the classroom's rear and everyone laughed.

"Alright Class," Miss Fyne called, clapping her hands. "Do I have your attention?"

Erik turned away and stiffened when he noticed a shadow of a man lingering near the classroom entrance. Before he could alert the teacher about the unknown visitor outside, the shadow left its place from the door. Erik blew a hard sigh as she approached her desk and grabbed a stack of papers.

"Hey man, I wasn't tryin' to be hard on you or anything," Antony Gregg said and Erik turned his attention to him. "I just wanna hear all sides and what you *really* think, not spittin' out other people's stuff."

Erik nodded. "I guess you're right…"

"Man, you gotta make your own opinions. Think for yourself; otherwise, if you don't question everything, the establishment will control you."

Erik swallowed hard as Antony Gregg turned back around in his seat. *"The establishment trying to control me?"* he mused. *"What kind of crazy idea is that?"*

"I have some paperwork that I want you all to read," the teacher announced moments later. "All of them are different, so you can't cheat." She then handed smaller stacks to the students who sat in the front row of desks and they took a sheet then passed the stack behind them. "You'll have to write a report answering all the questions of who, what, where, when, why and how. Only write down your responses if it answers any of these questions. Now I'm going to hand this social skill--" There were moans and groans before she could finish and the teacher laughed in response.

"What's wrong?" Erik asked to no one in particular. "It can't be that bad, is it?"

"Man, it's helluva worse," grumbled Antony Gregg. "It ain't nothin' but useless bullshit tryin' to control our minds!"

Erik leaned forward. "Why do the others call you by your full name?" he inquired, ignoring his statement.

"There's two more fellas named Antony: Jones and Washington."

"Why don't you go by your last name then?"

"There's a Greg Spardek in this class."

"So what about your middle name then?" Antony Gregg did not answer.

"I'm going to hand out this social skills worksheet," Miss Fyne continued. "It'll take you five minutes. You can do this for the remaining twenty-five minutes, or do this as homework. You can finish your homework for those who hadn't had the sense to do it at home, Caelan." Laughter followed.

"Homework and me don't connect," Raider replied as he sat up, stretching. "We just ain't there." He yawned loudly then leaned over, pulling out his books from under his desk.

"Erik, your books are in the office," the teacher said to him. "You can find it downstairs on the right from the foyer. It has the name 'Box Office' on the door."

"How did an office get a name like that?" Erik asked as he sat back in his seat.

"Someone put it there and it was never removed; it's been there for all the years I've been teaching here." She waved a hand idly in the air. "Well, I've got papers to grade."

Miss Fyne returned to her desk, grabbing a pen from her cup nearby and started the task of grading the mountain of homework assignments there.

Erik leaned forward and tapped Antony Gregg on the shoulder.

"What's up?" Antony Gregg answered.

"Do you have a pen I can borrow?"

"Yeah, you can keep it." Antony Gregg handed Erik the pen he had over his shoulder and Erik took it. "I got tons at home."

Erik murmured his thanks, feeling slightly guilty for asking. Antony Gregg leaned over, grabbing his pen case from under his seat and Erik noticed several sheets of paper had sketches on them, with the topmost sheet a realistic drawing of Miss Fyne at her desk.

"*What impeccable skill!*" Erik thought as Antony Gregg withdrew his pen and grabbed his worksheet, covering up the drawing. While Erik returned to his own work, he chastised himself for rushing in the morning and forgetting his backpack hanging on his bedpost.

The backpack itself came from the orphanage where Erik used to stay, donated along with the binder, paper and the box of pencils and pens. He clenched his teeth, remembering the crayons that were in there as well.

No matter how much Erik complained to Jane Greenfield about keeping them, she continued to insist and he yielded, not wishing to hurt her feelings.

"Any Art Appreciation class would cover what the students need to know about colors and basic drawing," Erik protested.

"Well, with eight colors, you can learn how to make new ones," Jane Greenfield said brightly.

"You have a point..."

"Now why make all that fuss and trouble over such a little thing like that?"

Erik sighed, thinking about the Greenfields who worked at the office complex in downtown Keely. He couldn't quite place when he met them or his life before being adopted by them, finding it odd that they wanted to skip childhood altogether and jump into dealing with an adolescent.

Slightly disturbed when no memory came to mind, Erik grunted and tucked the pen behind his ear.

"*It's like there's something I want to forget,*" Erik mused. "*It's not like I lived a hard life and the Greenfields are kind to me, so why can't I remember anything?*"

If you remember, it'll only destroy you...

Erik rubbed at his temples that thudded dully in pain. "There's nothing to worry about," he muttered under his breath. "Everything will be okay…"

Keep telling yourself that!

Erik swallowed hard and ignored the sinking feeling in his guts.

SIX

After finishing the worksheet, Erik tucked the pen behind his ear, grabbed his homework assignment and put it in the space under his desk for holding papers, then folded his schedule and placed it in his rear pocket.

He left class, heading downstairs for the office. Erik grew annoyed when he entered a congested hallway full of students after the first pass time of the day. Pushing his way through, Erik sighted his cap bobbing and weaving through the crowd.

"Hey," Erik yelled. "Hey you, wait!"

Rushing over, Erik pushed several students out of his way as he advanced. Before he reached the thief who spoke to a lanky young man with long platinum blond hair in denim vest and ripped jeans wearing mirrored glasses, Erik suddenly received a heavy smack directly to the face with a book, forcing him spiraling back and strike a nearby locker, dazed.

"You better not step on my sneaks again, fool!" a harsh voice yelled. Erik let out a yelp as someone grabbed his collar and pulled him forward, forcing him around.

Erik faced a pale student with spiky green hair who wore a bright orange track jacket, heavy gold chains around his neck, and baggy jeans that threatened to fall past his hips and to his knees, even though he wore a worn brown leather belt. The student stood with an awkward gait, trying to keep up his pants for the sake of courtesy.

"I don't care about your expensive high-tops," Erik snapped and pushed him back, blowing a disgruntled sigh.

"You wanna rumble, man?" the bully growled, standing ready to fight at the first chance of a hostile reaction.

Erik clenched his hands. "I don't want to fight you!" he protested, taking a hesitant step rearward. "I have to get to the office!"

"The office is right there, dumb nuts!" the student yelled, his dark gray eyes narrowing. "But you ain't steppin' foot there 'til you get through me!"

"It probably wasn't even me who stepped on your shoes, it was--!" Erik searched through the gathering crowd, spotting his cap on the thief standing behind a group of girls. He ran for the hat; the potential bully ran after him and the thieving student in Erik's cap took off.

"Where you think you goin'?" shouted Erik's aggressor.

"Hey, you!" Erik hollered, "Give me back my hat!" He finally broke through, entering an empty hallway and ran down the corridor, being chased by the other student.

When he came to the end, wondering if the thief went right or left, Erik's opponent caught up and grabbed his collar, throwing him forward. Erik yowled when his face struck the door of an open locker.

"You better say you sorry, you dumb ass fool," the bully growled, "or you'll meet my friend Mister Locker again."

"But I didn't do it!" Erik cried and the metal slammed into his face again. "I--!" Erik's head ravaged in pain as the bully continued banging his face with force. Hearing a pop, Erik cried out when his already crooked nose became disjointed. "My nose!" he wailed and another pop followed as the bully ignored his protests of wrongdoing. "I'm sorry!" Erik screamed, giving in for some show of mercy after the agony became too much.

"That's better!" The angry student pushed Erik onto the floor and grabbed the end of his shirt, wiping the dirt off his white sneakers.

"Why do you want to wear the only color that's the best thing to pick up dirt?" Erik groaned, slightly dazed. "Do you have enough sense to have that thought occur to you?"

"Tryin' to get smart, huh?" Erik's opponent snapped and kicked him in the side. Erik coughed and doubled over, moaning. "If you bleed on my kicks," the bully sneered, "you're gonna pay with all the shitty junk you own!" He let go of Erik's shirt and shoved him away.

"I don't own that much, you jerk!" Erik hissed and stood unsteadily to his feet. "Now it's my turn to kick you around!"

"I'll just have to beat it out your scrawny ass, then, huh?"

Anger flaring, Erik clenched his hands, ready to throw a punch, only to pause once he heard heavy steps come down the hall. He turned, spotting Heinrich's bulky frame approaching them.

"You wouldn't want to do that, Erik," Heinrich called. "Calm down."

"What...?"

Erik grunted when pushed back to the floor by the student who smugly smirked down at him. Kicking at Erik again, Erik yowled and clutched his side. The bully turned to Heinrich, rolling his eyes.

"What grade are you in?" Heinrich demanded.

Erik groaned and sat up, hissing in pain. "Don't worry about me," he muttered. "I got this."

"I'm a junior," replied the student, unfazed. "What's it to you?"

"That doesn't matter," Heinrich snapped.

"So?"

"What matters is that you're picking on someone I know and I don't like it; you busted his nose and I really don't like that."

"*How does he know me?*" Erik thought, stunned.

"What about it?" The bully snapped, crossing his arms. "I can take your ass on in my sleep, homeboy."

"Come with me." Heinrich's face became unreadable. "You and I have to talk." Heinrich grabbed him by the pants waist that almost fell past his hips and yanked them up, going down the rest of the hall.

The bully protested, only to have the pants hitched up higher, forcing him yowling in pain. They turned the corner and Erik got up, wiping the crimson blood from his nose with the back of his hand. He grimaced when he touched his nose, fearful it would be broken again.

"What a lousy first day," Erik grumbled to himself. "Luck's already shot and sinking fast."

Heading to a nearby water fountain, Erik ran the cold water over his nose and hand, washing off the blood. Glancing at the clock above a classroom door, he saw pass time had run out and ran the rest of the way, making up for lost time.

Approaching the main artery, Erik paused, taking notice of the wall signs that directed where the offices were located. He raced for the office door down the hall, only to be stopped by a whistle. Erik froze and looked around, finding nobody connected to the whistle. He continued on, only to hear it again.

"No running in the halls!" a voice called. Erik slowed his running, but walked briskly. "Do you have a hall pass?"

"Do I have a hall what?" Erik stopped and glanced over his shoulder, spotting an elderly man in a white sport shirt and khakis with a clipboard in hand walking up to him. "I don't want to be any later for class than what I'm already in!" Erik protested, turning about face toward the hall monitor. "I need to get going!"

"Can't you hear what I just said?" the monitor grumbled loudly. "I want a hall pass: the yellow paper with your name and destination." Erik gave the monitor a wary glance then spotted a small beige hearing aid above his right ear.

"This is just great," Erik grumbled, running his hands through his hair. "Really? Universe, do you have to do this to me?"

"What did you say?" the elderly man snapped, withdrawing a pen from the pocket protector in his shirt.

"I, um, don't have one," Erik stammered. "I..."

"I see." The monitor clicked his pen and quickly scribbled notes in his clipboard. "So, what is your name?" Erik gave his name and the monitor scoffed. "You're hot? It's only seventy-five degrees out!" The elderly monitor pointed his pen in Erik's direction. "What's your name? Speak up." Erik yelled his name and the monitor huffed. "Erik Hart, you have three days detention." He wrote more on his notepad before handing Erik a pink slip.

Erik snatched it away and scanned it, realizing he held a detention notice with his name jotted down on the front. "What did I do wrong?" he spat. "It's not like I was trying to skip class, Mister! I was trying to *get* to class!"

"Next time you'll think before you go lollygagging without a hall pass," the hall monitor snapped, not hearing his objection. The elderly man walked away, leaving Erik with the offensive colored sheet.

Looking down at the pink slip, Erik read what was written more carefully. To his dismay, he found he had an after school detention tomorrow, the next day and the day after. Erik puffed a disgruntled sigh and crumpled the paper in hand.

"What a bad day already!" he growled, kicking at the floor.

Shoving the notice in his pocket, Erik finally approached his intended destination, finding a door with an aged brass nameplate naming the lonely room 'Box Office'. He knocked on the door, only to hear a sharp buzz.

"Yes?" questioned a hollow voice after a moment's silence.

Erik gave his name. "I need to pick up my books," he stated, "and I'm a new student here."

"They will be in the bin on your right in a moment." Another buzz followed, accompanied by sudden silence.

Disturbed by the lack of human contact and the faceless clerk with only, its voice talking at others the other side, Erik noted the lonely boxed-in existence surrounded by books and files in such a small space. He chuckled to himself, considering the cynical humor for the placing of the nameplate on the door.

Coming onto the right side of the enclosed office, Erik stood in front of what resembled the outer end of a wood chipper. His books spat out of the small-shafted hood, dropping them into a mid-sized wire mesh bin underneath. He caught a slip of yellow paper tucked inside one of his books and took it out to read. To Erik's irony, lay a hall pass.

Grabbing his books from the containing bin, Erik pulled out his schedule from his back pocket with his free hand, glancing at his next class for the morning. Finding he had Geometry, Erik lugged his books threatening to fall out of his grip up the stairs while constantly checking his schedule, making sure he headed in the right direction.

Scanning the doors and their number plates above them, searching for Room 340, Erik followed the numbers to the end of the hall and walked up another flight of stairs, finally approaching Classroom 340.

Nudging the door open with his foot, Erik stumbled inside and his books fell from his arms, striking the floor with a loud clatter. A wiry man with thinning dark hair combed over to the right of his balding head turned from the chalkboard scribbled with equations and gave Erik the iciest of glacial glares he had ever encountered.

"You're late," the instructor spat venomously.

Erik introduced himself nervously, giving a shy wave. "I... ah... well..." He swallowed hard as the teacher's mean glower burned through him. "With a look like that, you can light paint on fire," Erik quipped and some of the students laughed.

"Oh, we have a clown, huh?" the teacher snapped then held out a hand. "Mister Hart, where's your hall pass?"

"Hold on, let me find it." The thin teacher with the comb-over tucked the piece of chalk behind his ear and folded his scrawny arms across his small chest, growing impatient as Erik searched his pockets. "Schedule, detention notice, lint…" Erik murmured under his breath.

"Stop wasting my time!" the teacher growled.

"Give me a minute," Erik protested. Finding nothing, he crouched down on his haunches, searching his fallen collection of books. After flipping the last hardback, he froze when he remembered taking his books from the bin, but leaving the hall pass behind. Erik put the heel of his hand against his forehead, moaning. "Why is this happening to me?" he griped. "I left it at the office!"

"You idiot!" Hanalei snapped and some students giggled.

Erik's face burned once he scooped up his books in his arms and shrugged his shoulders awkwardly at the teacher. "Well, you know, I don't have one at this time…" he said timidly, "but I just had it a little while before; it was in my possession, I honestly swear!"

"Then possess this," the teacher grumbled and stomped towards his desk. Erik blew a distressed sigh as the teacher picked up a pen and a small piece of paper, scribbling a quick note on the sheet.

"Really?" he groaned when the teacher beckoned to him.

"Today, Mister Hart," the teacher snapped.

Erik winced and approached the side of his desk, wilting under the teacher's irate stare. Handed the yellow slip of paper,

Erik grunted and shifted his books in his arms. "Not again," he grumbled in dejection, taking the paper.

"Oh, quite the troublemaker already, eh?"

Erik shook his head vehemently. "Oh no," he protested. "I'm no troublemaker! I'm a good guy, really!"

"Alrighty then, Mister Good Guy, go down to the downstairs office and give them this. You will receive your pink slip there." Erik heard someone snicker and the thin man whirled around, glaring at everyone. "Work out this equation and shut it!" he barked.

Slipping the sheet in his pocket, Erik walked with heavy steps, exiting the various halls and stairs, before finally approaching the door. He rapped on it with the back of his hand.

"Yes?" replied the faceless, nameless clerk after the buzz.

"I have a message from..." Erik pulled out the sheet and glanced at the back of the hall pass, reading the teacher's name inscribed. "Mister Deverel wants a pink slip for Erik Hart."

"It's in the bin on your right."

Stepping up to the bin, another pink slip fell out after the buzz. Erik snatched it up before it fluttered away, reading the date stated three days after he served his first three days. Crumpling the sheet and stuffing it into his pocket, Erik hurried back upstairs without delay.

Forcing himself to slow down before his feet left the ground; Erik shouldered in the door of the classroom and entered, taking an empty seat in front of Hanalei. Dropping his books on his desk with a bang, Erik slumped in his seat as Deverel droned on about the current lesson.

Hanalei tapped Erik on the shoulder and he leaned back as she leaned forward. "Turn your book to page one-hundred eighteen," she whispered in his ear.

Erik nodded and pulled out his ratty Geometry book, flipping the worn pages to the destination. Reading over the instructions in the book to make sure he would do them correctly, Erik assessed what he needed and put the rest of his books under the desk before scanning the lesson one last time.

"Hana, do you have some extra paper?" he asked, pulling out his pen from behind his ear. She flicked Erik upside his head and handed him a pencil and several sheets of paper from her binder.

"Math is always done in pencil, you idiot!" she whispered sharply. Erik sighed and rubbed his sore ear before tucking the pen back there.

Doing the lesson on the Polygonal Theory took Erik only several minutes and he went ahead, doing the next section as the teacher Deverel continued on in monotone about the Theory. After completion, Erik decided not to wait and continued other assignments included in the remaining chapter.

After checking his work three times to make sure the equations were correct, Erik realized while overlooking the many math problems, he had finished two chapters of Geometry before the teacher stated the time to go. Hopeful Deverel would give him some slack as he confidently turned in his work, Deverel paused to examine them.

"Wait," snapped the instructor and Erik cringed as he neared his desk to collect his books. "Stay after class... I want to give this a more critical eye."

Erik hoisted his books in his arms and waited near the door after the other students left. When new ones came through, the teacher set his jaw as his face turned bright pink.

This can't be good, standing out like that...

"What is it, Mister Deverel?" Erik asked faintly. *"Please don't give me a verbal kick in the head,"* he prayed silently. *"Your attitude is bad enough!"*

"Do you think this is funny, Mister Hart?" Deverel snapped, shaking the fistful of papers at Erik.

"No, but I did complete them," Erik protested. "Check them yourself!"

"I just did," Deverel growled. "No one can do two chapters of Geometry in thirty minutes, even with me talking! That alone cannot be done in ten!"

"Maybe I'm pretty decent in math," Erik spat. "Have you ever thought about that?"

"Don't talk back to me," Deverel snarled.

"Mister Deverel," Erik objected. "I can tell you what I read."

"Tell me." Deverel glanced at his watch. "You have five minutes."

Erik told him what he knew of the Polygonal Theory, including the entire chapter sections he had done by name and section and what contained in each section as well as the chapter reviews covered in the section.

"So you have a photographic memory," Deverel grumbled. "That doesn't amount to much!"

"Stop insulting me!" Erik protested. "I'm not stupid!"

Deverel suddenly smirked as he set Erik's papers aside. "What's an angle?" he asked.

"When two rays have a common endpoint," Erik replied without hesitation, "or vertex."

"What is greater than zero degrees but less than ninety degrees?"

"That's an acute angle."

"What is an obtuse angle?"

"It's greater than ninety degrees, less than one-hundred and eighty."

Deverel crossed his arms across his thin chest, giving Erik a superior stare as he glowered down at him in disdain. "You have lines AB and RS. The two lines intersect at point P. Angles one, two, three and four are formed. You now have lines A, B, C and D. What is perpendicular since they've all formed right angles?" Deverel gave a slight smile. "You have thirty seconds."

"Line AB is perpendicular to line CD," Erik answered. "Am I correct?"

Deverel grunted. "Alrighty then, smart ass," he grumbled, "I'll grade your papers, but stay with the flow of the class next time, please? Now," Deverel's hardened expression returned on his face, "go to class!"

"Fine by me," Erik said as he readjusted his books in his arms and quickly left for his next class.

SEVEN

Erik encountered a rowdy crowd of students once he entered his English class. The students talked loudly or threw paper balls around at each other, completely ignoring the teacher named Whitley, an elderly woman who had a limp in her right leg. Around her neck, she wore a pair of bifocals on a lanyard.

"Class! Class, simmer down now!" she called in frustration, trying in vain to control the students who undermined her authority. "Simmer down!" Whitley clapped her hands when no one paid attention to her calls. "Class, simmer down!"

Approaching an empty seat at the front of the class, Erik dropped his pile of books on the desk's face with a bang. The students suddenly fell silent, stunned and staring at him as if he had just lost his mind.

"Shut up, please!" Erik yelled in irritation. "You see the woman's trying to teach you idiots!"

"Damn," a student muttered nearby. "You're bold!"

"I want to learn," Erik snapped, "and if you don't care, then make it your care!"

"Well, I don't give two shits," snapped another student from the room's other side.

"No wonder your English is so bad," Erik spat. "You're not learning a thing!"

"Thank you, young man," Whitley rasped and cleared her throat.

"*She must yell at them often*," Erik considered, glaring at the other students. "*These jerks don't give a flying care...*"

"Alright, we get it," a voice jeered in the back. "Sit your skinny punk ass down!"

"What is your name?" Whitley asked and Erik gave it as he sat in his seat. She smiled warmly in return. "I was told I may receive a new student." Whitley returned to her desk at the head of the class and thumbed through her papers scattered there. "A young man wanting to learn... I don't get many of those these days."

"What a suck up!" someone crowed and laughter followed.

Erik turned in his chair, giving the rear of the classroom the worst glare he could muster. "If you guys would be so nice," he snarled, "I'd actually enjoy listening to what she's got to say!"

"Man, this is English class!" a voice piped from the rear. "Ain't shit worth learnin' anyways."

"Right, there ain't nothin' to say," said a student behind Erik, "so just take it easy!"

"What's wrong with wanting to learn something?" Erik spat and clenched his teeth when the student body laughed and jeered in return. Grunting when someone threw a paper ball at his head, he turned, facing the teacher's desk and slouched in defeat.

"Alright, you hooligans," Whitley snapped as she put on her bifocals and scanned her planner. "I want someone to put together a sentence using a noun, an adjective and a verb and we'll go over today's lesson." She sat at her desk, puffing an exasperated sigh.

"I'll do it," a student piped up and he walked up to the front of the class. Picking up the chalk, he wrote on the chalkboard and the students started laughing once he finished his sentence. The student returned to his seat, grinning.

"What's so funny?" Whitley turned in her chair and her face grew red in rage. "*Fuck off, you fucking fuck*," she read back.

"Hey, it's got a verb, an adjective, and a noun!" the student replied smugly. "I reads, lady!"

Whitley rose to her feet and slapped a hand across the worn desk. "I've been wasting my time teaching you hoods since September, spending most of it controlling you all in vain when you don't care to learn a thing!" she shrilled. "Now it's March and we're still on November's lesson!" Whitley put her hands on her hips, glaring at the students. "If you won't learn English, Composition, or Literature, leave now. Only the ones left are the ones worth teaching." She pointed to the door. "If you decide to leave, then you fail!"

"Whatever, old bag," spat the student who wrote the offensive sentence. "I'm outta here!"

"Me too!" someone else said.

Chairs scuffed across the floor and feet moved about; voices floated in the air as the classroom emptied. Once the general commotion ended, only Erik remained at his desk.

"Well, I guess it's just me left here," Erik murmured.

Whitley nodded. "Yes, it seems that way," she agreed sarcastically.

"I'm nothing like those punk kids, you know," Erik replied. "I like learning new stuff!"

Whitley returned to her seat and blew a discontent sigh. "If you say so, young man," she muttered wearily.

"Ask me anything you want to know," Erik pressed.

"Well then, what *do* you know about English in today's modern society?" She folded her hands on top of the worn wood. "You sound well-read."

"English shouldn't be that difficult," Erik considered. "I'll tell you the best I can..."

After Erik completed a month's worth course load of English and composition tests, Whitley appeared slightly disturbed. "Have you ever finished work this quickly," she said, "and yet, comprehend it?"

"You can ask Mister Deverel," Erik said nervously, "but he doesn't believe I did two chapters out of the book in thirty minutes."

"No one has completed a chapter by themselves in Richard's class. The way he talks on and repeats himself... it's a complete shame, I tell you."

"Is it all right if I do it here?" Erik asked. "I know I have a lot to catch up on."

Whitley gave a terse smile. "We'll have plenty of time," she replied warmly.

"Well, I need to get going before I'm late again." Standing to his feet, Erik then collected his books.

"I'll tell you what," Whitley said seriously, beckoning to Erik. "Go down to room 213-G and ask for Counselor Callaghan. Tell him I've sent you and I'll forward down the extra criteria."

"Do I need a hall pass?"

Whitley raised an eyebrow and Erik explained his dilemma from earlier. "I'll clear your name of it; this is my only favor." Erik nodded. "Keep up the outstanding work and I'll consider."

"Yes, Missus Whitley." Erik palmed the yellow paper she handed him and hurried out the classroom, rushing down the corridor.

Bypassing other students who were heading for their next class, Erik raced downstairs then slowed his stride, searching for the room 213-G.

Finding the brass nameplate outside the heavy wood and glass door, Erik shifted his textbooks to one arm and rapped on the glass.

"Come in," a voice called from the inside.

Erik opened the door with his free hand and stepped inside, placing his books on the edge of the muscularly built middle-aged man's desk.

"There's a note on the back," Erik announced, handing over the hall pass.

"Thank you," Callaghan answered.

Erik noticed Callaghan had narrow steel blue eyes with wrinkled edges and light brown hair that had silver streaks tied back in a loose queue. Erik felt uncomfortable without knowing why and looked away, his gaze falling upon shelves of trophies from weightlifting and wrestling in competitions behind Callaghan and the anxious feelings worsened.

He's nothing but trouble…

"Sit, Erik," Callaghan suggested, gesturing to an empty seat beside his desk. Erik took the chair facing the desk while Callaghan turned in his chair, facing a small desktop computer and typed at the keyboard.

Ill at ease, Erik swallowed hard as a sinking sensation penetrated his guts and folded his arms across his chest, tucking his clenched hands beneath.

"*I shouldn't feel afraid*," he thought as the machine beeped when Callaghan typed at the keyboard and brought up several electronic records. "*Everything will be okay… I'll be fine.*"

Callaghan scanned the screen and nodded to himself, then turned to Erik with a warm smile on his face. "I see we have some extra talents, Mister Hart," he said brightly.

So you say…!

"I don't have that many," Erik murmured, cringing. "I'm just your average geeky dork. My friends call me 'Doofus' for a reason."

Callaghan chuckled. "You're no punk idiot kid, I can tell," he replied. "Alright, I want you to take some tests. You don't mind, do you?"

"Tests are okay and everything. There's nothing to it, right?"

"As long as you finish these for me today, then I'm okay."

Callaghan nodded to Erik and turned away from him, kicking back his chair. He rolled to a file cabinet on the office's other side and opened a drawer, pulling out a folder and a spiral-bound book.

Elbowing the cabinet shut, Callaghan wheeled back to his desk and set the folder aside. He opened the book and unfolded a long sheet of paper tucked inside that had a grayscale scene of people at a park. Placing it in front of Erik, Callaghan reached into his inside jacket pocket and withdrew a stopwatch.

"What's this for?" Erik asked.

"You have sixty seconds to find all the flaws on this page," Callaghan answered. "Now start."

Erik unfolded his arms and leaned forward, scanning the paper. "You have flaws on this paper here," he remarked, pointing to the page, "also here... here, here and there." Callaghan paled, putting down his stopwatch. "Where is the real test, Mister Callaghan? Is it open-book or do I have to already know this stuff?"

"You were supposed to find the flaws in sixty seconds," Callaghan said irritably. "You found them by half that!"

Erik's face flushed and he looked away. "What do you mean?" he murmured, running a hand nervously through his hair. "I'm sorry, Mister Callaghan."

"You don't have to be sorry," Callaghan said cheerfully and chortled. "That's okay."

Setting the book and long paper aside, he opened his folder and thumbed out a sheet. Placing it before Erik, Callaghan set the second sheet in front of him and withdrew a pen and pencil from a drawer in his desk.

Erik leaned forward, finding the page full of questions in list format with lines underneath for written answers. "And I thought it'd be multiple choice," he cracked.

"Then that'll be too easy," replied Callaghan, grinning. "I want you to take this test. It has sixty questions that cover the four main subjects: English, Science, Mathematics and History. All the questions start easily and then get harder. You have five minutes."

"What, no Social Studies?"

Callaghan raised an eyebrow. "What kind of question is that?"

"Which history are we covering?" Erik pressed.

Callaghan rolled his eyes. "It's obvious, kid." He handed Erik the pencil and took up the stopwatch in his free hand, clicking it. Erik took the pencil as the watch ticked and scanned the test, writing down answers as he went down the page.

After finishing the test, Erik pushed his paper toward Callaghan once he clicked his stopwatch. Glancing at his test, then at his stopwatch, Callaghan's face paled.

"*I don't like the way this feels...*" Erik thought, growing more on edge. He sank back into his seat, slightly disturbed as Callaghan wrote a note on his paper.

"You've finished that test in two minutes and forty-five seconds," the counselor murmured.

"Well, it was pretty easy," responded Erik. "Where's the challenging stuff, Mister Callaghan?"

"Give me a moment to check your answers," Callaghan muttered, giving Erik a wary glance.

"Sure, I can wait."

Callaghan compared Erik's paper with his master copy, checking off Erik's answers simultaneously noting against his master list. Erik sucked in a shallow breath once Callaghan stiffened after finishing and set the papers aside.

"All questions answered and correct," Callaghan said and looked up at Erik as he leaned back in his chair, blowing a short sigh. "Well..."

"Well, what?"

"Are you trying to jive me, kid?" Callaghan snapped and folded his arms across his chest, appearing tense. "Did you memorize these tests and their answers?"

"I never saw that kind of stuff before in my life," Erik retorted, clenching his hands at his sides. "No one's ever tested me like that, not ever!"

"I believe you," Callaghan uttered evenly, with the countenance on his face changing from unbelieving to cheerful.

"You disgust me," Erik thought. *"I've never seen an expression so fake!"*

Callaghan leaned forward and opened his folder, withdrawing another sheet with various words in columns. He handed one to Erik, keeping the master to himself.

"I want you to read this to me, going down the column," Callaghan ordered. "This has eighty words, starting really easy and getting harder as you go along. When I say 'go', do it, okay?"

"Okay..."

Callaghan narrowed his eyes and clicked his stopwatch. "Go."

Erik gripped his chair's edge, starting with the word 'ad'. As he read the list's words aloud, he realized the words were in alphabetical order. Coming to the last word 'Zhuangjiakou', Erik clenched his teeth as the sinking in the pit of his stomach worsened.

"*Some of these words I never heard of,*" he mused. "*Probably made up or something, like they were* _supposed_ *to be harder than normal...*" Erik blew an unsettled sigh. "*What is up with this?*"

Do you really believe that?

"Okay..." Callaghan murmured, taking the sheet back and scribbled a message on it. Placing it next to his duplicate that had notes in the margins, he reached into his bottom desk drawer and withdrew a wooden pegboard with pegs inserted. "Here's another test I want you to take."

"That looks fairly simple," Erik noted. "What are you trying to do, play me for the idiot punk kid you think I am?"

Callaghan's jaw tightened and he clenched the pegboard harder in hand. "I want you to put all the pegs into this pegboard," he said through gritted teeth, "and the point of this test is that I'm timing you on speed and accuracy." Callaghan banged the pegboard, voiding it of its contents.

Erik quickly scooped up the pieces before they rolled away and the counselor slapped the empty board before him. "I don't see the point of this," Erik complained. "What does this have to do with me?"

"Start." The click of the stopwatch underlined Callaghan's words.

"*What a horrid beast of a test!*" Erik thought and tensed as Callaghan's eyes betrayed another emotion altogether, brewing in exasperation beneath the fake pleasant smile he had plastered on. *"I know what you're feeling... hiding it on the outside!"* Erik stared back with a stony glare after he finished the trial. *"Inside you're feeling a mix of rage, of disarray and defeat..."*

"Erik..." Callaghan started.

"I don't know what you want from me," Erik snapped, cutting off the counselor. "I put all fifty pegs in the holes and you're still not satisfied!" He immediately stood. "If you're done trying to make a fool of me, I'm going back to class."

"I'm not done yet," Callaghan retorted, writing a note on his paper. He glared at Erik and pushed back his chair then leaned against his desk with an elbow. "Why do you feel you need to be perfect at everything you do?" he demanded.

"I told you I never saw these tests in my life," Erik objected. "What more do you want me to prove?"

"What is your IQ?"

"What does that matter?" Erik shot back. "I'm above average at best, I guess."

"Don't put me on and answer the question, Mister Hart."

"I don't know my Intelligence Quotient, Mister Callaghan," Erik muttered, looking down at the floor. "I've never been tested like that before."

"Do you know if you're a genius or not?"

"I really don't care to know." Erik ran a hand through his hair. "What difference does it make? It's not like I'm going to college at sixteen."

"You can go to the gifted class, Erik," Callaghan chirped, smiling warmly. "You'll still be in the same school as your friends."

Erik scoffed, giving Callaghan a wary glance. "Where are you going with this?" he pleaded. "You want to brand 'FREAK' on my forehead so your schools can win awards or something? I'm not into that, so forget it!"

Something doesn't feel right about this situation...

"Don't you want a more productive future?" Callaghan urged. "Don't waste your life being a lazy dumb ass, talking about what you could've done and wishing you did better when you had the chance."

"I'm not concerned with that," Erik grumbled. "I can choose what I want to do in life, even if I'm slinging burgers or pizza or whatever like that."

Callaghan snorted. "Total bullshit and you know it."

Erik folded his arms across his chest and narrowed his eyes at the counselor. "So, what's your point?" he sneered.

"Everyone's different, Erik," Callaghan said, still smiling. Erik grew unnerved by his wide smile as he continued. "You are unique."

"I don't care," Erik protested. "I don't want to stand out. I just want to be left alone and do my own thing. I enjoy hanging with my friends because we help each other out and our personalities complement each other, even though we come from very diverse backgrounds. They don't treat me different because I'm smarter than them. If anything, they rag me because of it as their weird way of accepting me into their group."

Callaghan's face twitched slightly. "Okay, whatever you say, Mister Hart," he warned in dejection, "but know this: you'll eventually have to grow up and get real with life. Why waste those smarts trying to fit in? It doesn't matter!"

"It matters to me!"

"You can go back to class now." Callaghan grabbed his pad of hall passes and wrote out Erik's destination. After tearing off the sheet, Erik held out a hand to take it and stiffened when Callaghan swiftly grabbed him by wrist, baring his teeth at Erik. "I'm sure you want to reconsider the offer, Mister Hart," Callaghan said through gritted teeth. "Why not better yourself?"

"I'm fine where I am," Erik declared. "Even if you don't agree with it, you can't make me do what you *think* is right. My life is *mine* alone, understand?"

"Are you *sure* about that?"

Erik tried to pull away, only to have Callaghan increase his grip. An invisible force pressed against Erik's head and he clenched his teeth.

Do you not understand what you have forgotten?

"What...?"

"Don't let popularity chip away at you," Callaghan sneered. "In the end, the popular ones end up working at some soul-destroying job while the smart ones lord over them."

It is for your own good...

Erik narrowed his eyes. "That's not what I want in life," he said through gritted teeth. "If I make bad choices, then it's my fault!"

If you refuse, then you may regret it...

"Fine then," Callaghan spat sternly as his face twitched again. He released his hold and Erik rubbed at his wrist. "Be that way, but you're only hurting yourself!"

"I'm not changing my mind," Erik growled, picking up his textbooks.

"Then what would you recommend instead?"

"I'm done with this!"

"Working in the mines isn't a good way to live, kid!"

"Whatever!"

Turning away, Erik slammed into the chair and hurtled over, striking the floor. He let out a cry as his books fell on him. Callaghan chuckled in response.

"You see what happens when you keep your head in the clouds, kid?" Callaghan jeered. "You break your face!"

Erik scrambled to his feet and grunted when he felt his nose burning. Running the back of his hand underneath it, he gasped when he found his blood dark blue instead of crimson.

"*What's going on?*" Erik thought, cupping his nose and glared back at Callaghan. Callaghan smirked, saying nothing. "*It hasn't been like this since--!*"

You're due for punishment... The incoming pain will be far more than what you're feeling now!

Erik bolted out the door, leaving his textbooks behind.

EIGHT

The time allotted for lunch finally approached. Going down the corridor, Erik entered the cafeteria and found to his dismay, a long line stretched around the corner and into the hall, filling the gap between his stomach and food.

"This can't be right," Erik griped. "Are the lines usually this long?" No one answered and he took his place at the queue's rear. Shoving his hands into his pockets, Erik idly listened to the surrounding conversation.

"Man, by the time I get my lunch," a nearby student complained, "I'll only have two minutes to drink da juice."

"Dude, I'll only have time to *smell* it if I ever get my lunch," said another next to him.

"Dude..." some others said in agreement who stood around Erik and the complaining students.

Glancing outside the line, Erik spotted the thief with his cap weaving through the assembled crowd, balancing a lunch tray in his hands as he headed toward a table. Erik pushed his way forward through the line, trying to sneak up on the student.

"Hey, man!" someone snapped, shoving Erik back as he wove through the crowd. "No cuts!"

Erik broke free and chased the student who dropped his tray when he heard Erik approach and bolted toward the door.

"Hey!" a voice called and a heavy hand fastened onto Erik's arm, yanking him back.

Erik whirled around and pulled out the stranger's grip, facing a tall athletic security officer who had olive skin, short black hair and narrow green eyes.

"No running," the guard snapped and Erik glared back at her.

"You're not going to cite me," he spat, "are you?"

"I'll look past it this time," the security officer replied, grinning darkly.

"What do you mean by that?"

"Whatever you want it to be, kid."

Erik swallowed hard, growing uncomfortable at the guard's unnerving smile. He turned away and walked past, only to get a hand clamped on his shoulder and pulled back. Stumbling rearward, Erik regained his footing and whirled around, facing the sentry.

"Why are you harassing me?" Erik snapped, clenching his hands at his sides.

The officer chuckled. "Where are you goin' in such a hurry, kid?"

"Somebody stole something from me and I'm getting it back." Erik blew an annoyed sigh. "Is that enough information for you or are you going to twist my arm?"

"Would you rather I did that?" Erik paled and the officer poked his chest. "Lookin' to punish, eh?" Erik coughed from the sudden pressure against his ribs when poked again. "Gonna put me outta my job, huh?"

"I'm not going to beat him up or anything," Erik protested. "I might rough him up a little though..."

"If you do that, then I'll have to rough *you* up."

"Can I go now?" Erik said in an exasperated tone.

"Aw, anxious to get back to some ass kicking, eh?" The officer chortled. "I never saw you 'round here before, kid."

"Same with you," Erik retorted.

"I been dealing with you punks all year and I know everybody." The officer gave Erik a long critical glance. "My guess is that you're new blood here."

"So what if it is?"

The officer pointed at her eye, then at Erik. "I'm keepin' my eye on you. I know you types."

"I'm no troublemaker."

"I'm sure you're not."

Erik backed away, suddenly baffled by the guard's hard stare. "What's that supposed to mean?"

I'm sure you know...

"Look, kid, don't cause problems here," the security officer said in a grim tone. "Kids like you love causin' me nothin' but difficulty and you don't wanna make me deal with it personally."

"You don't have to worry about me," Erik objected. "I'm not the kind that causes problems!"

"Sure, kid, they all say that!"

Erik cautiously stepped around the guard then took off in a run. Glancing over his shoulder, Erik saw the officer standing in the corridor, watching intently. Glad the woman didn't give chase; Erik rounded the hall and slowed his run once he approached a set of stairs, with one flight going up and the other going down.

"I doubt I'll ever come across that hat again with this school nearly bursting at the seams," he thought sourly. *"The only thing truly unnerving is that guard and counselor Callaghan; something just doesn't feel right about them!"*

A faint chill rushed through Erik as he descended the staircase.

You know otherwise...

Erik soon found himself lost downstairs in the school's bottom depths. *"I'm sure I passed the boiler room at least three times,"* he mused, walking past doors with huge locks on them. Finding the dimly lit lower levels warmer than anticipated, Erik found to his surprise he had not perspired.

Lights flickered on the brink of losing out power and a dank smell floated about; hearing a set of footsteps rush in, Erik searched hoping to spot his target. Another set came in moments later and Erik tensed as something brushed past him.

"Is there anyone down here besides me?" he called.

"Yep," a voice answered back, jarring him, "you're not alone."

Erik squinted, straining to see beyond the dim light shining in from afar; its source on the room's other side. He noticed a shadow against a wall with a broken light bulb on one end.

"Who's there?" Erik commanded.

"I'm nobody to you, Punk!"

A fist came out flying at Erik and he ducked, grabbing their hand. Pushing back his shadowy opponent, the mysterious fighter went sailing across the floor, crashing into the darkness.

Erik heard a groan and turned toward the sound, trying to catch his breath from holding it in. Another set of footsteps echoed through the room and Erik whirled around, straining his hearing trying to track them.

"Keep him busy!" a voice called back. Erik turned, searching for the source. "Sometimes you just underestimate your own strength, but thank you."

"What?" A groan came from nearby and Erik followed the sound, finding a faint outline of somebody sitting on the floor, rubbing at their head. "Are you okay?" Erik asked.

"I'm fine, you jerk!" The person below pushed Erik away. "Back off!"

"Behind you!" the voice offside called.

Erik turned to have his cap come back tossed at him, bouncing off his chest. He grabbed for it before it struck the floor.

"What's going on?" Erik demanded, putting the cap back on his head.

"Go on, scram," grumbled the voice behind Erik. "Leave me the hell alone!"

"*There are at least two people here,*" Erik figured, searching for the other person, now silent. "*Is the one upset with me chasing the one that's not really talking?*"

Suddenly, a hard push jolted Erik and he quickly turned around. Striking back, his fist hit nothing but air.

"I said to get the fuck out of here!" his opponent growled.

"I'm not leaving you here!" Erik declared. "If I hurt you, I want to make sure you're okay!"

"Heh, you should be more worried about yourself!"

Erik sensed the shadows moving and let out a yell once grabbed and pulled back in a swift hold. He yanked an arm free and raised it over his head, shielding his face as a cement block crashed into pieces on his arm when it made contact. Erik threw off whoever held him down and staggered back, stunned.

"What are you doing?" Erik yelled as his aggressor struck the floor with a hard thud.

"What does it fucking look like?" they snarled from behind.

"Are you trying to kill me or something?"

"Maybe!"

Erik tensed, whirling around when heard more footsteps echo throughout. "*I can't tell how many are down here!*" he thought, growing alarmed.

"Why are you down here?" the second voice shouted.

Erik strained to track them both and another person apparently bent on seriously injuring him.

"Why are you trying to hurt me?" Erik yelled. "All I wanted was my cap back; I wasn't going to beat you up!"

"Coming through!"

Erik cried out once plowed into and he struck the floor as a flash of light blinded him. The cap fluttered off his head, clattering to the ground behind him.

Sitting up, Erik noticed the swinging yellow bulb above him flickered dimly and shook his head, clearing his initial stun. Glancing at his arm, he saw his sustained cuts from the block crashing into it quickly healing on its own.

"I swear, I never intended on laying a hand on you!" Erik protested, watching his arm go from seriously injured to flawless. *"There are at least three people here!"* he realized from the confusion. *"What in the world is going on...?"*

"Yeah," the mysterious fighter scoffed, "right!"

"Really, I never want to hurt anyone!" Erik grabbed his nearby cap and stood, fixing the hat back on his head. "I don't like to see others hurt!"

"Liar and you know it!" Erik let out a yelp when suddenly grabbed in a stranglehold. His breath thinned as he struggled once their strength increased. "I'm through playing with you, Punk!"

"Let go!" Erik yowled and brought his foot down, followed by a muffled snap. "Why are you doing this to me?"

"You son of a bitch!"

Erik jammed his elbow hard into his aggressor, forcing a groan with two sickening cracks, followed by a faint cough. The door to the boiler room slammed open and Erik heard heavy footsteps storm in.

"Ay," Raider's voice called. "Don't make me come down there and tear you a new one!"

"Be careful, Raider!" Erik called.

The hold on Erik weakened, then released as the fighter slipped into a heap behind him. Turning, Erik faced them under the dim swinging bulb's light, and the glass broke as it charged and burned out. He knelt down and grabbed his former aggressor by the collar, shaking him.

"Get up!" Erik pleaded and cringed as sounds of Raider fighting grew intense.

"Get the fuck outta here you piece of shit!" Raider growled.

"Who else is down here?" Erik called once he heard footsteps running away after the fight. A faint chill rushed through him when he received no answer.

There's no one... But you're always being watched...

Focusing on his task, Erik dragged the body near the broiler room's doorway, getting them in better light. The wash of light revealed a young man around his age, apparently knocked unconscious.

The young man had a blond bowl cut with black roots growing out and pale white skin, almost as if he never saw the sun. The knocked-out fighter wore a blood-red dress shirt and slacks with white jackboots and had a tattoo on the side of his neck: 'PN13'.

"Why did you want to bust my head in?" Erik grumbled. "I never saw you before, let alone know you at all!"

"So, what'cha got there?" Raider asked upon approach.

Erik knelt closer over the young man's body, placing an ear to his chest and heard him breathing in shallowly, coming in slow and uneven.

"I have to get you to the nurse's office!" Erik murmured. "You need to wake up!"

"Ay, man," Raider snapped, taking Erik by the wrist, "leave him."

"Why?" Erik shook out of his grip and rose to his feet, glaring at him. Raider set his jaw, his expression becoming unreadable. "Why should I?"

"Just leave him alone." Raider turned away, clenching his hands at his sides.

"He came after me... I don't understand it!"

"Look, trust me on this one."

"What about the other one who was down here too?" Raider left without speaking, storming away. "So you're just going to ignore me?" Erik called after him.

Blowing a disgruntled sigh, Erik picked up the downed fighter and noticed though his body felt quite light, he had to pretend the young man weighed more than a sack of books as he carried him upstairs.

NINE

Arriving on the first floor of the school, where other students waited around until they had to go to class, Erik noticed most of them were either going to lunch or were coming back and about to head to class.

"Dude, like, what happened?" someone asked and before Erik knew it, a group of people surrounded him, talking excitedly to each other.

"He tried to smack me around and the next thing I know, I knocked him out," Erik replied in return. "Where's the nurse?"

"That way, man."

A plethora of fingers pointed the way and Erik carried the student to the nurse's office. Upon entry, Erik set him on a nearby cot then backed away. Before he sneaked out, the student started to stir.

"Damn..." he groaned, rubbing his head.

Turning around, Erik bumped into a burly-appearing nurse, who wore a pressed stark white outfit that consisted of slacks and short-sleeved dress shirt, black oxfords and black horn-rimmed glasses. Noticing the nurse had a navy tattoo 'PN04' marked on his right forearm, Erik suddenly grew nervous.

"*Are they related somehow?*" he wondered and immediately swallowed his dread, stepping back in mild fright.

"What are you doing here?" the nurse inquired as he pushed up his glasses on the bridge of his nose, his steel-blue eyes staring intently at Erik.

Erik swallowed hard and the sinking sensation firmly hit him in his guts in response to the nurse's presence. "He hit his head and I brought him here," he answered. "I really need to get to my next class." Before Erik made his escape, the nurse clamped a hand on his shoulder.

"You're not going anywhere!"

"Please, I don't want to get into any more trouble!" Erik pleaded. "It's my first day here and I just want to get through the day without more problems...!"

"You're not in any trouble," the nurse said gently.

"Then what do you want with me?"

"Don't act like you hardly remember me at all!"

"What?" The nurse let go and Erik turned around, studying him closely. "I..." The nurse smiled warmly and Erik clenched his teeth as a feeling of recognition flashed in his mind, quickly escaping before he focused on the thought. "I'm sorry," he murmured. "I don't recognize you."

We met once before...

"It's Stearne Gelnika!" The nurse said brightly. Erik gave a blank stare in return. "You called me 'Shot Glass' Stearne, don't you remember?"

Erik shook his head. "I'm still at a loss," he muttered.

Stearne folded his arms across his chest. "I left from Keystone several years ago," he said. "Don't you remember that day?" Erik shook his head again, unable to answer. "I was about eighteen when I left," Stearne filled in, "also around the same time; you were in talks with the Greenfields."

That doesn't sound right...

Erik reached forward and Stearne leaned back. Erik took his glasses and held them gently in hand while Stearne smiled sheepishly in return.

"Nothing's coming to mind," Erik said softly. "I don't know what else to tell you."

"I used to tease you," Stearne replied, "telling you I hated you so much for admiring me all the time."

"But how did you get a name like 'Shot Glass'...?"

Stearne chortled, flushing slightly. "Do you remember the drinking game we played?" Erik shook his head in response and Stearne grinned. "You know the one where we tossed quarters into an empty shooter."

A sudden memory flashed in mind and Erik recalled a younger Stearne opening a small case, revealing a small bottle of vodka and two shot glasses. Then another memory followed, with Stearne putting the flame from a lighter near the glass and it briefly caught fire.

"Two-hundred proof," Erik said slowly and Stearne nodded, smiling. "Strong enough to light up on fumes alone!"

"Whoever missed had to drink a shot of vodka and the game ended when someone passed out. You were amazed how I never became sick, never passed out drunk."

"What's with you then?" Erik asked. "Alcohol doesn't bother you or something?"

Stearne chuckled. "Heh, somewhat," he said. "Because I outlasted you, it was you who gave me my nickname." Erik grunted and Stearne jarred him with a hearty jostle to the shoulder. "Even so, you wanted to be like me in every way. I knew when you started to miss on purpose..."

"Yeah... I think." Erik shrugged his shoulders. "I doubt I'd do something stupid like that, though."

"You needed to loosen up some."

Erik stepped back, tense. "What are you doing here?" he demanded.

"I'm the nurse here," Stearne said proudly, standing taller. He flushed slightly and ran a hand through his cropped sandy hair growing out from fashioned into a flattop. "Well, assistant nurse." Stearne blew a sigh and smiled tersely. "I'm surprised you go to school here; I thought I'd never run into you again!"

"Again...?" Erik gave Stearne a wary glance. "How do you know me?"

"Oh..." Stearne chuckled as the flush on his face deepened. "Sorry, I forgot..."

"Forget what?"

"Never mind..."

"You're creeping me out being so happy to see me," Erik complained as Stearne continued to smile, though his eyes showed another emotion differently.

"We were quite close."

"How close are we talking here?"

"Like brothers."

"What's making you so sad?" Erik murmured.

"Well…" said Stearne as his voice started breaking. "I just wanted to tell you…" He sighed and took the glasses away form Erik, absently wiping at the lenses on his shirt's edge.

"Tell me what?" Erik asked guardedly.

"They say she died, not too long ago," Stearne said in a dead tone. "Drowning, they told me…"

"Who told you this?"

Stearne turned away from Erik, not looking in his direction and sighed heavily. "I didn't want to believe it, but I saw her… her hands were tied."

"What?" Erik cried, clutching his chest. He looked down at his free hand that grasped at nothing and vaguely remembered a necklace but the rest would not come to him. He watched Stearne struggle with his emotions as he continued. "But how can this happen? Who would do something so terrible?"

"Now you'll never see her again," Stearne said faintly. "I'm sorry, Erik."

Tears suddenly streamed down Erik's face, recalling the faded photograph Stearne always carried with him. Though he could not remember what she wore in the picture, he remembered her smiling face and bright indigo eyes as she reached for the camera, her long raven hair blowing around from the wind the day it was taken. The Stearne from back then pointed to the picture, then back at himself and Erik.

"Erik, are you okay?" Stearne asked from far away.

Erik shook his head and staggered forward towards a nearby chair. "I need to sit," he grumbled and grabbed a chair against the wall, falling into the seat.

The younger Stearne of the past smiled brightly, appearing so much different from the one with the fearsome presence and hardened looks.

Even his face can't hide the weariness and the pain of those terrible years...

"*You're one of us, because she's one of us; we're the same as her,*" the proud Stearne of long ago said, "*I'm your brother and don't you ever forget it!*" Erik shook his head, trying to get his brain straight with the present. Stearne approached, standing before him.

"You remember me telling you, before I left," Stearne said softly, breaking his thoughts, "but it's not true."

"Stop it," Erik muttered, gripping his head in his free hand while the other clutched hard to the armrest. "Don't say anymore!"

"Listen to me," Stearne pressed and slipped the glasses on his face. "I told you that you were my brother, but really, we're not. She was never our mother, though she cared for us..."

"How?" Erik sputtered, "why not?" He clenched his hands, pushing them to his forehead. "We're the same!" Erik cried.

"We are not and never will be!" Stearne yelled.

"You liar!" Erik shouted and sprang to his feet. He grabbed for Stearne and Stearne quickly stepped back, suddenly on guard. His face twitched and his hands curled into fists, though he did not raise them. Erik grabbed his shirt, shaking him. "You monster! Why would you tell me something so horrible?"

"No," Stearne said evenly as he shook his head. "No, Erik." He pried his fingers from his shirt. "The woman you remember... don't go looking for her. She's not around anymore."

"Who was she?" Erik demanded.

Stearne's back and shoulders tensed. "We're through with this, Erik," he growled.

"But--!" Erik took in a sharp breath. "But how? Who is she really?"

"Someone already dead!"

"Stearne, stop this!" Erik protested.

"Please, let it go," Stearne said in a more controlled voice.

"You tell me right now!"

"Get out before I get angry!" Stearne snarled. "You know what happens when I get angry and I have to try really hard not to!"

"Stearne!" Erik grabbed him by the arm and Stearne reacted by taking Erik's hand in a swift strong grip, breaking his hold and shattering the bones in them. Erik let out a stunned cry once let go and pulled away, stumbling over his steps as he neared the door. "Stearne, why...?" he yelped, disturbed.

Stearne's breathing turned irregular as he tried to keep his composure and his dark blue eyes grew blank. Erik yanked open the door and bolted, not wanting to contest him.

Erik's head reeled and he looked down at his wrist, flawless as usual, with some fleshy tone to his paleness. It mattered not how long he stayed out in the sun unprotected; he never became any darker than he currently saw himself.

Erik clenched his hand and it worked perfectly, though only moments before the same had nearly became destroyed, rendering it useless.

"*I'm imagining things,*" Erik thought, taking in a breath and wiped his eyes with the back of his hands. "*I'm just stressed out...*"

The woman in the photograph generated little of all he could remember, with any names or other memories seemingly wiped out. He knew resolutely in his mind in which he firmly held onto the woman had been his mother, Stearne existed as his brother, and she cared about them both.

There is something not quite right with this...

The threads of recognition were too fragile and the more he held on trying to piece them together, the more the lines were misplaced. Erik agonized over the woman he barely remembered now dead and the only brother he knew wanting to forget him made him want to vomit.

They will only erase you, torture you then kill you if you get too close...

Erik grew chilled and came to a sudden stop in the middle of the congested corridor, surrounded by students who packed the halls.

"*I refuse to believe she's gone, just like that,*" he mused. "*Such a nice and kind person punished so harshly... What is it she could've done to deserve such bad treatment?*" Pain radiated in Erik's hands and he looked down, noticing he clutched them tightly. He released his hands and blew a shaky sigh. "*Get it together and leave it alone. If Stearne got so broken up over that, then it must be true.*"

Erik yelped in surprise when abruptly grabbed by the arm and wrestled into a hammerlock. He fell slack, waiting for his aggressor's next move.

"Where have you been?" a familiar voice snapped in his ear. "I'm about to pulverize these idiots who said you knocked some jerk cold and I know *to the fact* you hate fighting!"

"Francisca, it was an accident!" Erik protested. "I was caught off guard, for real!" Francisca let him go and glared at him. "Honestly, I tried to reason with him and he just jumped me!" Erik put his hands up in surrender. "You believe me, right?"

Francisca blew an annoyed sigh. "Come on, Doofus," she muttered and pushed past him, going down the hall. Erik hurried to her side, following in step. "We have History class."

Entering a silent classroom where a tall young man with frizzy red hair lounged on the desk, snoring loudly, Francisca shoved Erik into a desk.

Francisca sat in the desk in front of Erik and pulled out a worksheet to work on. Erik glanced around the room, noting the other students appeared to be working on various papers. He grew slightly disturbed by the sheer normalcy of the actions taken around him and leaned forward in his seat, looking over Francisca as she wrote in answers.

"I thought he's supposed to be teaching," Erik said softly.

Francisca leaned back slightly. "He is," she answered. "We get these worksheets and he gets his afternoon nap." She turned to face Erik. "Just don't wake him up, okay?" Francisca poked the eraser end of her pencil at Erik's forehead. "He's a monster if he doesn't sleep after lunch!"

"Well, what can I do?" Erik complained. "I don't have anything to work on!"

"Find something!" She turned back to her work.

Erik sighed, growing bored as he watched the class listlessly. Moments later, a student stood up and stepped silently toward the desk, making a grab for the box of tissues.

The student gingerly pulled out two sheets and tried to place it back as quietly as she could. Erik tensed as the whole room became frozen in fear when the box clattered on the floor. The teacher rigidly shot up in his chair, his eyes extremely bloodshot.

"What's going on?" he barked, whirling around. "The bell doesn't dismiss you; I dismiss you!" The girl cringed and Erik immediately rose to his feet.

"Get back in your seat," Francisca hissed, elbowing Erik's side.

Erik pushed her away and walked up to the teacher's desk. The teacher glowered at the other students and they hunched at their seats, pretending to be busy. Glaring at Erik, the teacher bared his teeth.

"What the hell do you think you're doing?" he growled through gritted teeth.

"It's my fault," Erik said, picking up the tissue box. "I wanted to ask you something, but I didn't know your name. I know it's no excuse since I'm new here, but if she's in trouble, let me get whatever punishment you deem is just."

Erik set the box back on the edge of the desk. The girl gave Erik an expression of relief and he smiled assuredly at her in return.

"Eh? Yeah? Well, don't do it again and it's Marion to you!" Marion crossed his legs and placed his hands behind his head then reclined back in his chair. Once he closed his eyes, snores escaped him again.

"Thank you," the girl whispered and hurried back to her desk.

Erik sighed, his moment of adventure over with. Heading reluctantly back to his desk, Francisca smirked and rolled her eyes at him as he sank into his seat.

"You can't get out of everything by moving that mouth," Francisca said to him.

"How am I supposed to know all this?" Erik grumbled and groaned, holding his head in his hands. "I never had classes with that beast!"

"Please," Francisca drawled and made a razzing sound. "You don't know, Doofus, you learn!"

Erik sighed. "This is going to be a tough semester," he spat.

"You think?"

Erik moaned in frustration and put his head on the desk.

TEN

Walking home, Erik listened to his friends talk about their day at school. He gave noncommittal responses, fretting they would misunderstand even after explaining to the best of his ability about his misadventures.

Raider noticed Erik deep in thought and poked him in the side to get his attention. "Ay, wassup in there?" Raider asked. "Something wrong with ya?" Erik shook his head. "What's the matter?"

"There's nothing wrong," Erik replied. "I'm just thinking, you know?"

"You see this here?" Raider tapped the side of his head with his hand. "I don't do too much thinking with this melon of mine. Me and the brain... we just ain't cool; it ain't a good mix."

Erik laughed as Raider gave him a wide smile and jostled him playfully by the shoulder. "Almost everything with you doesn't mix!"

"Did I tell you guys he almost got chewed out by Mister Marion?" Francisca interjected. "I was about to bust Erik's caps out for bothering, but he charms the old man."

"Always working like you usually do, huh?" Raider said, shaking his head. "Man, you and your stuff!" He jumped up and seized Erik in a loose holding lock, making false jabs into his side. Erik giggled and pushed him away and Francisca laughed, grabbing him by the arms.

"I'll hold him down for more punishment!" she crowed.

"Make sure he doesn't squirm!" Hanalei cheered. "I'll keep score!"

"You're such the advocate, Hana!" Erik said brightly and worked a hand free, making a weak swipe at her. She squealed and jumped away.

"You know what?" Raider said, pretending to slap Erik across the cheek. "I ain't worried." Hanalei tousled Erik's hair and he blushed, smiling at her.

Erik pushed Raider away, grinning as he pulled out from Francisca and Raider put his arms around them both. "Why is that?" Erik asked.

"That's 'cause you learned how to be awesome from me!"

They all laughed as Raider let go and jabbed lightly at Erik. Erik giggled and pushed him back.

"I know I can never be as intimidating and coolheaded as you," Erik said, "but given the chance, I can just about talk my way out of any situation…"

"Well, don't talk yerself into trouble, dig?" Raider replied and grabbed Erik, pulling him close. "I can't always be there to help you rumble!"

"I promise," Erik said and Raider chuckled, tousling his hair.

"Alright, you suckers," Raider called as he let Erik go. "This is where we split!" He gave them a salute before running down the beaten paths leading to his house. "See you jerks later!"

Erik and company waved him goodbye.

"Well, we'd better get going," said Francisca as she headed up the steps of her house.

Hanalei followed and poked Francisca's chest hard. "We're going to exchange papers to check for correct answers," she said sternly. "You'd better pay close attention this time!"

"Yeah, I know," Francisca griped, rolling her eyes, "and knowing me, everything is going to be wrong as usual." She made a razzing sound. "Believe me, if I could learn by osmosis, I would!"

"There's a reason for that: you don't study!"

Francisca made grand, wide sweeping gestures as clutched her chest, staggering as if she were shot. "Leave now, Erik!" she wailed dramatically. "Leave and save your brain before Headmistress Hana beats you with her ruler!"

Erik laughed as Hanalei started ranting. "See you," he said and waved them off, then left on his own way, cutting through the corn and wheat fields.

"My friends are great," Erik thought. *"We work together so well, though our personalities are all so vastly different."* He smiled as he continued on his way home. *"They accept me despite..."*

Erik suddenly drew a blank and it dawned on him he couldn't recall how they met. He *knew* Raider from *somewhere* in Aynslea and that Raider was friendly with Hanalei and Francisca. Raider even made his way to introduce them to Erik when he moved into the neighborhood.

Erik's unease worsened once he finally reached the Greenfield residence when he realized the memory seemed misplaced with what he knew.

Erik could rattle off their likes and dislikes such as colors, food, clothes, and their birthdays and hobbies, yet couldn't account for any history between them.

Nothing came to mind, not even a special day or year when the four of them worked together on a project, made any plans, or spent summer vacation as a group of friends. He swallowed hard, growing increasingly uncomfortable at how he knew such information or for how long.

It seems far too perfectly normal...

Reaching the steps, Erik came to pause in front of the door. Looking around on the porch, he noticed how everything around him seemed somehow *off*.

A little too perfect, in fact...

Stepping back to get a better view of the house, Erik noted the housing itself, built of brick, had red paneling to match the foundation. The trim, accented in white, including the nameplate near the white screen door had wrought iron leaves and vines as the pattern, seemed flawless.

The mahogany Monticello door did not look as if was very old. The whole house itself, from the large bay windows to the spacious carport appeared too new, including the paint on the side of the house where the sun shone often did not seem chipped from the weather.

The only personality of the house was Jane Greenfield's pastel colored glass wind chimes, as well as John Greenfield's bamboo chimes hanging over the carport - mundane at best.

"They're just *normal*," Erik muttered under his breath. "I'm just freaking out over nothing..."

Or so you think!

A queer sinking sensation penetrated Erik as he came up the steps and opened the screen. Placing his hand on the doorknob, the door swung silently open and an eerie silence followed him as he entered a dark empty house.

Erik noticed John Greenfield's briefcase missing from the parlor's cocktail table and Jane Greenfield's purse void from the counter along with her pearls. He knew she would usually be in a clean apron, preparing something sweet while her husband sat at the kitchen table with the free newspaper he picked up from the office, but on this afternoon, neither one left any trace of their presence.

Erik drifted into the kitchen after taking off his cap and set it aside the chair's post. He ran a hand over the stainless steel electric stove then glanced at the refrigerator door, finding no notes posted there. The telephone rang moments later and Erik quickly grabbed for the phone on the far wall near the kitchen entrance.

"Greenfield residence," he greeted, only to hear the sound of steady breathing and haunting background music. "Hello...?" Growing unnerved, Erik immediately placed the receiver back in the cradle and leaned against the wall, disturbed. Hearing the floorboards creak, he whirled around, noticing movement from upstairs. "Is anyone here?" Erik called.

Rushing up the staircase to the master bedroom, he opened the door and saw John Greenfield punching a man in a dark suit and throw him against the door. Erik cried out, jumping back when the man's weight smashed against the panel, slamming it shut.

"What's going on in there?" Erik called and knocked frantically.

You're only going to get yourself killed...!

"Are you okay?" Erik demanded. "Please, open the door!" Before he could grab for the knob again, the phone rang downstairs, startling him. Erik looked down the hall, afraid to answer it.

You're in danger if you stick around!

A soft click followed and Erik grabbed the door handle. He turned it, finding it locked.

"Father, answer me!" Erik called, knocking.

"Answer the phone, Son," John Greenfield's voice called from the other side in a strained tone.

"Why?" Erik demanded, knocking again as the phone continued ringing repeatedly. "Your room can get the main line as well!" He received no answer in response.

You know why...

"Please, Son," John Greenfield pleaded moments later.

"Don't you lie to me!" Erik said angrily, giving one final bang in frustration. "I will hate you forever!"

"Please, don't say things like that," answered John Greenfield.

Unable to say anything else, Erik retreated to his room. Opening the door, he cried out when he found it trashed from someone searching for something of importance.

"What the–?" Erik yelped.

"So, think you can escape, eh?" a voice suddenly said to Erik and he froze.

Whirling around as his door slammed shut, Erik faced a tanned woman with long raven hair who wore a simple black A-line dress and calf-high leather boots. On her slender face, she wore a pair of darkly colored mirrored glasses and long cuffed leather gloves on her hands.

"Don't be afraid," she said softly.

"Who are you?" Erik demanded, backing away. "What are you doing here in my room?" He clenched his teeth as pain flashed behind his eyes at the sight of her. "What are you looking for?"

The woman smiled faintly at Erik then her overall expression turned serious. "If you don't remember my name," she answered, "then there is no use telling, is there?"

Erik gasped when sharp pain quickly struck the back of his neck, traveling down his shoulders and arms. His wrists ached and he rubbed at them when sudden raw bruises appeared on his hands traveling as angry red lines up his arms.

"I'm not sure if I want to remember..." Erik retorted. "Besides, you didn't answer my question!"

"It matters not what we want," the woman replied. "What matters is you."

"We?"

An arm roughly grabbed Erik by the chest, pulling him back and he stiffened when a gloved hand clamped over his mouth. Glancing over his shoulder, Erik saw a young man with high cheekbones and two gold hoops in his left ear and a silver one in his right, wearing smoky glasses and a dark navy yachting cap covering his shaggy dark blond hair.

The young man, dressed in black turtleneck, jeans, and motorcycle boots had a titanium watch with both analog and digital readings hanging from his left wrist. He grinned at Erik and Erik had a flash of faint recognition as pressing fear gnawed him.

Why are you here?! You're not supposed to be--!

"Just listen to the lady," the young man said and snapped Erik's face forward at the woman who approached.

"Let me go!" Erik growled, struggling with his captor.

A low whine droned in Erik's ears once the young man wrestled him to the floor with ease. He heard faint voices speaking from afar as the woman knelt down to him, pressing her fingers to his chin and lifted his head.

Don't fight us...

"Here's what it is," she said evenly. "Your father is fine; so don't bother calling for him."

Erik pulled back and the young man tightened his grip. "What about Mother?" he pleaded. The woman frowned and said nothing. "Please let me go," Erik begged. "I won't do anything!"

"No, you will."

"Why are you here?"

"We're here to make sure things go as planned."

"How am I part of your plan?"

"So you *do* remember?"

Erik gave her a blank stare. "Remember what?" His fear intensified when the man tightened his grip.

"As for you, you are not satisfactory. You are going to become a risk and if you want to keep your happy little life as you know of it, you do as we say."

Erik shook his head. "I'm not listening to you," he snapped. The drone in his ears worsened, turning into static and Erik clenched his teeth as he shut his eyes, shaking his head when the voices grew louder.

Hurry with it...!

Stop scaring him...!

I'm not trying to...!

"Don't come looking for any others who are like you," the woman continued.

"Shut up!" Erik shouted.

"You will only end up dead in the process," the woman pressed. "As for us, they assume we are dead."

Erik's eyes snapped open. "I'm not going along with it if it means harming my family!" he yelled and shouldered the woman back, knocking her rearward.

Breaking free from the young man's grip, Erik elbowed him back in the side and turned, socking him in the chest. The young man stumbled then grabbed his wrist and Erik reversed him. Throwing the young man back, Erik sent him sailing into his chest of drawers, crashing into them. The young man groaned and staggered to his feet.

The woman jumped to her feet and made a grab for Erik. He pushed her arms aside and slapped her away, forcing the glasses off her face. Erik gasped when he saw her pained indigo eyes as she looked directly at him, touching her sore cheek. Erik backed away, clenching his hands.

"You're that woman in the picture!" he cried. "You're supposed to be dead!"

A saddened expression shadowed her face and before she could say more, the young man's watch beeped.

"Genovera, we need to go," he said and hurried for Erik's bedroom window, throwing it wide open.

"Genovera?" Erik squawked as Genovera approached.

"We need to go, *now*!" the young man yelled.

Erik pushed her away and raised his fists. "Don't touch me!" he spat. "I will hit you, woman or not!"

Genovera pushed down his hands and leaned forward. "There is no need to fight," she said softly in his ear. "Fight when you are protecting the weak and never forget who you are. Let your spirit prevail at any given cost."

"But--!"

"Keep yourself alive and we'll meet again."

The static Erik heard worsened into white noise and he cried out, clamping his hands over his ears as he doubled over in pain. "What are you doing to me?" he screeched. Genovera appeared concerned and touched Erik's shoulder.

"Forget him," the young man snapped and jumped out the window, landing several feet below on the ground.

"Don't hold it against me," Genovera said softly and broke away, hurrying for the window.

Erik stood as she climbed out and he ran for the pane after it slammed down shut. He watched her grab onto the branch of the tree, swinging down and land steadily on her feet next to the young man waiting below. He grabbed her hand and both ran away to a motorcycle parked behind a larger tree on the other side of the street.

A heavy chopping sound resonated at Erik's door and he turned, overcome by instant dread washing over him as the mirror rattled.

They're coming to punish you... Tell them nothing! You know nothing!

Erik heard the motorcycle outside turn and revved its engine then sputtered. The slight pain saturating his arms and neck spread further, rising to his back and head. He held his hands over his ears as the low drone screeched louder in his head, forcing him to his knees.

Don't fight me... I will punish them for you...

The mirror on the back of the door crashed to the floor, spraying silvered glass everywhere as the panel split open and a red mast axe came through.

"*Who wants to hurt me?*" Erik thought frantically as the axe yanked back and hammered again through the wood. "*Are they going to kill me?*"

The ones who want you are mindless sheep... The one who wants you dead is the wolf...

Erik's skin grew cold as his breathing turned into a chore. "I don't understand...!" he wailed. "What are you talking about?"

Beware of his illness... for once it overtakes you, you'll be no more!

"What does it mean?" Erik cried.

The numbing pain took over and he went blind.

ELEVEN

Erik's eyes snapped open and he gasped when he found himself staring up at the overcast sky. He blinked, trying to clear the cryptic letters and glowing green numbers scrolling and flashing across an invisible screen.

Erik groaned and rubbed at his eyes once pain began to register in his body, though the flashing text did not disappear. Sitting up, he rapped the side of his head, jarring the continuously scrolling numerals, and then tilted his chin until the bones popped in his neck, forcing the glowing digital lines vanishing completely.

Blowing a sigh of relief, Erik frowned when his green-tinted vision hadn't cleared to color. He looked around, disturbed when he saw he lay in a deeply cracked impact crater on the sidewalk below a towering apartment building.

"There's no way I caused that!" Erik muttered. "I'm not that heavy!"

A heavy object smashed against Erik's head and he wailed in pain as his vision flashed momentarily in red. Clattering beside him lay a broken suitcase and several cartridges.

Erik rubbed his head and looked up, noticing a woman in a dark uniform standing at his apartment's broken balcony window. She waved and disappeared back inside.

Erik grunted and punched at the suitcase, sending it flying. Beneath the case lay the translucent blue pen with a golden nib. He picked it up and slipped it in his pocket.

Sudden noise screeched in his ears and abruptly gave way to screams and cries of general panic around him. Rising upright, Erik turned in the direction they ran from, spotting a young man in a dark suit standing on the roof of Farmless Tower.

Erik's vision cleared to vivid color once he focused and studied the man, noticing he had long wavy silver hair, blue skin, and glowing red eyes. Cackling blue-violet light surrounded his body and the mysterious stranger raised his hand, forming greenish-black daggers.

Thrusting down his hand, the shards multiplied, raining on the people below, instantaneously killing some while wounding many others. The survivors ran for safety, trying to avoid another attack.

"*What is that?*" Erik wondered in awe, amazed at the being's incredible power as it towered over everyone else on the tallest building in the city.

The man jumped from the edge and smashed into the pavement a thousand feet below, forming deep cracks in the surface as he landed on bended knee.

Standing with ease, he turned around and thrust forward a charged hand, releasing a navy sphere. The ball of flame crashed Farmless Tower's side, instantly destroying the observation deck. The building caught aflame, throwing dark heavy smoke in the air.

"I need to get it together!" Erik said to himself as the blue-skinned fighter turned away and started crossing the lot.

Looking around, Erik noticed an abandoned security cruiser near the apartment complex he stood in front of, its radio cackling. He approached and listened in.

"All defense units, report to Farmless Tower at once," stated the voice of the dispatch operator over the radio. "There's been what appears to be a terrorist attack in Menoka at Farmless Tower. I repeat..."

Erik made haste for the tower, feeling his own energy flare as he sprung into action.

"It's him," he thought. *"It has to be..."*

Overhead several helicopters belonging to the Defense Force division cut through the skies, heading toward the mysterious being. Sirens wailed from security cruisers racing toward Farmless Tower, followed by ambulances and fire corps engines.

News crews in their vans attached with huge satellite dishes sped for the scene, intent on capturing the unfolding story.

The blue-skinned battler raced ahead, dodging gunfire the militia unleashed from their machine guns. He made a leap, bulleting toward the three helicopters flying above him and threw a sphere of blue flame. The fiery globule smashed into one copter and the vehicle imploded on impact.

The silver-haired fighter waved a hand, unleashing another fireball. The concentrated flames bashed into the second and the crippled copter crashed onto the third.

Screams erupted as the police scurried away and the citizens dove for cover when both aircraft fell from the sky into a burning heap of twisted metal, scattering gravel and glass.

The fighter hurled another blast of azure flame toward the ground, colliding on the security vehicles scattered below. The force of the blast threw Erik as he approached the perimeter, forcing him back on his rear, slightly dazed.

Getting up, Erik shook his head, clearing the fog and clenched his hands as his power flashed stronger around his body.

"Now's my chance," Erik mused as the fighter dropped down from the sky, stomping on a security cruiser for his landing as he touched down with a bang.

Stepping off, the warrior kicked the crumpled metal aside, sending it flying several feet. He drew near a wounded woman who held her young child close, paralyzed in fear. The fighter grinned darkly, stepping toward her and she recoiled, clutching the wailing boy close.

The fighter raised a charged fist and Erik rushed forward, taking a stand before them. He immediately blocked the crushing blow over them with his arms.

A police officer and a soldier armed with a high-powered rifle ran over to the woman. The officer grabbed the woman by the arm, dragging her away as the soldier kept his gun trained on Erik, backing away toward the safety of his unit.

Struggling against the force, Erik then threw back his silver-haired opponent, tossing him head over heels on the ground.

"You shouldn't hurt innocent people," Erik snapped. "They didn't hurt you!"

"Get out of my way," the battler growled, leaping to his feet. "Or you'll be the next to die!"

"Now leave them alone," Erik snapped. "Or I'll have to break you!"

"Bring it!"

The blue-skinned fighter shot off a dark charge of light and Erik thrust both glowing hands, creating a shield of light immediately diffusing the sphere.

"Is that all you have?" Erik vaunted. "You're not strong enough!"

"I'll show you!"

Erik raced ahead and threw a powerful punch infused with bright blue-white light, slamming his empowered fists into the fighter's face before he could react. The man's head whipped back and he crumpled onto the ground. Erik stood over him, heaving for breath.

"This is your last warning!" spat Erik. "I doubt you can take more punishment."

"What immeasurable strength...!" a nearby officer cried.

"He defeated the monster!" said another.

"Not yet," Erik called to the crowd. "He might get up again, tough as he is..."

"What are you?" bellowed a third.

Erik looked up, spotting a uniformed officer wielding a high-powered pistol standing offside. He noticed the officer wore a lanyard around his neck, holding a silver badge.

"I should ask you the same," Erik called back.

"I'm the district public security chief," the officer snapped. "First of all, explain all this commotion and watch your answer." He waved his pistol at Erik. "If it's the wrong one, I might have to pump you full of lead!"

"I'm sorry for all this," Erik said, "but this monster - he was created to destroy."

"Created? Monster?" The police chief let out a short laugh. "Look, kid, don't talk nonsense! I've about had it with you!"

"I don't have time to explain - it's too dangerous for you to be here!"

"What the hell?" the officer spat. "Don't tell me how to do my job!"

Thunder rumbled overhead and violet lightning crackled around them. Erik grew tense as harsh cold winds blew forcefully around the area. He looked up, noticing falling snow.

"*Thundersnow...*" Erik thought. "*That means...!*"

"On my count," the chief shouted. "Ready!" The other assembled officers raised their weaponry.

"Wait!" Erik cried.

Haunting manic laughter filled the street and a stroke of violet lightning struck near Erik, unleashing a blast of crystalline spears spiking up from the ground.

The fighter leapt to his feet, snarling at Erik. Erik took a step away, frightened of his opponent still able to stand.

Pale porcelain white skin appeared under parts of the young man's dark blue exterior that cracked and fell off in places. Black and dark navy streaks appeared in his silver hair and one eye glowed violet.

"What the flying hell?" the chief of police screeched. "That monster got up!"

"Thought you had the drop on me, eh?" the mysterious fighter sneered. "You awakened too late, however..."

"I'll reduce you to ashes," Erik snapped. "You need to stop!"

"I can't go against programming... And neither can you!"

"Men, be on your guard," the chief officer called and pointed his pistol at Erik's opponent. "This one looks pretty nasty..."

"Don't shoot!" Erik screeched and the officer opened fire. Erik ducked as the bullets tore into the blue-skinned battler.

"What's this?" Erik's opponent grumbled as the bullets slammed into him, denting upon contact. "Interesting..."

"Fire!" the chief officer shouted and the rest of the Public Security officers joined by the Defense Force soldiers let loose a torrent of bullets with their pistols, shotguns, rifles and machine guns. The warrior wailed in terror as his body was consumed in a hail of gunfire and he fell back, crashing into the earth.

Erik cautiously stepped forward once the soldiers and officers ran out of bullets after the dust cleared. Standing over the young man, he found his body still and his eyes closed.

Bending toward him, Erik gasped as the once-dead eyes snapped open. The fighter grabbed Erik by the throat and Erik yelped when thrown back with force. His body smashed into a security cruiser, crashing out the windshield.

"Did you enjoy tearing me to bits, gentlemen?" the silver-haired young man asked, standing with ease. The cracked dark skin under the barrage of bullets crumbled and fell away, revealing more pale skin underneath.

"What the hell...?" the chief wailed, backing away.

Erik grunted, wriggling out of his crumpled position and fell over the hood of the car, landing on his face in the pavement.

"Get away," groaned Erik, staggering to his feet. "He's too strong to take on at your level!"

"I might have to kill you now," said the young man and clenched his hands sparking in green electricity. "But oh well, you get it, eh?"

"Everyone," Erik screamed, "get out of here, now!"

A high whine emitted from the young man when he raised his electrified hands, his body surrounded by green light. Erik charged, hurrying before the group of officers and took a direct hit from the spewed blast of flame aimed at him. The shield of energy around Erik's body flickered out and he clenched his glowing hands glimmering in golden light.

"Wilhelm, there's no reason for you to hurt these people," Erik snapped. "Take your aggression out on me, not them."

"Why should I bother with that, Ferdian?" Wilhelm spat. "They can't be saved. All they do is destroy, fight, and kill - they need to be stopped!"

"If you kill them, then what will happen to you?" Erik retorted. "Without them, you can't live."

Wilhelm scoffed. "I don't care about life, obviously!"

"I'll restore whatever you destroy every time," Erik snarled. "Don't make me break you!"

"I've yet to see you even try to cancel my destruction..."

"If you keep this up, then I'll have to!"

"Tch, then stop pretending to hesitate!" Wilhelm beckoned to Erik. "Come on, do your worst. You know we were made to oppose each other!"

"Yes, for me to keep you in check!"

"Then check!"

Erik grunted from a lightning-fast blow to the face, sending him hurling fast forward to the ground. He slammed into the pavement below, throwing up large chunks of concrete flying in the air.

Erik struggled to sit up as Wilhelm generated a large sphere of black light, cackling in violet electricity. The air around them plummeted to below freezing and the officers panicked, scattering at once seeking warmer air.

"Are you satisfied, Wil?" Erik groaned. He reached into his pocket, withdrawing the pen and it cackled in white light, transforming into a golden long sword with a winged hilt. "I didn't want to use this... but now, it's my turn to destroy!"

"You're still too weak!"

Erik staggered to his feet, holding the sword in both hands. "*Ieoshira!*" Erik dashed ahead and thrust forward the blade before Wilhelm let loose his charged attack. "*Sirajen!*" He sliced down, followed by a wing of silver light. "*Kenzan Karin!*"

A giant blast of white light erupted, blinding Erik completely and a high whine droned in his ears as intense pain washed over him. His vision slowly turned to red, then faded to black.

TWELVE

"Erik, dear," Jane Greenfield's voice called from afar. "Erik, do you hear me?"

Erik stirred, coming out of his dark fog and his eyes fluttered open. "What happened?" he murmured. Looking up, he saw Jane Greenfield kneeling beside him, appearing troubled.

"Well..." Jane Greenfield sighed and looked away.

Erik sat up and turned to her line of sight, finding John Greenfield standing offside with his arms folded across his chest. At his feet was a pile of split wood and the shattered mirror. Leaning against the hacked-open door frame lay the large red mast axe.

"Did I cause this?" Erik asked. "I'm sorry..."

"We heard you screaming," Jane Greenfield answered softly. "We couldn't get in and the door was locked."

"That's a bit extreme," Erik murmured. "Did you lose your key?" He stiffened when squeezed in a firm embrace.

"I was so worried!" Jane Greenfield cried.

"I'm not hurt or anything," Erik said once Jane Greenfield let go. He rose upright and lent her a hand. She took it and Erik pulled her to her feet.

"Are you sure you're all right?"

"Yes, Mother, I'm fine." Erik approached John Greenfield and he pulled away when touched on the arm. "Father, are you all right?" Erik asked gently.

John Greenfield turned away, grunting. "I'm fine," he muttered.

"Do you know a woman named Genovera?"

"Please, Son," John Greenfield said exasperatedly and pushed him away. "I don't want to talk about it."

"Face me, Father," Erik pressed. "Are you all right?"

"Nothing happened," grumbled John Greenfield. "Everything is all right now, Son."

"*But there's something wrong,*" Erik thought, sighing as Jane Greenfield approached her husband's side and touched him by the elbow. "*It has to be something about that woman...*"

Once they left the room, Erik looked around the trashed bedroom and picked up the dark glasses the woman named Genovera left behind, finding them snapped in half.

Glancing at the mirror's part left standing; he noticed it seemed older than the rest of anything in the house. Erik walked up to it, facing his reflection and touched the large fragment's silvered surface, noting its unnatural sheen.

"What happened?" Erik muttered at the disoriented teenager in mussed clothing staring back at him. "Why can't I remember? Why are they acting like what just went on never happened?"

You'd like to see, wouldn't you?

"I don't know," Erik murmured. "Would it hurt me to see?"

I don't know... Is that all you can say?

"Then what is it?"

117

*Seeing will drive you cold and numb and to the fringe of
madness...*

"What do you mean?" Erik clenched his teeth as cuts and
punctures slowly began to appear on his arms.

You need to remember...

"Remember what?"

Remember what they did to you...

"What did they do?" Erik cried out as the wounds deepened
and dropped what he held, clutching his chest as deep
excruciating pain ate away at it.

They're trying to control you... destroy you...

"Who is trying to control me?"

Erik heard a snap and staggered back as his right arm
turned lame. He collapsed onto his knees as dark burns
covered his left arm and the biting infliction spread throughout
his body. Erik struggled to breathe and the pain slowly grew
stronger.

Would you still like to see, Ferdian?

"Ferdian?" he moaned. "Who is he?"

Look into the mirror.

Erik looked up and saw his reflection standing with his
hands folded across his chest. Puzzled since he lay on the floor
wounded whereas the reflection stood in perfect health
uninjured, Erik gasped when he noticed the reflection had high
cheekbones, narrow blue eyes and earrings in his ears.

"Wait--! You're that guy...!"

A series of knocks outside Erik's window made the pain
vanish and he turned, searching for the sound. Looking at the
mirror, he saw his own reflection on the floor and let out a

shaky breath. Standing to his feet, Erik approached the pane, finding Raider hanging from the tree, grinning brightly.

"Yo," Raider called and waved.

The last of Erik's soreness faded away and he opened the window then poked out his head.

"Hey," Erik greeted and gave a terse smile. "What's up?"

"Nothin' but word on the street," Raider replied.

"What's the word?"

"Crazy shit's gonna go down soon, dig it?" Raider gave Erik a wary glance. "Wassup with the firewood over there? Some farmer did a job on yer door fer sure!"

Erik glanced back at the broken door, the cracked mirror and leaning mast axe. "I know; it's crazy..." He laughed nervously and rubbed the back of his neck. "It's not a big deal, really..." Erik turned back to Raider who let the branch go he held onto and hung upside down by his legs.

"Ah, no biggie... I get it." Raider ran his hands through his scalp as his hair hung free. "What 'bout them 'rents of yers?"

"I don't know. Mister Greenfield won't even look at me!"

"Say what?" Raider said, astonished. "What you do, clock 'im or somethin'?"

Erik shook his head. "No, I would never do that!" He scoffed. "What makes you think I'd do something like that?"

"I dunno man," Raider replied. "You got a helluva temper."

Erik gave Raider a blank look. "Okay, what?"

"Never mind what I said," Raider snapped. "So, your old man okay or what?"

"I mean... He looks fine to me, but I don't know for sure." Erik grabbed the windowsill's edge. "I don't know what happened." He shook his head. "I wish I could remember..."

"Ay, don't be worried 'bout them so much, Erik!" Raider reassured. "He's prolly freaked out like you is, ya dig what I'm sayin'?" Erik nodded. "Give him some time to chill; he'll get it back together!"

"I hope so..."

"Dig this: I'm gonna check this shit out, man; so don't freak on it no more while I'm makin' a few calls."

"I'll try not to."

Raider swung up and vaulted off then ran away from the house's side, tearing through the fields. Erik turned around and stiffened at the sight of John Greenfield standing at his door.

"So it's Mister Greenfield?" he said simply.

Erik clenched his teeth as he took in a shallow breath. "I-it's not like that!" he sputtered. "Please, don't take it the wrong way!"

"It's only Father and Mother to our faces, but Mister and Missus Greenfield to everyone else you meet."

"No," Erik cried, "it's not like that!"

"Do you hate us?"

"I--!" John Greenfield stormed out the room. "Father, wait!" Erik called and hurried after him.

Reaching the door, Erik grabbed John Greenfield by the arm before he left. John Greenfield turned out of his grip and shoved him back by the chest, throwing him head over heels.

Erik slammed into the bed and scrambled to his feet. He clenched his hands at his sides, watching John Greenfield storm down the hall.

"*Why the sudden hostility?*" Erik thought, terrified. "*He never laid a hand on me before!*" He hurried out into the corridor, catching sight of John Greenfield hastily pulling on a heavy cotton overcoat from the hallway closet.

"Dear, where are you going?" Jane Greenfield called from the bedroom.

"For a walk," John Greenfield said simply.

"Be careful," Erik said gently.

John Greenfield gave Erik a piercing glare in return and Erik stepped back, slightly terrified.

"Why would you care?" John Greenfield snarled.

Erik stepped forward, standing in John Greenfield's way before he made his way down the stairs. "I care nonetheless!" Erik protested. John Greenfield grabbed Erik's shoulder and he took his hand. "Please, don't leave like this!"

"I just need to clear my thoughts," John Greenfield said evenly. "It's nothing you did."

"Then why are you acting like this?"

John Greenfield narrowed his eyes. "I should ask you the same."

"What?" Erik let go and stepped away, then cringed when grabbed by his shirtfront. "Please don't hit me again!"

"I–!" John Greenfield tensed when he heard Jane Greenfield step out the room. He let Erik go and pushed past him, hurrying downstairs.

"He'll be all right," Jane Greenfield said upon approach.

"He's not going to hurt us," Erik asked, "will he?"

"No, don't think such things."

She's lying!

"I'm unsure about Father," Erik murmured. "He's acting strange."

"What do you mean?"

"Was it something I did?"

Jane Greenfield blew a disconcerted sigh. "Just don't do that again," she said sternly.

"What did I do then?"

"I... I really don't know."

"I didn't mean to upset him like that."

Jane Greenfield said nothing else and returned to the master bedroom. Pausing at the door, she turned back to Erik. "Are you well?" she suddenly asked.

"I feel fine."

"Are you sure?"

"I guess."

"No headaches or anything?" Erik clenched his teeth, afraid to say and nodded. Jane Greenfield smiled. "Good."

Erik returned to his room and sat on the edge of his bed. Holding his head in his hands, he stared off in the middle distance, disturbed by the unsettling atmosphere.

Later that evening, Erik picked at his dinner, highly upset when John Greenfield had not returned. Jane Greenfield sighed as she got up from her place at the table.

"I guess I'll put his plate to warm in the oven," she murmured, picking up John Greenfield's serving from the head of the table.

"May I be excused?" Erik asked.

"Sure, Erik."

Leaving his chair, Erik headed for the front door while Jane Greenfield put her husband's meal away. He frowned when he found it ajar and John Greenfield's keys tossed aside on the nearby end table.

"*Why did he rush out of here?*" Erik thought as he opened the door and stepped out onto the porch. "*What is he running from?*" A chilled wind blew through him and Erik shuddered as faint pain coursed through his arms and down his back. "*Which direction did he take?*" Before he took a step down the stairs, Jane Greenfield called for him.

"You didn't put away your dishes!" she snapped.

"Sorry, Mother," Erik called back and re-entered the house, scooping up the keys. Pocketing them, he pressed the front door shut with his hip and hurried into the dining room.

"Please be more mindful," Jane Greenfield reprimanded and Erik nodded in response.

Clearing the table, Erik glanced at Jane Greenfield who sat at the table's far end, her hands clasped in her lap and her food still on the plate, untouched. "Do you want me to take that?" he asked.

"Please leave it," Jane Greenfield answered.

Erik shrugged and headed for the kitchen. After washing the dishes, he returned to the table and took the empty seat across from her. After sitting in silence for several moments, Erik cleared his throat.

"What is it?" Jane Greenfield responded.

"I wish what happened earlier never occurred," Erik said softly. "I didn't mean to upset you or anyone else."

"It's all right," Jane Greenfield said gently.

"What was with that violent reaction then?" Erik pressed.

"Oh, Erik," Jane Greenfield said irritably, "Don't say such things!"

Erik winced from her irate glance. "I can't help it!" he declared, standing to his feet. "He hit me pretty hard, so hard in fact; it nearly threw me across the room!"

"Please, don't tell any more horrible stories!"

"It's not a false story, Mother!" Erik cried, clenching his hands. "He walked out on us, if you hadn't noticed!"

"Erik, hush up!"

"Why is he acting like this? Apparently you know more than I do."

"There's nothing left to discuss about the matter."

"Then set me straight; I'm afraid and I don't know what's going to happen!"

"We're done talking about this, Erik!"

"But, Mother--!"

"That's enough!"

Erik clenched his teeth, knowing he reached the conversation's end. He wanted to say more, but by Jane Greenfield's icy glare, he figured she would not allow him to speak any further.

Erik dug through his pockets, pulled out John Greenfield's keys and threw them on the table. She gasped and Erik grabbed his cap left on the chair's post then stormed out the house, slamming the front door shut behind him.

THIRTEEN

Erik squinted from the setting sun's bright light casting the sky in harsh shades of pink and orange. He jumped down the porch and headed out onto the walk.

Erik came to a stop and grew tense at the sight of a tall broad-shouldered man walking toward him from the opposite direction. He wore a long double-breasted belted olive raincoat, wide-brimmed hat set low on his head and dark wool scarf covering the lower half of his face.

The mysterious stranger paused several yards away, standing across the street before the Greenfield residence. They stood for several moments, staring at each other. The man made no movements as he observed Erik and Erik watched back.

The man then withdrew his hands and pointed them at Erik in the shape of guns, mimicking sounds of gunfire. The stranger chortled in response when Erik jerked, startled in response.

Erik paled and hurried away for the townhouses. He heard footsteps from behind and glanced back at the man following him. Erik took off in a run.

Racing up to Francisca's house, Erik banged frantically on the door. Turning, he caught sight of the olive raincoat-dressed man not too far away, watching silently. The door opened and Erik let out a yelp once pulled in roughly by the arm and slammed against the wall.

"What the hell is wrong with you?" Francisca yelled and kicked shut the door. Erik put up his hands as she pointed the head of a sawed-off double-barreled shotgun at his chest.

"Someone's following me!" Erik cried.

Her worried expression turned irate and she smacked him upside the head. "Stupid Doofus!" Francisca shouted. "So you bring them *here* so they know where I live?"

"I'm sorry!" Erik wailed as she smacked him again.

"What's going on back there?" Hanalei called.

"It's Erik," Francisca called back and peeked outside through the heavy curtains.

Hanalei exited from the rear rooms and folded her arms across her chest, irritated. She shook her head, puffing a hard sigh. "You know I'm helping her study!" she scolded. "If she gets another 'D' letter grade on her next test, *you* are going to tutor instead!"

"Sorry, Hana," Erik said ruefully and held out his hands. "I'll make up for it, I swear." Hanalei approached, taking his hands into hers and he gave a firm squeeze. "If I don't keep my promise, I'll give you the next two weeks of my allowance."

Hanalei smiled briefly. "I *will* hold you to it." She came out of Erik's grip and took a seat on the couch near the door.

"I don't see anyone," Francisca grumbled after studying the outdoors. "What does this thing or whatever look like?" Erik gave the stranger's general description and Francisca shook her head. "There's no one like that out there." She left

127

the window and gave Erik a worried glance. "Are you sure you're all right?"

Erik nodded. "I'm sure."

"No fever or anything?"

"Really, Francisca!" Erik exploded. "Why is everyone asking me this?"

"Then what do you want?" Francisca snapped, ignoring his statement and set aside the rifle near the door.

"Tell me I'm not crazy," Erik pleaded.

"Okay, you're not crazy."

"Let's go back," Hanalei interjected. "You can sit with me and help me quiz Franny."

Francisca glowered at Hanalei who grinned slyly and Erik chuckled.

"Okay, I'll help,"said Erik brightly.

Hanalei left, heading for the house's rear where Francisca's room was and Erik followed. He looked around, noting despite its exterior front the apartment was small. Erik felt heat from the kitchen and glanced in the doorway, finding the old oven open.

"Is it going to get frigid tonight?" Erik asked and Francisca pushed him forward.

"Don't worry about it," Francisca muttered.

"It's dangerous using that oven as a space heater trying to warm the rest of the house."

"Maybe I should toss you in there and feed you to Collin!"

"Sorry for asking!"

Erik entered the short corridor where one door was open, washing light into the hall. He saw the apartment's largest rooms were the kitchen and parlor, compared to the bedrooms and water closet down the hall.

Entering Francisca's bedroom, Erik noticed its essentials, save for a desk near the door and stacks of books in the corner beside her closet. He sat next to Hanalei on the floor while she sifted through her backpack, withdrawing books and papers.

"Once it gets warm enough, I'll shut it off," Francisca said as she entered and closed the door. "Last I need is to leave it unattended at night and have Collin light his dumb ass on fire!"

"Why not let him?" Hanalei snapped. "With the way he beats you--!"

"Shut up!" Francisca shouted, shaking her fist at her. "I can handle myself fine!"

"Here, this is the last test," Hanalei said to Erik and handed him a paper. "Quiz her on it."

Erik took the sheet and looked down at it, noticing it was a photocopy of the instructor's textbook. "Hey," he said, "where'd you get this?"

Hanalei gave a mischievous grin as she rose to her feet. "My secret," she replied, tapping the edge of her nose.

Erik cracked a smile and waved the paper at her. "You're a bad girl," he teased.

Hanalei giggled and took her place nearby the student desk. Francisca blew a heavy sigh and sat across from Erik on the floor, crossing her legs. She set her hands on her knees and Erik took off his cap, setting it aside.

"Let's have a go at this," Francisca grumbled.

"Okay," Erik answered and glanced down at the paper. "What is the length of the hypotenuse in an isosceles right triangle?"

"The hell?" Francisca squawked. She groaned and rubbed her temples. "Um, length of a leg times the square root of two?"

"Right on!" Erik praised.

"About time!" Hanalei jeered. "My teachings are finally sticking in that mucky brain of yours!"

Francisca glared back at Hanalei and shook her fist at her. "I'll show you muck!" she sneered.

Erik grabbed Francisca by the wrist and leaned out of a backhanded punch. "Cool it," he said gently.

"I'm sick of her ragging on me," Francisca groused and shook out of his grip.

"She does it because she cares," Erik said and snorted. "Besides, she's a cheater anyway."

"Please don't tell my parents," Hanalei said quietly as her face flushed bright scarlet. "If I fail, they'll take away my college fund!"

"Then have Erik help you study," Francisca shot back. "He's smart but acts like a lazy dumb ass."

"Hey, don't turn this against me!" Erik protested.

"Why are you wasting your time with us anyway?"

Erik sighed and ran a hand through his hair. "I don't know what I really want," he murmured.

"Why did you come here? We can't help you!"

"I'm not asking for help," Erik complained. "I just needed to get away..."

"Problems at home?" Hanalei inquired. "We understand."

"Which one was it?" Francisca implored.

Erik glared back at her. "What kind of question is that?" he snapped.

"Collin smacks me around after my mom ran off and Hana's mom beats both her and her wimpy dad," Francisca answered. "So, which one hit you?"

"I'm not going to answer that."

"Please don't let it get to you," Hanalei said softly. "Just put up with it."

"I'm not going to hit them back, if that's what you're worried about."

"That *is* what we're worried about."

"What?" Erik raised an eyebrow. "What are you talking about?"

"You have a nasty temper," Francisca said, looking down at the floor. "You used to do horrible things..."

"Please don't lie to me," Erik said faintly. "Don't say nasty things like that."

"Don't you remember being at the hospital last year?" Hanalei asked. "We always brought your school work so you can keep up. That's why you're going to school so late in the year."

Erik let out a nervous laugh, despite the dull ache returning in his head. "Where are you going with this?" he pleaded. "It sounds like you're saying I used to be a violent monster."

"You were."

"But I'm not anymore, obviously."

"You may be Mister Nice Guy now," Francisca murmured, "but we're worried that this might set you off."

"That's why we keep the conversation light around you," said Hanalei. "Raider asked us to, since he said violence is a trigger for you."

"You guys smack me around all the time!" Erik protested.

"That's because you know we're just goofing off," Francisca retorted. "We used to talk to you about everything, but after *that* happened…"

"*What* happened?"

"Just know that you're much stronger than you look."

"What do you mean?" Erik complained.

"You're not stupid, Erik," Francisca snapped. "You know exactly what we mean!"

"I'm no fighter; I'm as geeky as they come!" Erik shrugged his shoulders. "I'm just a mild-mannered book reader!"

"Sure, keep telling yourself that," Francisca said, rolling her eyes. "You're a monster, always have been."

Hanalei nodded in agreement. "You can get quite scary sometimes," she muttered. "I'm glad you can't remember."

"What are you talking about?" Erik demanded. "You two aren't making any sense!" He shook his head. "You're talking out your butts; you're just trying to play me, that's all!"

"We're serious," Francisca said coldly.

"You act like I hurt you before!"

"Just that one time," Hanalei said vaguely. "But we know it wasn't your fault."

"Come on!" Erik exploded. "I'm not like that! I was never like that! I don't want to hurt anyone."

"You can *kill* if you wanted," Hanalei murmured. "You're insanely strong."

"Right, what she said," Francisca admitted.

"Under that sweet exterior, you're a total beast!" Hanalei noted.

"You're scaring me," Erik said faintly. "Please, stop."

"If you need to run, just do it." Francisca declared. "I'll help you disappear."

"You don't have to stay with them," Hanalei chimed in. "Just think about it!"

Erik found breathing difficult as the atmosphere grew awkward between them. "Monster?" he squawked. "You said that I'm some kind of beast?" He stood immediately growing irritated. "Now I really know you're talking out your butts! You're crazy!"

"Erik..." Francisca started.

"You mean not hypothetically, but as pure fact, right?" Francisca's expression turned grim and Hanalei sighed, not answering. Unable to get the words fully out, Erik's head reeled as he kicked up his cap and caught it. "Well, I... ah... I should go then," he said timidly, changing the conversation. "I have to search for Mister Greenfield."

"What happened to him?" Francisca questioned and Erik turned away as his face reddened. "Did you hurt him?"

"Don't start with me about that," Erik growled and fixed the hat on his head. "It's not like I made him hate me for some reason."

"So you *did* do something," Hanalei murmured.

Erik clenched his hands, glaring back at her. "Not that way," he snarled. "Now stop with this, please!"

"Fine, we'll drop it," Francisca grumbled. "But our offer still stands."

"We'll run off together," Hanalei said and gave a faint smile. "Just let us know when you want to go."

Erik left the room and hurried for the front door, letting himself out. He came to a dead stop when he saw the raincoat-dressed broad-shouldered man walking away from his spot across the street. Shoving his hands into his jeans pockets, Erik stomped down the path, going in the opposite direction.

Erik kept his sights on the loose gravel road crunching under his sneakers, then looked ahead at the skies slowly darkening around him with the fading of the setting sun.

He stiffened when he heard the quick and even steps of another out on the path. At first, Erik paid them no mind, continuing onward and getting lost in his own thoughts. When the steps came closer, he cringed, unnerved by the person offside still following.

"*Maybe I'm making too much over it,*" Erik mused. "*They're probably heading down to Keely for something to do.*"

Or, so you think...

Erik abruptly turned around and the mysterious person following him paused in step, startled. Erik squinted in the dim lighting, making out a slender pale person in boots and oversized dark navy overcoat draping their thin frame. The stranger had short spiky dark hair and wore dark glasses, hiding their eyes.

"What do you want?" Erik called.

"Nothin'," came the reply.

"Then why are you following me?"

"Who said I was?"

"I said so and I want to know who you are!"

"I'm nobody... nobody at all."

"You'd better stop it or--!"

"Or what?" The stranger smirked. "You're not going to hurt me, are you?"

"I'd better not see you around here again!" Erik snapped and stomped past, heading for home.

When he heard the stranger behind him, Erik stopped in his tracks and whirled around, throwing a punch. The stranger swiftly leaned out of the blow and grabbed Erik's fist with their opposite hand. Erik grunted when pushed back and sent crashing onto the ground.

"Hey!" Erik barked as the stranger took off running. "Come back here!"

"No dice!" the person shouted.

Immediately scrambling to his feet, Erik gave chase and lost his opponent once they took off for the fields. "Forget it," he grumbled and started the trek back to the Greenfield residence. "They're not worth my time!"

A sharp blow abruptly smashed into the back of Erik's head. The force knocked off his cap and threw him forward on the ground. He crashed into the dirt with a hard thud, knocking the wind out of his lungs.

Erik ground his teeth in pain as he grabbed the back of his head, feeling sticky warmth. Looking to his side, he saw a mid-sized stone with a smattering of blood on it. Turning over on his back, he looked up, finding the mysterious person standing before him, smiling deviously.

"Oh, did I hurt you?" they teased.

"You--!" Erik sprang to his feet, only to get a fast stomp to the groin and groaned in pain, sinking to his knees.

"I just wanted to talk..." The stranger grabbed his hair in a firm hand and forced him looking up.

Erik ground his teeth when his neck pulled back in a painful angle. "What do you want with me?" he hissed through clenched teeth.

"You'll find out soon enough."

"Do you have a name?"

"Sure I do..." The winds picked up, and the mysterious person's overcoat blew open, fluttering back. Underneath the coat, the winds revealed the person wearing a dark sweater, pleated skirt, black tights and leggings over short boots. Erik gasped when he noticed a blue steel dagger strapped to her thigh. "It's Danae," she answered.

Danae let go and socked Erik's jaw, the force flipping him over onto the ground. She kicked Erik again, striking his chest and the power spiraled him back, facing the muted clouds overhead. Danae stood over him, blocking his view of the evening sky.

Erik spat blood at her and she raised her heel. He quickly grabbed her foot and pushed her away.

"I thought you wanted to talk," Erik snapped as he cupped his stinging face. "Not kick me around!"

"We already exchanged names... I don't have to tell you any more."

"I never told you my name!"

"I already know who you are." Danae stepped over him and walked away, hands in her coat pockets. "When I want you," she called over her shoulder, "I'll get you later."

"Get back here!"

Erik jumped to his feet and a sudden pitch of sound screeched in the air. He let out a cry and held his hands over his ears as the noise became louder.

Erik's vision flashed red and he slipped to his knees, swamped by agonizing pain. He struggled to get up, finding it difficult to move. Once Danae left Erik's line of sight, the mysterious sound died and Erik staggered to his feet, panting hard for breath.

It's only going to get worse from here...

Erik's heart skipped a beat in fear when he recalled the mysterious raincoat-dressed man following him earlier and John Greenfield leaving the house. He took off for home.

FOURTEEN

Bursting through the front door, Erik plowed into John Greenfield just as he had come indoors and pulled out of his coat. John Greenfield stumbled rearwards and grabbed Erik's arms, keeping him from falling over. The coat he came out of fluttered to the floor behind him.

"Where are you going?" John Greenfield asked as Erik sank to his knees, nearly fainting. Lifting Erik to his feet, John Greenfield gazed down at him with concern. "Son...?"

Erik pulled away as Jane Greenfield entered with her purse and picked up the fallen coat.

"He was upset that you suddenly left like that," Jane Greenfield said softly, answering for Erik as she put away the overcoat in the nearby closet.

John Greenfield's worried expression changed to hurt. "No, Son, I didn't leave," he said sternly. "I just took a walk to clear my head!" John Greenfield gave a faint saddened smile. "I promised to never leave, remember?"

"But you said...!" Erik started and clenched his hands as the crushing fear intensified. "You had a talk with that man, didn't you?"

"What man, Son?"

"That guy in the scarf and Mackintosh and that hat," Erik stated. "He was following me! Did you run into him?"

John Greenfield appeared puzzled then suddenly let out a nervous laugh. "There's nothing to get upset about," he replied. Erik stiffened when John Greenfield hugged him firmly. "Please, don't worry," he murmured. "Nothing's going to happen to us."

"Okay." Erik returned the embrace halfheartedly. "So where did you go?" he asked once let go.

"I stopped by the drugstore and picked up some sherbet."

"Where is it then?"

"Oh?" John Greenfield chuckled. "I was so lost in my thoughts, I probably left it."

"I'll go pick it up for you, dear," Jane Greenfield said from behind and approached, touching his arm. "I'll be back right away."

"Do that for me, will you?" John Greenfield requested and gave her hand a gentle pat, smiling tersely. Jane Greenfield then stepped outside and shut the door behind her.

"What are you thinking about so deeply that you're forgetting stuff?" Erik inquired.

John Greenfield headed into the parlor toward the glass-accented cherry wood mini-bar in the corner. "What goes well with lime sherbet, Son?" he asked instead, ignoring Erik's question.

"I'm not sure," Erik responded.

"I'm out of sherry, so I think some brandy might do it..."

John Greenfield pulled out a bottle of brown liquor and grabbed for a highball glass, filling half of it. Erik entered the parlor moments later, taking a seat on the couch. John Greenfield put the bottle away and approached offside, glass in hand.

"Do you want any ice or anything?" Erik asked.

"Nah, this is fine as it is," John Greenfield answered then gave Erik a concerned glance. "Will you be okay, Son?"

"What do you mean?"

"What happened?"

"What are you talking about?"

"Did you get into a fight?"

"Er, someone tried to rob me," Erik lied. "When they found out I had no money, they beat the stuffing out of me." He smiled nervously. "I'm fine, really!"

"You've got a pretty nasty gash on the back of your head there."

"It's not as bad as it looks."

"If you say so..."

Erik nodded. "Will *you* be okay?"

"Oh, I'm just fine, Son." John Greenfield took a seat next to Erik and downed his drink in a large gulp. A distant expression appeared on his face as he held the glass.

"How long have you been drinking?" Erik suddenly asked.

"Beg pardon?" John Greenfield murmured and his distant expression vanished as he smiled warmly. Erik repeated his question and John Greenfield appeared perplexed. "I... well..." He looked down at his glass. "I don't remember, Son," he demurred. "I honestly don't remember."

"Never mind," Erik muttered, shaking his head.

Leaving John Greenfield's side, Erik headed for his room and leaned against the doorway's frame. He blew a troubled sigh at the sight of the mussed bed and the rest of the trashed room.

"*I wonder what they were looking for*," Erik thought. "*Why would they think I have it, whatever it is?*"

Hearing John Greenfield coming upstairs, Erik stepped out into the hall and John Greenfield tousled his hair upon passing.

"Please don't worry about me," John Greenfield pressed while loosening his tie with his free hand. "I'm the one who's supposed to worry around here."

"About what?" Erik asked after him as John Greenfield entered the master bedroom.

"Oh, about a lot of things... mainly you, perhaps." John Greenfield slipped off his tie and pulled out of his blazer, throwing them into the chair set in the room's corner.

"Perhaps?" Erik spat. "What's that supposed to mean?" He stood at the door as John Greenfield sat on the edge of the bed, pulling out of his black oxfords.

"Please, let me relax," John Greenfield pleaded and set the shoes aside on the floor near the bed. "I need time to think."

"Think about what?"

"The meaning of life, the universe, and everything in it."

"Don't kid around, Father."

"I'm worn out right now," John Greenfield grumbled. "Please, leave me be for a bit."

"Father..."

"Not now, Son."

Erik grew silent and stepped out, then returned silently to the door. He watched John Greenfield's expression turned blank as he unbuttoned his shirt and sighed heavily, staring off into the middle distance.

John Greenfield's right hand suddenly twitched violently and he grunted, holding his wrist as his face twisted in painful concentration.

Erik gasped and John Greenfield looked up, startled. He stood, letting the shirt slip off his broad shoulders and Erik winced, noting the numerous scars and old burns across his arms and chest.

"What happened to you?" Erik asked faintly, cringing behind the frame when John Greenfield approached with his right hand clenched at his side. "W-what is it you want?" Erik sputtered.

"What I want...?" John Greenfield gave a crooked smile. "Why do you ask?"

"H-how...?"

"Oh, this?" John Greenfield tapped at his chest with his free hand. "It was an accident, long ago. Nearly burned all over."

"Yet..."

"Yes, I got lucky, though most of my friends didn't." John Greenfield poked Erik in the chest with a firm hand. "Are you done asking me such personal questions?"

"Is it because I had something to do with it?"

"Now where did you get that idea?"

"My friends mentioned it..."

"Oh..." John Greenfield's expression hardened. "Then you must remember."

Erik shook his head. "I don't."

"Don't tell me you forgot!"

"Forget what?"

"About who you are."

Erik gave a blank stare in return. "Father, please lie down," he finally said. "I think you're drunk."

John Greenfield cracked a devious smile and chortled. "Oh, I'll need more than that to get me drunk!"

"I'll keep that in mind."

"I have something else to ask you..."

"Sure, anything you want."

"Did you run into anyone else while you were out and about this evening?"

"No..."

"Please don't lie to me, Son. I won't punish you, if that's what you're worried about."

"Well..."

"Don't you trust me?"

Erik swallowed hard. "I..."

"Do you think I might hit you?"

Erik gestured to John Greenfield's side. "Your hand..."

"It seizes up sometimes," John Greenfield answered and lifted his arm. "See that scar here? Cut right into the tendon." Erik took his wrist and traced the deep scar down his arm from the crook of his elbow. He took in a shallow breath when the pain behind his eyes increased and he let go, clutching his head. "Did you just remember something?"

"No," Erik moaned. "I just hurt, that's all."

"Is it from the beating earlier, then?"

"Er, sure," Erik lied.

"I don't believe you."

Erik sighed and looked downward toward his feet. "Some girl named Danae," he muttered. "She attacked me for no reason at all..."

John Greenfield's eyes widened and the color drained from his face. He turned away and clutched his chest, gasping weakly for breath. Erik snapped to attention and grabbed for John Greenfield when his knees buckled and he fell.

"Father!" Erik cried, turning John Greenfield onto his back. He grew afraid, overwhelmed by the man's brown blank and glassy eyes and blood seeped from his nose. "Father, wake up!" Erik shook him firmly by the shoulders then leaned forward, putting an ear to his chest and heard his heart beating wildly.

"Oh, Erik!" Jane Greenfield's voice cried. She stepped in and knelt toward Erik's level, touching her husband's face.

"What's wrong with him?" Erik demanded. "Why is he like this?"

"He's having another one of his nervous attacks," Jane Greenfield answered.

"Nervous attacks...?" Erik parroted. "Is it related to that accident he mentioned?"

"Go get the medicine for me in his nightstand," Jane Greenfield ordered. "I'll take care of him, so please, don't worry."

Erik scrambled to his feet and hurried over to the nightstand. Rummaging through the drawer, he pushed aside envelopes, other papers and a cigarette tin. Finding an amber bottle closed by a yellow cap and white label on the face with a blue and red sticker on the side, he tossed it to Jane Greenfield and she caught it.

"Mother..." Erik started.

"Please let me stress over this," Jane Greenfield said firmly.

"But--!"

"Please, honey."

"Okay," Erik answered weakly and hurried out the room. He ran to his bedroom, stepping over the debris at his doorway and paced frantically, wringing his hands.

Moments later, the light switched on in the hall and Jane Greenfield appeared at his door, clutching the amber bottle. Erik tensed at her shadow reaching across the floor and stopped his pacing, turning to face her. She blew a heavy sigh and Erik folded his arms across his chest, staring back.

"Will you be all right?" Jane Greenfield asked before Erik could say anything. He nodded in response. "Why don't you turn in for the night and try to get some rest?"

"I don't think I can sleep," Erik answered.

"At least try, honey," Jane Greenfield insisted.

"Will he be okay otherwise?"

"Let me take care of this and everything will be brighter tomorrow, okay?"

Erik clenched his teeth and ran his hands through his hair, groaning. "Fine," he muttered. "I'll let you worry about it."

"That's good," Jane Greenfield said gently as Erik slumped onto the edge of his bed, blowing a short sigh. "You have bigger worries to stress about, like getting good grades."

"Sure, Mother," Erik grumbled, "whatever you say."

"Sleep well, honey."

"Good night."

Jane Greenfield left the doorway and Erik lay back in bed with his hands behind his head, staring at his darkened ceiling. He later fell into a dreamless sleep.

FIFTEEN

Erik awakened early to the sound of the telephone ringing. It continued to chime then stopped, only to start again moments later. After another round and stopping, the phone started again.

"Why aren't they picking up?" Erik grumbled as he sat up, rubbing at his eyes.

Slipping out of bed, he yawned and paused when he found the debris from yesterday cleared, leaving behind the mirror leaning against the wall. The mirror's bottom was broken out and the top half was left with a jagged edge and a large crack through the middle.

Erik shrugged his shoulders and padded out into the hall where the phone continued to ring. He approached the master bedroom door and knocked, only to hear no answer.

"Are they out?" Erik wondered and tried the handle, finding it locked.

When the phone stopped ringing, Erik heard muffled voices on the door's other side and put his ear against it, straining to hear.

"You need to stop!" John Greenfield suddenly shouted.

"Don't start with me," Jane Greenfield shrilled back. "Lower your voice before you wake up that monster!"

"How dare you--!" Erik cringed when he heard something crashing inside. "My boy's no monster! If anything, *you* created him to be that way!"

"How dare you say that to me!"

"Don't tell me you didn't mean to say that then, heh!" John Greenfield retorted.

"You need to be careful with what you say," Jane Greenfield protested. "I'm warning you, *telling* you, watch your words around him! You don't know how he would've reacted!"

"What are you trying to say?"

"Why did you do such a thing?"

"What nonsense is this?"

"He nearly freaked out, thinking you left him for good, John!"

"If I were to leave for good, then I'm taking him with me!"

"You can't have him worrying needlessly over you!"

John Greenfield blew a heavy sigh. "I'll be more careful then," he said dejectedly. "I'll try harder..."

"He's a troublemaker and we can't have him getting upset over you!"

"He's not and he never was," John Greenfield snarled, "nor will he ever be!"

"See to that he doesn't," Jane Greenfield said firmly. "I'll forgive you of your mistake this time... just don't do that again!"

"What's that supposed to mean?" Erik thought.

The door suddenly opened, revealing John Greenfield in bare feet, wearing a dark brown smoking jacket and beige silk pajama pants. Erik gasped and stepped back, mildly stunned.

The phone rang again and John Greenfield gripped tighter to the handle. "Erik," he said, then hesitated.

Erik immediately turned away and headed downstairs, approaching the desktop phone on the end table at the staircase's bottom. He looked up at John Greenfield standing at the top of the staircase, leaning against the banister. When the phone rang again and Erik heard no other orders from John Greenfield, he picked up the receiver.

"Greenfield residence," Erik answered. A soft melody played in the background on the line's other end, accompanied by the sounds of even breathing. "Whom do you wish to speak with?" Erik received no reply and looked back at John Greenfield as he put the receiver back in the cradle. "No one answered," he said to him.

"It's quite fine, Son," John Greenfield replied as an unreadable expression shadowed his face.

"Were you expecting a call?"

"No, I was not."

Erik shifted nervously on his feet. *"You're lying,"* he thought, distraught. *"They didn't answer because I did!"*

"Well, Son...?"

"Since I'm up early," Erik said instead, "do you want me to cook you something?" He gave a nervous smile.

"You should really get ready for school, Son," John Greenfield said flatly. "Eggs and toast should be fine."

"I won't be late," Erik promised and made his way into the kitchen. He pulled out a carton of eggs and a loaf of bread from the refrigerator, setting them aside on the counter.

"Will you get the paper for me?" John Greenfield asked once he entered moments later and grabbed a mug from the drain board.

"Sure, I guess..."

Erik left the counter and hurried to the parlor, opening the front door wide to early morning. Stepping out, he grabbed for the newspaper on the porch and paused once he stood, catching sight of a person in black walking down the road.

Clenching his teeth, Erik hurried inside and slammed shut the door. He returned to the kitchen and set the paper aside on the table.

John Greenfield grabbed the kettle from the electric percolator and poured himself a cup of coffee. "Are you all right, Son?" he asked and returned to the table, setting the kettle aside.

"Do you want anything in particular?" Erik answered instead.

John Greenfield sipped his coffee and shrugged his shoulders. "What you have is fine."

"Other than eggs and toast?"

"It doesn't matter to me."

Erik grabbed the apron hanging on the oven's handle and tied it on over his bedclothes. He opened the refrigerator and sifted through its contents, dismayed at finding mainly ingredients to make meals by scratch.

"I haven't taken Home Economics yet," Erik cautioned. "I only know basic stuff." John Greenfield chortled. "I hope you don't mind toast and fried eggs."

"I don't know what to say...!"

"Oh, what do you know?" Erik sighed in frustration when the only items he found easy to cook were a box of oatmeal and some sticks of margarine. Pulling them both out, he scanned the oatmeal box's back. "It shouldn't be that hard," Erik grumbled.

"Do you want my help, Son?" John Greenfield inquired. "I'm a pretty decent cook myself."

Erik scoffed. "I've never seen you step foot into the kitchen!" he jeered.

John Greenfield snorted. "My wife didn't like my presentation skills."

"Really, I can do this myself!"

"I can show you how if you like."

Erik looked up and John Greenfield smiled faintly. "Let me give this a try, okay?" Erik complained. "I think I can cook oatmeal. It's all about following directions, right?"

"Well, if you need any help, feel free to ask."

"If I can't do this right, then I might as well die," Erik fussed as he set the oatmeal and margarine aside. "With the way I like to eat, I'd starve!"

John Greenfield chuckled, taking a seat at the kitchen table with his mug of coffee. "You can start and if you're really stuck, let me know."

Relieved when John Greenfield seemed in stable spirits, Erik smiled warmly at him. "If it kills you, you were warned," he teased.

"Then that'd be a happy death for me, I suppose."

Erik stiffened, unsure what to say. Searching the cabinets for an appliance, he grunted and turned to John Greenfield. "Where's the toaster?" he asked.

"We don't have one."

"Microwave then?"

"Why you want to do that?"

"Then how--?"

"With the oven."

Erik groaned and John Greenfield bit his fist, trying not to laugh. "What kind of black magic sorcery is this?" Erik protested and John Greenfield set his coffee aside as he doubled over, howling in laughter.

"Too cute," he said once he calmed down from his riant fit and wiped his eyes with his sleeve.

"I can do this, just you watch!"

"I will, Son, I will…"

SIXTEEN

"Jane, do you think he'll be all right?" John Greenfield asked softly to his wife.

Jane Greenfield replied in response, but Erik could not tell what she said. John Greenfield picked up his newspaper and opened it, scanning the headlines. Erik failed to catch what he said in return to his wife, growing frustrated.

On edge, Erik picked at his meal of thin watery oatmeal, hard toast, very lightly scrambled eggs with cheese and burnt bacon while John Greenfield already had his coffee and Jane Greenfield had orange juice to accompany her meal.

Erik bit into his piece of jam-covered toast, frustrated once it crumbled from a small bite. Piercing his fork into the bread, it cracked in several pieces.

"This is terrible," he grumbled and gulped down his glass of milk.

"You did a swell job, honey," Jane Greenfield replied in assurance. "It was a fine attempt."

Moments later, a knock resonated on the front door.

"I'll get it," John Greenfield announced and set his paper aside as he rose to his feet.

"Who would it be this early?" Jane Greenfield asked when her husband left the table.

"I hope it's nothing too serious," Erik murmured and pushed his food around on his plate.

Glancing aside as John Greenfield spoke to the person at the door, Erik strained to hear what was said and grunted when static squelched in response.

"What the--?" Erik thought, stunned. *"Why can't I hear them...?"* Using his spoon, he barely caught a glimpse of the unnamed visitor wearing a dark pea coat and baggy jeans with a hood pulled forward over their head. Erik clenched his teeth when the scrambled sound worsened. *"Something's blocking me out; this doesn't make any sense!"*

John Greenfield shut the door moments later and Erik set down his spoon.

"What is it?" Erik asked as John Greenfield returned to the table at Erik's side with a harried look on his face.

"Is something wrong?" Jane Greenfield asked tentatively.

John Greenfield's expression immediately changed from troubled to pleasant. "You never told me that you had a friend named Danae," he said in fake cheerfulness with a hint of disdain in his voice. "Did you meet her on your first day of school?"

"What?" Erik yelped and quickly rose to his feet. "I don't know that girl!" John Greenfield's face twitched slightly. "She was the one that beaned me with a rock yesterday!" Erik tapped at his head. "I got the lump on my head to prove it!"

"I'm sure it was a simple misunderstanding," John Greenfield said in a strained tone. "Don't be so quick to judge, Son!"

"What...?"

John Greenfield's face twitched again and he grabbed Erik firmly by the arm, pulling him closer. He leaned in, whispering in his ear.

"Listen, she is more dangerous than she looks," John Greenfield said in a low tone. "Don't let her appearance fool you!" He let Erik go, his expression suddenly turning painful and staggered back, clutching his head.

Jane Greenfield swiftly sprang to her feet as Erik grabbed for John Greenfield's arm, keeping him from swaying and striking the floor. Jane Greenfield pulled out the nearby chair and her husband collapsed into it.

"Get ready for school," Jane Greenfield ordered. "I'll take care of things here."

Erik let go and backed away, distressed. "What's happening to him?" he asked as Jane Greenfield hurried into the kitchen. "Is it another one of those nervous attacks?" Upon return, Jane Greenfield glared at him and Erik hurried upstairs to his room.

Grabbing one of his many button-down shirts, Erik paused and pulled out the drawer more so than partway. All the shirts were similar: button-down flannel shirts with slight variation in its striped patterns.

"They're always cream or yellow or beige," Erik muttered as he pulled out several shirts. "Navy stripes or black stripes and the alternating colors are yellow or blue or red…" He threw the shirts aside on the floor as he picked through them, growing more disturbed. "There's green and gray, brown and violet…" A sudden chill rushed through Erik and the room seemingly closed in around him.

You're starting to see…

Erik yanked out the entire drawer, letting it strike the floor with a bang, forcing the remaining shirts falling out over the sides. He clutched his chest as his breath thinned.

"*This is crazy,*" Erik thought. "*This doesn't mean anything!*"

Open your eyes!

Kicking the shirts aside, Erik browsed through the framed photographs on the top of his chest, finding he wore the same clothes in the pictures.

Pain entered his mind as he faintly recalled the photographs from another time and place that once rested on his dresser, consisting of another boy with his face who excelled in sports.

You remember... it's there, deep down...

Shaking his head to clear the altered vision, Erik picked up one framed photograph, noting one carefree moment playing basketball against John Greenfield at the local park.

In the photograph, John Greenfield wore his white dress shirt without his dark tie and blazer. His sleeves were cuffed and he wore dark slacks with high-top basketball shoes instead of his usual oxfords.

"*That's so unlike him,*" Erik thought. "*I don't remember this at all...*"

Erik swallowed hard when he saw his past self in the picture wearing a yellow flannel shirt over a white T-shirt and jeans with low-top sneakers.

"*I'm wearing the same thing again! What gives?*"

Erik's throat tightened as he browsed the others of himself and John Greenfield in various locations: at the racquetball court, at the community gymnasium, at the lakefront.

You're starting to understand...

"He's always wearing his work clothes," Erik muttered. "This doesn't seem right..."

Maybe because it's not real...

"It has to be!" Erik set the frame he held face down onto the dresser. "I can't be making up these locales!"

Only if you want to believe it...

Picking up the last photograph on the far end, he saw a younger version of himself against a blue background, grinning brightly at the camera. Disgusted at the tow-headed boy with slight freckles on the cheeks, bright blue eyes and straight white teeth, Erik set it face down as well.

"*This one is supposed to be a school photo from the looks of it,*" Erik mused as a chill rushed through him. "*Why don't I ever wear anything different in these pictures; why don't I ever wear anything different at all?*"

It's there. It's all there...

Erik ran across the hall into the master bedroom and opened the Greenfield's closets, finding Jane Greenfield's clothes in variants of beige, with a similar style, from her dresses to her skirts and blouses.

Opening John Greenfield's closets, he found his dress shirts and ties in a variety of pastels, with the exception of his suits that were shades of black, navy, brown or gray with a variety of pinstripes ranging from blue to lavender to bright red. Even with these splashes of color, the outfits were all cut the same.

"This can't be real," Erik moaned, backing away from the closets when overcome by the sinking feeling in his guts.

You know it's all a lie...

Erik rushed back to his room and opened the other drawer for his jeans, dumping them all out on the floor. To his stark horror, he realized they were styled the same as well: high waist with a loose leg and the only variants were the over-stitching on the back pockets.

"This can't be--!"

The feeling of vomiting came stronger and Erik ran into the bathroom, collapsing in front of the toilet as dry heaves wracked his body.

What a shame! You know death is imminent once they realize you can no longer conform...

Erik looked up, facing his reflection in the mirror hanging on the bathroom door. He saw himself kneeling at the toilet, though the alternate variant of himself leaned against the sink, smirking.

"What do you mean?" Erik spat. "I'm not dying!"

I mean this. The altered reflection pulled at the collar of his flannel pajama top. *All of it's fake! The house, the people, the town, even your parents... You need to wake up before it's too late!*

"Am I losing my mind?"

I don't know. His reflection gave a devious grin. *Are you?*

"Who are you?"

I should ask you the same.

158

Blowing a frustrated sigh, Erik stood unsteadily to his feet then undressed and stepped in the shower.

Turning on the cold water, he winced and touched his shoulder that suddenly radiated in pain from the water striking it, only to find nothing in particular.

"*I didn't hit my shoulder,*" Erik thought. "*That girl smacked me on the back of the head!*" Touching the back of his head, he ran his fingers across his scalp and through his hair, also finding no breaks in the skin.

After showering, Erik stepped out and glanced at the mirror, watching his variant adjusting the lone silver earring in his right ear.

Instead of standing nude as Erik, his counterpart had a towel about his waist. Erik clenched his teeth, noting the numerous old scars from cuts and burns covering his arms and upper body.

"Why are you here?" Erik griped. "Why is it I can only see and hear you?"

Maybe I'm a part of your imagination?

"Oh, now I'm crazy?"

Erik blew a sigh and stomped out the bathroom, returning to his room. Kicking up a pair of clothing to pull into, he hurried into his clothing and turned to face his reflection in the broken mirror.

His counterpart with the earrings stood there fully dressed, staring back with an annoyed expression.

"Have you always been here?" Erik demanded.

Maybe I'm part of your subconscious, trying to tell you something you're trying in vain to suppress.

"I've got nothing worth remembering!"

The young man snorted and rolled his eyes. *Obviously you do, otherwise you wouldn't have everyone asking about it!*

"That doesn't mean anything!"

The young man's jaw tightened and he clenched his hands. *Keep ignoring me and I'll do more than haunt your sorry ass!*

"I'm sure you will, but I obviously don't want to remember, hence me suppressing it!"

It will only kill you, just watch!

Erik cuffed up his jeans then stepped into his loosely laced sneakers nearby. "Why is it important for you to bother me?" he grumbled as he stomped to the nearby bed. Sitting on the edge, Erik bent over, tightening the laces.

I'm bothering you because you'll need the help!

"For what? With what? From what?"

Oh, you'll see; you'll see clearly!

Erik glanced up at his reflection leaning against the inner edge of the mirror, picking at his nails nonchalantly. "What is it with you?" he spat.

I'm not spelling it out for you.

"What does your being here have to do with anything?"

His reflection pinched his nose and shook his head, grumbling under his breath. *Details, is that what you're worried about?*

"But why is it *now* that I can *see* you? When I heard you before, you were never *there*."

Erik's variant shook a fist at him. *Listen, Ferdian, just be glad I'm able to talk to you at all!*

"Why should I?"

You still have your life, right?

"... and you don't?"

His reflection scoffed again. *Understatement of the week!*

Erik grabbed the comb lying nearby his nightstand and ran it through his short hair. He heard a grunt and turned to his reflection. "What's got you in a bad mood today?"

You'll find out later...

Erik threw the comb at the mirror. He gasped when the reflection caught the comb and tossed it back. Erik backed away, stunned when the plastic landed at his feet and his eyes widened in fear.

"I'm losing my mind for real!" he cried.

Really now?

Erik took off downstairs and paused when he found his backpack resting on the lower banister.

"*I know for sure I left my backpack on my bed yesterday morning*," he mused as the unsettled sensation grew worse once he picked it up. "*Why would it be moved and why does it feel a little heavier than it should?*" Erik lifted the backpack, noting the weight. "*I don't have my books in here because I left them in Callaghan's office!*" He blew a disgruntled sigh and slung the bag over his shoulder. "*I just don't have the time to check it here. Besides, there's probably nothing in there for them to feel suspicious over...*"

Heading into the kitchen, he found John and Jane Greenfield still at the table.

"Have a good day at school, honey," Jane Greenfield said.

Erik approached John Greenfield and touched him gently on the arm. "Aren't you going to work today?" he asked.

"Today's an off day from the office," Jane Greenfield answered. "We'll be in tomorrow."

Erik grunted. *"How convenient,"* he thought sourly and gave John Greenfield a firm embrace, only to receive no reaction. "Please be okay," Erik murmured in his ear.

"I'll be fine," answered John Greenfield flatly.

Letting go, Erik adjusted the backpack over his shoulder. "I'm off to school," he announced. "I'll come straight home."

"Do well, Son."

SEVENTEEN

Leaving home, Erik came down the steps and spotted Raider coming up the walk. Raider wore a black leather motorcycle jacket with fringes along the arms, a pair of ripped jeans and heavy work boots. His hair, usually feathered, was slicked back this particular morning.

"Hey, man," Raider called to Erik. "How's it cooking?"

"Totally faded," Erik replied and he walked in step with Raider toward Francisca's house. "Don't you have a ride today?"

"Usually, but I wanted to get a walk in so we can talk!"

"What about?"

"*You*, dummy!" Raider jabbed Erik's chest with his elbow. Erik giggled and pushed him back. "No, really man, with all this shit goin' down, you gonna need some help!"

"What kind of help?" Erik gave Raider a wary glance. "Does it have something to do with yesterday?"

"Yeah, Franny called me up and said you're not doing okay."

"I was a little shook up, but I'm fine now."

"Ay, man, come to me whenever."

"Sure."

They approached the house and Francisca came out with a messenger bag in one hand, wearing a yellow blouse, brown jeans and black riding boots. She threw an obscene gesture to her father inside with her free hand and stomped down the steps as the door slammed shut after her.

"So, no ride today?" Francisca inquired as she ran up to Raider and Erik who kept on.

"Did Hana beat the homework into you?" Erik teased and Francisca swung her bag at Erik. He quickly dodged the attack, chuckling. "I guess that's a 'yes'!"

"Whatever, Doofus," Francisca snapped and slipped the messenger bag over her shoulder. "We were up 'til three in the morning! I walked her home and her parents chewed her out hard."

"I'm sure she won't hold it against you."

"If I get another 'D' she will!" Francisca punched Erik on the arm and he yowled in pain.

"What was that for?" Erik yelped.

"If she's in a bad mood today, it's your fault!"

"I'm sorry!" Erik yelped.

"Chill out," Raider interjected. "You know he was illin' the other day. Give him a break."

"Stuff it, Raider," Francisca huffed.

"Why are you making your rounds so early this morning?" Erik asked, changing the conversation. "How did you know I was up?"

"I just know stuff, dig?" Raider answered vaguely.

"Don't tell me you're spying on me," Erik complained. "That's creepy."

"I ain't gotta spy on ya," Raider replied. "I called yer old man this morning!"

"Was it you making those freaky phone calls?"

"What the hell, man?" Raider snapped, glaring back at Erik. "What freaky calls?"

"Somebody's been phoning with weird music and heavy breathing!"

"Yeah, right," Raider spat and shoved his hands his jacket pockets. "When I want somethin', I get it. I don't hafta be a jerk 'bout it. I get it, and I'm gone, man."

"Somebody's been bothering your folks or something?" Francisca asked in a concerned tone.

"Lately they have," Erik answered. "I don't know why."

"Maybe they pissed somebody off at work?"

"I'm not sure..."

"That explains why you're in a poor mood today," Francisca murmured. "I'd be creeped out too if someone was calling the house like that!"

"Whatever it is, I dunno nothin' 'bout it," Raider grumbled. "I don't do that weird shit, man." He suddenly turned, socking Erik's chest and Erik staggered back, stunned as the air left his lungs. Francisca quickly grabbed for Erik before he fell back.

"What the hell, Raider?" Francisca cried.

"Don't you trust me?" Raider shouted.

"Of course I do!" Erik wailed. "I never doubt it at all!"

"Better act like it, man!"

"I'll try harder..."

"I don't know what the hell's in yer head," Raider growled, "but don't talk outta yer ass like that again!"

"Got it," Erik groaned and pulled out of Francisca's grip. "I'm all right," he muttered.

"Please calm yourself," Hanalei's voice said from behind. "We don't need violence."

Erik jumped from the sound of her voice and turned, finding they were already past her house. Hanalei smiled gently as she shifted the books she carried in her arms. "You almost scared me to death!" he yelped.

"She comes up unannounced all the time," Francisca interjected. "We're used to it."

"Yeah, Hana's like some kinda ninja, man," said Raider, smirking. "She just sneaks up on you and bam! She's over here; she's over there, like the damn wind."

"I'll have to get used to that," Erik muttered.

"Are you all right?" Hanalei asked.

"It's okay," answered Erik. "I know he hit me because he cares."

"Is something bothering you; is it about yesterday?"

"What kind of question is that?" Erik squawked. "I thought we were done talking about it!"

"You jumped like I was going to hurt you," Hanalei said quietly.

"You got me," Erik grumbled. "So, I'm a little jittery. You would be too if some weirdo girl in black suddenly jumped you for no reason."

"Weirdo girl in black?" Francisca repeated.

Erik frowned when he noticed Raider grow tense. "She didn't beat the stuffing out of me or anything," Erik said quickly. "But she put up a pretty good fight."

"Was her name Danae?" Raider suddenly asked.

Erik nodded. "That's what she told me."

"Shit!" Raider growled and clenched his hands. "I should've sent that bitch to the grave a long time ago!"

"Now hold on--!" Erik cried.

"I don't believe it!" Francisca complained and punched a fist into her palm. "I thought we kicked that girl's ass the last time! She was in traction and everything!"

"Traction?" Erik yelped. "What are you talking about?"

"She's the reason you can't remember," responded Hanalei.

"Obviously she's better and is coming after you for revenge," Francisca grumbled. "She's going to fight us again and'll probably go harder than before!"

Raider's dark brown eyes narrowed as he shook in rage. "And knowing her," he growled, "that nasty bitch'll bring in her slimy ass brother Seraphine!"

"Please Erik, don't get involved again!" Hanalei pleaded. Erik stiffened when she grabbed his arm and buried her head into his shoulder. "I don't want to lose you."

"What the--?!" Erik yelped.

"Don't fuck with her, Erik," Raider said seriously and turned to Erik. "We got this, dig it?"

"If she wants me," Erik retorted, "then I'll take the fight to her."

"No, I mean it!" Raider kicked at a rock, sending it sailing several yards. "Both of 'em's gonna get a pummel of a lifetime. I ain't losin' ya again, not if I can help it!"

"Why do they hate us so much?"

"It's not just us they hate," Hanalei replied. "They hate you the most for the terrible things you did."

"What did I do?" Erik inquired.

"It ain't nothin' for you to know," Raider spat. "All you need to know is I'll kill that son of a bitch with *my own hands* if he rolls up on you, Erik! I'll kill him and that sister of his a thousand fucking ways from Sunday!"

"Just know they're dangerous people," Francisca warned. "Don't be a dummy get yourself involved!"

"Please, *stay away!*" Hanalei begged. "Let us take care of it!"

"But I don't understand," Erik protested, "what did I *do?*" No one answered.

"Ay, don't ya worry yer blond head 'bout it," Raider said surely and jabbed Erik's ribs with his elbow. He suddenly brightened as fell in step beside Erik and put an arm around his shoulders. "I got my peoples covered!"

Erik smiled warmly, despite his misgivings. "I'm glad you all are my friends," he said. "You're just too good to me."

"Hey man, that's how we roll."

At school, Erik approached his locker and did the combination. He stiffened when he found his books stashed inside and a slip of folded notebook paper taped to the top book. Erik ripped off the note and grew ill when he read the message scrawled inside: *We are watching you closely.*

Crumpling the paper, Erik tossed it aside in his locker and opened the backpack. He gasped, finding a notebook computer stashed inside.

"So *that's* what's making it heavy!" Erik murmured in mild surprise. "Why is Father Greenfield's work laptop down in here?"

Pulling it out, he examined it, finding a sticker of a man with arms outstretched, holding scales with symbols of swarming atoms around a nucleus in the background on notebook computer's bottom. Underneath the logo read 'Property of Gen-Tech'. Placing it back in the pack, Erik shut his locker and threw his bag over his shoulder, walking briskly to the library.

"*I don't care if I get in trouble for skipping class,*" Erik thought and slipped into the room as the other students filtered into their various classes. "*I need to know why he would put this in my bag...*"

Approaching the far rear of the library, Erik sat an empty table and pulled out the laptop. Turning it on, the boot screen loaded and an access lock appeared, requesting a password.

Pondering what it could be, Erik first tried 'password', only to be denied. A message came onto the screen, stating he needed an alphanumeric code.

"*Since this belongs to Father Greenfield, maybe he used his birthday,*" Erik considered and typed it out in long form only to get access denied again. He sighed, noting he had three tries left and tried Jane Greenfield's birthday, then their wedding date. "*I got one last shot before I'm locked out for good... What would this password be?*" Glancing at his open bag with his needed books and papers spilling out, Erik grinned to himself as he slapped his forehead. "*I'm so clueless! Why else would he put it in my backpack? Those people would know all the information I just put in, but not my birthday!*" He typed it in and the locked screen vanished.

Proud of himself as the virtual desktop came into view, the various program icons appeared. Once it finished loading the data needed to run, Erik noticed a document file displayed offside of the other icons on the bottom right hand corner of the screen, titled 'Physical Revelation - Case Study'.

"What's this?" he muttered. "Why would that be out of place, unless Father Greenfield *wanted* me to read it...?" Before Erik could access the file, he heard the door to the library swing open.

"Yo, I been lookin' fer ya," Raider's voice called. Erik quickly shut the top of the notebook computer as Raider approached, grinning. "Hey man, ya got detention with me, don'cha know that, right?" He gave Erik a playful jab on the shoulder.

"What did *you* get in for?" Erik asked and Raider snorted.

"Rumblin' with Seraphine, what else?" Raider scoffed. "Gotta get my licks in early, yo."

"You don't have to do that."

"So, wha'cha lookin' at?"

"It's nothing important..."

"But you look helluva ill, man. C'mon, lemme see what's on the lappy, huh?" Erik put an arm over the notebook computer.

"I can't," he murmured. "It's private stuff."

"Why's that?"

Erik shook his head, his face flushing. "I just can't right now. Besides... the files, they're unreadable."

"C'mon, man, ya trust me right?" Raider placed a hand on the desk and leaned forward. "Lemme look at 'em."

Erik blew a resigned sigh. "I can never say 'no' to you..."

"It's just 'cause I'm too awesome fer yer ass to handle."

"Now you're talking out your butt!"

Raider chuckled and Erik opened the notebook computer's top, revealing the electronic documentation. Raider glanced over Erik's shoulder as Erik accessed the file and his expression became unreadable once the document came open.

"*What's this?*" Erik thought. "*Molecular Rearrangement of Subcutaneous Matter? Measures for Enhancement of Physical Capabilities Through Improved Regenerative Medicine*...?"

"Move it," Raider snapped and pushed Erik out of his chair.

"*What is he thinking?*" Erik wondered as he stood and Raider moved over, scrolling through the document. "Well...?" he snapped.

Raider shook his head as he closed the document. Standing, he stuffed his hands into his jacket pockets. "Trash that shit, man," Raider said in an even tone. "Don't look at it or it'll destroy ya."

"What are you talking about?"

"Look man, there's stuff that you don't wanna know 'bout yer old man's business, dig what I'm sayin'?"

"What kind of business is he in?"

"The kind where if ya know too much, they'll get rid of yer ass."

"But--!"

"Don'cha trust me?" Erik nodded. "So don't look at it and junk it."

"Fine..."

Erik approached the laptop and sent the 'Physical Revelation - Case Study' document to the electronic shredder. A message appeared, stating it successfully no longer existed. Erik then turned off the computer and put it away in the backpack.

"*I didn't get a chance to learn anything important,*" Erik thought in irritation as he hoisted the bag over his shoulder. "*Is that part of the reason why I can't remember?*"

"Ya got Gym Class with Mister Lachlan, man," Raider said, breaking his thoughts. "You know me and the water thing... I ain't there."

"Afraid of getting wet, are you?" Erik teased.

Raider chuckled. "Naw, man, it wrecks my hair."

Erik laughed. "You're too much!"

"Hey man, I gotta keep my good looks; I'm like a pimp man, nothin' touches my face, dig?"

"Then what's with you getting into all these brawls?"

"Hey, I hit 'em hard, fast and early." Raider threw a few swift mock jabs at Erik. "My moves are like lightning - they never knew what hit 'em!"

Erik giggled and pushed Raider aside. "You're crazy."

"Last I checked I was okay in the head."

"You know they make swim caps, right?"

"It don't matter, man. I gotta keep lookin' good for them hip ladies." Raider grinned. "They don't want no old prune. They like 'em young and sexy, like me."

"Now you're really nuts."

Raider left the library with Erik and they walked together down the hall.

"Ay, man, never knew you was a swimmer," Raider said moments later. "Thought you'd be in into runnin', like I'm doin'."

"I never gave it much thought," Erik answered and gave a fake smile, feinting aloofness. "So, what do you have for Gym?" he asked instead.

"I got Track with Miss Auchinakie," Raider answered and smiled brightly. "She's okay, if you know what I'm sayin'."

Erik chortled, shaking his head. "Is she pretty to look at like Miss Fyne?"

"You know it!" Raider nudged Erik's side with his elbow. "Now if all the teachers in my classes were that foxy, I'd work harder to better my grades, man."

"So the only passing grade you're getting is Gym?" Erik burst out laughing. "Keep that up and they'll hold you back a year!"

"Hey man, I pass all them tests they throw at me!" Raider squawked. "Don't hate on my photographic memory! I look at it once and it's all in here." He tapped the side of his head. "I ain't gotta do shit. I murder those exams and they're like 'what the hell?' so I tell 'em straight up: C's still passing!"

"I can't argue that."

"Hey," Raider continued once they reached a break in the corridor and came to a pause, "our class is at the same time, now I think about it." He poked Erik's chest. "I'll catch you at your locker after class lets out, dig it?"

"Alright, Raider," Erik responded.

"Be cool, man."

"You too."

Raider saluted him ran down the hall while Erik took the opposite direction.

EIGHTEEN

Returning to his locker, Erik did the combination and put his backpack inside. The door abruptly slammed in his face and the pale student with the black and blond hair stood on the other side, glaring at him with dark green eyes.

"What do you want?" Erik demanded, looking down. He noticed the young man stood a head shorter than he, wearing a navy dress shirt, slacks and matching jackboots.

"Why," the student snapped, smirking, "don't you remember me?"

"Of course I remember, Shorty!" Erik took a quick step backward. "You tried to smack me with a brick!"

"Heh, no kidding, Punk!" The student booted Erik in the shin and Erik let out a yell in pain as he faltered. "But there's more than that!"

"What is wrong with you?" Erik yelped, clutching his leg. "What was that for?"

"My name's not Shorty, Punk!"

"My name's not Punk, Shorty!" Erik snapped. "Why can't you be civil?"

His aggressor scoffed. "Aw, want me to be civil to you?" He let out a short laugh. "I have no reason to be after the last time!"

"What last time?" Erik grunted when he received another swift kick in the other leg and he lost his balance, striking the floor on his knees.

"The next time we meet," the young man snarled, "I'll curbstomp your ass!"

"I want you to leave me alone!" Erik shouted. "I'm not scared of you, Shorty!"

The young man's shoulders and back tensed and he grabbed Erik by the face, throwing him against the lockers. "I told you," he sneered, "my name's not Shorty!"

"Then who are you?" Erik asked weakly and clenched his teeth as the student tightened his grip. "Obviously I don't remember you!"

"I'll crush you!" Erik's opponent growled.

"Do it then, Shorty!"

The student banged Erik's head back into the lockers and Erik returned with a groin kick, causing him staggering rearwards and let loose his grip. Erik sprang to his feet and shouldered his opponent in the chest, knocking him to the floor.

"You come after me again," Erik bellowed, "and maybe I'll knock *you* around for kicks!"

The young man jumped to his feet and charged Erik, grabbing him by the waist and hurled him down to the floor. Pinning Erik down, he punched Erik's chest, then leaned his elbow against Erik's neck, forcing Erik gasping and choking for breath.

"My name is Seraphine," the young man hissed, "and don't you ever forget it!"

Erik worked a hand free and grabbed at Seraphine's face. Heaving him off, Seraphine rolled to his feet as Erik struggled to stand. Seraphine rushed him and ducked, grabbing Erik by the leg and flipped him onto the floor on his back. Erik banged his head on the tiles and groaned as his vision flashed in red.

"Dude!" a voice called.

Seraphine rose to his feet, panting hard for breath. "We'll finish this later," he spat and stormed away.

That nutcase is nothing but trouble... With him back in the picture, you know your end is coming soon!

Erik sat up, holding his head. Looking up, he saw Seraphine shove past a tall thin student who had long bleached hair and wore ripped jeans, black T-shirt, denim vest, scruffy low-top sneakers and silver mirrored-lensed wraparound glasses on his face.

"Dude, hey!" the tall student yelled, whirling around and glared at Seraphine who stomped past. "Your butt's not a bumper!"

"Fuck off," Seraphine called over his shoulder.

The lanky student shrugged his shoulders and continued down the corridor. "Dude, hey, you okay?" he asked, approaching Erik.

"I'm fine," Erik moaned.

"You look pretty scrambled. You need a hand up or anything?"

"Don't worry about me... just give me a minute."

"Want me to get the nurse or whatever?"

"No, don't worry about it."

"Whatever you want, Dude." The lanky student walked away, going down the hall.

Erik shook his head and the reddened vision cleared to color. He staggered to his feet and made his way for his swimming class, inundated by the suffocating fear threatening to weigh him down.

"Class, I'd like you all to meet a new student," said the swimming instructor as Erik entered the large beige and gray tiled room with wide bright spotlights, lighting the room and massive ten-lane pool.

The instructor, a tall slender young man with long shaggy brown hair and small hazel eyes with wrinkles around the edges, wore red shorts with orange stripes on the side, a plain white T-shirt and leather strapped sandals. A bright orange whistle hung from a black cord around his neck and he held a clipboard in his hand.

Erik smiled timidly and gave his name, noting he stood out of place wearing his street clothes when everyone else wore swimming trunks and school issued T-shirts. He folded his arms across his chest when the instructor asked him if he had done any competitive swimming before.

"No, Mister Lachlan," Erik answered, "I've never done any swimming much."

"Man, a beginner!" a student complained. "Great!"

"I'm just as good as you guys!" Erik snapped back. "It's not that hard, is it?"

"Well, go see my assistant to get you fitted into a pair of trunks," Lachlan said. "When you get back, go to Indoor Pool Three. We're doing laps."

Erik left the room, heading into a small hall leading to the locker rooms and found a door with Lachlan's name on it. Knocking, he heard a gruff voice telling him to enter and Erik opened the door. "I was just told..." he began.

"Yeah, I know," snapped the assistant hidden from view behind the swamp of papers on the desk. Many trophies and medals lined the rear room on shelves. "What's your waist size?"

"Um... medium."

The assistant rose from his seat and headed into a cabinet, sifting through several articles of clothing. Erik caught a T-shirt with the school's mascot on the back and a pair of shorts, followed by a pair of swimming trunks.

"Don't lose these," said the assistant. "If you do, then you owe ten bucks apiece." Erik nodded. "You get locker fourteen."

Erik left the office, finding his locker already occupied. After clearing the top shelf of articles jammed inside with books and papers from the other student, he quickly stripped out of his clothes then pulled into the trunks and T-shirt. Tossing his clothes in the locker, he slipped into his sneakers and ran back for the gym.

Searching the pool area, Erik entered a glass hallway and found three large separate pool rooms with various colored tiles and holding different sized pools. One room had alternating blue and white tiles holding an eight-lane pool and the other with green and yellow tiles containing a six-lane pool.

He saw the class grouped in the beige and gray room and Lachlan shouting instructions to those doing laps in the water. Erik approached one slender student who had shoulder-length dark red hair and cool green eyes. His face had three long dark thin scars across the right cheek.

"Hey," Erik said brightly.

"Hey," he answered back. "I'm Garcia Leuong." He put his hands to his hips, rocking back and forth on the balls of his feet.

"Why aren't you in the water?" Erik asked.

"I'm not here for the sport. I just swim because it's a favorite thing of mine." Garcia turned to Erik. "Coach says you swim okay."

"That's right." Erik crossed his arms.

"Lose the kicks. I wanna see if you can really be a fish."

"Oh, alright." Erik slipped out of his shirt and shoes and then headed for an empty lane. Before he could take a breath, a violent shove threw him in. Erik immediately surfaced, glaring at Garcia grinning madly down at him. "Have you lost it today?" Erik yelled.

Lachlan approached them both, appearing concerned. "What's the matter, boys?" he asked.

"He claims he's not a good swimmer," Garcia protested. "He came up like it was nothing!"

"What are you going on about?"

"If he wasn't a good swimmer, he'd be flailing his arms and throwing up water!" Garcia pointed to Erik accusingly. "He's trying to downplay it all; he wants my medals!"

"What?" Erik sputtered, treading water. "I didn't even sign up for this class; someone else decided what I was taking!"

"I don't recall you in my class before."

"Apparently I have enough skill to be in this class so late in the semester."

"Maybe I should talk to your parents."

"My father wouldn't mind it at all."

"What's his name?"

"Greenfield."

"John Greenfield...?" Lachlan's face blanched, and then he cleared his throat loudly. "Do you do any diving?" he asked instead.

"*What's with that look?*" Erik wondered.

"Well...?" Lachlan pressed.

"A little," Erik answered sheepishly. "Why do you ask?"

"Get out and come over to the board. No cannons, okay?"

Erik sighed, wiping away his hair from his eyes. "*That can't be right,*" he thought. "*I don't remember, yet...!*"

Maybe it was erased from before...

Erik swam to the pool's edge and lifted himself out. Garcia kicked Erik back by the shoulder and glared down at him viciously when Erik fell back in. Erik clenched his teeth as he gripped the edge and glared back at Garcia.

"What's your deal?" Erik snapped.

"Why aren't your eyes red?" Garcia retorted.

"You seem smart," Erik said caustically as he hoisted himself up. "Figure it out."

"The chlorine makes everyone's eyes red!"

"So?" Erik got to his feet and shrugged his shoulders. "Big deal." He followed the instructor Lachlan to the diving board, sensing Garcia's burning gaze at his back.

"*Why isn't the chlorine bothering me?*" Erik mused after realizing the other students clustered nearby wore goggles and grew immediately sick in the pit of his stomach. "*What is it about me...?*"

"Class, for those still in the water ought to get out. We're going to do a diving test," Lachlan announced. "For those interested, please line up behind Mister Leuong. Those who aren't sit on the edge and don't horse around!"

Erik looked up at the ladder leading to the springboard. "What could I have possibly done to tick Garcia off?" he muttered.

"Oh, before I forget," continued Lachlan, pointing a pen in his direction. "How deep can you swim?"

"I'm not sure," Erik replied nervously. "Deep enough, I suppose..." Putting his hands to his hips, Erik waited to see if anyone else were going to take the diving test as well. He found to his dismay he alone stood the only one.

"I'm assuming you can do more than five feet. Now, please, climb up the ladder for me." Erik did as told. "Whenever you're ready, just dive in, Mister Hart."

Erik looked down at Garcia who fumed in silent anger. "*What is his problem?*" he thought, turning to the water.

Looking down at the true blue color, Erik backed up and then ran forward. Diving in with a splash, he swam to the edge pool's edge and surfaced; tapping the end, then swam back and grabbed the other side's edge. Erik came up for air, finding shocked looks on Lachlan's face and the other students.

"No way!" a student said in awe.

"What," Erik asked, "did I do something wrong?"

"Are you sure you never took diving lessons before?" Lachlan asked and Erik shook his head, afraid to answer. "Don't be so modest!"

"Well..." Erik's face burned scarlet in response. "I can't really remember; I was in terrible accident last year and my memory isn't the best anymore."

Is that so...?

"I'm sorry to hear that," Lachlan murmured.

"Liar!" Garcia howled. "He's trying to take my medals!"

"I don't want anything!" Erik yelled back. "Keep your precious medals; I'm just here to pass the class!"

"You just performed a somersault with a half-gainer," Lachlan said in a matter-of-fact tone as he clicked his pen. "That's a diving technique." He wrote a note down on a sheet attached to his clipboard.

"Listen, I'm not joining the team," Erik snapped as he pulled himself out the water. "Especially if I have to be bothered by that screeching wingnut!"

"The hell you say!" Garcia screeched.

"You heard me!" Erik shouted back. He stormed to where his sneakers and discarded shirt lay and retrieved them. "At this point, you can fail me, Mister Lachlan," Erik grumbled as he slipped his feet into his shoes and pulled into his shirt. "I'm not returning to class tomorrow!"

"I bet you he'll be back!" Garcia yelled. "He's trying to take everything I've earned!" Erik stormed away for the locker rooms. "I've worked hard for this!"

"Shut up, Leuong!" a student snapped.

"He's gonna show you up good, Leuong!"

Gay laughter followed.

"Shut up!" Garcia screamed.

The locker room doors swung shut behind Erik.

NINETEEN

Coming out of his trunks, Erik squeezed the water out of them in the showers and the material dried after a few wrings. He slipped out of his gym shirt and headed for locker fourteen.

"Hey!" Garcia yelled, "They gave you my locker!" Erik cried out in surprise and jumped back, immediately throwing the shirt in front of himself.

"Some warning would've been nice!" Erik snapped as his face burned bright red.

"I don't care if you don't have clothes on," Garcia screeched. "I'm still better than you!"

"Either hand me my clothes or get out of here!"

"No way," Garcia grumbled, "I'm not doing a damn thing for you, Hotshot!" He clenched his hands, baring his teeth at Erik. "You think you're so great, trying to pretend you suck and then show off!"

"I'm not really trying that hard!" Erik protested. "Please, I just want to grab my clothes and go home!"

"Stop lying to me!" Garcia stormed out the locker room.

Erik puffed a hard sigh and approached his locker, immediately changing into his clothing. While tying up his sneakers, Garcia returned with a metal bar and swung at him, striking Erik across the shoulder.

Erik stumbled forward and held his shoulder in mute shock when the bar twisted and part of it shattered from contact. Garcia dropped it as if it was hot and shock shadowed his face.

"Why are you trying to hurt me?" Erik shrieked and shrugged his shoulder, checking for breaks. He gasped when he registered no pain and nothing had become dislocated.

"*How can that happen?*" Erik thought, taken aback. "*A bar that heavy--!*"

"I *was* making sure you didn't join the team," Garcia snapped, "but I see you're taking Junk! I'll let the coach know for sure!"

"Taking what?" Erik spat. "I don't know what you're talking about!"

"You're not slow in the head, Hotshot, now come on!"

"Whatever, Garcia!" Erik grabbed his assigned clothes. "If you were paying attention and not squawking, you'd heard that I said I lost my memory; obviously I forgot I could swim like that!"

"Bullshit!" Garcia crowed. "I don't care if you can't remember your own damn name; I'm making your life hell!"

"Join the line!" Erik pushed Garcia back by the chest and Garcia stepped away, clenching his hands. "Whatever you're talking about, I'm not taking it," Erik said evenly. "Just leave me alone, Garcia; I'm no different from you!"

"Is that so, Hotshot? Nobody I know can take a hit like that and keep standing!"

"So what? I'm just tougher than you are, so accept it."

Garcia's smug expression turned stony. "Oh yeah?" he retorted. "What are you trying to say, huh? That you're one of *those* freaks?"

"You're not worth my time!" Erik grumbled and stormed past him, leaving the locker room. "You can't prove I'm taking any Junk," he called over his shoulder, "even if you could!"

"I'm onto you!" Garcia shrilled.

"What is with that guy?" Erik muttered and headed upstairs.

Exiting through the back door of the school, Erik spotted the runners in red trunks and yellow shirts on the track. Their feet hit the pavement unevenly and they gasped for breath, trying to beat the others ahead of them.

Catching sight of one student who passed everyone up, Erik realized with no mistake at the athletic swarthy young man and his feathered black hair blowing behind him to be Raider. The teacher, Auchinakie, hollered at the others to catch up.

Erik made his way down the field and approached the area where everyone dumped their bags. He tucked part of the t-shirt and shorts in his back jeans pocket and sat next to the collection of bags, wrapping his arms around his knees while waiting for class to end. Raider spotted him and waved. Erik returned the gesture.

Raider left the path and jogged up to Erik. "Hey," he called, "they let you bums out early?"

Erik took in a weak breath when he noticed Raider wasn't winded at all. "*He's not sweating either!*" he thought, stunned. "*What did Garcia mean by 'those freaks'? Does he know more than he's letting on?*"

"Ay, got water in yer ears?" Raider said louder.

Erik shook his head. "No need to yell," he replied and explained what happened. "I didn't want to start with that guy," he concluded. "I'm not feeling up to fighting him today."

"Want me to take care of him fer ya?" Raider asked, giving a malicious grin. "Sounds like a chump."

"Don't do that."

"Lemme know his name then," Raider pressed. "I'll only rough him up a little, I swear."

"His name is Garcia Leuong."

"Damn, I know that punk; he's a total kook!" Raider perched down to Erik's level. "Look, man, he's a total headcase and he'll try *anything* to keep ya from beating him. Stay away from his crazy ass, dig it?"

"He'll try anything," Erik asked warily, "like causing some serious harm to my bones or something?"

"Nah, not a scuffle... it ain't gonna go down like that." Raider shook his head. "The wimp can't even hold his own in a fight, but he can trip up your samples, makin' it look like you're taking Junk." Raider shrugged. "So the kook's got some brains and can cook up some shit..."

"You know I'm not taking anything!" Erik protested. "I don't even take painkillers!"

"Just be careful!"

"Even if Garcia did try, he can't put one over on my older brother, Stearne," Erik declared. "He's the assistant nurse here and he'll put that nutjob in a half-nelson for trying!"

"Man, that ripped guy nurse is your brother?" Raider grinned. "Way cool!" Auchinakie yelled at Raider to get back on the course. "Gotta jet; I'll see you when she lets me out."

"I'm not going anywhere soon," Erik replied. "Have fun though."

Raider stood. "Hey, you wanna run with me?" he asked. "I know you can keep up."

Erik put up his hands. "No, I've had a long day, so maybe I'll race you some other time. Besides, I got homework to catch up on and so much to think about..."

"Aw, come on!" Raider complained. "Let's give it a merry-go-round once about the track!" He held out a hand. "I swear I won't kill ya!"

Erik laughed when Auchinakie screamed at him again. "Okay! I'll give it a go, just once." He reached out and Raider pulled him up by the wrist.

Getting to his feet, Erik kept pace with Raider as he returned to the track. "*This is the slowest I've ever run,*" he thought, putting more effort than usual to keep his speed.

Raider kept shaking his head, laughing at him. "Man," he said and Erik glanced over his shoulder, noticing the other students from behind who were close to passing out glaring at them in envy. "You do this often?"

Erik grinned. "Not for fun, if that's what you mean."

"I dig what you sayin'," Raider answered.

"Why do you run?"

"I run because I want to be good like my cousin." Raider threw back a strand blown in his eyes. "He was tight; the star in the family, doing better than any of these bums in any sport thrown at him: football, baseball, basketball, tennis…"

"He must be really good," Erik said respectfully.

"Kevin could amaze ya," Raider continued, "especially in the gymnastics. He was strong…" His eyes became distant. "I wasn't good at nothin'. I was tiny… a shrimp like these bozos behind us. I run 'cause if I don't, then I'm the next to go."

Kevin…?

Erik came to a stop, utterly blown as Raider kept ahead of him. "That name--!" he murmured.

The other runners shoved Erik aside, forcing him out of his daze.

"Watch it, Stupid!" someone snapped.

"*The next to go!*" Erik thought, incredulous. "*What kind of trouble is he in…?*"

He left the track after getting pushed several more times and headed to where he left his bags. After collecting them, Erik heard Auchinakie blow her whistle and shout. Turning to the racecourse, he waited on Raider. When Raider continued about the paved path with no intention of retrieving his articles, Erik headed back for the exit.

Passing other students limping away from the track, he saw several lying in the grass from exhaustion, while one retched far from the group, his limits broken.

Auchinakie waved to Erik and he waved back. She waved again then jogged up to him. "You're the only one who can keep up with Zeadeas!" she said upon approach.

"Is that a bad thing?" Erik asked.

"Say, do you run often?"

"No, and I'm not planning on joining anytime soon."

"There's a spot open if you're still up to it," Auchinakie called after Erik as he walked away to where the students were filing into the locker rooms.

"Hey," another voice called to him, "you're Raider's friend?"

Erik turned around as a thin young man with tanned freckled skin ambled up to him. "No concern of yours," he grumbled and turned away.

"Hey, wait," the young man protested and grabbed Erik's arm.

Erik shook out of the young man's grip. "What does it mean to you?" he asked apprehensively.

"I just wanna tell you something," the student said brightly and leaned towards Erik. "Now don't get me wrong," he said in a low voice. "I don't know him all too well, but I hear stuff."

"What's your name?"

"Vicente Chavez." He leaned back, sticking out a hand and Erik shook it. "Listen, I heard that he's in this thing... you catch it?"

"... not entirely."

"Just watch your back, you catch it? Word was that Seraphine had somebody trash Raider's family real bad 'cause he wasn't too careful. Heard that his cousin's neck got broke in the wings."

"What are you talking about?"

"Hey, here's more juicy gossip," Vicente continued, ignoring Erik's question. "Was you in class today?"

"I..."

"Well catch this: Antony Gregg got tore up when Danae crashed his party last night. She put his homegirl Rotobot in traction and shot up Sharif!"

"You're talking out your butt!" Erik snapped and shoved Vicente away. "Get out of my face with that talk; you can't be for real!"

"Ain't no lie, man," Vicente prattled on. "Hartlan got spooked and took off, leaving Special Kaye and Two-tone Tony with the mess. Man, they got their heads busted into gravy and shipped to Centerville, never to be heard from again!"

Erik put up a hand. "Okay, that's enough!" he spat. "Why are you telling me this?"

"Because that girl told me to tell you she went easy on them!"

"You're nuts!"

"Hey!" Vicente grabbed Erik by the arm before he could walk away. "Look, man, some free advice: don't mess with that girl if you know what's good for you!"

"I'm good, thanks." Erik yanked his arm out of Vicente's grasp. "I need to get going..."

"Imma tell ya, man, she's not alone. When those guys in suits showed up..."

Erik blanched as the pain returned full force in his head. He sucked in a sharp breath and swallowed hard. "What guys in what suits?" he asked faintly. "Are they from Centerville?"

"Naw, man, much worse than that. But that's all I'm allowed to say."

Erik shoved Vicente aside and backed away. "You stay away from me!" he cried. "Don't talk to me anymore!"

"Vinny Chavez don't lie, just spreads what he hears." Vicente approached and poked Erik's chest. "And from what I heard, it's important if you still want some friends!"

"Get away from me!"

Erik pushed Vicente to the floor and took off, too disturbed to stick around.

TWENTY

Grabbing his backpack from his locker, Erik kicked it shut and stuffed his swimming gear inside. Hoisting it over his shoulder, he headed for the end of the foyer toward the school library, hoping to find Francisca and Hanalei.

Coming to a stop, Erik grew worried when he ran into Danae instead. She wore her black pea coat over her hooded sweatshirt, dark jeans and black leather work boots. Perched atop her head she had dark glasses.

"Are you obsessed with me or something?" Erik derided. "Is that why you're following me around?"

"I don't have to follow you around," Danae answered. "I already know everything I need to know about you."

"Then you already know I want you out my face."

Danae snorted. "Not this time!"

"Then what do you want with me?"

"I want nothing out of you right now," Danae said evenly and smirked. "I'm watching you though, real close."

Erik clenched his hands, growing enraged. "While you're at it, tell your brother to leave me alone!" he exploded. "I don't want to fight him either!"

Danae laughed in response. "You can't hurt me!" she crowed. "You're too weak!"

"You wanna prove it?" Erik slipped off his backpack and set it on the floor, then beckoned to Danae. "Come on, let's do this!"

Danae stepped up to Erik, glaring hatefully at him with narrow hazel eyes. "Trust me," she snarled, "you touch me and I'll have to hurt you."

"I told you to leave me alone. If I need to rough you up for you to understand, then you're dumb as a box of rocks!"

"I'm warning you - you're not built to defeat me, so save yourself the trouble and just give up while you still have the chance!"

"Forget it!" Erik put up his fists at the ready. "You keep pushing me and I *will* push back!"

"Don't make this harder than what it is!" Danae shouted.

"Don't test me, girl!" Erik snapped. "What's your deal?"

"My deal, huh? You wanna know?"

Danae swung at Erik and he leaned out of the attack, whirling around her. He threw a punch and crumpled when she booted his crotch. Danae then threw a powerful backhand forcefully across Erik's face, whipping back his head. Erik stumbled back and struck the floor with a dull thud.

"You–!" Erik held his stinging jaw and spat blood on the floor. "Why are you so intent on hurting me?"

"Because I can!" Danae stepped up to Erik as he scrambled to his feet and again stood back on the defensive. "I'll hurt your friends too without remorse if I don't get what I want."

"Not happening," Erik snapped back.

Danae leaned in, poking Erik's chest. "I always get what I want," she said sweetly, "even from you."

Erik slapped her hand away. "What if I don't want to give you what you're looking for?"

Danae grinned darkly. "Then I'll break every bone in your pitiful, scrawny body!"

"I don't believe you," Erik hissed.

"You'll always be weak, just like Genovera," Danae sneered. "And just like her, you'll end up dead too!"

That can't be--!

"What do you know about her?" Erik clenched his hands harder, his nails cutting into his palms as his anger flared. "Don't tell me–!"

"Fine, I won't, but you already know the answer!"

Erik threw a punch and Danae grabbed his hand, then immediately twisted his arm behind his back in one fluid motion.

"You really shouldn't hit girls," Danae snarled in his ear.

"You're an exception," Erik growled back. "Apparently I beat you down before!"

"Oh, who told you that?" Danae kneed Erik's back, forcing him down to the floor. "Back then, you could beat me, but not now!" Erik struggled as she pushed his face to the tile. "Admit it, you're weak!" she crowed. "I want you to say it!"

"Stuff it!"

Danae pushed him harder onto the floor. "If you keep resisting me, then I'll break your face!"

"Over my dead body!"

"Prove it!"

You're stronger than that! Get up!

Erik clenched his teeth and pushed back. Danae increased her strength and slammed him into the tile, busting his jaw. Erik let out a restrained yell and finally threw her off. Danae struck the floor stunned and Erik scrambled to his feet, clutching his face. Pushing against his chin, he heard a pop and the pain he felt immediately faded.

"Leave me alone!" Erik thundered. "I swear I will break you if you keep coming after me!"

Danae laughed at him and stood with ease. "Don't worry," she vaunted. "You'll get all the alone time you'd like!" Danae dusted off her coat and stalked off in the opposite direction.

Along with torturous punishment...

Erik whirled around about face to the nearby locker, half expecting to see his counterpart there. Instead, he saw his usual reflection against the polished metal.

Growing abruptly ill, Erik grabbed his backpack and ran to the nurse's office. Upon entry, he blew a sigh of relief when he found Stearne at the desk, filling out paperwork.

"Is something wrong?" Stearne asked, glancing up.

"I could use your help," Erik answered.

"With what?" Stearne pushed up his glasses slipping down the bridge of his nose. "Don't annoy me with worthless requests."

"You don't know what I'm about to ask you!" Erik snapped.

Stearne sighed and set down his pen, then leaned forward on his desk on his elbows. "I'm listening."

After Erik explained about his troubles with Danae and Seraphine, Stearne then pinched his nose and shook his head.

"What do you want me to do about it?" he grumbled. "Scare them off for you?"

"What kind of response is that?" Erik squawked. "I'm not asking you to fight my battles!"

"Then what do you want? You seem to have handled yourself fine."

"Stearne–!"

"You have nothing to worry about." Stearne picked up his pen and resumed his work. "Please leave me alone."

"Stearne," Erik pleaded. "Please, just listen to me! Danae mentioned something about Genovera..."

The writing stilled and Stearne glared at Erik, narrowing his eyes. Erik swallowed hard and backed away for the door when Stearne abruptly rose to his feet.

"What did she say?" he asked in a controlled voice. Erik told him what happened and Stearne's expression hardened.

"I didn't know what she meant," Erik continued. "Obviously you do."

"She's probably not planning anything harmful just yet, but you need to be careful."

"While we're on that subject, there's something I think you should hear..."

"Out with it already!"

Stearne turned pale after hearing about Erik's meeting with Genovera. "Why are you saying these things?" he growled.

"I'm not making it up!" Erik cried. "Stearne, please tell me, what's going on? Why is this happening?" Stearne clenched his teeth, putting a finger to his temple as the veins fleshed out in his forehead, jaw and neck. "Tell me, who are these people and why are Danae and Seraphine trying to hurt me? Is it related to my not being able to remember stuff?"

"Just go," Stearne said hoarsely. "Go home. I'll do what I can."

"What are you going to do?"

Stearne said nothing and Erik stepped out the nurse's office, shutting the door behind him. Unsettled, he spotted Raider stomping down the corridor.

Erik waited on him to catch up and Raider gave no greeting once he followed his stride. As they walked, Erik noticed his friend's dark brown eyes narrowed in concentration.

"Are you okay?" Erik asked timidly. "I thought we had to serve detention together."

"Man," Raider snapped, "we ain't got time for that shit!"

"What's more important than that?"

"I heard Seraphine and Danae shook you down."

"I put them in their place, if you're so concerned."

Raider came to a stop and grabbed Erik by the arm. "Don't, man," he begged. "I'm *telling* ya, don't fight 'em!"

"I'll try," Erik answered and pried off Raider's firm grip. "However, I highly doubt it can be helped."

"I don't wanna tell your folks you're tied up in the hospital again!"

"I'll be fine!" Erik grinned. "You trust me, right?"

"Don't forget I got your back."

Erik nodded and Raider said no more. Approaching the library, they were met by Hanalei and Francisca as they stepped out. Francisca appeared agitated and Hanalei fumed in visible anger as they continued for the school exit.

"What's wrong, Hana?" Erik asked.

"That ugly girl Danae broke Hana's best racket," Francisca answered for Hanalei who was too steamed to reply. "So now she's stuck playing the worst position on the team after failing Mister Crane's tennis test!"

"I'm sorry that happened," Erik said.

"The nerve of that bitch; what a total dick move!" Francisca went on. "Hana saved all that money for that damn thing for nothing!" She kicked at the wall with her boot. "If I wasn't away in my crappy Algebra class, I would've been down Danae's throat!" Francisca punched her free hand into her palm. "Then to make it even worse, she damaged Hana's French books! Now Hana owes the school money!"

"You can borrow my books if you want," Erik gently offered. "I'm not really paying attention to French anyway..."

"That's not the point," Hanalei spat. "The point is I'm getting a beating when I return home!"

"Then take it out on me if you want." Erik took Hanalei's hand and squeezed gently, making her blush slightly in response. "It's my fault all this happened. I started this nasty chain reaction in the first place."

"It couldn't be helped," Francisca muttered. "It was only a matter of time before that bitch recuperated and found out where you were!"

Erik sighed, frustrated. "Well, I'll still be there for you when you go to tennis practice, Hana!" he said instead.

"Fourth doubles have you far in the back where no one can see you," Hanalei said quietly.

"Don't worry," Erik said, grinning. "I'll be there to watch you practice."

"You're only going to drool over her because she's in that tennis skirt, Doofus!" Francisca snapped and punched his chest. "Be serious, Erik!"

Erik turned away and coughed, stunned as his heart skipped a beat. "What do you want me to do?" he moaned, holding a hand to his chest. "If I fight her like she wants, I'm in trouble. If I let you guys fight her, I'll feel guilty."

"We're asking you as your friends," Hanalei pleaded. "We don't want you to get involved!"

Erik blew a heavy sigh and ran his free hand through his hair. "I can't take this," he groused. "I really can't!"

"Man, don't sweat it!" Raider assured. "We've been dealing with her longer than you've been in my crew!" He grabbed Erik's arm and gave a firm squeeze. "Look, man, she ain't makin' us fall apart here! She gonna be comin' after us too, but we ain't freakin' the hell out or nothin'!"

"You're not the one with the messed up head!" Erik retorted. "She has some apparent skill and scrambled me! To think what she could do to you guys!"

Raider's grip turned vise-like and he shook Erik, suddenly becoming visibly irritated. "Don't let that ugly cow make ya spit bricks!" he shouted. "We're gonna show her and that son of a bitch Seraphine we're on her game!"

"How do you expect me to deal with this?" Erik objected. *How long has it been really?*

"If you gonna be stupid and go out there anyway, I ain't savin' yer neck!" Raider shrilled. "I ain't puttin' my ass on the line fer ya this time! You're on yer own!"

Erik wrenched free of Raider's grip, glaring back. "I didn't ask for your help!" he snapped. "You offered and I accepted!"

"Then I take it back!" Raider took off down the hall and kicked the exit doors open, storming outside.

"What are you planning?" Francisca asked.

Erik pulled away from Hanalei and ran a hand through her hair. "I'll meet up with you later," he said.

"Please be careful," Hanalei murmured and took Erik's hand, pressing it against her cheek.

"I guess you made up your mind," Francisca grumbled. "You want any reinforcements?"

"I'll call you if I get too banged up," Erik promised, releasing his grip from Hanalei's.

"Then tell me how it goes," Francisca commanded and tapped Erik's chest hard. "I *will* be waiting by the phone!"

"You have my solid guarantee." Erik put out his hand and Francisca grasped it. He clasped his other hand atop hers and squeezed firmly. "I mean what I say."

She nodded and let Erik go. "Give them hell!" Francisca called after him as he raced outdoors.

TWENTY-ONE

Erik hurried up the porch steps and stopped short when he found the front door ajar. Pushing it open, he peered inside, noticing the home devoid of light and life. Glancing outside, he searched past the porch, noticing the car gone.

"Father must be sicker than I thought," Erik thought upon re-entry and dropped his backpack near the door. *"They left in a hurry..."*

Pushing the door shut, he went through the house, turning on most of the lighting. Entering the kitchen, Erik checked the refrigerator's message board, finding nothing left for him to read. He leaned against the chrome-accented refrigerator, overwhelmed with dread.

The telephone's shrill ring cut the silence and Erik cried out, startled. He reached up, grabbing the nearby receiver. "Greenfield residence," Erik answered and froze when he heard the haunting melody on the other end. "Hello?" When no one answered, he put the receiver back in the cradle and headed upstairs.

Erik stiffened when the air in the hall dropped in temperature. Switching on the corridor light, finding the other doors closed, aside from his room. Entering through the hacked-in door, he turned the light on and froze at the sight of Danae standing at his open window.

"What are you doing here?" Erik growled.

"I thought you'd never come," Danae said in false cheer.

Erik clenched his hands. "How dare you break in here!"

"You left your window open, dumb ass," Danae retorted, smirking. "Besides, who are you going to tell? Public Security?"

"Did you leave the front door open?"

Danae shrugged. "What are you talking about?"

"Stop lying to me!"

"Whatever; it doesn't mater now. You know what I want." Danae took off her coat and dropped it to the floor. "We've got a fight to finish."

"Are you soft in the head?" Erik shouted. "I'm not playing your game!" He advanced and Danae blocked his swift punch for her face with her arm and pushed back. "I want you gone!"

"You keep saying that!" Danae spat. "You'd better show me how much you mean it; otherwise, I'm not going down easily!"

Erik bared his teeth. "I'll tell you all right," he snarled and grabbed her by the shirtfront. "I'll just have to put you in further pain for you to understand!"

"Do it then!"

Erik reversed Danae and hurled her forward, tossing her out the door. Danae rolled with the fall and sprang to her feet, withdrawing the dagger from the harness she wore strapped to her thigh. She rushed toward Erik and he leaned out of her attack, grasping her wrist and flipped her forcefully to the floor.

"How many times do I have to tell you?" Erik screamed and stomped on her chest. "Leave me and my friends alone!"

"Forget it!" Danae jammed the blade into his thigh and Erik cried out in shock and pain, gripping his leg as she drove the steel through. He staggered rearward and Danae grabbed his foot, flipping Erik over on the ground. She sprang to her feet and stepped on Erik's throat as he grabbed her ankle, struggling to push her off. "I don't care what I have to do," Danae shouted. "You're going to pay for what you did!"

Hearing footsteps in the corridor, Erik looked past Danae, spotting Seraphine entering the room, dressed in a dark trench coat. Danae turned and frowned at the sight of him.

"What took you so long?" she spat. "You should be doing this, not me!"

"Came in for scraps, Shorty?" Erik interjected. "I thought you planned to curbstomp my ass!"

Seraphine bared his teeth and withdrew a sleek black pistol from inside his coat. "I don't need my sister's help," he sneered and pulled back the safety. "Move out of my way, Danae."

"Have at it," Erik egged. "Obviously you've got the advantage with your sister holding me down!"

"Shut up!" Seraphine screamed and aimed the gun at Erik's head with a shaking hand.

"What are you waiting on, Shorty?" Erik pressed. "Do you need a target?"

Everything became washed out after a loud bang, swiftly going dark.

Erik slowly came to and found himself in a pitch-black world. He couldn't move his limbs and when he tried to speak, no words came.

"This ultimate power you have," said a voice in the darkness, "you can use it for good or for evil. I can't make you decide; it's your choice."

"*I don't understand,*" Erik thought. "*I can't talk... Can't move... Is this Limbo or something?*"

"You two are polar opposites in both heart and mind... I just hope you don't destroy each other."

"*Who is my polar opposite? It can't be Danae! Please, don't let it be her!*"

"We will take care of you... He needs you here, otherwise he can't go on."

"*What? Who is he?*"

A warm gentle hand touched Erik's cheek and his eyes snapped open to blurred vision. The fog slowly cleared and Erik found himself in a white room, with cream-colored walls and ivory tiles.

Looking up, Erik faced a middle-aged man with tired gray eyes and long brown hair peppered with silver streaks pulled back into a braid. The mysterious man wore a dark navy suit and sat at his side, appearing dispirited.

"Can you move you toes?" The doctor asked and Erik tried, sensing his feet twitch slightly. "What of your fingers?" Erik concentrated and his fingers tapped the surface he laid on at his side. "Can you speak?"

"Who..." Erik rasped, "who are you?"

"I'm a friend," the stranger answered. "I made a promise to help you in case something happened."

"What happened?"

"I'm afraid the fighting may start again. You might be sent to fight over there, but your father doesn't want that."

"What are you talking about?" Erik fought to sit up and the man stood, taking Erik by the arm and helped him upright. "Fight where...?" Erik gasped, noticing he was dressed in a brown jumpsuit and rest on a metal table with broken harnesses on the sides.

The war's long over...

"Their hatred still hasn't fully disappeared..." said the stranger. "We're reluctant to use you for purposes like that again..."

"What war? What purpose?"

The man began pacing, holding his hands at his back. "That's why I allowed Schumacher to reprogram you as he did."

"Programming...? Schumacher...?" Erik felt at his face and head, finding no injury. "What happened to me? I thought...!" He drew a blank, unable to recall what he wanted to say.

"Doctor," a voice called from afar.

The man in the dark navy suit turned away, frowning. "In a moment," he called back and resumed pacing.

"You're not making any sense," Erik muttered. "Doctor..."

"Between the two of you," the doctor continued, "you both possess great abilities. Powers of destruction, powers of restoration... When the final war looms, you will each return."

"I'm sorry, I don't understand..."

"There is still something in which you lack, something not even I can give you."

"What do you mean?"

207

"You can't go on living without it; therefore, you will always overcompensate for it. Be mindful, for you were born to discover something important."

"Living without what? What am I to discover...?"

The doctor paused before Erik, his face expressionless. "You are a curse upon this world," he said seriously. "Eventually, I will have to watch what you bring to this realm from beyond this life..."

Finding his voice, Erik gripped the table's edge. "Please don't die!" he cried. "You don't have to do that!"

"I can't make you save them from their grave errors. Like I said, it's your choice." The doctor turned on his heel and stalked out.

Erik stared down at the floor, hindered by pain and fear. *"What is it I lack?"* he wondered. *"Why is he going to die?"*

"I'm sorry, Doctor," a malicious voice called from outside the corridor. "Your time ends now!"

"Don't do that!" the doctor cried.

Erik felt the feeling return to his numbed body and jumped down from the table. Hearing a shout, Erik rushed out into the hall and halted at the sight of the doctor facing a young man who had Erik's likeness, wearing a dark green jumpsuit. The young man blocked the doctor's path, wielding a violet crystalline long sword.

"It's him again...!" Erik thought, stunned.

"Please, reconsider," pleaded the doctor. "You don't have to do this."

"Oh, but I must," said the young man. "Of course, you might not like this..."

"What are you doing?" Erik yelled.

Why do you keep following me...?

"Silence is what I want from you, Ferdian!" the young man snapped. "You get in my way and you're next!"

"Ferdian?" Erik cried. "Why are you calling me that?"

"Put that away, Wilhelm," the doctor said calmly. "We can talk about this."

Wilhelm chortled. "I promise to kill you quickly, toymaker," he snarled and held the sword at ready. "Now don't make a sound..."

"No!" Erik cried and dropped for a tackle, grunting when Wilhelm lashed out at him, slicing at his chest.

"You can't strike me down!" Wilhelm hollered. "I will crush you!"

"You leave him alone!" Erik shouted. "I don't care if you cut me to ribbons... You can't go around killing people!"

"You touch me," Wilhelm snarled, "and I will devour your soul!"

Wilhelm swung again and Erik leaned out of the attack. He dodged the young man's ferocious blows, barely keeping away from the sword's path.

"You must let your hatred manifest," the doctor called to Erik. "Don't hold back!"

"I don't know how!" Erik yelped.

"Hurry and obey!"

Erik jumped out of another strike and stumbled forward when hit in the back by a hard slash. He turned out the way as Wilhelm struck again, forcing the blade smashing into the wall. The sword shattered on contact, breaking off at the handle.

Erik turned and kicked Wilhelm's chest, sending him crashing to the floor on his back. Wilhelm groaned and scrambled to sit up. Panting hard for breath, Erik stormed over.

"I'm tired of fighting you," Erik declared. "You need to stop!"

"Then put me in my place!" Wilhelm growled as he sat up. "You can't do it; you're not strong enough!"

Erik clenched his hands, growing irritated. "If I hear that one more time!" he snarled. "I *am* strong enough - just don't push me!"

"You need to wait," the doctor pressed.

Wilhelm staggered to his feet and clutched the broken sword handle, shaking in rage. "Wait for what?" he screeched. "We've been waiting forever! Ten years now, or have you forgotten?"

Ten years...!

"How can I forget when no one will ever let me?" the doctor retorted.

"Then do it so I can get rid of you!"

"I can't do it!"

"Why?" Wilhelm pointed the broken sword handle at the doctor. "If you don't, then I will!"

The doctor narrowed his eyes. "I dare you!" he sneered. "You only have one chance!"

"*Sirachet!*" Wilhelm generated navy electricity around his hands and a golden steel saber formed from the handle, shining in crimson light. "I will get rid of you, toymaker," Wilhelm roared. "You, all of you, will stay dead! You deserve to rot in Hell!"

"Stop!" Erik shrieked and pushed the doctor aside. Wilhelm thrust the cutlass into Erik's chest, infusing him with the energy emanating from the blade.

"*Kenzan Kaisen!*" Wilhelm thundered and white flames blasted into Erik. Erik let out a wail when his skin burned from the flash flare and Wilhelm withdrew, kicking him aside. Erik staggered rearward and fell forward on his knees, gasping weakly for breath. "You're next, toymaker!" Wilhelm bellowed.

"I can no longer salvage you," the doctor said, backing away. "You're making me resort to what I don't want to use."

"Save your breath; it'll be over quickly."

Wilhelm charged and the doctor withdrew a pistol hidden beneath his blazer. He let off a single shot before the young man raised his sword and Wilhelm fell back from the force, collapsing to the floor with a borehole between his eyes. The sword he held clattered away, shattering into shards.

"I exist to protect," stated the doctor. "You did what you had to do, but to protect, there's no other way, other than to destroy..."

Why must we continue destroying?

Erik watched in stunned silence as the doctor sheathed the pistol and walked away down the lone tiled corridor. Erik struggled to get up and frowned when he noticed dark blue burns covered his arms.

Touching the charred skin, part of it peeled away, revealing titanium underneath. The shock caused Erik's world slipping from him and he fell forward as a heap on the floor.

TWENTY-TWO

Erik woke up with a start, finding breathing difficult. He panicked and realized he couldn't scream once he noticed his mouth taped shut.

Unable to move, Erik looked around his surroundings and saw he lay on the floor of a darkened room with his limbs tied at his back. He fought to get out of his binds, trying to loosen the ropes around his wrists and ankles.

Hearing indistinct noises and heavy footsteps coming from another room, Erik stiffened; worried the intruder may come for him. When he heard nothing else, he turned over onto his knees and rose unsteadily to his feet.

Taking a hop forward, Erik stumbled when his injured leg gave way to spasm and crashed on a sharp edge, striking his chest hard. Erik grunted and rolled over, hitting the floor on his shoulder. He let out a muffled scream in agony when his shoulder popped out of place.

Sitting up, Erik perked when he heard a faint dial tone. He pushed back against the wall and part of it gave way when a heavy object fell on his legs. Erik shook his head violently, crying in pain and pushed off the metal, forcing it clattering aside.

Erik leaned over, straining to hear the dial tone. His uninjured shoulder pressed against a wheel and Erik stiffened in surprise.

"*Is that an office chair?*" he wondered. "*Am I in Father Greenfield's study?*"

Erik pushed across the floor and his back finally met a cool hard surface. Leaning against it as leverage, he pushed up with his legs and finally stood. The dial tone turned louder and Erik bent forward, rapping his head against the desk. He winced then felt with his nose, making his way around.

Bumping into the phone, Erik used his nose, pecking at the touch-tone keys. He grunted when the tone was wrong and pushed the switchhook, then tried again. The call went through and he heard the buzz of the call connecting. Sinking to the floor in exhaustion, Erik moaned and leaned forward. Several rings later, the line clicked.

"Hello?" a tinny voice answered. "Hello, is anyone there?" After a moment of silence, the voice spoke again. "Erik, is that you?" Erik stiffened when he heard the door handle turn across the room. "I'm coming right over!"

Erik fell over on his side and held his breath as the door opened, washing light into the room.

"Is he dead?" a woman's voice called from outside in the hall.

A bright light flashed in the room, making a sweep. Erik shut his eyes tightly, breaking out in cold sweat when the light landed on him.

"Yeah, out cold," a man's voice called back. "What you want me to do with him?"

"Leave him there. They'll get the message."

"Did you find it yet?"

"Not yet."

The door shut after the man and Erik listened to his heavy footfalls descending the staircase.

"*What are they looking for?*" Erik thought as he sat up.

Moments later, sudden gunfire blasted outside the house, followed by shouts and return fire.

"Get the fuck outta here!" Raider's voice screamed.

"I got him!" Francisca called and another blast resonated in the night.

Harried footsteps stormed the stairs and the office door slammed open. The light switched on and Erik let out a muffled cry in pain, shutting his eyes from the stinging light.

"Shit, man!" Raider yelped and ran up to Erik. He dropped by his side and ripped off the tape.

"Hey!" Erik yelped. "Go easy on me!"

"Sorry." Raider grabbed Erik by the arm and pulled him upright. Erik wailed in pain and withdrew, doubling over in agony. "What is it?"

"My shoulder's messed up," Erik complained.

"Here, lemme fix it."

"How are you going to do that?" Erik spat.

Raider gestured at Erik to stand. Erik blew a heavy sigh, doing as told and Raider put one hand on Erik's shoulder near his collarbone while the other pressed at his back near his shoulder blade.

Raider pressed into Erik and Erik clenched his teeth when pushed against. The force popped the socket back in place and Erik slipped against the desk, exhausted and in agony.

"I thought I was never gonna run into ya!" Raider said. "Franny rang me up freakin' out, thinkin' something heavy happened."

"Obviously!" Erik spat.

Raider untied the ropes around Erik's wrists, then bent down, taking off the ties around his ankles. "The hell's going on, man?" he demanded once he stood. "What shit you got yerself into?"

"Like I would know!" Erik complained, rubbing his sore wrists. "Danae and Seraphine jumped me when I showed up here."

"At least they didn't kill ya."

"Is that all you can say?" Erik exploded.

"Looks like you handled it without my help," Raider grumbled and shrugged his shoulders. "Still kickin' and that's what matters, right?"

"Raider, they could've easily shot me dead!" Erik screamed. "He did–!" He gasped and felt his face. "I should have a wound somewhere," Erik said in horror. "Or at least be dead! Nobody can survive getting shot point-blank like that!"

"Lucked out or something, huh?" Raider said coolly. "That kinda thing does happen, ya know. Like this dude got a six-inch knife up in the skull..."

Erik grabbed Raider by the shoulders and shook him hard. "Damn it, Raider, Seraphine shot at me *point blank*!" he exclaimed. "He shot me *in the head* and the sound was

215

unmistakable!" Erik poked Raider's forehead with his finger. "A bullet between the eyes kills *everyone* - no one can *survive* such a thing!"

Raider narrowed his eyes and slapped Erik's hand away. "You look fine to me," he grumbled. "Prolly dreamin' up shit from gettin' kicked in the head!"

"This isn't funny!" Erik squawked.

"I ain't sayin' it is!" Raider snapped in annoyance. "I ain't gonna be surprised if they come back here with some *real* party toys!"

"Raider!"

Raider snorted. "Dig this man: not everything leaves holes in ya," he explained. "I mean, even dart guns are helluva shiny these days; so what you think is some forty-five cal, is actually holdin' some green juice!"

"Oh, comforting," growled Erik and limped past him. "*He's taking this a little too well,*" he thought warily. "*What's his deal?*"

"Fine, then!" Raider yelled at his back. "Don't ask me to help you rumble next time!"

Hurrying down the steps, Erik entered the parlor and put up his hands when Francisca pointed her shotgun at him.

"Damn, don't scare me like that!" Francisca exclaimed and lowered her weapon. "I damn near shot your face off!"

"Thanks, I suppose," said Erik.

"I thought I saw Danae take off 'round the back," Francisca said and sat on the edge of the overturned couch.

"Yeah," Raider chimed in as he came down the steps. "See, I ran into 'em on my way here and gave 'em the ol' one-two."

Erik blew a hard sigh and ran his hands through his hair. "What were they looking for?" he moaned. "What trouble are my parents in?"

"So you weren't robbed?" Francisca asked, surprised.

"I don't know what's going on," Erik grumbled. "I'm just glad they knocked me out."

"You heard the ones who tore up your house?"

Erik nodded. "It was someone else other than Seraphine and Danae. One of them saw me and either thought I was dead, or lied..."

"Did you recognize the voice at all?"

"I–!"

The rear door slammed open and all three turned toward the sound's source. Erik took off for the kitchen, followed by Raider and Francisca. Erik came to a stop when he saw Seraphine pointing a high-powered pistol in his direction.

"The hell you doin' back here?" Raider snarled and pushed Erik aside, standing before him.

Seraphine aimed in Raider's direction and grinned maliciously. "I got orders to take all of you out," he said. "This is the last time you punks show me up!"

"I'm gonna take your ass down, sucker," Raider shouted, "and you ain't gettin' back outta Hell!"

Erik grabbed Raider by the sleeve as Seraphine withdrew the safety and waved the gun at their general direction.

"Try me!" Seraphine shouted.

"Before you get rid of us," Erik pleaded, "at least tell us what you're going on about!"

"You got those schematics somewhere and we need you out the way."

"What makes you think I don't have those schematics?"

Seraphine scoffed. "Someone as stupid as you wouldn't have them!"

Erik grunted. "You never know," he said. "Go on and give it your best shot. You might be making a mistake!"

Seraphine growled. "I really gotta kill you now. You saw too much... You know too much."

"You kill us and everyone will find out!"

Seraphine laughed. "Who?" he crowed. "Once the cleaners come, nobody will notice a thing."

"Don't think about it," Francisca sneered and readied her rifle. "I'll blast a hole in your ass so wide, I can stick my foot in it!"

Raider charged and delivered a heavy punch at Seraphine's jaw, snapping back his head. He crashed to the floor and Raider stormed up, kicking Seraphine down with his foot.

"Stay down!" Raider grumbled and stepped on Seraphine's wrist, forcing him dropping the handgun. Erik ran up and took the pistol, holding it in both hands.

"Tell me what's going on!" Erik hollered. "Or so help me, you're going to suffer lead poisoning!"

Seraphine laughed. "You can't do shit!" he crowed. "You don't have the heart in you to kill!"

"Well, I do!" Francisca said and raised her shotgun.

Erik pointed the pistol at her and her eyes widened. "Back off!" he thundered. "I don't want him dead!"

218

"Are you fucking nuts?" Raider bellowed and grabbed Erik by the arm, turning him around. "This son of a bitch has orders to wipe us all out!"

"You kill him and more will keep coming!" Erik protested, yanking out of his grip. "I want answers." He pushed Raider aside and stood over Seraphine, pointing the pistol down at his head. "Tell me what you know, or you're losing some body parts."

"You're full of shit," Seraphine hissed and spat at Erik. Erik growled and wiped the spittle away with the back of his hand. "All you do is talk out your ass!"

"Really?" Erik snapped, stomping on Seraphine's chest. "Don't push me!"

A blast of gunfire shot through the room and Erik cried out, jerking back in pain.

"Damn it!" Francisca cried, taking off for the front door as Erik dropped the handgun and clutched his shoulder. The pistol discharged its bullet, ricocheting off the counter, and chipped off part of the marble.

Raider pulled aside when Seraphine grabbed for the fallen weapon, leaning out and aimed, firing from his place on the floor. Erik screamed, gripping his neck as white-hot agony seared through him and sticky warmth ran through his fingers. He staggered against the kitchen counter then slid to the floor.

"How's that for shitting you, Punk?" Seraphine vaunted. "I got thirteen more in here. We can party all night."

"Shit!" Raider growled and charged again, brought down by shots to his leg and arm.

"However you want to die," Seraphine said, standing. "I don't care." He waved the pistol in their direction. "Easy or hard, you're gonna suffer either way!"

Raider struggled to get up and Seraphine stood over him, firing again. Raider cried out and Erik cringed in pain.

"This can't be the end!" Erik thought as he fought to stand. *"I can't have my friends dying over me!"*

Holding onto the counter for support, Erik reached over the drainboard and grabbed a butcher knife. He ran and ducked when Seraphine turned to him, carving into Seraphine's side with the blade. Seraphine doubled over and Erik kicked him back, sending him crashing into the basement door. Seraphine struck his head then slumped forward, unconscious.

Holding the knife between his teeth, Erik bent down and grabbed Raider, hoisting his arms over his shoulders. A forceful push slammed down into his back and he staggered forward, dropping Raider. Erik whirled around and leaned out of a slice from Danae who held a foot-long dagger.

"Give it up," Danae spat. "I already took care of your bitch outside!"

Erik held the knife at ready in his free hand. "I can still try!" he yelled. "I can never forgive you for hurting my friends!"

"Bring it, asshole!" Danae beckoned to him. "You don't know who you're fucking with!"

Erik lunged at Danae and she turned away, withdrawing another dagger from a holster at her back. Erik blocked one strike aimed at his face with the spine of the knife, then again for his side. He grunted when slashed across the chest as he stepped away, then around when she swung again.

Turning out when she threw her dagger, Erik spun around when he heard Raider shout in pain. Raider clutched his profusely bleeding shoulder and held Seraphine's pistol weakly in his hand.

"You bitch!" Raider snarled and yanked the out blade out with his free hand. "I'll fuckin' murk yer ass!"

Erik kicked Danae back and retreated as Raider charged Danae, making a swipe at her. Danae turned out of his attack and slashed back, cutting into his arm as Raider blocked the blow.

Raider slammed the pistol over Danae's head with his other hand, knocking her dazed and stomped on her chest, sending her crashing to the floor. Raider pointed the pistol down at Danae and Erik ran up to him, grabbing his arm.

"Don't," Erik pleaded.

Raider glared back at Erik, appalled. "The fuck is wrong with you?" he shouted. "That bitch is tryin' to kill us here!"

"Before you get rid of her, I want to know why she's doing this."

"You already know why," Danae hissed. "Just give up... There won't be just us; there's more out there!"

A loud blast resonated in the kitchen and Erik staggered back, clutching his chest. Looking toward the kitchen doorway, he spotted a woman dressed in a dark suit, hat and glasses, pointing a revolver in his direction.

Erik immediately grew weak as his blood ran through his hands and he slipped to his knees, gasping. His hands suddenly burned and the fiery sensation spread up his arms.

Brace yourself!

Raider jumped the counter and the woman turned to fire, only to miss as Raider kicked her back by the chest, sending her crashing on the floor. Raider jumped down and the woman rolled out the way to her feet, releasing the remaining rounds. Raider screamed when the bullets ripped into his leg, side, thigh and torso.

Danae scrambled to her feet and Erik stood, grabbing her by the wrist when she rushed him. Yanking forward, he ducked down and reversed her as a man dressed the same as the female killer came through the back door with a rifle. Danae screamed when blasted in the back and fell forward.

Pushing her aside, Erik reached down, picking up the fallen knife. He sidestepped the man's attack with the gunstock and made a mad slash, carving into the man's arm and across his chest.

The man punched Erik's face with his uninjured hand and slammed the rifle into his chest, sending Erik smashing against the kitchen table.

The knife clattered to the floor and Erik groaned in pain as he slipped down on his face. The man stepped up to Erik, holding his rifle at ready.

"It's over, kid," the man said.

"Why?" Erik moaned. "What are you looking for?"

"Obviously you're lying; otherwise you wouldn't fight back so hard." The man pulled back on the bolt, releasing the spent bullet. "Now tell me where it is and I'll send you on your way."

"What makes you think I know?"

"Where else would he hide it? It's not in the most obvious place. It has to be in you. Now tell me."

"I don't know what schematics you're talking about…"

"Stop stalling and just spit it out."

Erik looked up and squinted at the man standing before him. He gasped when he saw someone else in dark navy at the back door and shook his head.

No! No, this can't be!

"Are you going to tell me or what?" the man commanded.

"I don't remember!" Erik cried. "Honestly, I don't!"

"You got one last chance!" the man growled. "Where is it?"

"What is it you're looking for? I told you I don't know!"

"The schematics or the weapon! Cough it up!"

Erik held his breath as the other person sneaked behind the man with the rifle. A loud screech abruptly squelched in his head and Erik cried out as fierce pain throbbed behind his eyes. He turned on his side, clamping his hands over his ears, unable to drive out the sound.

The rifleman dropped dead with a large borehole between his eyes and Erik looked up, facing a slender woman who wore a dark helmet with a reflective visor. She set her pistol into a holster at her thigh and withdrew a miniature machine from a small pouch she wore at her waist, turning a switch. The sound cut off and Erik sat up, sagging back against the table.

"What weapon are they looking for?" Erik moaned once the woman approached and knelt at his side. "Is it some kind of machine, or a gun or something?" The woman put away her handheld device and took out a penlight. Clicking it, she shined the blue light in Erik's eyes. He winced and turned away. "Hey, don't do that!"

"Sit still," snapped the woman.

Several others dressed the same as the woman entered, carrying bags and buckets of chemicals.

"You didn't answer my question," complained Erik.

The woman set the penlight aside and grabbed another pen with a clear body, holding orange liquid inside. She slipped a slender violet liquid-filled cartridge from her pack and thumbed out the orange one, snapping the new one in place.

"What are we gonna do with him?" a man's voice called from the next room.

"Lady, please answer me," Erik begged. "What are they looking for?"

"They're looking for you," the woman replied and jammed the pen in the side of Erik's neck. His world fell away and a loud hiss sounded in his ears, then turned red and silent as he slumped forward, unconscious.

In the darkness, Erik screamed, consumed in fiery pain throughout his body. His limbs refused to respond, held down by invisible forces. Around him, many voices spoke to him at once.

Who are you...?

Where are you...?

224

Where have you been...?

Where are you going...?

What are you...?

Why are you here...?

How will you return...?

When will this finally end...?

Breaking free, Erik scrambled to his feet and raced toward the light at the end of the long corridor stretching into a tunnel. Another voice, louder than the rest Erik faintly recognized called to him frantically.

"Don't go into the light! Come back..."

I have to go...

"Please return to me... stay here, stay here...!"

I promised...

Erik finally reached the brightly lit door and flung it open, revealing on the other side the mirror hanging over his bedroom door. He touched it and it fractured in many places, its pieces all showing different facets of Erik who had his likeness but different hair and eye color.

"They're me, and yet not me," Erik thought, touching the face in the glass reflecting back a redheaded young man with cool green eyes and freckles across the cheeks.

"Justin!"

Erik whirled around, searching for the voice. "Who's calling for me?" he shouted.

"Ferdian!" another voice called.

"Wait...!"

"Erik!" called a third.

"Stop it!"

"Wake up!" all three voices called at once.

Erik turned back around, facing the young man who had his exact appearance inside the mirror. Instead of blond hair, blue eyes and freckles across the cheeks, the young man had dark green eyes, black hair, and thin scars across the nose and cheeks. In his left ear, he wore an earring containing a single silver bullet.

Stepping out of the cracked reflection, the young man gained form and grabbed Erik by the throat. Erik winced when searing pain tore into his side and looked down, finding a blade embedded there.

"It's nice to see you again, Brother," Erik's reflection hissed in his ear. Erik gasped as the blade turned swiftly in his side, releasing more blood. "But I'm sorry to see you go..."

"Why...?" Erik moaned.

"Because only one of us can live!"

The young man withdrew the short sword and Erik slumped forward onto his knees, growing faint as his life slipped away. "What did I do to deserve this?" he wheezed as the young man sheathed the bloodied blade at his side into an empty harness.

His dark counterpart knelt down, grinning sardonically and gave Erik's cheek a gentle pat. "Nothing at all," he answered and drew a golden revolver from a rear holster. Reaching to his earring, the young man snapped off the silver bullet. "Let's see if you're lucky..." Erik grunted when the gun struck his face and kicked in his chest, throwing him on his back.

"Don't do this," Erik pleaded as his opposite loaded the revolver and spun the chambers before flicking his wrist to snap it shut.

"Get the fuck up," the young man snarled and pointed the gun down at Erik.

Erik staggered upright, clutching his side with burning hands. "Please, don't," he begged and the young man waved the revolver at him.

"On three, run." Erik clenched his teeth as violet light erupted around the gun, charging it and his dark counterpart placed the flat of his hand against the hammer. "Three!"

Erik turned to run, hearing five clicks before the blast. Everything darkened instantly.

PART TWO

Outside Within

TWENTY-THREE

Erik slowly opened his eyes to blinding white, besieged by a faint antiseptic smell permeating the air. Many blurry colors moved back and forth and he heard low tones and beeps from machines. Pain swamped his body and Erik shook his head, clearing the fogginess.

"Am I dead?" Erik groaned and glanced to his side once his vision returned slightly hazy. Facing a large pane window, he caught a glimpse of his reflection from the darkened nighttime atmosphere and gasped, noticing the many bandages on his body.

Sitting up, Erik heard footsteps enter from behind and turned, looking up. His eyesight sharpened when he saw John Greenfield standing over him, wearing a pale green dress shirt, dark olive tie, and chinos. He took Erik's hand, grasping it firmly.

"Hey, Ace," John Greenfield said softly and gave a gentle smile. "Please tell me you're all right!"

He hasn't called me that since–!

Erik sucked in a shallow breath when fierce pain banged in his temples. He whimpered, pulling out of John Greenfield's grip and held his head as he shut his eyes.

"What's wrong with me?" Erik moaned. "I swear, my head's going to explode!"

John Greenfield sat at Erik's bedside and pried his hands away. "Tell me," he pressed, "how long has this been going on?"

Erik looked around the room and noticed from his surroundings that he lay in a hospital bed. "Are you the only one here?" he asked. "Where's Mother?"

"She's waiting outside," John Greenfield replied. "Please, answer me. I only want to help."

Erik shook his head. "I'm not sure," he muttered. "For a while now..."

"How long of a while? A few days, a few weeks...?"

"I've always had headaches..." Erik shrugged. "I guess I can say they started to get worse a couple of days ago."

"Why didn't you say anything to me about that?"

"I didn't want to worry you."

"Remember, Son, you can always come to me when anything happens," John Greenfield assured. "My job is to worry about you; I'm your dad, remember?" Erik smiled weakly and John Greenfield chortled, tousling his hair. "So tell me, is there anything bothering you?"

"Aside from passing class, school bullies and my friends..." Erik took in a sharp breath, recalling the fight from home. "My friends!" he cried. "She killed them!"

"Wait, what?"

Erik pushed John Greenfield aside and tried to get out of bed, only to be yanked back by fiery pain ripping through his arm. He looked down, finding intravenous lines and monitoring cords taped to his skin. "I need to see them!" Erik wailed. "I need to know they're still alive!"

"Calm down, Son; they're fine!" John Greenfield grabbed Erik by the wrist before he tore out the tubes attached to his arm and pulled him downward back into bed. "Please, just listen to me."

"Why would they want to brutally hurt me?" Erik lamented and broke down into tears. "Why is this happening?"

"Son, I–!" Erik grabbed onto John Greenfield's sleeve, sobbing into his shoulder. John Greenfield blew a heavy sigh and ran a hand through Erik's hair. "I'm sorry," he murmured. "Please know that everything *will* be okay. I'll get to the bottom of this... There's nothing too small for me to handle."

Erik began to calm and pulled away, sniffling. John Greenfield withdrew a cotton handkerchief from his shirt pocket and handed it to Erik. Erik nodded his thanks and wiped at his eyes, then blew his nose. "Where did you go earlier?" he murmured.

"I had to get a few tests done," answered John Greenfield apprehensively.

"Is it because of those nervous attacks?"

John Greenfield nodded. "Things have been tense lately at work, but it's not for you to fret over."

"What is it you're working on?"

John Greenfield gave a pensive smile. "It's nothing really important."

"Why are you so secretive about it?"

"All I can say that it's a government program."

"Is it dangerous?"

"I can't confirm nor deny anything." John Greenfield pet Erik's head. "Please rest and get better." He embraced Erik firmly and Erik fell slack, unable to return the gesture.

"I'm sorry for acting like such a big kid," Erik grumbled. He pulled away and wiped his eyes with the back of his hands.

"This is quite stressful for you, I'm sure."

"I..." Erik blew a shaky sigh and glanced back at the window. His reflective variant, also in bandages, stood offside in the window, leaning against the foot of the bed with his arms folded across his chest. He sighed heavily, blowing the strands of his hair fallen in his eyes.

You need to tell Jerry! He can't help you if you don't say anything...

"Well...?" John Greenfield pressed. "Something seems to be weighing heavily on your mind."

Erik's alternate wagged a finger at him. *However, if you tell him, he'll get hurt too.*

"What if I don't say?" Erik asked.

"Then I can't help you," John Greenfield muttered.

Erik's counterpart said nothing in return and Erik groaned, holding his head in his hands. "This is so hard!" he moaned. "I can't do it!"

"Do what?"

"You might get in trouble..."

"I told you not to worry about me." John Greenfield touched Erik's shoulder. "Just say it."

Erik hung his head, sighing. "The one you warned me about," he mumbled. "It was her and her brother..."

John Greenfield's face twitched and he immediately stood, clenching his violently shaking right hand. "They did this?" he snarled.

The machines hooked to Erik chirped wildly, then buzzed before making a high-pitched drone. A nurse rushed in the room before John Greenfield could say another word and checked the cords hooked to Erik.

"You're not unplugged," said the nurse as he analyzed the connections. "So it shouldn't be flat-lining like this..."

"Maybe it's faulty," quipped Erik timidly.

The nurse struck a few buttons to reset it and a chirp followed after it rebooted. "There, that should fix it." He turned to John Greenfield, his face terse. "Visiting hours are now over with, Mister Greenfield," he said gently.

"Leave," John Greenfield growled, glaring at the nurse.

The nurse took a step away, startled by his reaction. "Um...!" The nurse turned on his heel and hurried out the room.

"Don't worry, Son," John Greenfield said weakly and ran his free hand through Erik's hair. "I'll take care of it."

"But I hadn't told you anything!" Erik protested.

"You don't have to."

Erik frowned, watching his father stalk out the room. "*What a strange response,*" he mused. "*What is it he knows?*" He stiffened, hearing a crash outside his door and a woman's scream.

"John!" Jane Greenfield shrilled.

Erik grew tense, hearing the frenzied chatter of doctors and other medical personnel.

Moments later, Raider appeared at the doorway, shirtless and wearing green scrub pants and his unlaced leather boots. Taped to his forehead he had a large piece of gauze and bandages wrapped around his arms and torso. In his hand, he held his torn leather jacket.

"Ay, man," Raider said and jutted a thumb behind him. "Your old man ain't doin' so hot."

"Why, what's wrong with him?" Erik clutched the sheets. "Don't tell me–!"

"He ain't dyin' or nothin', so chill the fuck out!" Raider shrugged his shoulders. "Look, while they were busy, I had to slip outta there. I fuckin' hate hospitals."

"Don't tell me you're going home like that. How are you going to sign yourself out?"

Raider scoffed. "Watch me bounce, man."

"Don't leave, please."

Raider approached the bed and leaned against it, giving Erik a critical look. "Man, you look like shit!" he cracked.

Erik grinned. "Says you," he retorted. "You got it worse than I did!"

"You should've seen how much blood they had to pump back into me!"

Erik looked away, growing uncomfortable and Raider sighed, running a hand through his greasy hair.

"Look," Erik started, "I..."

"You're cool, man," Raider replied. "It's my fault... I got hotheaded and wouldn't listen."

Erik glanced back at Raider, stunned. "But I was the one who didn't listen!" he protested.

"You couldn't help it," Raider shot back. "That bitch rolled up on you in your *own damn house*! You had every right to whoop that ass!"

"Because of me, you nearly got killed and Francisca too!" Raider paled and Erik's eyes widened. "She'd better not be!" he cried. "You tell me she's dead and I swear–!"

"Naw, man, she's kickin'," Raider admitted. "She's tough... Ain't shit those bastards can do to her that her old man ain't done to her already."

"I don't think I can take this." Erik fell back, rapping his head against the wall. "I swear, when Danae said..."

"Forget what that bitch says," Raider interjected. "She says nothin' but lies, just shit to work yer nerves."

"I can't take the insanity!"

"Hey man, you're tougher than you look, okay?"

"How would you know?" Erik spat and rolled his eyes. "You're talking out your butt!"

"Look at ya, man; you're still standing! Anybody else would've died already!"

Erik stiffened at his words. "*He's right,*" he thought, stunned. "*Raider should be dead too with all the injuries he's sustained... so what's going on here exactly?*"

"Hey, ya gotta trust me on this one," Raider said and approached Erik's bedside. "Besides, I just got a knack for this shit."

"What do you mean?" Erik asked, giving him a wary glance.

"Your old man's not gonna let some punk assholes do 'im in, now come on!" Raider jabbed Erik's arm and he winced.

"He's tough like you is, besides, where do ya think you got it from?"

"I'm just worried," Erik murmured. "What if all this mess was started by some suits Father Greenfield's working with?"

"Where'd you hear that shit, man?"

"Vinny warned me."

Raider's countenance changed as Erik explained the conversation he had with Vicente.

"That sick–!" Raider let out a scream of rage and slammed his fist against the wall, punching a hole in it. Erik jumped back, startled. "Fuckin' hell, man! Fuck!"

"That's a strong response," Erik thought, taken aback when Raider punched the wall again.

"Hey!" a voice called and both Erik and Raider turned to the sound, finding an orderly near the door. "You're not supposed to be here!" She gestured behind her. "You need to go back to your room!"

"Ay, man, can't I visit my friend?" Raider snapped back. "Besides, I'm only down the hall. It ain't like I'm upstairs or nothin'!"

"Go back to your room!" the orderly ordered.

"When I'm done visiting!" Raider spat.

"Visiting hours are over with!"

"Okay, gimmie a sec, damn!" The orderly stepped out and Raider turned to Erik. "Look, Franny's waitin' on me downstairs," he said. "Just watch yer back out there on them loose screws, yeah?"

"I'll try," Erik replied.

Raider slipped into his jacket and stuffed his hands into the pockets. "There might be a day when I can't catch them chumps tryin' to trip ya up, dig?"

"You're tough, Raider, so don't give me that!"

"Hey, I'm gettin' too old for this shit."

Before Erik could say anything else, Raider turned on his heel and stomped out the room.

This is only the beginning...

Erik turned to the glass, only to see his own reflection instead.

After a week's stay in the hospital convalescing, Erik grew apprehensive when the injuries he sustained healed quickly. He masked his unease, chatting to the nurses who came in for his vital statistic readings and relaxing when they spoke cordially to him in return. When the nurses wanted blood draws, Erik resisted, only relenting once the orderlies were called.

"How long will I be here?" Erik asked a nurse who came in to get his vitals again.

"A few more tests," he replied, "and then the doctor will decide to release you."

After the nurse left, a food service attendant dressed in a red and white striped uniform entered, delivering a plate of mashed potatoes, a piece of turkey in gravy, some carrots and zucchini, a cup of decaffeinated lemon tea, and two pear halves for dessert. Erik asked the hospital attendant neutral questions, and attendant spoke candidly for some time as he relaxed against his cart. The attendant then checked his watch and flushed red when he noted the time.

"I'm running late!" said the attendant, smiling sheepishly. "I guess we'll talk later after lunch." He hurried out the room and pushed his cart down the corridor.

Erik sighed, poking at his cold meal with the plastic spoon. *"Why are they keeping me for so long?"* he wondered. *"Wouldn't they find it weird I'm nearly healed from the cuts and bullet wounds?"* He stiffened when he heard voices outside the room's door.

"... Coming in here," said a woman's voice. "Is it okay for him to have roommates?"

"Yes," answered a man's voice. "We've had no problems with him."

"Good, wheel him in."

Erik watched an orderly with short black hair and blue eyes wearing a white scrub shirt, pants and walking shoes push in a hospital bed. A doctor who had sandy brown hair and dark green eyes wearing a white consulting jacket over a dark gray suit entered moments later behind the orderly, followed by a nurse in her white uniform.

In the bed laid a young man who had dark bronzed skin and many cuts and other scars to his arms, neck and face. His shaggy dark brown hair hung in his sleepy light brown eyes, hiding his overall expression. He lay almost lifeless on his side, cradling his arm with his free hand wrapped in gauze bandages.

Erik's heart skipped a beat when the young man stared directly at him before closing his eyes. He grumbled under his breath and the doctor and nurse glanced at Erik. Erik waved shyly, only to receive a less-than enthused expression in return.

"Wait up!" a third voice called and another orderly with blond hair and brown eyes entered the room, holding onto an ice pack. "Here's some ice for that, Johnston."

"Bah, I'm good," said Johnston as he took the ice pack and set it aside near the head of the bed. "Help me with this little troublemaker and remember Carlsbad, *don't touch him*!"

Carlsbad nodded and both orderlies yanked out the sheet on the old hospital bed, picking up the young man and placing him in the new bed.

"See, that wasn't too much trouble," said the doctor. "You made it seem like it was such a hassle!"

"You try getting kicked *and* cooked in the nuts," Johnston muttered, grabbing the ice pack.

"That's one helluva meal, eh Johnston?" Carlsbad cracked. "Toasted frank and beans and it's not even our lunch hour yet!"

"Argh, shut it," Johnston grumbled.

Erik looked to the other patient who grunted and turned on his side away from him. *"He's smiling,"* he thought, slightly puzzled. *"I wonder what he did..."*

Taking the young man's chart, the nurse reviewed the material with the doctor while the orderlies wheeled away the old bed.

"He's stable for now, Doctor," said the nurse.

"We'll be back in an hour for that sample, okay?" the doctor said gently.

The young man refused to answer as the nurse set the chart back in the bin at the end of the bed. Once the nurse and doctor left the room, Erik pushed away his tray and planted his feet on the floor, facing the young man across from him.

"What's your name?" Erik asked, hoping his friendliness would help his roommate relax and speak to him freely and candidly. Erik blew a disconcerted sigh when he received a grunt in return. "Have you eaten lunch yet?" The young man grunted again and turned on his side, facing Erik. "What happened to you, if I may ask?" Erik stiffened when the young man opened his eyes, the light brown voids giving him a hard stare.

If he told you, it might kill you...

"You're staring at me like you know me," Erik said nervously.

"I do," the young man muttered.

"But I don't know you at all!"

"I know you're another one, otherwise you wouldn't be here!"

"What's that supposed to mean?" Erik snapped, glaring at him.

The young man turned on his side away from Erik once more, saying nothing else.

Facing the large glass window, Erik spotted his reflective counterpart sitting on the bed's edge with his arms folded across his chest.

He'll speak to you sooner or later... Just relax.

Erik sighed and pulled up his tray. He stared at his food, waiting on his nerves to calm to keep from getting ill later.

TWENTY-FOUR

Later, the food service attendant returned, taking the lunch tray.

"You didn't eat anything!" he reprimanded.

"I don't feel well," Erik responded.

"I'll let the doctor know then."

Erik shrugged and left his bed, approaching the large pane window.

"Do you want to eat anything?" the attendant asked Erik's roommate. "I can send up a sandwich and milk if you like."

The young man grumbled an answer and Erik listened to the attendant leave. Staring outside, Erik saw they were on a higher floor and people below appeared like miniatures as they crossed the courtyard.

Leaving his bedside, Erik approached his roommate, who was now lying on his back and staring up at the ceiling. Erik noticed he wore a silver chain with a white-gold lotus flower charm.

"What do you want?" the young man growled, glancing at Erik.

"Why did they allow you to keep your jewelry?" Erik inquired.

"They don't." Erik's roommate returned his gaze to the ceiling.

"Is that why you did something to them?" The young man smirked, but gave no answer. "How are you otherwise?"

"What's it to you?" Erik's roommate answered gruffly.

"Just trying to make conversation, that's all."

"You're annoying."

"I'm Erik and how do you do?" The young man smiled briefly and Erik grinned. "See, I knew I could crack that mask of yours!"

"Whatever..."

"Do you watch television or anything?" Erik grabbed for the bedside remote. "I'm not much of a telly watcher but without any books to keep us entertained, we can see what's on."

"I really don't care."

Erik pointed the remote at the overhead television and the set turned on, broadcasting an afternoon news report about energy corporations.

"Well, since you don't seem to feel like talking much," continued Erik, "I'll blab my face off and see what hits."

"You talk too much," the young man snapped.

"Your voice sounds like sandpaper."

"Yours will get that way too if someone hacks at it."

Erik paled and folded his arms across his chest. "So the scars on your neck... Throat cancer, is it?"

"Not quite..."

Erik blew a short sigh. "Well, I don't mean to annoy you. It's just that it gets pretty lonely sometimes..."

"Huh, really?"

"Well, feel free to say anything when I reach a subject you like!"

Erik talked about his misadventures at school, what he felt about his classes, and his experiences with his friends. When Erik mentioned his family, his roommate appeared interested.

"Are the Greenfields really your family?" he probed.

"Oh, well, as far as I'm concerned, they are," Erik replied and shrugged his shoulders. "I know they adopted me long ago, but I don't remember too much about it."

"Your memory is bad, huh?"

"Well, I have an older brother named Stearne, I think..."

"I see now..." The young man gave a dark smile. "It makes sense..."

Erik raised an eyebrow. "What are you getting at?" he hedged.

"Maybe with all that stressful stuff going on, it was too traumatic for you and you blocked it out."

Erik nodded. "I guess you can say that... I do suffer from headaches, after all."

"Oh?"

Erik sat on the edge of the other patient's bed and he grunted in return. "Do you want me to move?" Erik inquired.

"No, you don't have to get up," he muttered. "You can stick around if you want."

"We're not going anywhere any time soon, so I might as well." Erik set aside the remote on the nearby nightstand.

The young man blew a heavy sigh. "My family..." He looked away as his brown eyes turned distant. "They hate my guts and want nothing to do with me."

"How can you say that?"

"I just said it!"

"Is it because you're sick?"

"They like to trash me and it's *not* because I'm sick - *they're* the ones who are sick!"

"I'm sorry..."

"At least your family treats you well from the way you tell it... You belong; you don't stand out like I do."

"What do you mean you 'stand out'?"

"You'll find out later..."

"I'm as bland as they come," Erik replied and gave a nervous laugh. "I'm just your average geeky dork."

"Well, I guess you're right." The young man turned on his side, holding his head in his free hand as he looked up at Erik. "I'm Chico Ramone," he muttered.

"That's an original name," Erik commented. "Sounds neat!"

"It's short for Chicago." Erik grinned brightly in response. "That's right. I'm Chicago Ramone." He grunted and glared back when Erik continued to smile. "What, don't you think it's funny?"

"What... should I?" Erik's goofy grin became wider. "You expected me to burst out laughing, right?"

"Right," Chicago replied sullenly. "Especially because I'm short too."

"Well, I'm not 'cause I like your name." Erik shrugged. "So what if you're short? You're a solid-looking guy anyway."

Chicago razzed him. "Oh, shut up."

"Seriously!" Erik continued. "If someone yelled your name in a crowd, you'll be the only one who'll look up. As for me, at least four or five other kids will be looking around."

Chicago gave him a wary glance. "Well, since you didn't laugh, I'll let you call me Chicago. If anyone else is around, then it's Chico to you!"

"Sure thing!" Erik promised and rose to his feet. Chicago turned on his back, placing his hands behind his head. "Hey, Chico, why are you in here?"

"Couldn't you tell?" Chicago answered and gestured toward his heavily scarred arms. "I tried to off myself." He ripped off the gauze wrapping, showing Erik the deep cut starting from his elbow and ended at his wrist. "Attempt five-thousand-twenty-something, give or take."

Erik stiffened, gulping hard. "You're not serious, are you?" he pressed, unable to tear away from the deep wound Chicago displayed. "Um, you're kidding, right?" Erik cleared his throat as Chicago sat up, giving him a piercing gaze in return.

"Don't like dark humor, huh?" Chicago snapped. "You ought to get used to death, Erik. Our lives are short…"

"You're being a bit creepy…"

Chicago let out a hacking laugh and Erik tensed, unnerved by the sound. "Oh, I'm creepy now?"

Erik swallowed hard and shuffled back, looking downward. The flush darkened around his cheeks and spread to his ears. "Okay," he muttered, "I believe you!"

"Don't worry about me going off on you; I won't," Chicago muttered and folded his arms across his chest. "The folks say

I'm pretty sane - more or less - so I'm waiting for more tests; they know me well here."

"Why would you *want* to do that?" Erik questioned, returning to his bed and drew up his knees. "Why is it that you don't like your life?"

"What makes me?" Chicago glared at Erik. "You don't have parents who hate your mere existence! The ones that the State calls parents only just want me for the checks -- the spineless lying bastards just clean house and make everything look decent when the soc's call a few hours before -- otherwise it's back to the basement for me!" He grunted and lowered his head, shutting his eyes as he let out a hard sigh.

"How terrible," Erik murmured. "I wish you had it better."

"Oh, wish I had it better, eh?" Chicago groused, "I'd rather be with my *real* family... six feet underground." Erik sucked in a thin breath, stunned at what Chicago said.

Moments later, the nurse came in and Chicago lay back in bed, throwing the covers over his head.

"You have to get up," the nurse snapped.

"Burn in Hell," Chicago growled.

"Oh, so he speaks!" The nurse yanked the covers back and grabbed Chicago by the wrist, forcing him sitting up. As he checked Chicago's vital statistics, Chicago muttered answers when the nurse asked him various questions. "You just vie to be difficult, eh?" the nurse spat in exasperation.

"I make it my duty," Chicago rumbled in his gravely voice. "So, back off!"

"The quicker you comply, the faster we can get this done." He sighed when Chicago refused to answer anymore and left in frustration.

"What..." Before Erik could finish his question, Chicago began speaking.

"We were on the highway, on our way to see some distant cousins," Chicago said softly. "One of them got married and it was supposed to be a great blast! It was storming the whole way there..." He sighed, leaning back against the headboard and stared up at the ceiling.

"We made it in one piece and the whole thing was awesome," Chicago went on. "For three days, you couldn't complain about the rain. It was bright, sunny and the winds were cool, light. I hung out on the waterfront and it was always '*Oye, primo!*' the whole way, asking me to do this and do that. They wanted to see my skills out on the water. It was the best time of my life; I was alive then." He settled back into bed and turned on his side, facing away from Erik.

"What else?" Erik prodded.

"Rare comic books, cool movies, playing around at the park... all it was good memories, you know," Chicago said sadly. "Seemed like yesterday, those old days; I could do it again." He blew a short sigh. "We had to go after it was over and I refused to go home. These distant cousins of mine, they were the best I've known and I just *knew* that if I left this sure thing, something bad would happen."

"Like what?"

"My folks had to drag me kicking and screaming..."

"What happened after that?"

"The summer was officially at an end and I had to start school the next week. It began to storm again on our way back. I was sitting on Papa's deaf side, so he couldn't hear me shout to him about the car coming too close. Mama tried to grab the wheel, but it was too late. We were hit broadside and the whole thing went upside down!"

Chicago quickly sat up, heaving for breath as he clenched his hands and his distant brown eyes gave way to hatred.

"I'm sorry," Erik murmured.

"Don't!" Chicago roared. "Don't feel sorry for me! Feel sorry for that bastard who kept going! Feel sorry for the damn rain that flooded the creek that drowned all of them! But don't you *ever* feel sorry for me!"

Erik stammered, trying to find his words. "H-how did you survive?" he carefully queried.

Chicago softened somewhat, wiping the tears streaking his face with the heels of his hands.

"I don't know," muttered Chicago, his guttural voice cracking. "The belts were trashed and I was able to slip out easy... but everyone else... everyone else was still stuck and they couldn't get out..." Chicago sniffed as his voice began to trail. "The water... it came in so fast..."

Erik decided not to press further as Chicago grew silent. He slipped out of bed and stood at the large pane window, looking outside at the unchanging scenery.

TWENTY-FIVE

In the glass's reflection stood a tall, athletic man wearing black horn-rimmed glasses, dark overcoat and cap. Erik turned around as Stearne entered the room, taking off his driving cap.

"I just heard about it," Stearne said in a low tone. "Your friend... he told me everything."

"I might get released soon," Erik replied. "I'm not sure if I want to go home, though."

"I want you to take this." Stearne dug through his pockets and pulled out his wallet, withdrawing several old worn photographs he carried with him. In doing so, others fell out of his bulging wallet and onto to the floor.

Erik gasped once he noticed they all consisted of the smiling young woman named Genovera. "Why do you have so many pictures of her?" he wondered aloud and picked up one photograph of many.

In it, Genovera sat tall in a large stuffed royal blue chair surrounded by shelves of books and smiled brightly toward the camera. She wore her long dark hair pulled up in a chignon held in place with pearl and ebony hairpins and an elaborate kimono-style maxi dress with many layers. In her left hand, she held a white sword sheath decorated with moonstone and gold accents and while her right held an intricately engraved white-gold saber with an ivory handle and brass bell-pommel.

Erik's gaze fell to the necklace she wore around her neck, a long silver chain with golden charm of the sun and moon.

Why is this one different from before…?

"I…" Stearne started and sighed, shaking his head as he pocketed his wallet. "It's been a long time…"

"May I keep it?" Erik asked instead.

"You can keep it if you like," Stearne murmured and bent down, picking up the fallen pictures. "You need it more than I do."

"Why?" Erik demanded. "Who is this woman and why is she involved with us? Why is it that I can't remember anything about her?"

"I'm not sure about that…"

"Why are you giving me this?"

"I thought it might jog your memory…"

"Well, apparently it's not working." Erik handed the photograph back and Stearne shook his head.

"Go on, it's yours."

Erik held it close and brushed his fingers across the face of the photo, then turned it over, reading the faint unsigned inscription on the back: *May your spirit prevail at any given cost.*

Glancing over Stearne's shoulder while he collected the last of the fallen pictures, Erik's heart skipped a beat and he grabbed his arm, noticing Genovera in a red dress.

"Let me see that one," insisted Erik.

"This one?" Stearne held it up for Erik to see.

Erik took the photo of Genovera smiling brightly as she stood on an unfamiliar beachfront in a cherry red sundress, holding onto a mid-sized light blue parasol. In that, she also wore the same necklace.

Erik's heart pound hard in his chest and he heard a weak gasp for breath. Turning toward the source, he saw his counterpart in the glass, shaking in fury with his hands clenched at his sides as tears streamed down his face.

Why are you doing this to me?

"I thought Genovera..." Erik started.

Stearne put up a hand, cutting him off. "You're going to need all the support you can garner," he said evenly and pocketed the photographs in his coat pocket.

"But--!"

"She wanted you to have something to remember her by, in the case..."

No!

Erik cringed and held his painful throbbing head. "Please, stop!" he moaned. "Just stop it!"

Shut up! Shut up, you piece of shit!

Stearne grunted and yanked Erik's hands from his head, pulling them down at his sides. "What is it you want me to say?" he snapped. "You want the truth or keep living a lie?"

And even you agreed!

"That's not true!" Erik yelled. He wrenched from Stearne's grip and turned away, facing his own unaltered reflection instead.

"They only want to hurt you."

"Who are 'they'?" Erik demanded.

"If you believe they will kill you, then they will," Stearne answered vaguely.

"Why are you telling me this?"

"Just remember that invincibility is a state of mind." Erik nodded and Stearne grabbed his shoulder as his reflection also fleshed out in the glass. "Please, try to remember before it's too late."

"I don't know what I'm supposed to remember."

"It'll eventually come to you."

"Do you know what it is?" Stearne's grip tightened and Erik looked up at him. Stearne grew tense as his jaw set and veins fleshed out in his neck. "Stearne, tell me."

"I don't have anything to say to you," Stearne spat.

"But–!"

"I'll see you soon." Stearne let Erik go and stalked out the room.

"I hate this!" Erik complained and dropped back in his bed, clutching the photograph to his chest. "This is too much." He winced when his shoulder ached again in faint throbbing agony.

"May I see it?" Chicago requested. Erik held up the picture and Chicago left his bed, approaching offside. "So, is that your brother you mentioned?"

"Yes, Chico, that was... Though I'm not so sure anymore..."

Chicago took the photograph and frowned as he studied it, then set it aside on the nightstand. "I saw him before, you know," he murmured. "I hate to break it to you, but that's not your brother."

"Then who is he?"

"He's somebody assigned to protect you."

"If you say so."

"He'll make sure you won't take those tests. You don't want to do them, just know that."

"What kind of tests? Why shouldn't I take them?"

"A part of your soul is taken away each time!"

"What do you mean?" Erik sat up on his elbows, giving Chicago a wary glance. "Stearne never mentioned anything about tests to me."

"It was a short stay where he went," murmured Chicago as his eyes grew distant. "They had him before he finally got shipped back."

"*I might as well play along,*" Erik mused then grunted. "When did that happen?" he asked.

"Some time or so ago." Chicago returned to his bed and sat on the edge, looking off into the middle distance. "Anyway, they complained about his anger and how he couldn't take control of it. I have the same problem..."

"Who are *they*?" Erik demanded. "What *kind* of problem?"

"We were in this place where the doctors asked us a million questions," Chicago went on, ignoring Erik's initial inquiry. "They thought we were too different and made us do all sorts of tests and simulations."

"How so?"

Chicago continued, disregarding him completely. "I accidentally killed a few people there and they kicked me out. Stearne was there for a little while longer until he could control it all and they finally let him go."

"Killed a few people...?" Erik shuddered. "*He's got to be unbalanced talking so casually about killing others!*" he

255

considered. "I don't remember too much about Stearne to form an opinion," Erik said. "Yet from what I can tell, he looks like he lived a hard life."

"He didn't leave willingly," Chicago grumbled. "He was *forced* to leave earlier than he had to."

"Forced?" Erik sat up and leaned forward. "What are you getting at?"

"Don't you understand?" Chicago growled. "You're going to end up where he was and not come out the same!"

"I don't want that to happen."

"He's lying to you to protect you."

"Thanks for letting me know."

"Are you putting me on?" Chicago spat and jumped to his feet, visibly irritated.

"No, I'm not!" Erik cried and held up his hands in surrender. "It's just I don't remember what he's talking about – It's nothing to me, not at all!"

"You just said your memory was bad, right?" Chicago accused.

"Well...!"

"So there!"

Erik blew a hard sigh. "You have a point," he admitted.

Chicago immediately calmed and sat back down. "Anyway, they won't let me go," he concluded. "But sometimes I forget and I try to do things that I'm not allowed to. Then I end up here for a few days for adjustments."

"What kind of adjustments?"

"You'll eventually find out."

"Er, can you control it now?" Chicago glowered at Erik and Erik cleared his throat instead, avoiding his harsh gaze. "What kinds of things do you try to do?" Chicago shook his head when the doctor entered the room with a thick chart.

"How do you feel?" asked the doctor and approached the foot of Erik's bed.

"I feel good," Erik replied. "Will I be leaving any time soon?"

"Not so soon..." The doctor opened the chart, flipping through the pages. "We have a few more tests to run."

Erik gave the doctor a wary look. "Like what?" he asked guardedly.

"Oh, these are so minor..."

Erik swallowed hard, immediately growing ill when the doctor smiled at him. "*He's hiding something,*" he thought as the doctor wrote several notes in his chart. "*That smile is so fake... his eyes are still dead serious!*"

"We'll be ushering you out later this afternoon," the doctor continued and shut the file.

"I'm done playing along," Erik snarled and stood. "I'm going home."

"No, you're not," the doctor snapped and dropped the chart back in the bin. He grabbed Erik by the shoulder when Erik tried to walk past and Erik winced as sharp pain traveled down his arm.

"What are you trying to do?" Erik pried off the doctor's fingers and shoved him away. "Don't touch me!"

"You're not leaving against medical advice!" the doctor sneered.

"I'm leaving!" Erik spat. "If I have to fight my way out, then I will!"

"I run you just as I run this floor," the doctor said through gritted teeth. "You're staying whether you like it or not!"

They continued to stare each other down and Erik grabbed the doctor's tie, yanking hard. The doctor raised his hand to strike Erik and paused when the nurse entered the room.

"Doctor, I have the serum you ordered," she called.

Erik let loose his grip as the doctor let go and the doctor turned away, approaching the nurse. He paused dead in his tracks when the nurse withdrew a small bottle of dark bluish-green liquid from her pocket.

"What are you, mad?" the doctor hissed, snatching the vial from her hand. "You were supposed to deliver it directly upstairs to Doctor Cor... er, Doctor *Colbert.*"

The nurse's eyes widened and she blushed as she put a hand to her lips. "I'm sorry," she whimpered, "I forgot, Doctor Blazejewelski!"

"I'll send it directly to Doctor Colbert myself," Blazejewelski protested, pocketing the vial. "Here, go over the procedure notes and make sure it's matched up."

The nurse nodded and took the chart as the doctor left the room. The nurse scanned the file and wrote in adjustments then placed it back in the container at the foot of the bed.

"*Who is this Doctor Colbert?*" Erik wondered. "*It's not even his real name -- why would he lie?*"

"Couldn't you tell?" Chicago insisted once the nurse hurried out the room.

"He's lying to me," Erik said, terrified. "What does he plan to do?"

"Just expect to be lying on your back often."

Erik glared at Chicago, disgusted. "What do you mean?"

Chicago scoffed. "Oh, you'll find out soon enough."

"What's *that* supposed to mean?"

Chicago lay back in bed and turned on his side. "If you don't mind, I'm going to catch some sleep," he murmured.

"How can you be fine with this?" Erik protested.

Chicago grunted, saying nothing else in response.

Too nervous to relax, Erik paced the room.

TWENTY-SIX

Chicago sat up in bed, watching Erik pace. "Stop that running around!" he complained. "You're making me dizzy with you wearing out the floor like that!"

"Sorry, Chico, but this is really bothering me," Erik answered. "I don't mind tests, but I don't like it when I'm forced to do them and they're lying to me about what they are."

"Do you ever get angry often?" Chicago suddenly asked.

"No, why?" Erik stopped his pacing. "I'm as mild-mannered as they get. I'm no dangerous guy."

"I don't mean angry; I mean really, *really* angry."

"I might get upset sometimes, but I'm no raging maniac."

Chicago scoffed. "Raging maniac, huh?"

"So, what about it?"

Chicago crossed his arms. "Does the name Giuseppe Petra mean anything to you?"

Erik shook his head. "Sorry, no clue." He shrugged his shoulders. "I never heard of him."

"Johann Schnell then?"

"Nothing at all."

Chicago blew an exasperated sigh. "Don't you understand?" he exploded.

"What are you saying?"

"You *have* to be him, I mean; you look like this guy... He wasn't in testing for long since they found him crazier than I was and I thought *I* had some issues." Chicago grunted. "But *damn*... that guy was a sensitive one, I'll tell you." He shook his head. "*¡Por supuesto!*"

"What does this mean for me?" Erik pressed. "Where are you going with this?"

"How long were you bounced in and out?" Chicago asked in response.

Erik came to a pause in his pacing, bewildered. "Okay, what?" he yelped, turning to Chicago. "What kind of conversation is this?"

"The kind where you answer questions!"

Erik threw up his hands. "I really don't know what you're talking about!" he protested. "You're confusing me!"

"Were you moved from place to place like the others?" Chicago demanded.

"I can't answer that..."

"At least try!"

Erik resumed his pacing, pondering how to best respond to Chicago's persistent questions. "What do you want from me?" he complained. Chicago narrowed his eyes and Erik glanced his way, then blew a heavy sigh. "Don't give me that look!" he groused. "I vaguely remember growing up in an orphanage." Erik shrugged his shoulders. "The Greenfields adopted me from there... I don't have anything else to say about that."

"Oh, really? Is that what they told you?" Chicago snorted. "What a big one, *buey mudo!*"

Erik stopped his pacing and whirled around, glaring at Chicago. "Hey!" he squawked. "What did you call me?"

"Where did they say they picked you up from?" Chicago spat. Erik gave Chicago a blank look and Chicago let out a short laugh. "Don't tell me you can't remember, because it doesn't exist!" he crowed. "They're lying to you!"

"Father Greenfield would never lie to me!" Erik shouted. "You don't know anything about me; you were never there!"

"Oh, I was there," retorted Chicago. "You *have* to be him, because he was always at The Center with *me* and you look just like him!"

"I don't know you!"

"Well, I remember *you* and you were at The Center with me *and* Stearne!"

"Now you're making stuff up!" Erik thundered. "I don't recall anything about this Center place and I'm not sick in the head!"

Chicago scoffed. "Oh yeah, you are," he said, rolling his eyes. "You're more fucked up than me!"

"That's enough." Erik clenched his hands and the burning sensation returned, traveling up his arms.

"After the stint at Keystone," Chicago went on, "they bounced Stearne back with us and then you were taken away with Doctor Schumacher and I never heard from you again."

Erik gave him a lost expression. "I'm sorry," he said flatly. "I *honestly* don't remember anything."

The pain increased in his hands and Erik looked down, realizing they shook. Releasing his grip, Erik slowly opened his fingers and sucked in a shallow breath at once noticing how deep his fingernails dug into his palm, drawing small lines of blood.

"*Why am I having this kind of reaction?*" he wondered. "*He's talking crazy out his butt; there's nothing worth believing, nothing at all!*"

You do remember, deep down in your soul...

"How can you *not* remember?" Chicago screamed, drawing his hands into fists. "You promised me!"

"What did I promise you?" Erik cried, glaring back at Chicago. "I *don't remember!*"

You don't want to remember...

"Stop lying to me!" Chicago bellowed.

Erik gripped his hair, blowing a hard sigh. "My head is killing me!" he moaned. "Stop talking about this!"

It's too deep, too painful to face, now is it?

Turning away, Erik faced the large pane window, half expecting his counterpart to be standing there. "*Okay,*" he mused, "*if I play along, let's say that maybe somewhere in that crazy mind of his, he might be telling the truth.*" Erik looked down at his hands that continued having the burning sensation coursing through it. "*But this can't explain the pain, the headaches, and hearing voices... Unless I'm crazy too?*"

Somehow it's deep enough that your body remembers...

"*Everyone's telling me to remember something... If it didn't exist, then they'd all be crazy too!*"

Release it! Become one with it!

"*If he said I was that mad to begin with...*"

Only because they made you that way!

Chicago growled and Erik whirled around, watching the young man step out of bed. His light brown eyes glazed over and Erik tensed as Chicago stomped over to him.

"Please, don't," pleaded Erik.

"Why can't you remember?" Chicago thundered and grabbed Erik by the shirtfront. "Wake up in there! Remember!"

"Let me go!"

Chicago shook him violently and Erik grabbed his wrists, struggling against him. Chicago reversed Erik and Erik stooped down, shouldering his chest. Chicago let out a yelp when the force of the blow launched him across the floor.

Erik quickly backed away and stood on the defensive as Chicago rolled with the fall and jumped to his feet. His shoulders heaved as he seethed in rage.

"I dare you!" Chicago snarled and beckoned to Erik. "*Vamos!*"

"Don't make me do this," Erik protested. "I don't want to hurt you!"

"You don't have the guts!"

"Chico, please!"

Chicago let out a scream and charged. Erik grabbed Chicago's fist aimed for his face and reversed him, throwing him against the window. Chicago's body struck the tempered glass, cracking it and he slumped to the floor.

Approaching Chicago's downed form with caution, Erik let out a terrified cry when Chicago suddenly grabbed him by the foot and yanked his leg out from under him. Erik crashed to the floor and Chicago pounced atop Erik's body, holding him down by the throat while he drew back with his other hand.

Erik grabbed Chicago's clenched hand aimed for his head, struggling against his strength while his other hand clawed at Chicago's wrist.

"Please," Erik wheezed. "Don't..." Chicago applied pressure against Erik's throat and he choked, gasping for air.

Erik saw red and the burning in his hands and arms increased. Letting go, Erik turned his head as Chicago slammed his fist into the floor beneath him, cracking the tile.

Erik bashed his fist into Chicago's temple in return, stunning him. Chicago inadvertently released his grip around Erik's throat and Erik used his chance, grabbing Chicago by his collar.

Erik hurled Chicago violently overhead and Chicago tumbled upside down, striking the bed across the room. Erik immediately scrambled to his feet as Chicago sat up and shook his head, then stood unsteadily.

"You keep this up," Erik threatened, "and I might seriously hurt you!"

"Try it," Chicago retorted. "Show me how sincere you are!"

"*He's tough _and_ crazy!*" Erik thought, astounded. "If you hurt yourself," he warned, "it's not my fault."

"Shut up!"

Chicago charged and Erik dodged out of his low blows aimed at his body. Erik turned away and reversed Chicago again, then drew back, throwing the hardest punch he could muster. Chicago sidestepped the attack and Erik's fist connected into the window.

Erik's breath caught in his throat when the whole pane shattered, raining rose-colored glass onto the miniature people in the courtyard below.

"There's no way–!" Erik cried.

"Heh," Chicago muttered behind him. "That's what I thought..."

"Safety glass can't break that easily..." Erik looked down at his uninjured hand, flexing it in awe. He frowned when he noticed the burning sensation in his fist released. "The pain I felt... is it tied to that?"

"What are you talking about?"

Erik staggered rearward and slipped to his knees when the blood drained from his face. "This can't be real," he moaned. "I'm not that strong!"

"You're not going to faint, are you?" Chicago asked in concern. He approached Erik's side and lent a hand. "Come on, get up!" Erik took it and Chicago pulled him upright.

Moments later, two nurses came running into the room and Erik turned around, stunned as the pain in his hands returned.

"What was that noise?" the nurse on Erik's right demanded. "What's broken?"

"The glass," Chicago answered.

"What the hell?" the other nurse cried. "Carlsbad, get in here!"

"What happened?" the orderly Carlsbad asked as he entered.

"Restrain him!"

Chicago stepped aside as Carlsbad approached Erik. Erik backed away and let out a yelp when Carlsbad grabbed for him. He struggled against Carlsbad then slackened when wrestled to the floor and his arms painfully twisted behind his back.

Erik made no attempt to struggle as Carlsbad dragged him back from the edge and pulled him toward the exit. The doctor who made Erik uncomfortable returned, pausing at the sight of them both as he stood at the door.

"What's going on here?" the doctor demanded.

"Doctor Blazejewelski," Carlsbad said simply, "he tried to jump."

Blazejewelski stormed in and grabbed Erik by the hair, yanking back his head. Forced to look up, Erik glared back at the doctor who glowered down at him.

"Trying to fly, eh?" Blazejewelski sneered.

"I'll try that later," Erik replied weakly.

Blazejewelski gave a hard backhanded slap, whipping back Erik's head. "Say that again," he snarled.

"Go kill yourself," Erik spat and grunted when punched in the face.

"Get him out of here!" Blazejewelski ordered.

Erik looked to Chicago and Chicago turned away, acting as if he didn't exist. Johnston appeared at the door behind Blazejewelski and grinned as he cracked his knuckles.

"Alrighty now, where's the sneaky bastard?" Johnston rallied. "I got a knuckle sandwich ready for his ass!"

"Not him," Carlsbad responded and shoved Erik forward. "His roommate."

"What he do?"

"Nothing yet."

Carlsbad adjusted his grip and Erik jumped, pushing back against Carlsbad and kicked Johnston's crotch. Johnston grunted, faltering and Erik fell forward, using the momentum to toss Carlsbad over his head.

Carlsbad let out a yelp when thrown; crashing into Johnston and both spiraled out the hall. Standing, Erik stiffened when he felt a prick to the back of his neck.

"That's enough out of you," Blazejewelski said over Erik.

Erik fell slack to the floor as a heap and Carlsbad returned to the door, followed by Johnston.

"Shit," Johnston moaned and grabbed for Erik's feet.

"Today's ain't your day, eh?" Carlsbad said as he picked up Erik by the arms. "All day, everybody's been picking on your family jewels."

"I'm going to start wearing a cup," Johnston complained. "They're not paying me enough to put up with this shit!"

Carlsbad laughed and helped haul Erik out the room.

TWENTY-SEVEN

Thrown violently into a small padded room with bright plate lights, Erik crashed face-first into the wall and slumped on the floor. He groaned as he came to and behind him, the door slammed shut with the locks turning on the outside. Erik quickly stood and rushed the door.

"What are you doing to me?" he screamed and struck his fists against the panel, putting in dents. "Let me out!"

"We can't do that," a hollow voice called.

Erik looked around for the sound's source and spotted three cameras fixed on the ceiling. The monitoring devices made a sweep every few moments in different directions.

"This isn't a real hospital!" Erik shouted and kicked the door, giving it another deep depression. "Let me out!"

"You must stay calm," the hollow voice continued. "The tests will be over soon."

The fiery pain flared in his hands much stronger than before, traveling up to his arms. His aching shoulder throbbed in response and Erik grit his teeth, overwhelmed.

"I don't want to take any tests," Erik screeched, "I want to go home!" He gave the door another hard strike then flew into a rage, punching and kicking against the panel until exhaustion set in.

Erik fell to his knees, fighting tears. "*Why would the doctors do this to me?*" he thought in despair. "*Where are the Greenfields; why can't they rescue me?*"

The white plate lights above Erik flickered and he cried out when they brightened, washing the room out of color. Crawling to the corner, Erik drew up his knees and put his head down in his arms, blocking the light. He moaned in agony when his eyes continued to burn and his vision turned foggy.

After some time, the door opened, and Erik looked up, unable to discern who stood before him as a pale haze.

"Who are you?" Erik demanded and scrambled upright as the person entered the room.

"This will hurt just a tiny bit," Blazejewelski's voice said with fake gentleness. "This is just a serum to calm you down."

"Go away!" Erik yelled once Blazejewelski approached. He grabbed the doctor's wrist when taken by the arm and violently pushed back, sending him crashing to the floor.

"How is it you can still see?" Blazejewelski thundered and immediately stood. "You're supposed to be blind!"

"I want out of here!" Erik shouted. "If you stand in my way, I will fight you!"

"You're not going anywhere!"

Erik drew back when two heavily armed men dressed navy uniforms with silver buttons and black caps appeared at the door. Erik stiffened, taken aback by the show of force.

"Don't like my friends pointing guns at you, hm?" Blazejewelski vaunted and chortled. "If you're smart, you'll do what I say!" Erik clenched his teeth and hunched down, anticipating Blazejewelski's next move. "Oh, so you're serious about trying to fight?"

"I'm not afraid of getting shot," Erik spat. "It's already happened once before!"

"Men, stand ready," Blazejewelski ordered. The armed officers withdrew their rifles and aimed them at Erik.

"Don't push me!" Erik thundered. "I will tear you apart!"

"We'll see about that!"

Blazejewelski charged and Erik sidestepped the doctor's grab, then ducked down, shouldering the man's chest. Blazejewelski grappled with Erik, attempting to take him down and Erik reversed him. Reaching down, Erik punched Blazejewelski's leg and flipped him over onto the floor when he faltered.

Turning, Erik rushed to the open door and the bright lights switched to an intense blue-white. Erik screamed, his eyes searing once he saw full whiteout.

The armed guards fired and Erik staggered back, struck in the shoulder and leg. He stumbled and fell back, striking the ground with a hard thud.

The guards entered the room as Blazejewelski rose upright and stood over Erik's downed form. The doctor kicked Erik's side and he yelped in pain.

"Now that's a good boy," Blazejewelski said as he knelt beside Erik and grabbed him roughly by the arm. Withdrawing a syringe with a clear serum from his coat pocket, the doctor popped off the safety cap and jabbed Erik, injecting him with the syringe's contents. "All you had to do was follow orders, and we wouldn't have to go through all that trouble."

Releasing his hold, Blazejewelski stood and backed out the room, followed by the armed guards. The door slammed shut after them with a bang.

Erik struggled to sit up, finding it hard to move as the wooziness came on strongly. *"I hope Stearne will find me,"* he thought as tears ran from the corner of his eyes. *"I don't know how much more of this I can take..."*

Erik swallowed hard, fighting the nauseous sensation permeating his being when his body felt as if he were stuck in a violently spinning room.

The vertigo ended and his world fell out from beneath him.

Erik woke up with a start, gasping for breath and fought with the sheets tangled around his limbs. Breaking free, he sat up, trying to recall where he was. Looking around, Erik sighed in relief once realized he was back in his bedroom in the Greenfield residence.

Feeling a sharp pain in his side, Erik pulled up his nightshirt, finding a faint scar starting from his right hip and across his torso. He traced it with his finger, trying to recall how he got the old injury. Nothing came to mind and Erik grunted, rubbing at his face.

"These bad dreams are going to be the end of me," he mused and padded out of bed.

Facing the broken mirror hanging over his door, Erik took in a weak breath when he saw his altered counterpart instead of his usual reflection. "Hey!" he yelped.

The young man in the mirror folded his arms across his chest. *I'm telling you, you're becoming too dangerous to keep alive!*

"What are you going on about?" Erik demanded.

You're nothing more than a copy of the boy you replaced.

"What's that supposed to mean?" Erik yelled.

You're starting to remember, aren't you? His reflection leaned forward, sneering. *There are things you've done in there that you'd rather forget, right? The things you know you've done and the things you think you remember are clashing, causing you to go mad. I'm merely here to sort it out for you.*

"Don't tell me that you're here to kill me!" Erik scoffed. "You're not real!"

His counterpart clenched his hands at his sides. *If it means salvaging you, then I just might!* Erik took a step away as his reflection stepped through the mirror, gaining form. *Burn out and die... before you destroy everything you're trying to save!*

"Now hold on--!"

Your original assignment was to destroy everything that belonged to them, but some kind of disturbance took place within you and new directives were assigned instead. Erik's double grinned darkly. *I temporarily maintained a connection with you to fix that disturbance, but any memories you had - anything you had touched or were involved in - they were already gone, forgotten because you technically exist no longer.*

"So what you're saying is... that I'm long dead?"

Erik's reflection nodded. *That's right; you're no longer Erik Hart - he does not exist.*

"But of Ferdian... I've been called that too."

He's dead as well.

"So you want me to just 'burn out' as you say... just up and disappear?"

If I can find the code that activates the self-destruct sequence, then I may be able to do it remotely. Until then, I'm hoping to wear you out so you can start the sequence yourself.

"You're kidding!"

Just telling the truth.

Erik turned away, gripping his hair. "This has to be some kind of horrible dream..." he cried. "You're making no sense!"

It's only reality. You became too self-aware, now you have to die.

"That can't be – that's just too awful!"

"Erik!" John Greenfield's voice called from down the hall. "It's time to wake up!" Erik pushed past his counterpart and paused when grabbed by the arm.

He can't save you... You were originally to replace something that he lost.

"But if I were to cease to exist now, what would Mother and Father Greenfield do?" Erik shook out of the young man's grip. "Suddenly becoming childless would mean they've wasted years raising me..."

Oh, come on! His counterpart shook his head and waved a dismissive hand. *You know and I know they're used to it by now. Besides, just disappearing is better than outright dying. Death would mean grieving, you see.*

"You're a sick bastard!" Erik pushed his counterpart away. "Just leave me alone!" He stomped across the hall for the bathroom.

After showering and changing clothes, Erik exited downstairs and approached the table where the Greenfields were having breakfast.

"Good morning, Erik," Jane Greenfield greeted and left her place at the table, withdrawing his plate left to warm in the oven.

"Is something the matter, Son?" John Greenfield asked as he picked up his mug of coffee. "It's unusual for you to oversleep like this."

"Everything's fine," Erik replied nervously and nodded to Jane Greenfield who set his plate before him. "Thanks, Mother."

John Greenfield nodded, sipping his coffee and Erik picked up his fork, only to pause when he spotted his alternate passing the kitchen doorway. He stood, dropping what he held.

"Erik!" Jane Greenfield cried, startled.

"Son…" John Greenfield started.

"I just realized the time," Erik said quickly. "I've got to get going!"

"Take care then…" Jane Greenfield murmured as John Greenfield set his mug aside and rose from the table.

"You're right," John Greenfield said, taking up his briefcase resting near the table's leg at his feet. "Get your things, Son."

Erik left for the parlor and discovered his counterpart gone, leaving the front door open. He hurried outdoors, finding no one there and was later joined by John Greenfield.

TWENTY-EIGHT

Once dropped off at school, Erik headed for his locker in a daze. Glancing around, he breathed a small sigh of relief.

"*At least Seraphine and Danae aren't around to bother me,*" Erik mused and took his needed books.

Kicking shut the door; he froze when a hand clamped on his shoulder. Turning around, Erik grunted when he found no one there.

He hurried to Home Room and concentrated on completing his missed homework. As the morning wore on, Erik felt increasingly worse and broke out in cold sweat.

"What's wrong with me?" he muttered and bit the end of his pen, moaning when the sickness progressively worsened.

Once class ended, Erik left his books behind and ran to the restrooms. Kicking in an empty stall, Erik fell to his knees and vomited painfully into the commode. He groaned, pressing his face against the cool tiles.

"*I don't understand it,*" he thought, "*I didn't eat anything that could make me this sick.*" Sitting up, Erik frowned when he saw blood in the bowl and flushed it down. "*I'll ask Stearne about it later...*"

Staggering to his feet, Erik returned to the classroom and collected his books, then entered his next class. Taking his assigned desk, Erik set his books aside and pulled out his geometry text when the instructor Deverel announced a test.

"You're late for class, Ferdian," a harsh voice sneered from behind.

Whirling around, Erik let out a stunned cry and stumbled out of his seat. "What are you doing here?" he yelped, immediately standing to his feet. "You're not real!"

His counterpart chuckled. "Oh?" he teased.

"Do you want to go to detention again?" Deverel snapped.

Erik returned to his seat and the young man behind him moved his desk closer to whisper in his ear.

"First of all, I'm as real as it gets," he hissed. "And second of all, I need to stick close by to you in order to get rid of those that have you in their sights as a target."

"What should I call you then?" Erik muttered.

"Anything but late for dinner," he quipped.

"So you're not going to give me a name, nor let me name you."

"Savvy."

Erik groaned and put his head on the desk. "Why me?" he moaned.

"Thirdly, I don't visit these kinds of places often," said his counterpart. "So I thought to get in some sightseeing before I have to move on to my next assignment."

"What do you mean?" Erik grumbled.

"You're dying, Ferdian. Your existence is soon to pass and you'll be nothing but a faded memory, if any at all."

"That's why I'm losing my mind, right?"

"Or you could be merely dreaming..."

"What?"

"Taking over an existence that is no longer is not about trying to imitate the original..."

Erik sat up and turned in his seat, glaring at the young man who shared his appearance. "Who are you?" he sneered.

Erik's double grinned. "I'm whoever you want me to be." He shrugged his shoulders. "What is there to understand?"

Erik turned back around, rubbing his temples while trying to sort out the information. *"I've completely lost my mind!"* he mused. *"The medicines the doctors gave me; it's finally breaking me down!"*

"I'm here to play my part, and so are you," the copy grumbled from behind. "Once you burn out, then I'll be gone."

"But why exactly?"

"You think you had other plans?"

"It just doesn't feel right. I wouldn't be sent here on some kind of suicide mission, only to forget it. Even you said there was some kind of disturbance..." Gaining the tests, Erik turned to his counterpart after passing the papers back. "So how does it feel to be a high school student again?"

"I'll let you know about it later."

When his lunch period came, the mysterious young man with Erik's appearance rushed out into the corridor, unleashing a blue steel rapier. Erik raced after him, bypassing other students in the hall.

"Give me one good reason to spare you!" Erik's counterpart shouted. Turning the corner, Erik found him standing before a student speared against the wall with the blade. The student gasped, coughing up blood. "*Kenzan Hussaru!*" A blast of violet flame surrounded the student, eradicating him completely.

"Hey!" Erik cried as his double withdrew the rapier and it vanished once he sheathed it back into an invisible scabbard. "Why did you kill him?"

"He used to be Human... He was contracted out to report on us."

"What difference does it make?" Erik spat. His counterpart huffed and pushed past him. "You can't decide who lives and who dies!"

"So you say *they* can? They have killed and will not hesitate to kill again!"

"Who's 'they'?" Erik demanded. "Why are we their targets?"

"You already know," answered Erik's copy, turning the corner. "The reason they target us is the same reason you target them."

Erik stood there dumbfounded. "*Maybe I <u>am</u> crazy,*" he considered.

After getting shoved past in the corridor, Erik hurried after his counterpart who stepped outside the side entrance leading to the courtyards. Pushing open the doors, Erik found him at the rear wall, striking a rubber ball against the brick surface.

"Hey," Erik called after him. "Why did you go so far like that?"

Erik's double caught the ball and turned toward him, forming a blue and gold sheath in hand. "What are you talking about?" he grumbled as the handle of the blade appeared in gold with a blue steel bell pommel. He pushed his thumb against the hilt, unclicking the blade from the sheath.

"Ah," Erik said nervously, backing away. "Forget it…"

"It's obvious that you wanted something," his alternate groused. "Why else would you be here following me?"

"Other than skipping class?" Erik asked sheepishly.

"What is it you find so fascinating about me?"

"Just that… I don't remember a whole lot, yet I also remember so much as well. It's like I'm scared of you, but deep down, I know I have no right to be."

"What are you saying… that you're somehow intimately drawn to me?"

"It's something like that, but not quite. I know we're supposed to be close somehow…"

The young man smirked and turned away, facing the wall. "You have memories of another time and another place in there," he explained, "but it's not of this time or place. You as who you thought you were… you can't manifest that part of your will to the world anymore. Just let it go."

"I need to know who I am!" Erik cried. "I need to know and remember so I can stop hurting like this!"

"You're under contract to do as told and only obey your master."

"*No one* masters me!" Erik yelled. "I am a human being with free will!"

"That doesn't mean anything, not anymore. I mean, look at you; you're an outright mess to even *dare* calling yourself human. It's a damn near shame that you can barely pass as it is."

"Hush up!" Erik screeched and charged, throwing a punch.

His copy swiftly blocked with the scabbard and kicked Erik aside, sending him rearward on the ground.

"You've been allowed to live freely long enough," Erik's counterpart grumbled. "You have lost sight of your original goals and can't even keep hold of your abilities. They're too erratic, just as you are becoming."

"You know nothing about me," Erik snarled, standing to his feet.

"You can't control the transformative powers anymore. You're nothing but a ticking time bomb waiting to go off at any moment."

"I'm not a problem to be fixed!" Erik screamed. "I have every right to live and I won't be exterminated by any means!"

"Then prove it," declared Erik's double, withdrawing a golden saber. "Show me that you are worthy of manipulating the powers of existence for the greater cause!"

"You're not making any sense!" Erik thundered, holding his hands up in guard. "I'm sick of this... you're crazy! All of this is crazy!"

"Maybe *you're* the crazy one."

"I'm not your enemy here."

Erik's reflection hurled his sheath and Erik slapped it aside. He turned, finding the young man suddenly at his back. Erik froze, sensing the golden steel pressed at his throat and ducked before his counterpart slashed the blade across. Erik stomped down, striking the young man in the side with his elbow.

Erik's double grunted, staggering back and Erik turned, facing his counterpart who held his side in pain. Erik clenched his teeth, noticing a dark blue stain slowly spreading on his shirt.

"I didn't cut you," Erik retorted. "Why are you bleeding like that?"

"What does it matter?" the young man snarled and stood, pointing his saber at Erik. "You'll eventually meet your end too!"

"Then why do you keep attacking me?" Erik hollered. "I did nothing to you!"

"For you to stay in this world, you need to remember your original purpose!"

"I don't believe what you say anymore!" Erik slapped the saber away and shoved past him. "You're just lying to me!"

"You're a deviation of the natural law," the young man called after him. "You technically shouldn't exist in this world because you're a danger to everyone around you!" Erik came to a stop and ground his teeth as his hands trembled and burned. "Therefore, you're to be hunted down and exterminated, wiped out!"

"You think by fighting me like some kind of monster, you'll maintain some kind of balance that someone's screwed up with, right?" Erik yelled, whirling around. "Aren't you one of *them*? How are you fine with hunting down people like me?"

Erik's counterpart shrugged. "Because I was given new orders."

"But what of *you*? What do you think of all this?"

"Thinking is merely a game for fools, a set of materials to be easily molded and manipulated. There are no facts, but baseless feelings and half-formed ideas!"

"But that's what makes us human... it separates us from animals, you heartless bastard!"

Erik's reflection pointed his electrified golden saber toward Erik that cackled in green energy around the blade. "You know nothing about me!" he shrilled.

"You're the one who's crazy!" Erik bellowed. "Back off!"

"I'll deal with you later!"

Erik's copy stormed off and Erik blew a heavy sigh, clenching his hands at his sides. He walked away, heading back indoors once the bell rang.

"*I must be getting close to the truth,*" Erik mused. "*If he's upset, then it must be true...*" He came to a pause once he spotted Wilhelm sitting on the steps, picking at his nails with a nail file. "Now I know I'm dreaming," Erik moaned.

"Have a nice chat, Brother?" Wilhelm asked, glancing up.

"What do you want, Wil?" Erik grumbled.

"You don't have the power to prevent the extermination process."

"Such encouraging words," Erik spat sourly, rolling his eyes. "What are you doing here?"

"You'd better be careful with what you do," Wilhelm replied. "You never know who's watching nearby..."

"Don't provoke me, Wil," Erik snarled. "You get too close and I might just become aggressive."

"Maybe I might just do that..." Wilhelm rose to his feet and Erik stood back as the nail file in his hands glowed dimly in golden light. "*Reijin Furiaga!*"

A violet circle of light formed beneath them both, followed by a high whine and silver sparks blasted through them. Erik cried out and staggered back, stunned. Wilhelm also fell against the wall, panting weakly for breath.

"Why use a technique that hurts us both?" Erik moaned.

"That way we can be evenly matched, Brother."

"You mean to say," yelped Erik, "that I'm stronger than you?"

"*Rarin!*" Wilhelm called. "*Sirachet!*" The nail file vanished, transforming into a golden saber. A white gold rapier appeared strapped to his waist and he withdrew it in his free hand.

"I don't have time for this, Wil!" Erik roared.

"Then defeat me to pass!"

"*He's serious this time!*" Erik confirmed as Wilhelm tossed him the rapier. "But why *now*?" he protested and caught the blade. "What changed?"

"The only thing that's changed is *you*, Brother," Wilhelm snapped. "I want you to fight me!"

"What makes you think I can use this?" Erik yelled. "I haven't changed!"

Wilhelm rushed Erik, swiping at him with incredible speed. Erik screamed when he lost his right hand and quickly picked up the fallen rapier with his left, only to lose his arm. Turning, Wilhelm slammed the saber in his chest and stomped him off onto his back with his foot.

Striking the ground, Erik coughed up blood and gasped weakly for breath. Looking up at the cloudy sky overhead, Wilhelm came into view and grinned devilishly down at Erik, standing over him.

"You're a little slow," Wilhelm said, hoisting his bloody saber over his shoulder.

"Really now?" Erik snarled, narrowing his eyes.

Wilhelm stomped on Erik's chest. "I thought you'd be better than that!" he complained.

"I'll get you for this," Erik wheezed.

"Oh?"

Erik spat at him and Wilhelm grunted. "Just you wait," he growled.

Wilhelm's eyes darkened and he wiped away the bloody spittle on his cheek against his sleeve. "We'll see about that." Wilhelm impaled Erik directly between the eyes, marking out his world.

TWENTY-NINE

Awakening much later, Erik found himself lying on a cold steel table with many monitors surrounding him. He noticed his numerous bandages and hospital gown were removed and only a sheet covered his lower body.

Many people stood around him, wearing pale blue-green scrub suits, surgical masks, surgical caps, and latex gloves.

"Let's try this again," snapped Blazejewelski's voice irritably. Erik closed his eyes, listening to what went on around him. "The scalpel broke again?"

"Yes," a second voice answered. "When Corbin had him injected, it went through fine. Even when he ordered blood drawn, it went fine."

"I know that, you prick!" Blazejewelski growled. "You're nothing but an incompetent shit..."

"I'm incompetent?" The second voice scoffed. "Look who's talking!"

"You--!" Blazejewelski growled. "Let me do this myself!"

"Fine, you'll see the hard way..."

"Shut the fuck up!"

"Corbin wants us to find out why blood reports stating that it's not cobalt -- it's normal red... Type O negative."

"Don't make me gut you, you son of a bitch!"

Erik stiffened when heard the clinging of metal.

"Hey, cool it!" another voice cried.

"Suber, get Nelson out of here before he loses a thumb!" a fourth voice said nervously. "You guys are freaking me out... I'm already trying to quit as it is!"

"You're still getting cancer anyway with all the smoke you're inhaling, Hernando," Suber cracked. "You might as well clamp your lips over a factory stack!"

"Shut it you two," Nelson grumbled. "He's been injected with everything to suppress his genetic material; I made sure of it."

Erik sensed someone near him and stiffened when nicked on his arm. Metal shattered in response.

"Damn it!" Blazejewelski growled. "What the fuck's going on?"

"I'm not the one to ask," Suber replied.

"Is that bastard awake?"

"No," Nelson answered. "The machine reads that he's still unconscious."

"That can't be right," Hernando muttered.

"Corbin says it's been reported that when he's powered down, little activity will result on our monitors," Suber interjected. "But as for why things keep breaking against his skin, that's abnormal."

"But the medications should've suppressed it," Nelson complained. "Even this freaky shit he's displaying!"

"Did you use the max?" Hernando asked.

"Yeah, we've used the max without killing him!"

"Maybe it's some freak thing...?" Suber murmured. "This is highly unusual..."

"Nelson, hand me the drill," Blazejewelski ordered.

Erik opened his eyes, spotting a large hand-held machine come his way and passed over him to the annoyed surgeon.

"*I can't believe they're actually going to use that on me!*" Erik thought, stunned. "*Why are they trying to cut me open?*"

Blazejewelski grabbed the drill and yanked out the older bits. He snapped his fingers to one of the three men who stood nearby.

"Give me the size six bits." Blazejewelski ordered and Erik closed his eyes again as the surgeon reset the machine. The drill started whirring away, only to jam suddenly. "What the fuck?"

"What's wrong with it?" Nelson demanded. "It worked fine before!"

"I need a new drill!" Blazejewelski thundered and the machine clattered to the floor. "Tell Corbin that we can't do it."

"We won't get paid..."

"Don't you think I know that, you stupid shit?"

A small ring penetrated the room and Erik heard a phone flip open. A voice squawked faintly on the other end followed by a click.

"Doctor, Corbin has requested more tests to be performed on the Ramone boy," Suber announced. "He feels that he's the source of our trouble for Product Number Three."

"Damn it!" A loud bang rattled the table Erik rest on. "Fine!"

Erik opened his eyes, watching Blazejewelski storming out the room. His aide Nelson glanced down at him, then his eyes widened, noticing Erik lay awake.

"Hey, he's up!" Nelson looked up at the nearby monitors, then back at Erik. "But...! The machine -- the monitors still state you're unconscious!"

Erik said nothing and sat up, watching Nelson race out the room. The other assembled surgeons stepped away in apprehension.

"Don't you think he'll go nuts on us?" asked Hernando. His gray eyes looked to Suber. "I don't think I can take this anymore..."

"Why are you asking me this?" answered his companion Suber, narrowing his pale violet eyes at Hernando. "*He's* the one looking at *us*."

"Be nice to him; maybe he won't try to kill us."

Three more doctors raced into the room with Nelson following close behind. "See!" Nelson protested, waving a hand in Erik's direction. "The medication wore off too quickly!"

"Now, don't agitate him!" Suber cried and the doctors slowly approached.

Erik tensed when he noticed one doctor reaching for a gun tucked in his waistband at his back. "What are you going to do to me?" he demanded, clenching his hands. "I just want to go home; I want to be left alone!"

Around him, the machines in the room began to beep erratically and the overhead lights started flickering wildly.

"Oh my goodness," Hernando moaned, "the kid's going to fucking go nuts!"

"Shut up, you pansy!" Suber yelled.

"We can't allow that right now," said one of the doctors. "You'll just have to bear with us."

"Why won't you let me see my family?" Erik hollered and clenched his teeth when the pain coursed through his hands and traveled up his arms at full force. "Why are you trying to cut me open?"

"You're sick, kid," said another doctor. "We're just trying to help you!"

Erik ripped out the intravenous lines connected in his arms and jumped down from the table, forcing the sheet fluttering to the floor. The assembled team of doctors and assistants stepped back, afraid of what he might do next.

"Leave me alone, you liars!" Erik shouted. "You're trying to harvest my organs or something!" The doctor in front of Erik immediately withdrew his pistol and Erik kicked the gun from his hand, sending it sailing across the room. Shoving the doctor down to the floor, the force threw him back hard, sending him bowling head over heels. "Don't touch me anymore!"

"Get him!" Nelson barked.

Erik raced out the room, bypassing orderlies and guards who tried to grab him. He twisted and turned out of their reach, also jumping over them when they dove at him.

Finally reaching the hall's end, Erik found a locked door and pulled on the handle. The door refused to budge when he tried to force it open. A guard in low black cap and dark uniform approached, smirking.

"That door only locks from the other side," the guard declared as Erik turned around, facing her. The sentry came prowling closer, holding a pistol at ready. "Now, come peacefully and you won't be harmed."

"I don't want to stay!" Erik protested. "I just want to see the Greenfields!"

"Tough shit," the guard snapped. "You're not leaving out of here!"

"Aren't they even worried about me?"

"Hell, no; now stop your whining and come here!"

"Stay back!"

Erik pushed the guard away as the corridor's lights flickered and dimmed, close to losing power. He clenched his teeth from the increasing pain emanating from his arms and hands, biting away at his skin. The other patrol filling the hall backed away when the lighting above them blinked and buzzed loudly.

"Calm down, boy! We won't hurt you again," one of the doctors yelled over the noise. "We just want to make sure you're safe!"

"Again?" Erik screeched, pressing his back against the wall. "You're lying to me!"

"You have no choice!"

Erik shoved the guard onto the floor when grabbed for. "I want to be left alone," he screamed, "and I don't want to hear anything more about testing!"

The lights above them burst, sending crashing glass on the floor over Erik and the guard. Erik ducked as the guard screamed when a piece of fallen glass cut her on the side of her neck.

The guard staggered back, clutching her throat as liquid crimson spurt out, spraying through her fingers. She struck the floor, twitching as blood pooled on the floor beneath her. The other sentries and doctors paled at the sight and backed away.

"Stop him!" Nelson shouted.

More lights overcharged with electricity and burned out, crashing out the bulbs as it lead down the corridor, encasing the hall in darkness.

A blast of electricity ripped through the guards and other doctors and they cried out in pain as blood burst from their eyes, noses and ears. The wounded collapsed into a heap on the floor and several gagged, wheezing as they choked on blood. Others screamed when their uniforms caught fire, their shrieks tapering as they immediately burned to death. Another blast charred the remaining, turning them to ash once the flames died.

Erik pressed against the wall, heaving for breath. He swallowed hard, trying to keep down the acrid burning in the back of his throat, growing nauseous from the stench of burnt flesh permeating the hallway.

Erik wavered and sank to the floor as his legs gave out from underneath him, shuddering in fear. Shutting his eyes, he moaned and clutched his head, unable to escape the bloodied scene seared into his mind. He tensed, hearing heavy footsteps thudding in the hallway.

"Please, don't hurt me," Erik pleaded. "I don't deserve this."

He opened his eyes when the footsteps thumped closer and saw a faint light illuminating the corridor. Moments later, a tall middle-aged man with long curly platinum-blond hair and narrow violet eyes wearing ripped black jeans, black leather boots, and a thin white T-shirt molded to his semi-muscular upper body appeared at the corridor's end.

Erik clenched his teeth when he saw a glowing white staff strapped to the man's waist in a low-slung harness. The staff had two golden ornately decorated handles on the shaft's top and bottom, with a set of dark red tassels in the center with a small bell knotted on the end.

"I'm not here to hurt you," the man said gently upon approach. "I'm here to help."

"Please leave me alone." Erik drew up his knees and buried his head in his arms. "I can't do this anymore..."

"If you stick around, they'll bring reinforcements," the mysterious stranger said and tugged at Erik's arm. "Do you want them to capture you again?" Erik glanced up and the man held out a hand to him. "Hurry, if you still want to live! I'll escort you out this place."

"Why are you helping me?" Erik asked. "Why bother?"

"Because I promised someone..."

Erik took his large calloused hand to get pulled up. Released from the pain as a sudden bright light blinded him, Erik fell forward from exhaustion.

THIRTY

Erik gasped and sat up, finding himself in a dimly lit room of unfamiliar origin and dressed in a dark green hospital gown. He glanced around, noticing the room barely furnished, with a simple bed, nightstand, and water closet.

On the wall's other side across from the bed, a small nightlight illuminated the room with a soft glow. Erik left his bed and approached the door, trying the handle. He grunted when the handle didn't turn.

"Why can't I leave?" he thought. *"Why lock me in here?"* Erik tried the handle again, and then banged his fist against the panel. *"How did I get here? This can't be General!"*

Erik's hands suddenly burned and he turned around, facing his pale reflection standing before him. He backed away as his counterpart formed a faintly glowing ornate silver saber in cyan light.

"Hey," Erik demanded, "what happened to that guy who helped me?"

There is a swirling darkness in your heart... a fog in your memory...

"What are you talking about?"

I can see it... your past, your future...

"What do you want from me?" Erik cried. "You're not real!"

I am very much real... as you see I'm standing before you.

"That doesn't mean anything - you're just a figment of my imagination!"

Erik rushed ahead and threw a punch, only to have his double swiftly sidestep the attack and slash at his back. Erik cried out and fell forward onto his knees once his skin split open.

Know this... that nothing will ever be the same again...

"You're lying!"

That's so far from the truth and you know it!

Erik grunted once kicked in the side and fell onto his back, yowling in pain. He crawled rearward as his counterpart stepped up to him.

"What do you want me to do?" Erik pleaded.

As soon as you get close to the truth, you must act. The young man with his looks pointed the blade's tip at Erik's throat. *You are a force to be reckoned with!*

"How would I do that?"

You have two choices... Either you protect those you care about, or...

"Or what?"

The door to the room unlocked and Erik seethed when his hands flared in pain as the young man struck the saber into the floor once he vanished, leaving the sword behind. Erik scrambled to his feet and picked up the saber, holding it at ready once the door came open.

A tall thin young man with tanned freckled skin, long black hair in a braid hanging down the middle of his back, narrow blue eyes and a large crooked nose from a previous break entered the room, wearing all white: scrub shirt, slacks and walking shoes. Clipped to his shirt was a nametag with his employee picture and the name Nelson with his last name covered by dark tape.

"What the hell are you pointing that at me for?" snapped Nelson. "You bastard, are you looking for a fight or something today?"

"I want out of here," Erik growled and slashed at Nelson. Nelson sidestepped the humming sword's path. "I'm not asking you, I'm *telling* you: let me go!"

"What the fuck you think you're doing, eh?"

"If I have to fight to get out of here, then I will!"

"I don't like your answer."

"Then I'm kicking your butt!"

"Are you certain about that?" Nelson rushed Erik and Erik slashed back, keeping him away. Nelson sidestepped the attack and kicked Erik against the wall, stunning him. Nelson grabbed Erik by the throat, leaning in. "You really don't want to mess with me, little boy," he sneered. "I'm warning you."

"You don't scare me!" Erik hissed.

"Then do it," Nelson jeered. "Cut me." Erik released the saber and it clattered to the floor. "I thought so." Erik grunted when struck heavy-handedly across the face and dropped to the floor as Nelson stood over him, cracking his knuckles. "If I had the time, I'd punish you."

"How so?" Erik asked weakly.

Nelson laughed darkly. "You'll know in time." He withdrew a capped syringe from his shirt pocket. "But, unfortunately, you're due back to return."

"Why drug me before taking me back?"

"Because we need to finish our tests. This time, you're not escaping and we're taking precautions so that your hero doesn't show up again."

"And how is that?"

"You're going downstairs."

Erik grunted when grabbed roughly by the arm and Nelson flipped off the cap. Nelson stabbed Erik in the arm and pushed the plunger down, releasing the clear serum. The fog filled Erik's head quickly, whiting out his world.

Waking up in a shadowy realm, Erik sat up, gasping for breath. Looking around, he saw a door at the end of a long corridor and scrambled to his feet. Racing for the exit, it extended far out of reach. Erik ran until he collapsed on his hands and knees, heaving for breath.

Do you know what happens after the end...?

"What?" Erik called. He stood, searching for the voice's source. "What end?"

Don't let the enemy lead you astray...

"How would I do that?"

The gears of time are constantly moving... The enemy's aim is to destroy you...

"I figured that out... So what should I do? I keep getting conflicting advice!"

You are only here to observe...

"Really?" Erik let out a short laugh. "Observe my loss of mind, is that right?"

Don't let the enemy provoke you!

"Too late for that!" Erik stomped onward, clenching his teeth when the door moved further away.

A warning for you...

"If I'm allowed to leave after you tell me, then I'm listening."

You are the cause of their destruction... Though you had great power, your failure to act caused such collapse...

"So what should I do? If I'm here to watch, then I necessarily can't fight, now can I?"

There is no way one can turn back time and make it so that everything that has happened will have never been...

"So you're trying to say I'm doomed to repeat my mistakes?"

Your motive is to stop the destruction...

"Now I *know* you're lying!"

What a miserable existence...

"Then I'll make the best of it."

The door at the corridor's end slowly opened. Erik ran for it and stepped through.

Erik stirred and opened his eyes, facing Chicago looking down at him, appearing distraught.

"I thought you'd never wake up," Chicago murmured and ran a hand through his shaggy dark brown hair. "You scared me."

"Chico..." Erik murmured. "What happened?"

"A lot, Erik," Chicago answered, taking his hand, "a lot that I can't tell you right now."

"Who brought me back here?"

"A friend of ours," Chicago said vaguely. "It'll be a while before they replace that window, so we're in another room right now."

"*Maybe I shouldn't press further,*" mused Erik once Chicago let go. "Are my parents coming to see about me?" he asked instead.

Chicago nodded. "The doctors said that you had a bad reaction to some painkillers," he explained. "Quite naturally, I broke the damn window."

"Thanks, Chico; I don't know how I can make it up to you." Erik tried to sit up and Chicago put a hand on his chest, pushing him down.

"Don't worry about it."

"Chico, I was just wondering..."

"What?"

"Do you know anyone named Ferdian?"

"I've heard of him," Chicago muttered, "but I don't know him personally... why?"

"People have been calling me that lately."

"Maybe you look like him then?"

"I'm not sure..."

"Is there something about him that they want?" Chicago wondered. "Is he part of the reason for all these doctors trying to cut on us?"

"Why are you asking me?" Erik asked. "I don't know the reason."

"I wish I knew..."

"Do you think he's somehow related to some government program?"

Chicago raised an eyebrow. "What are you talking about?"

"Why are these people targeting me and my family?"

"I don't have the answers."

"I'm tired of the madness."

"Me too."

Erik groaned and put an arm over his eyes. "I want to wake up out of this nightmare," he moaned. "I wish it was all a bad dream."

Sleep came immediately, drowning out his doubts and everything else.

THIRTY-ONE

Someone shook Erik's shoulder with a firm hand, taking him out of dreamless sleep. Rousing, Erik found Chicago standing over him, appearing extremely distressed.

"What is it, Chico?" Erik muttered and sat up.

"My fake parents are taking me away!" Chicago cried, gripping onto Erik's arm. "I don't want to go with them!"

"What do you want me to do about it?"

"Please, let me stay with you for a while!"

"What makes you think you can stay with me?" Erik protested. "I don't know you!"

"I won't cause trouble; besides, you won't even notice me there!" Chicago's grip tightened on Erik's arm. "Please, promise me... I already gave you my word!"

"*What did I promise him?*" Erik wondered, frowning. "*He said I made a commitment before... now another one?*" Chicago's frightened eyes tore at him and Erik nodded in response. Chicago quickly relaxed and let go then sat on the edge of Erik's bed, hugging his knees. "*I wonder what it was that he says he's assured me in return...*"

Moments later, Raider's voice shouted out in the hall. "Ay, I visit him when I feel!" Raider entered the room, wearing dark jeans, boots, denim jacket and T-shirt. An irate nurse followed him in moments later.

"You have two minutes!" the nurse snapped. "You're not supposed to be up here anyway!"

"Piss off, man!" Raider approached the bed, ignoring the nurse who sighed in frustration and stormed out. "Ay," he said to Chicago. "Who you is?"

"That's Chico Ramone," Erik answered. "He's my roommate for a while and wants to hang out at my house until he feels like going home."

"What," Raider chided, "the 'rents don't love ya no more?" He chuckled. "Check this: I can get some calls 'round to some folks and have ya livin' in a nice place fer a few days. Won't nobody know 'bout it, dig it? Ain't even gotta freak out his folks or nothin'."

"You'll do that?" Chicago asked, amazed. "No one's ever done a nice thing for me!"

Raider grinned. "If you a friend of Erik's then you's a friend of mine."

"You're looking better," Erik commented.

"Ya don't look too bad, yerself," Raider replied. "Now, down to business..." He began pacing, his expression becoming serious.

"What's going on?" Erik asked, suddenly overcome with dread. "Is it about Father Greenfield?"

"Somethin' like that," Raider replied. "You gotta remember why Danae kicked yer face in so we can stop her shit, man."

"Apparently, I don't," Erik murmured. "She claimed she had unfinished business with me from last year." He shrugged his shoulders. "What difference does it make? You know more about it than I do, obviously!"

Raider glared back at Erik. "That's between you and her!" he retorted. "I just helped yer ass out and damn near got myself killed!"

"Then stop trying to help me then, if I'm such a danger to you!"

"You don't get it!" Raider thundered. "That bitch ain't never gonna stop until they off you, man! I mean it: they wanna wipe yer ass off the face of the damn planet!"

"Why?" Erik cried. "Why do they want me *dead*?" He threw up his hands. "What could I have done to them? I don't know what they want me for!"

"Damn it, Erik! Why the hell you holdin' back then?" Raider clenched his hands, pausing in his pacing. "Just fucking do it already!"

"Forget it!"

Raider approached and grabbed Erik by the shirtfront, shaking him. "You better *get with it* or we ain't gonna be 'round here no more to keep savin' yer ass, Erik!" he thundered. "Wake the fuck up!"

"I'm awake!" Erik spat and punched Raider's arm. "I'm not going to hurt anyone; I don't fight and I don't kill, so get that idea out your head!"

Raider let go, appearing pained. "So you just gonna let us die, just like that?" he roared. "You can go to Hell, 'cause I ain't puttin' up with that shit!"

"Tell me what it's like down there," Erik snarled and stood. "Because you're really working my nerves!"

"Oh, gonna kick my ass, huh?" Raider pushed up his sleeves. "Am I pissin' ya off that much?" He beckoned to Erik. "Alright then, let's go!"

"I've had enough with you!" Erik growled and put up his fists. "Bring it!"

Raider leaned out of Erik's swing for his face and ducked down, throwing a powerful blow to Erik's side. Erik grunted and staggered back against the bed.

Growling, Erik lurched forward and Chicago sprang to his feet, immediately grabbing Erik by the arm and swung him around. He caught Erik's fist and threw him back, sending him crashing into Raider. Raider stumbled rearward and both fell toward the floor.

"Both of you, stop," growled Chicago, glaring down at them both. "Save it for them!"

"I'm tired of everyone telling me to remember," Erik groused. Chicago lent a hand and Erik took it, getting pulled upright.

Erik tensed when the lights above them flickered wildly. He turned to Raider as he stood, dusting himself off. "What's going on?" Erik complained. "What's with these power surges?"

"Hell if I know," Raider groused. "Maybe something 'bout that energy plant outside town..." He shrugged. "I don't watch the news."

Erik grunted as pain flashed behind his eyes.

"He's not the bad guy here," Chicago said to Erik. "I agree with your friend... If you don't keep yourself alive, then we might never see you again!"

Erik let out a cry and gripped his head as intense pain ripped through it while white noise buzzed in his ears.

"Make it stop!" he wailed.

What is the ultimate power?

Erik clenched his teeth when the fiery pain cleaved through his arms and spread throughout his chest. Small fissures appeared on his skin as dark cuts and burns appeared, weeping dark blood. "Why are you doing this to me?" he moaned and doubled over when the agony worsened, penetrating his skin and driving deep into his bones.

Would you still like to see, Ferdian?

Erik shut his eyes and clamped his hands over his ears, screaming. "Stop it!" he screeched. "Stop tormenting me like this!"

I'm sure you remember, Ferdian! You see, you feel...

"Get out of my head!"

Let's show them! Hate them, degrade them, fight them, destroy them...

"No!"

The noise suddenly stopped and Erik dropped his knees, immediately drained.

"Get out of my way!" another voice thundered in the room.

This power is not a weapon nor ability, but when the heart and mind do not hesitate...

Erik yowled in pain when a sharp blow struck the back of his head, jarring him. He opened his eyes and scrambled to his feet, facing the man who constantly posed as Erik's reflection, with the exception of narrow pale blue eyes, high cheekbones, and several earrings in his ears.

The young man wore a navy sleeveless shirt underneath a leather motorcycle jacket with many buckles, navy slacks, and black boots with chains lined along the calf. He pushed up his sleeves, revealing steel bracers on his arms matching the buckle of his belt. The belt held suspended bullets, hanging loosely about his slender hips.

People have opposing forces and yet they hesitate...

Erik backed away and put up his hands in surrender, growing nervous when he could not see his overall expression, given the black fishing cap the young man wore low on his face.

"Please don't hurt me," Erik begged.

The young man smiled maliciously. "Do as I say and I won't have to," he answered.

"Arizeh, leave him alone!" Chicago bellowed.

Arizeh turned around as Chicago charged. The young man grabbed Chicago's fist aimed at his face and yanked him forward. Throwing Chicago across the room, he sent him crashing into the opposite wall. Raider ran up to Chicago's fallen form and pulled him up by the arm.

"Ay," Raider yelled at Arizeh as he drew back, "what the fuck is wrong with you, man?"

"Shut your face," Arizeh snarled.

"What are ya tryin' to pull?" Raider demanded.

"He attacked me," Arizeh snapped. "But I'm not here to deal with him."

Yet you are different...

Erik backed away when Arizeh turned to face him. "Don't tell me you're here for me!" he cried.

"Are you tryin' to get us killed here?" Raider shouted when Arizeh gave no immediate answer.

"What are you doing here?" Erik demanded.

Seeing will drive you cold and numb and to the brink of madness...

Arizeh reached for his side and withdrew a dark blue scabbard with gold accents appearing on his left, glowing faintly in green light. The sword's grip, wrapped in black leather and reinforced with dyed navy sharkskin, appeared worn from heavy use.

"I'm here to destroy you," Arizeh answered and unhooked his sword from his sheath with his thumb.

If you fell off the edge, you will never return...

"The hell you ain't!" Raider screamed. Both he and Chicago advanced, flanking Arizeh from both sides.

"If you hurt him," Chicago snarled, "I'll send you to Hell myself!"

"I came here to destroy that monster over there," Arizeh declared, "and you weaklings aren't strong enough to stop me!"

"What are you talking about?" Erik demanded. "You can't mean *me*!"

"Remember, Ferdian," Arizeh grumbled, "the games of fools and madmen never end, no matter where in the world they reside!"

Thinking is merely a game for fools... There are no facts, but baseless feelings and half-formed ideas!

Raider charged and Arizeh withdrew the blade with his free hand, slashing down in one fluid motion. Raider staggered back in shock as his blue-violet blood splattered against the walls and floors from the diagonal cut across his chest.

"What are you doing?" Erik screamed.

Arizeh turned to Chicago and made a diagonal sweep, slicing at his side. Chicago jerked back and Arizeh skewered him through the shoulder, then stomped his chest with a forceful kick. Chicago cried out and fell against the bed before slumping forward on the floor.

You're a deviation of the natural law... you're to be hunted down and exterminated...

Raider jumped Arizeh from behind and Arizeh hurled him forward, sending him bowling over on the floor. Arizeh jammed the sword into Raider's leg and Raider screamed in pain.

"Stop hurting my friends!" Erik shouted as Arizeh withdrew the glowing blue steel.

"What they created us to be," Arizeh thundered, "*they are the ones to blame!*" He turned, slashing at Erik. Erik shielded his face with his arms and hands, grunting when sliced into. "We are *never* outside their influence!"

Chicago shook off his stun and let out a scream in rage, lunging at Arizeh's back. Arizeh swiftly stepped down, striking the sword from behind without turning around. Chicago moaned and slipped to his knees when stabbed in the stomach, his dark indigo blood seeping from his side.

You have lost sight of your original goals... You're nothing but a ticking time bomb waiting to go off at any moment!

Erik clenched his hands at his sides, growing enraged. "I will kill you if you keep doing this!" he thundered.

"We are *nothing* but toys to them," Arizeh bellowed, "and they will never stop until they *use* us at our ends!" He withdrew his sword. "What you can do is stop pretending it will all go away!"

Erik ran up to Arizeh and froze at the bloodied blade directed at his throat. "Are you here to kill us?" Erik demanded. "I thought you were here to destroy me, not my friends!"

"I'm doing whatever it takes to get you to understand," Arizeh sneered. "You need to kill those snakes in order to right the wrongs done to us!"

"I'm not going to kill!" Erik said evenly. "I don't kill, so forget it!"

"*Sirachet!*" Arizeh sneered, forming another blue steel blade with gold accents in his right hand. Erik leaned back as they were both pointed at him and he sucked in a shallow breath, noticing Arizeh's narrow pale blue eyes blank in his head. "You will kill, and you'll do as you're ordered to do!"

"No one orders me!"

"Tough!"

Erik sidestepped a wild slash and ducked out of another swing, then stepped under Arizeh's reach, shouldering his chest. Throwing Arizeh against the wall, his cap fell off, revealing shoulder-length curly platinum-blond hair.

Grabbing Arizeh's throat, Erik leaned in and Arizeh's eyes widened, stunned at Erik's quick reaction. "You--!" Erik growled.

"You--!" Arizeh said faintly.

Erik tightened his grip. "I--!"

Arizeh chortled. "You remember," he gasped, "don't you?"

"Remember what?" Erik hissed.

"Justin!"

We may never meet again... but we'll never forget each other.

Erik gasped when sharp pain erupted behind his eyes and he pulled away when a young man with black curly hair and dark blue-violet eyes stared back at him.

I already died for you...! What more do you want...?

Rubbing at his eyes, Erik looked again, seeing Arizeh normally and Arizeh gave a sinister, knowing smile in return. Erik took in a weak ragged breath as nervous sweat broke out over his face and he struggled to find his words.

"*I don't understand,*" Erik thought. "*Why am I seeing things?*" He clutched his head as the throbbing pain worsened. "I think I'm going to be sick," he moaned.

"Either release me," Arizeh snarled, "or finish what you've started!"

"You're crazy!" Erik spat.

"And so are you!" Arizeh bared his teeth. "I have no compunctions about cutting your sorry ass in half!"

"You don't have the guts!"

Arizeh kneed Erik's groin and Erik cried out as he released his grip, crumpling to his knees.

Arizeh raised his swords then suddenly paused as his hands shook violently. He took a step back as a vacant look appeared in his eyes and he lowered his blades. A trickle of blood escaped Arizeh's nose and his breathing became labored as he struggled with his emotions.

"I thought you were going to cut me in half," Erik grumbled from below as Arizeh dropped the weapons he held. "Have you lost your nerve?"

"You...!" Arizeh sneered, grabbing Erik by the collar and yanking him upright. "I'll destroy you!"

Arizeh backhanded Erik, throwing him on the floor and stomped his chest, pinning him down with his weight. Arizeh struggled to breathe as the muscles worked in his face and he let out a strained laugh.

"What--?" Erik started.

"I have to kill you," Arizeh hissed, cutting off Erik. "So stay down and let me torture you slowly."

"Do it then!" Erik retorted.

"W-what's wrong with me?" Arizeh murmured. "Why...?" He let out a pained shout and gripped his head, staggering back in agony. "I--!"

Erik sprang to his feet and grasped Arizeh's shirtfront. "Get it together!" he shrilled, shaking him.

Trying to regain his composure, Arizeh lost the battle and his eyes rolled to the back of his head. Erik let go, watching him crumple as a heap on the floor.

"What's all this?" a voice called.

Erik turned, facing the tall middle-aged man wearing ripped jeans, a patchwork dress shirt over a white T-shirt and a bright orange baseball cap covering his frizzy pale blond hair. He entered the room, holding the glowing white staff with ornate golden handles over his shoulder.

"What are you doing here?" Erik demanded. "Why did he attack us?"

"He had orders, I suppose," the man answered. "And besides, you seemed to have handled yourself fine against him."

"Are you nuts?" Erik hollered. "He nearly slaughtered my friends!" He gestured toward the carnage around him. "They're barely hanging on as it is!"

"They're tough old boys," the man said and grinned. "This is nothing."

"Who gave him the orders to kill me?"

"It wasn't me, if that's what you're concerned with."

"Then why did he freak out like that?"

"He went against programming for some reason." The middle-aged man snorted. "Lucky for you, I guess."

"You guess?" Erik shrilled.

"I've enough of this, old man," Arizeh muttered from his place on the floor. He grunted when the staff struck the back of his head.

"Do you want me to silence you permanently?" the middle-aged man retorted. "Stay there!"

"Shut up, Mahjin!"

"Clean up your mess!"

"Forget it!"

Arizeh snatched up the swords and quickly rose, slashing back with his blade. Mahjin quickly blocked the attack with his staff and pushed back as Erik stepped out the way.

Jumping behind Mahjin, Arizeh made a hard thrust and Mahjin turned away, letting the blade pierce the wall. Mahjin slammed the staff down into Arizeh, jabbing his face and Arizeh staggered back. Arizeh swung another wild lash and

Mahjin leaned out the way, then ducked under the blow and pinned him against the wall by the chest with the shaft.

"You need to check yourself!" Mahjin growled. "Or do you need another beating?"

"Stay out of my way!" Arizeh shouted.

"Atone for your sins or die!"

"You're coming with me!" Arizeh kicked Mahjin back and threw one saber at him. Mahjin swiftly stepped aside and it struck the wall.

"Your pointless rampage will get all of us killed!" Mahjin said evenly. "It's clear he doesn't remember anything!"

"Pointless, eh?" Arizeh pointed the other saber he held at Mahjin's chest. "Guilt is never pointless; responsibility is never pointless!" He thrust forward his sword and Mahjin leaned out the way, blocking with his glowing silver staff and shattered the blue steel blade. "Revenge is never pointless!"

Arizeh formed a golden-handled black-steeled sword with red tassels on the pommel and pointed it at Erik.

"You've been forewarned!" Mahjin growled, holding his staff at ready.

"You saw what they did, didn't you?" Arizeh bellowed. Mahjin's jaw set as his violet eyes turned into dark voids. "Those meddling imbeciles have more than rekindled the burning appetite for slaughter within me!"

"Don't remind me," Mahjin grumbled, lowering his staff.

"So let me destroy him... it'll save us all!"

"No one's destroying me!" Erik snapped and Arizeh turned to him. Erik reached out, grabbing the blade as Arizeh brought down the saber.

"How do you explain tragedy?" Arizeh demanded, struggling against Erik's hand gripping the sword, forcing dark blue blood running down his arm.

"I don't understand," Erik said and took a step back as Arizeh pressed forward.

"You, Dreamer, are walking a nightmare and the agony of the past can never be explained..."

"So tell me," Erik snarled, "otherwise, let me go!"

"You know I can't... Jerry can't either."

Erik sucked in a pained shallow breath when the skin on the back of his hands started to tear and split open. The muscles beneath turned taut and twitched as they warped, stretching nearly close to breaking. Erik let out a shout and pushed Arizeh back, forcing him staggering into Mahjin.

"I have lived it!" Arizeh screeched, swiping at Erik. Erik grunted when the blade's tip sliced across his cheek. "We all have lived it!"

"He has his own dreams to fulfill," Mahjin said, pushing Arizeh away with his staff. "You can't make him finish what you failed!"

"I will do whatever I wish, old man!" Arizeh hissed, glaring back at Mahjin.

"Let him be free to choose what he wants to do. If he is destined to fail, then he fails. If he's destined to be great, then let him be great."

"What he doesn't know will surely kill us all...!" Arizeh pointed his bloodied saber at Erik. "Know this, Ferdian... the torment will never end and this doomed quest is nothing but a fractured stained version of your self!"

"That's it," Erik declared, pushing past Mahjin. "I'm getting out of this madhouse!" He barely jumped fast enough as Arizeh lashed at him again.

"Get by me first!" Arizeh shrilled.

"You're really working my nerves!" Erik shouted. "Back off!"

"Good!" Arizeh thrust the blade forward, jamming it into Erik's side.

Erik's world immediately grew dark when the sword penetrated deep and the overwhelming pain caused a low drone buzzing loudly between his ears.

Growing disconnected from his body, Erik felt as if he were suspended elsewhere and heard many voices talking at him at once. Erik struggled to get out of the darkness, unable to find footing on reality.

Keep yourself alive...

Keep yourself...

So that we may meet...

Again...

THIRTY-TWO

Erik's eyes snapped open and he gasped as pain stabbed his side. Seeing he faced late-afternoon sky, Erik wondered how he got outside. He held his profusely bleeding side, trying to comprehend what just happened as he staggered to his feet.

Erik swallowed hard once he saw the hacked remains of many officers around him on the ground, dressed in navy uniforms, caps with visors and dark glasses.

"There he is!" a voice called and Erik immediately stood on the defensive as several other officers ran toward him, armed with an array of weapons.

"Thought your life would go on forever, eh kid?" snapped one officer who wielded a bloodied saber. Erik's mind finally grasped the situation and he took a cautious step back; noticing the one officer on his right held a shotgun and the other to his left held a high-powered revolver.

"What do you want with me?" Erik demanded, backing away.

"Seal off the perimeter!" called the officer who held the saber. "We got him cornered now..."

Before Erik could make his next move, a young man with shaggy crimson hair and narrow emerald eyes calmly approached the officers from behind. He wore the same outfit as the others except for cap and glasses, and carried a blue-steeled saber.

One officer noticed Erik's expression and turned toward his line of sight, facing the young man standing behind them. "Hey," he spat. "You're not supposed to be here!"

The officer raised his handgun to shoot and the young man immediately severed his head with a flash cut. He sliced the guardsman with the shotgun in half before he reacted and the saber-wielding officer quickly blocked the attack, then kicked the redheaded swordsman back.

"*Kenzan Hussaru*!" the young man thundered and released a blast of violet flame, knocking the officer off his feet. Slashing into him, he lopped off the officer's arm with a swift stroke. Before Erik could say a word, the mysterious redhead pointed the glowing saber at Erik's throat and Erik's eyes widened as he swallowed hard. "Give me one good reason why I should spare you!" he snarled.

"I don't have a good reason!" Erik wailed. He drew up an arm, generating a shield of violet light and blocked the swordfighter's rapid down-stroke, shattering the saber.

"*Sirachet*!" the redheaded warrior growled and Erik fell forward, stunned once he realized he had a golden variant of the swordsman's saber stuck through his chest.

"Who are you?" Erik wheezed. "Why do you look like me?"

"Because I *am* you, Brother," snarled Erik's counterpart. Erik grunted when the redhead pushed forth with his blade. "Pity that I defeated you so easily..." Erik cried out in agony once the swordsman twisted the sword. "You are a tool of

317

destruction," he shouted. "You shouldn't be giving up this easily!"

"I'd rather suffer in silence," Erik moaned, "if continuing on meant slaughtering others indiscriminately!"

"If so, let's hear you scream!"

"Wait!"

The redheaded swordfighter withdrew the blade and Erik quickly turned out as another young man with frizzy dark blond hair wearing a tan overcoat and driving cap calmly approached them from behind. Erik gasped, recognizing him at once.

"*What is Arizeh doing here?*" Erik thought as Arizeh unleashed a silver pistol.

"*Kenzan Toumetsuei!*" Arizeh shouted and fired, hurtling the red-haired fighter back.

Erik let out a cry as green flame burst around him. "What are you doing to me?" he wailed.

"I'm trying to make you remember, Ferdian," Arizeh growled, sheathing the silver pistol beneath his coat and withdrew a green-tempered saber holstered on his side.

"I wish you'd stop calling me that," Erik groused. "That's not my name!"

"And Erik isn't either!" Arizeh stormed toward Erik, poking the green-steeled saber at his chest. "You don't have much time left, you see... I am trying to *prevent* your destruction!"

"What are you talking about?" Erik complained. "Earlier you tried to kill me!"

"What are *you* talking about?"

Before Erik could explain, he heard movement from behind and immediately stood. Whirling around, Erik sidestepped the redheaded fighter's rushing attack. The swordfighter returned with a fast slice, taking of Erik's arm and carved through his torso, cutting him in half with the golden saber.

Erik vomited blue blood after gaining a severe gash to his midsection and sliced through his shoulder. Arizeh sprang ahead and the redhead turned to him, only to lose his head from a speedy attack.

"Heh, I forgot about that specific ability," Arizeh muttered when the red-haired fighter collapsed on the ground and his headless body burst into golden flame. Erik's eyes widened once the flames died, leaving behind charred remains and half-melted metal.

"What in blazes...!" Erik yelped, slipping to his knees.

"Shape up already, you nuisance!" Arizeh barked and kicked Erik in the head, forcing him on his back.

"But I've been cut!" Erik shouted. "It hurts like you wouldn't believe!"

"You're right, I wouldn't." Arizeh approached Erik, placing a foot on his chest.

"B-but...!" Erik sputtered. "How did he cut me when he wasn't even close to me?"

"Now why the fuss over getting cut up?" Erik groaned when jarred with a swift boot into the chest. "See here, the pain you're feeling isn't really pain... It's only remnants of a past life that makes your character. If you were truly human, those wounds you've received would've killed you instantly!"

"What are you saying...?"

"What I'm saying--!" Arizeh grunted and released his hold then wiped his stained green steel saber against his thigh. Dropping it back into the scabbard, he turned and stomped away.

Erik slowly rose upright, dumbfounded. *"If pain is only a memory,"* he thought, *"then <u>why</u> am I here?"* He shut his eyes and rubbed at his temple, trying to clear the fog inside his mind.

"Let's go, Ferdian," Arizeh called from afar. "Get up."

When Erik opened his eyes again, he sucked in a tight breath, horrified while watching the citizens go on their way, oblivious to the destruction around them. *"They're acting as if nothing happened!"* Erik mused, utterly floored. *"How could this be...?"*

Erik ran through the crowded city streets, spotting Arizeh walking along the sidewalk, wearing a white dress shirt and navy slacks with black oxfords, his long curly flaxen hair pulled into a loose queue down his back. In his arms, he carried his coat with his cap hanging out the pocket.

"You sure take your time," Arizeh grumbled when Erik caught up along his side.

"Hey," Erik said, "about what happened earlier... why aren't they aware of what went on just now?"

"Maybe because it's a daily occurrence for them," Arizeh answered nonchalantly.

"What?" Erik grabbed Arizeh's shoulder, forcing the young man around and Arizeh grabbed his hand, twisting it backwards. Erik recoiled in pain, crying out in shock by his swift reaction. "Hey! Ouch!"

"You really are an irritant," Arizeh growled. "You want me to erase you?"

"Erase me?" Erik yelped as Arizeh loosened his grip. "I thought you're on my side here!"

"Oh?"

"You saved me from dying back there...!"

"And that's supposed to mean something?" Arizeh pushed him back. "You got careless and I cleaned it up," he retorted and shoved Erik aside. "You've been a real bother lately and I don't see why I should keep watching over you like this." He stalked away.

"Why do you keep interfering then?" Erik yelled after him. "If you don't want to watch over me, then simply leave!"

"Oh, if it were that easy!"

"So what's holding you back then?"

"Do you really want to know the truth?" Arizeh came to a halt and turned around. "You are nothing more than a thing, a tool for destruction. Do I have to spell it out for you?"

"I'm *not* a thing!" Erik screeched and jabbed a thumb against his chest. "I'm Human, understand? Don't you forget it!"

"No, you're *not* Human. Not one part of you is organic. You're nothing more than a *thing*!"

"Stop treating me like some kind of machine!"

"Look at you," Arizeh protested. "Your arm is gone, you've been sliced damn near in half and yet you keep walking!"

"So what?"

Arizeh stormed ahead and Erik gasped as sharp pain met his side. Erik winced as Arizeh forced his hand through, causing him to stagger forward. "See, Humans don't bleed blue, black, or any other color." Arizeh swiftly withdrew his hand, displaying the dark stains painting them. In his palm, he held a small green circuit board that had copper contacts. "You are just a thing, so burn out and disappear already!"

Erik's world crashed around him into darkness.

THIRTY-THREE

The darkness slowly lightened and the weightlessness surrounding Erik began to fade. The static in his ears cleared and he let out a yelp when tackled.

"Don't hit him again!" Chicago's voice yelled from afar as Erik tumbled overhead and everything came back at once.

Erik wrestled off Raider holding him down and kicked him back, sending him crashing to the floor. Raider sprang to his feet as Erik stood and Chicago lurched forward, jumping on Raider's back. Raider hurled him off, sending Chicago smashing into the adjacent bed.

Chicago slammed his head against the wall and fell on his side unconscious. Erik grabbed Raider's fist aimed at his face and shoved him away.

"Why are you attacking me?" Erik cried.

"What the hell is wrong with ya, man?" Raider snapped. Erik leaned out of another punch and turned, slapping away a swift jab aimed for his side. Raider returned with another powerful blow into his solar plexus and Erik doubled over, coughing up blood.

"I should ask you the same!" Erik wheezed.

Raider growled and struck Erik's face with his foot, then shoved him on his back to the floor with his heel. "I don't know you no more, man!"

"I don't know what you're talking about!" Erik spat.

Raider bared his teeth and booted Erik's side before he could get up, forcing him to yowl in pain and crumple over. "I should kick your ass, Erik!" Raider said breathlessly and punted him again. "How the hell we supposed to be friends and you never keep my back?"

"Stop kicking me!" Erik wailed.

"That's it, we ain't friends no more!"

"Raider!"

Raider raised his foot and Erik grabbed him by the leg, pulling him down to the floor. Erik scrambled up and grappled with him, slamming Raider back against the ground.

"Let me go," Raider growled and Erik pressed his arm against his neck.

"Please, stop," pleaded Erik and Raider grabbed Erik's face, pushing back. "Don't do this!" Erik hissed. "This isn't you, Raider..."

"Shut up!"

"You know it's not and I know it's not... Just don't let whatever it is get through to you!"

"You hear me, don't you?" Arizeh called outside the door. "I'm not going to stop you from killing. It's his blood on your hands."

"Stop fucking with his head!" Raider screeched and jammed his fist into Erik's neck. Erik grunted, letting go and Raider released his hold, then struck Erik with a head butt, forcing him falling back, dazed. Raider sat up, blowing a hard sigh.

"I didn't set him off," Arizeh replied and Raider glared at him as he stepped into the room.

"Until you fix his crazy ass," Raider spat, "I'm gone."

"Fine, it's your choice."

Raider rose to his feet and stormed over to Chicago. Giving a swift kick to his side, Chicago sat up with a start, gasping for breath. "Get the fuck up, man," Raider grumbled. "We gotta bounce."

"What about Erik?" Chicago groaned, holding his side.

"Fuck him, man." Raider snapped. "Let's go."

"*Dame un momento*," Chicago muttered.

Raider stalked toward the door and paused when Arizeh blocked his path.

"Don't be gone too long," Arizeh said. "We have things to do."

Raider narrowed his eyes and shoved him aside. "Don't let this shit happen again!" he snapped. "I'm outta here."

"What are you talking about?" Erik protested, sitting up.

"Fuck you, man!" Raider spat and stormed out the room.

"Damn it," Chicago snarled, standing. "Damn everything!"

"What just happened?" Erik asked timidly. "What's going on?" Standing unsteadily, he held his aching side and leaned against the wall.

"It's not you he hates," grumbled Chicago. He punched the wall, forming a crater in the plaster. "It's the programming..."

"If you say so..." Erik blew a heavy sigh and ran a hand through his hair. "Where did Mahjin go?"

"He had elsewhere to be," answered Arizeh.

Erik glared back at him. "I want you gone," he snapped. "You're nothing but trouble!"

Arizeh smirked. "Says you!"

"Damn him and everything to Hell!" Chicago screamed. "I can't stand it!" He struck the wall again, heaving for breath as the veins in his neck and shoulders quickly fleshed out.

"Chico, please calm down!" Erik pleaded and left his place near the wall. "Don't get angry - remember, you said that you can't and terrible things happen when you do!" Approaching him carefully, he gingerly touched Chicago's arm and recoiled when a violent force shocked his hand.

"Don't," Chicago rasped.

Erik looked down at his hand, finding a third degree burn that quickly healed on its own. *Is that what happened to Johnston?* he wondered. "Chico, please!" Erik pleaded as Chicago leaned against the wall, resting his face on his arms and heaved for breath. "Chico... everything will be okay!"

"It'll never be okay, Erik!" Chicago roared. Erik stiffened when the room quickly grew warm. "It doesn't matter what happens in *here*; what matters is if it goes on out *there*!"

"I don't understand..."

The air in the room grew thinner and Erik clenched his teeth when he noticed Chicago's dark skin tanning and his own pale skin began to perspire. Erik stepped away when the plastic nightstand blistered and the metal bed frame near Chicago slowly turned red.

"Leave..." Chicago snarled. "I'll come later."

Erik backed away and turned to Arizeh who stood near the door, arms folded across his chest.

"What's wrong with him?" Erik inquired.

"You'll eventually find out," Arizeh answered.

A loud spark cracked overhead and the elevated television above Chicago caught fire. The fire alarm resonated loudly and Erik hurried out the room into cooler air as the sprinkler systems activated.

"Hey!" Suber's voice called to him. He grabbed Erik by the arm and Erik whirled around, hands up in guard. Erik relaxed instantly when Suber let go and put up his hands in surrender, his violet eyes showing concern.

Erik studied Suber, noticing he had a long wide scar over his left eye and ended at his cheek. He saw Suber appeared different from the other doctors, with his shoulder-length sandy hair, horseshoe-style mustache, opened-collared short-sleeved dress shirt, jeans and loafers. Suber appeared out of place from the other doctors who styled their hair short, had clean-shaven faces and wore suits with ties.

"Were you looking for me?" Erik asked nervously.

"What's going on?" Suber asked instead, relaxing slightly.

Erik pointed his room's general direction. "It's just--!" he started.

"I see," Suber said, cutting him off. "It's your comrade, isn't it?"

"I guess you can call him that..."

"I won't send the other nurses and doctors; I know they've hurt you too much."

"But what about you?"

"I'm going to send someone else to help him," Suber interjected. "Is that okay?" Erik nodded and Suber smiled warmly. "I'll let him know." Suber patted Erik's head and walked away. Erik stood there, stunned and unsure what to do.

"Oh," a familiar voice said to Erik. He turned around and Mahjin approached, pulling into a distressed leather jacket.

"You sure change out your work clothes quickly, eh Zachary?" a nearby orderly said upon passing.

"How else can I get my mind shifted into gear?" Mahjin called back. "If you can't enjoy play time, you might as well work until you die."

"Heh, or go insane!" The orderly laughed and Mahjin laughed with him.

"Mahjin..." Erik started once the orderly passed and Mahjin put up a hand.

"That's not my name here," he said in a low tone. "I'm just another faceless orderly named Zachary, understand?"

"Why are you here?" Erik demanded. "I thought you'd be against them, not working for them!"

"What does it matter?"

"Is Zachary your name?"

"That's my surname; however, my given name is Melvin." Mahjin grinned and leaned forward toward Erik's ear. "But if you want, you can call me Smiley," he said softly.

Erik clenched his teeth as pain flashed behind his eyes.

There's no way--!

Erik backed away and Mahjin leaned against the wall, pulling out a pair of driving gloves from the coat pockets.

328

"Am I going home soon?" Erik begged as Mahjin slipped the gloves on his large thin hands.

"It's being arranged," Mahjin replied and pushed up his sleeve, checking his titanium watch.

Erik sucked in a sharp breath. *"That's the same watch the one with Genovera has!"* he thought. *"Are they somehow related...?"*

"Hm?" Mahjin murmured, glancing up at Erik. "Is something wrong?"

"What are we waiting on?" Erik wondered aloud.

"We're waiting for something to happen," Mahjin said vaguely.

"Like what?"

Erik heard a shout and ran away to the door, spotting Arizeh kicking Chicago with force. He held his sword at ready as Chicago staggered back and clenched his hands erupting in flames. Erik gasped, noticing Chicago's shaggy dark brown hair, now flaming red and his brown eyes glowed deep ruby. Around them, part of the wall and the beds were charred.

"Dampen his abilities before he starts crashing," Mahjin ordered. Erik turned back, noticing him standing at the door. "Pull it in and neutralize it now!"

"Are you telling me this?" Erik snapped. "I don't know what you're talking about!"

Chicago charged and threw a punch at Arizeh who leaned out the way, blocking with his sword. It shattered and he grabbed Chicago's fist with his free hand, shaking as deep third degree burns covered his arms and ate away at his clothing.

"Die already!" Arizeh screamed and hurled Chicago across the room. Chicago's body burst through the window, shattering the glass.

"Chico!" Erik screamed as Arizeh raced past him. Before he took a step forward, Mahjin grabbed Erik by the arm, yanking him out the room.

"Let's take you somewhere safe so you can rest awhile," Mahjin said brightly and hustled him down the corridor.

"Are you unhinged?" Erik screeched, pulling out of his grip.

"I'm sure you'd love to meet some good people I know, but right now they're a bit busy."

"You don't say!" Mahjin pushed Erik into an empty room devoid of patients and dropped into a chair on the door's far side, folding his legs at the knee. "What are we waiting on now?" Erik asked nervously.

"Just relax," Mahjin said gently. Erik tensed and Mahjin grinned. "Oh, you don't think I'm going to hurt you, do you?"

"Please don't," Erik mewed and ran his hands through his hair. "I've had enough with that for now."

Hearing a hard thump, Erik turned, noticing a duffel bag near the room's door.

"Feel free to get what you want," Mahjin replied.

Erik approached the canvas bag and crouched down, opening it. Finding a variety of clothes stuffed inside, he pulled out a set of cargo pants, a long-sleeved T-shirt, and laceless sneakers. Erik slung the clothing over his shoulder and stood when he heard Mahjin leaving his chair.

"Now, don't run off anywhere," Mahjin ordered. "Go change your clothes and I'll be straight back."

"Sure, whatever." Erik grumbled. Once Mahjin left the room, Erik approached the bed and sat facing the door, folding his arms across his chest.

Moments later, Mahjin returned as promised, holding onto a backpack. "Why aren't you changed?" he protested.

"And risk a surprise attack?" Erik spat. "I'm no idiot!"

"Here." Mahjin tossed the bag to Erik and he caught it. "Get changed so we can get out of here. I should've clocked out twenty minutes ago."

Erik opened the bag, discovering his books and a black folder with a white sticker labeled *Number 3 - project data; Case file: Project CO-192A*. He withdrew it and Mahjin immediately took the folder out of his hand.

Erik glared up at him. "What's that about?" he protested.

"Where did you get that?" Mahjin demanded and tucked the folder under his arm. "This is classified stuff!"

"What's so important about those papers anyway?" Erik snapped. "Why do they matter so much?"

"It's for me to know," Mahjin retorted, "and for you not to ask questions about!"

"Do you work here?" Erik spat.

"In a way, yes." Mahjin grinned broadly. "Also, I'm here to make sure *you* don't go out and get your fool self killed with sensitive information like this!"

"Then why leave something like that behind with my stuff, unless you're trying to kill mc too!"

"Like I said, I promised someone to keep you alive..."

"Really now?"

"What does it matter?" Mahjin jutted a thumb toward the bathroom. "You're wasting my time," he snapped. "I need to see to it that you're sent home in one piece."

At unease when Mahjin's expression changed from lighthearted to disapproving, Erik sighed and took the clothing and backpack. He stepped into the small stall on the room's side and changed his clothes. Erik grew concerned when he heard Mahjin whistle a light tune on the other side while waiting for him.

"That song," he thought and shuddered in disgust. *"It's the same music in those freaky phone calls!"*

Leaving the hospital gown on the floor, Erik emerged fully dressed and hoisted the backpack over his shoulder.

"Are we ready?" Mahjin asked.

Erik frowned. "I guess," he muttered. "Is Mister Greenfield in trouble?"

"Why do you ask?"

"Never mind..." Erik shook his head. "Forget that I asked..."

"Then follow me," Mahjin ordered and Erik traveled along with him out the room down another set of halls.

"What about Chico Ramone?" Erik pressed as they exited the hospital entrance and stepped out into the late afternoon air. "Is he injured... or worse?"

Mahjin chuckled and shook his head. "What's with asking?"

"He wanted to come with me."

"He'll come." Mahjin tucked the folder inside his jacket and zipped it close.

Moments later, a black compact sedan pulled up to the hospital entrance's curb and Erik recognized it right away belonging to John Greenfield. He ran up to the car after it idled and put into park.

"Father!" Erik cried. "You're here!"

The door opened, revealing John Greenfield as he stepped out and leaned an arm against the car's roof. "I was coming for a visit," he said in mild surprise. "I didn't know you were released early."

Erik opened the passenger side and tossed his articles into the back seat. "Let's go home!" John Greenfield paused for a moment as Erik climbed in. "Is everything okay with you?"

"It's fine," John Greenfield murmured. "What of you? You look like you got into a fight."

"I got into it with my roommate," Erik replied. "He thought I was someone else."

"Oh?"

Erik pulled on his seatbelt and glanced out the window, finding Mahjin gone. "Do you know anyone named Melvin Zachary?" he asked.

John Greenfield reentered the driver's seat and shut his door, sighing heavily as he placed his hands on the steering wheel. Erik noticed the deadpan expression written on his face.

"The name sounds familiar," John Greenfield said thoughtfully, "but not entirely." Erik shut his door and John Greenfield switched gears, pulling away from the entrance. "Does he have a nickname?"

"He told me that everyone called him Smiley... it's unusual, don't you think?"

John Greenfield turned pale, but said nothing. Erik looked out his window at the passing scenery on their way home in silence.

THIRTY-FOUR

Pulling up into the house carport, John Greenfield cut the engine and gripped the wheel, forcing his knuckles white while his stony expression remained unchanged. Erik tugged at John Greenfield's sleeve and he grunted in response.

"Father," Erik said timidly, "are you all right?"

"Yes, Son," John Greenfield answered in a strained voice. "Go on inside; I'll put away your bags."

The almost mechanical response worried Erik and he swallowed his fear as he came out of his seatbelt. Erik hurried out the car and ran up porch steps, escaping the unsettling atmosphere.

The front door opened and Jane Greenfield greeted Erik warmly once he approached the stoop. Erik stood stiffly as she gave him a firm embrace and said nothing when let go. He frowned when he saw the house back in order and no bloodstains on the carpet and walls.

"*Seraphine was right about the cleaners,*" he thought. "*What else could they have done...?*"

Pain thudded in his head, drowning out his hearing. He saw Jane Greenfield talking and she took his hand, leading him inside to the kitchen. Erik took the plate of cookies and the glass of milk she handed to him and followed her into the dining room. Jane Greenfield gestured at Erik to sit at the table and he did so, nodding empathically when she continued to chat to him.

Erik said nothing as he ate silently, trying to ignore the overwhelming fear clawing away at him. *"She didn't notice how beat up I look,"* he mused and ground his teeth, growing tense. *"Only Father Greenfield did... Doesn't she care or does she already know somehow?"*

Erik downed his glass of milk and paused, spotting John Greenfield enter the house with his backpack and place it on the floor near the door. Erik set down his glass, keeping an eye on John Greenfield as he paced in the nearby parlor.

Erik's hearing returned and he grew irritated with Jane Greenfield's nattering. He yawned loudly and stretched.

"Sorry to cut you off, Mother," Erik interrupted, "but I think I might take a quick nap; I'm a bit tired."

"Oh, that's fine," Jane Greenfield replied and folded her hands in her lap. "Will I see you down for dinner soon?"

Erik nodded and grabbed another cookie then headed upstairs. Hearing the telephone ring along the way to the staircase, he grabbed for the receiver. "Hello?" Erik greeted.

"May I speak to Jerry?" a voice said over the line.

"There's no Jerry who lives here," Erik answered.

John Greenfield paused in his pacing and whirled around. "I'll take the call," he interjected.

"What?"

John Greenfield quickly closed the gap between them and snatched the receiver from Erik's hand. "What are you doing calling me here?" he snapped. John Greenfield turned to Erik and waved him away.

Erik hurried up the steps and ground his teeth when he approached his room, finding the door replaced. Entering, he sat on the edge of his bed and kicked off his shoes then lay back, looking at his window upside down. Near the window, he saw his chest of drawers were replaced as well.

You're still blind, aren't you?

Erik glanced up and around, unable to find the source of the voice. Putting the cookie in his mouth, he sat up and left his bed, kicking shut the door. The broken mirror hanging from the back clattered from the force and Erik grunted when he faced his own reflection in the cracked glass instead.

Withdrawing the cookie, Erik blew a sigh in relief and turned around. He let out a yelp when he saw his counterpart in a black and navy uniform standing across from him, appearing annoyed with his arms folded across his chest.

"What are you doing here?" Erik cried.

Now that's a dumb question!

"So I *am* going crazy, aren't I?" Erik let out a nervous laugh and ran his free hand through his hair. "Maybe I shouldn't have left General!"

What are you going to do?

"I don't know..." Erik clenched his hands, crumbling the cookie he held. "Do they know that I'm hearing voices and seeing things that aren't there?"

There's something wrong with you and you know it!

"I know because I'm just imagining things or something..."

You're not merely imagining things... you just don't want to remember!

"What is it I want to forget?"

So you're going to just hold back and let everything spiral out of control?

"I don't know what to do in the first place!" Erik snapped. "I can't remember!"

Try, Ferdian! Remember!

"Forget it!"

Fine then, don't believe me!

The apparition vanished and Erik returned to his bed, slumping on the edge. He held his head in his hands, moaning.

"I'm going crazy, for real," Erik grumbled. "What do I tell Father Greenfield?"

"It'll never be enough!" John Greenfield's voice abruptly thundered from downstairs. Erik stiffened when he heard glass suddenly shatter. "Never!"

Scrambling to his feet, Erik threw open the door and raced to the banister, spotting John Greenfield standing near the mini-bar, heaving for breath. At his feet lay a cracked bottle of cognac and at the bar were several broken glasses. Thrown on the bar lay the desktop telephone ripped out from the wall.

Jane Greenfield rushed in from the kitchen and John Greenfield pushed her away when she approached.

"I'm fine," John Greenfield said in a strained voice. "Please, leave me be."

"What's upset you?" she pleaded.

John Greenfield shook his head. "I need time alone to think."

"Something's obviously causing you great distress!"

John Greenfield loosened his tie. "I don't want to talk about it."

"Who's Jerry?" Erik asked.

John Greenfield whirled around, looking back at Erik.

"He's nobody," John Greenfield answered. "Nobody at all."

"Obviously he's somebody important; otherwise you wouldn't be destroying stuff."

"I need some air." John Greenfield pushed past his wife and stormed out the house, slamming shut the front door.

"Go to your room," Jane Greenfield ordered.

Erik opened his mouth to protest, then blew a heavy sigh and returned to his room. Upon entry, he paused at the sight of a young man with shaggy dark brown hair wearing a tan uniform lay curled in his bed, snoring softly. Erik clenched his teeth, growing irate when he saw his window left open.

"*I really need to get a lock for that thing,*" he thought sourly and shut the door with a bang. When the noise didn't wake the sleeping stranger, Erik kicked at his mattress. The young man groaned and tucked the pillow closer under his arm, turning on his face.

"Wake up!" Erik yelled. "Who are you; why are you here?" Kicking the mattress again, the stranger moaned and turned on his back.

"*¿Qué es?*" he muttered and ran a hand through his shaggy dark brown hair, pushing it out of his light brown eyes sleepily squinting at Erik. "What do you want?"

"Chico," Erik cried, "What are you doing here? I thought you died!"

Chicago sat up, rubbing at his eyes. "I'm no ghost yet," he answered and chortled. "I'm tougher than that."

"Why are you in my room?" Erik demanded.

Chicago stretched and yawned. "Raider told me to wait here until he could arrange something," he replied. "It won't be a problem or anything, right?"

Erik shook his head. "Never mind that -- what if the Greenfields find you?"

"Don't worry," Chicago grumbled, "I'm good as dead here anyway."

"You can't stay here forever -- you have to eventually go home sometime!"

"Heh, right, like my so-called family *really* wants me!" Chicago scoffed. "I'm nothing more than just their money maker," he growled. "The only time I get out is for school and shipped back and forth to The Center."

"What is this Center?"

"They're a part of this huge network; I'm sure you know by now."

Erik shrugged. "I'm sorry, I don't."

"The Agency controls everything," Chicago muttered. "The Agency controls The Center, Keystone, Centerville, and they work for someone even *worse* than they are!" He shook his head in disgust. "Those kinds of people control all the schools, the jobs, the hospitals and public security..."

"This Agency you speak of..." Erik said, "They can't be that powerful of a network!"

"It doesn't matter where you are," Chicago insisted. "Be it the big city Keely or in this fake little town Aynslea. Their reach isn't just the major cities, like Lestalt or Deranden either: it goes *everywhere*!" Erik clenched his hands at his sides, cutting into his palms as he struggled to find his words. "Now if you don't mind, I want to get this nap out before you bother me again."

"Before you go, tell me what about the hospital we were in," Erik finally said. "Does this Agency control it as well?"

"What do you think?" Chicago spat sourly. "General Hospital's under their thumb too. Like I said: it don't matter where you are, you're still going to get tested on." Chicago sighed and laid back, turning on his side. "We have a few friends that don't like The Agency, so make sure you're nice to them! They're the only help we've got since The Agency hates them too and wants to make them disappear, especially for their suits on high."

"Why if they're only a few people; can't they just go somewhere else?"

"Where can you go when The Agency is everywhere?" Chicago scoffed again. "Might as well stay in a dream!" His hacking laughter unnerved Erik. "If it's okay with you, I'm gonna sleep some more."

"But," Erik protested, "what if Mister Greenfield finds you...?"

"Like I said..." Chicago waved Erik away. "*¡Fuera!*"

Erik blew a disgruntled sigh as snores began to escape Chicago. Without any more reasons to get him to leave, Erik stepped into his shoes and stomped downstairs.

Finding the parlor cleaned of broken glass and the liquor rubbed out the carpet, Erik heard pots clanging in the kitchen and peered in at Jane Greenfield cooking.

Turning away, he heard the front door open and John Greenfield entered, tossing his keys aside on the end table. Erik watched him walk in the parlor, heading for the bar. Erik followed John Greenfield in and sat on the couch as John Greenfield poured himself a glass of scotch. John Greenfield returned, standing before Erik.

"What is it?" Erik asked. John Greenfield said nothing and gulped his drink. "Father, you're creeping me out."

"I'm sorry," John Greenfield muttered. He blew a heavy sigh and sat next to Erik, staring off into the middle distance.

"Do you need anything?" Erik asked after several moments of silence.

"Another shot please." John Greenfield handed Erik his glass.

"Of what?"

"Anything."

Erik grunted and went to the bar, opening the bottom drawer. Grabbing a random bottle, he opened the cap and stiffened when a firm hand clasped on his shoulder.

"Can't mix whiskey with vodka," John Greenfield said over him. "Unless you want me very sick."

"I don't want that to happen."

John Greenfield chortled and took the bottle from Erik. "Bah, who cares? I need to forget anyway."

"What are you trying to forget?"

"Promise me that you'll never mention this again." Erik nodded. Before John Greenfield could say, the phone rang again. John Greenfield tensed when Jane Greenfield took the call.

"Dear, it's for you," she called. "It's the doctor."

John Greenfield blew a heavy sigh and set the bottle aside. "Can't you take a message?" he called back. "I don't feel well."

"She says it's important."

"I'll take it upstairs," John Greenfield murmured and tousled Erik's hair. Erik winced and John Greenfield headed for the staircase.

Erik left the bar and stood at the kitchen doorway, watching Jane Greenfield place a pan in the oven. "What's for dinner?" he asked.

"Stuffed peppers," Jane Greenfield replied nonchalantly.

"I'm going to see Raider," Erik announced. "He wants me to pick up some homework."

"Don't be gone too long," Jane Greenfield called. "Dinner will be ready in a half-hour."

"I won't be late, I promise," Erik answered and hurried out the back door.

THIRTY-FIVE

Racing for Raider's house, he reached the complex and knocked frantically on the door. The door opened moments later, revealing a dour-appearing middle-aged man with nape-length dark reddish-brown hair and smoldering brown eyes. Erik recoiled, intimidated by the man who wore a dark sweatshirt and jogging pants underneath an old tan and green Defense Forces uniform jacket.

"Yeah?" the man snapped, glowering at Erik as he folded his arms across his chest.

"Is Raider here?" Erik asked nervously and jammed his hands in his pockets as the middle-aged man's piercing gaze probed him.

"Yeah, in the back..."

The man opened the door wider and Erik entered the small house, finding Raider easily in an overstuffed chair in the parlor. Next to Raider, lay a small box of sewing supplies and Raider held several stickpins between his lips while he sewed a rip in his leather jacket.

"Hey," Erik said softly, nodding to him.

Raider glared up at Erik and removed the pins he held.

"I don't know you," Raider snapped, jamming the pins into the chair's arm. "Commence to steppin', jerkass!"

"I just wanted to ask you something."

"I don't do favors for nobody, not no more."

"Please, Raider," Erik pleaded.

Raider narrowed his eyes at Erik. "Want me to remind ya what you done did to me?" he snarled.

"I'm sorry," Erik murmured and ran his hands through his hair. "How many times do you want me to apologize?"

"Then what the hell ya want?" Raider spat.

"I need some help." Erik avoided his gaze when Raider continued to glower. "It's about someone Mister Greenfield knows, apparently."

"What makes ya think I know?" Raider spat.

"You know a lot of people."

"So? What makes ya think I know the one you're talking 'bout?"

"Mister Greenfield freaked out about someone named Jerry."

Raider shrugged his shoulders. "Wish I could help, but never heard of that guy."

"Jerry?" the man suddenly said. Erik turned around, startled. "Was it Jerry Schumacher?"

Erik swallowed hard when he suddenly found it hard to breathe. "I didn't catch his last name," he answered.

"Oh, is that right?" The man left the room and Raider grunted.

"What is it?" Erik murmured.

"What are you getting at?" Raider grumbled. "What's with all these questions all of a sudden?"

"I'm worried about Mister Greenfield," Erik said softly. "He's having these nervous attacks lately and he's started drinking more..."

"What makes ya think I can help him?"

"Like I said, you know people." Erik shrugged his shoulders. "Besides, I need you to get Chico out of the house. He's making me nervous."

"Oh, that's what ya really came over for, huh?" Raider spat. He set aside the jacket and rose to his feet. "I might have somethin' to help ya, but trash me again and I ain't pullin' my punches next time!"

Erik snorted. "If it makes you happy," he said, rolling his eyes, "then you can slap me around any time you like."

Raider clenched his hands and swung at Erik. Erik flinched when Raider's fist stopped mid-punch, barely connecting with his face.

"This close!" Raider snarled. "You're *this close* to gettin' a big can of whoop-ass today!"

"Hey, I'm not trying to work your nerves here!" Erik put up his hands. "Do you want me on my knees; do you want me to beg?"

"Shut up," Raider spat and shoved Erik aside. "Come on." Raider headed for the kitchen and Erik followed him.

Entering the basement, Raider flipped the switch and descended the staircase. Erik ducked down from the low overhead, squinting to see as the dim orange bulb cast fluxing shadows in the room.

Raider approached an old desk that had several boxes of dusty letters and tattered briefcases with broken locks on them.

"What's all this?" Erik murmured as Raider sifted through the paperwork.

"I think this might be it," Raider muttered as he opened a box, pulling out a stack of envelopes held together by a rubber band. "Hey, check this out." He tossed the stack at Erik and he caught them.

"What's this about?" Erik asked and Raider blew an annoyed sigh.

"Just read the stuff that's on it," Raider ordered sternly. "I gotta see if ya remember, 'cause if you do, then I can ask some folks on our side to help yer ass out. But, I'm not gonna hold my breath since not err'body wants my help these days…"

Erik hunched his shoulders as Raider bristled, drawing out the last comment with an icy glare. He looked down at the envelopes, overcome by shock from upon closer inspection of the papers.

"This is Mister Greenfield's handwriting," Erik said, bewildered. "They're all written in his handwriting and addressed to Melvin Zachary…"

"Yeah," Raider said in a low tone, "they were hella tight then."

Back then, it wasn't so bad…

"*These all have postmarks from nearly twenty years ago,*" Erik thought as he set the stack aside. The pain started behind his eyes as he read the addresses. "*They used to stay in California…*"

Another time, another place…

"But why show me all this?" Erik groused and pulled out one folded yellowed sheet from an envelope. Scanning the writing, he read aloud the title. "*Contrabands that affect Core Irons - information contained herein...*" Erik glanced at the rest then looked up at Raider. "Why do you trust me with this?" he demanded, waving the letter at him. "This one list about Contrabands reads like some old alchemy text."

"Don't be a jackass," Raider snapped irritably.

Erik put it back and pulled out an envelope at random marked with a fifteen-year old postdate. A chilling sensation passed through Erik when he pulled out the paper, noting the date written was also on the day of his birthday.

"*Erik is now four today,*" it read in neat classical script. "*I doubt I can pull myself away. I think I'm starting to care. He is so normal in appearance, in his demeanor, that it's easy to forget that he's not truly normal, like the rest of us, but then again, we are all the same with our various faults...*"

Erik dropped what he held and clutched his chest as his heart skipped a beat. "What does this mean for me?" he cried. "This can't be right; this can't be right at all." Erik staggered as his heart thudded harder in his chest and he struggled to breathe. "Why are you doing this to me? This has to be some cruel joke!"

"I ain't jokin' with ya, Erik," Raider said seriously and pointed at his face. "You see this face? Does it look like I'm laughin'?"

"What is the meaning of this?"

"It means you're going to die soon if ya don't remember!" Raider snapped.

"That's the thing; I *don't*!"

"I see it on your face," Raider accused and poked Erik's chest. "There's somethin' in there working 'round. You look like you're 'bout to puke out yer guts when somebody says or does stuff."

"I couldn't tell you if I did," Erik protested. "Why doesn't anyone believe me?"

"You don't get it, do you?" Raider thundered and stormed away.

"*This has to be wrong,*" Erik thought. "*I was born in...*" He gripped his hair, unable to recall his birth date. "*But the date I used before...!*" The harder he thought, the more frightened he became when he drew a blank.

It's not true, is it? It's all a lie, it is!

"*I'm sure my certificate says so...*" Erik blew a heavy sigh. "*It's just the stress getting to me and mucking my memory! That's why I can't remember!*"

When did we live...? When? Where?

"*I'll have to check, that's all...*" Erik broke out in cold sweat despite his self-assurances. "*Father Greenfield wouldn't lie to me or make false documents, would he...?*"

When did we die...? How? Why?

"*But what if I'm wrong...?*" The tightening in Erik's chest grew worse as he crunched numbers in his mind. "*That can't be right...!*"

Why can't we recall? Why can't we know...?

"*I'm decent when it comes to math and I've never been wrong...*" Erik paled as he dropped his hands to his sides. "*Though by that letter, I'm not sixteen like I thought... I'm twenty!*"

Why is this happening to me?

Erik wavered as the pain in his shoulder radiated strongly and his feet suddenly gave out from beneath him. Striking the floor with a hard thud, Erik's ears rang and his vision grew cloudy.

"Erik?" Raider's voice called from afar. "Erik, get up, man! Get up!"

Erik's body turned numb and the ringing drowned out Raider's voice.

THIRTY-SIX

Erik felt the earth move beneath him and sat up with a start as an explosion rocked the ground in the distance. He looked up and around, finding he was on the ground surrounded by debris and burning trash.

Several paces ahead enclosed by a large gate loomed a large vacant apartment complex, with many of its windows boarded shut. The ground floor's door had been blasted open and fires licked at the crumbling concrete steps leading inside.

Erik staggered to his feet and crouched low when gunfire continued around him and from inside the apartment. He hurried over to the building's side and peered around the corner, finding a large swimming pool in the rear full of swampy algae-filled water, dirt and charred corpses. Further beyond the fence surrounding the apartments were a partially dried creek bed, with pockets of sludge and dirty water.

When the gunfire became sporadic, Erik ran for the building's rear and peered inside the blasted door, finding many slain fighters in black uniforms littered about the corridor, along with destroyed office equipment.

Making his way around the debris, Erik steadily made his way down the hall, glancing into the busted-open apartment doors and finding all manner of home living furnishings destroyed. Most of the studios were raided clear of anything of value.

Tripping over his steps, Erik glanced down at a body of a soldier in a navy uniform with a machete lodged into his head, blocking his path for the stairs. Erik yanked out the weapon, then immediately closed the corpse's blank eyes staring off into space with his fingers.

Hearing the gunfire moving upstairs, Erik hurried across the floor toward the door and pushed it open, listening to the men's footsteps and shouts as they continued to clear floor by floor. Erik kept his back pressed against the wall as he slowly ascended the staircase.

On the second floor, he found several men in black uniforms slaughtered in the corridor, riddled with bullets. Erik passed other rooms blocked with debris and entered a room at the end with its door blasted open. Peering inside, he found a dead man in a gray suit slumped against the wall, holding a stick of unlit dynamite in his stiff hand.

Kicking the trash out the way, Erik came across a large crate full of dynamite, flares, an ash-filled pot, several oily rags, bottles of lighter fluid, and boxes of matches. Erik grabbed a handful of sticks and a few flares, stuffing them in his pocket. Taking several boxes of matches, he put them in his other pocket and stiffened when he heard a clatter.

Immediately standing on the defensive, Erik silently made his way for the rear bedroom. Pushing open the door with his machete, he abruptly ducked back out when a spray of buckshot blasted at him.

"Leave me alone!" a voice cried. "I'm not the one you want..."

"Who are you?" Erik asked. "I don't want to kill you... I'm just trying to remember where I am."

"Who are you?"

"I can't remember."

"Let me see you and have your hands to the sky!"

"Don't shoot me!"

"Let's see you!"

Erik put up his hands, holding his machete over his head as he slowly stepped into the room. A young woman with dark red hair and indigo eyes wearing a navy uniform stood behind an overturned bed, wielding a shotgun in one hand. Her other arm and shoulder were tied in blood-soaked bed sheets.

"I'm not here to kill you," Erik said as the woman gasped and backed away, clearly frightened.

"Why else would they send you?" she shrieked.

"Who are you; what is this place?"

"This was company housing for retired Gateway scientists..."

"So why are they razing it down to the ground?"

"Our use ran out."

"That's horrible!" Erik turned back when he heard heavy footsteps storming the stairwell. "They're returning!"

"I don't have any more guns..."

"You stay back here," Erik directed. "I'll fend them off!"

Racing back for the parlor, Erik set aside his machete and rummaged through the box, taking a bottle of lighter fluid and a nearby rag. He twisted off the cap and stuffed the towel inside then threw it out the door, spraying fluids everywhere.

"What was that?" a voice called.

"There's some lifers over here!" called another.

Taking a flare from his pocket and the box of matches, Erik lit the flare and tossed it as well. The sparking signal struck the liquid and the bottle blew up, throwing flames down the corridor.

Several men shouted in terror at the sudden blaze and retreated upstairs.

"Come on," the young woman called. Erik picked up the machete and ran back for the bedroom, watching her break the window with the shotgun's stock. "Grab the ammo," she ordered and Erik scanned the room. He noticed a messenger bag full of shells near the bedpost and ran over, picking it up. "You can't handle the reinforcements with what you have!"

"We're on the second floor!" Erik cried. "You'll break your neck!"

"I can't have them kill me; I'd rather risk it!"

Erik handed her the bag and the woman slipped it over her shoulder, then crawled out onto the window's ledge. She took a leap and Erik ran forward, watching her land with a splash into the pool below, barely missing the edge.

Erik crawled through the window and paused on the ledge as a white sport utility vehicle suddenly barreled up, smashing through the rear gate. Gunfire from the roof rained down from above and the car screeched to a halt before flipping over into the pool. Erik jumped down, crashing into the water.

Erik tread water, noticing the driver who wore a dark suit slumped aside with a blank lifeless stare, dead from a large borehole between the eyes.

The passenger who wore jeans and denim jacket frantically kicked at the windshield. Erik waded over and slammed the machete against the glass, cracking it.

The glass burst open and the young man pulled himself out. Both immediately surfaced and the young man cried out in pain when struck by a bullet in the neck. He fell back, instantly sinking into the cloudy water.

Erik swam for the deep end where the cluster of corpses lay and dove underneath, waiting for the bullets piercing the water to end.

After several moments, he crested and quickly climbed out. The wounded woman with the bag and shotgun raced for the gate on the far side around the building, pulling aside a large part of the gate cut open from the bottom.

Running after her, Erik slowed his stride when she turned away once finding her potential exit blocked by overgrown shrubbery.

"This way," she said and took off for another part of the gate partially bent from a downed oak leaning against it.

Hearing shouts, Erik looked around, spotting several gunmen descending from the roof with cables and zip lines. Other gunfighters ran from the complex's other side untouched by fire. Erik followed the woman who scrambled over the tree and made a leap into the creek below.

Erik increased his speed and clamored up the tree, climbing up branches and crawled to the edge before leaping off. He struck the ground hard and everything went dark at once.

Erik's eyes snapped open and he sat up, sucking in a sharp breath as his shoulder ached dully. His face stung and he touched his jaw, running his fingers across split skin and a line of dried blood.

"*Another cut...*" Erik wondered and winced when touched. "*How did I get that one this time?*"

Looking up, Erik faced Raider who stood over him, holding a cutlass over his shoulder. The sword had a dark blue handle with gold tassels capped on the pommel's end. In Raider's free hand, he held a dark blue scabbard with gold accents.

"You okay, man?" Raider inquired.

"Why do you ask...?" Erik answered and Raider shook his head. "How long was I out for?"

"A few minutes... I tried wakin' ya up, but, man... out cold hellas..."

"Was it a seizure or something?"

"Nah, nothin' like that."

"Then what was it?" Erik scrambled to his feet. "Did I stop breathing or something?"

"Naw, nothin' heavy like that."

"So what's with the sword then?" Erik stepped back as Raider pointed the blade's tip at him and the silver steel glinted in the orange light.

"Don't lie to me, man," Raider growled. "You been actin' real shady lately and you keep pissin' me off!"

"How am I acting toward you?" Erik yelled. "It seems you just want an excuse to beat me around!"

"So stop fighting me!"

"You first!"

Raider jammed the scabbard into the side of Erik's neck and Erik stepped aside when Raider followed with the swing of his cutlass.

Turning out, Erik caught the blade between his elbow and side then stepped back, striking Raider in the face with a back fist with his other hand. Raider staggered back and Erik ducked then turned, facing him. He leaned out of a hard blow as Raider slammed the sword into the desk, splitting the wood.

Raider growled, struggling to remove the blade embedded into the writing table.

"Incredible," Erik murmured. "Never knew you to be that strong."

Flaring in anger, Raider glared at Erik and smashed the sheath upside his head. Erik staggered back, stunned and Raider knocked him aside with the scabbard before he had a chance to react.

Erik stumbled over his steps and Raider shoved the sheath's end into Erik's chest. The blow's force threw him head over heels on the floor.

"You dumb ass!" Raider screamed and dropped the scabbard. It clattered to the floor at his feet and he heaved for breath, growing enraged. "I could kill you--!"

"Then why don't you?" Erik wheezed as he staggered to his feet. "If I keep attacking you during periods where I blank out, why not? Apparently I'm some kind of monster!"

Raider let out a frustrated scream and kicked the desk. "I can't..." he grumbled. "I just can't..."

"Then what's your deal?" Erik demanded, clenching his hands. "You're the best fighter I know! Why not cream me by now; why hold back?"

"Because you can kill any chump with one hit!" Raider spat. Erik stiffened, stunned at his words. "You could kill *me* if you wanted to…" Raider kicked the desk again in agitation. "But I can't let you…"

"So you fight me back…" Erik tensed when Raider kicked harder at the table then grabbed the edges as he leaned forward, struggling to breathe. "You fight me back to live?"

"I don't wanna die for the wrong reasons," Raider muttered. "I don't wanna die fighting you."

"I'm sorry for making those feelings come back," Erik said softly. "I don't know what truly happened and again, I'm sorry." He turned on his heel and paused once Raider left the desk, storming over to him.

"Hold on," Raider ordered, grabbing him firmly by the arm.

"What is it?" Erik asked nervously, glancing back at him.

"Did you find anything that had stuff on it like C-O-one-ninety-two or whatever?"

Erik nodded. "I found a folder like that," he admitted, "but Melvin took it away from me before I had the chance to read it." Raider's face became unreadable as he let go. "Well…?"

"I dunno if I should tell you this, then…"

"Why not?" Erik poked Raider's chest. "Tell me what's going on here!"

"What's going on is that you ain't got long to live."

"Don't lie to me, Raider."

"Do you have a mark anywhere on you then?"

"What kind of question is that?"

"The kind that you answer!" Raider retorted.

"What's the point of you asking something like that?"

"Just answer the damn question!"

"No!"

"I don't believe you!"

Raider advanced and Erik backed away, ducking out of a swing. Raider swung again and his hard jab connected, smashing into Erik's jaw. Erik grunted, spiraling back on the floor.

Raider kicked Erik in the side once he landed, flipping him over on his front. Raider pounced on Erik's back before he could get up and held an arm under his chin, pulling back as Erik reached up blindly, trying to bat him off.

"Have you lost your mind?" Erik screeched.

"Sit still!" Raider growled and punched the back of Erik's head, leaving him dazed. He ripped at his collar, tearing off his shirt with his free hand.

Erik bucked, throwing Raider off and hurried to his feet, panting hard for breath as Raider struck the desk and growled. The cutlass clattered off the table and struck the floorboard with a twang.

"What's wrong with you?" Erik yelled as Raider stood.

"That's what I thought," Raider muttered.

"What are you talking about?" Raider pulled out of his shirt and tossed it to Erik. "*What did he see?*" Erik thought as he caught it and changed clothing.

"I can't tell ya anything else if you don't know what the fuck's going on!" Raider shouted. "Get with it and remember already, Erik; you're the last line of defense here!"

"I can't if Melvin took it away!" Erik snapped. "I keep trying and it's getting harder - I'm losing my damn mind!"

"Them papers don't matter. You gotta feel, really *feel* it in yer head, in yer heart! Without it, we're all fucked!"

"What the hell am I supposed to remember?" Erik screamed. "Everyone keeps telling me that!" Raider harshly slapped him, whipping his face to the side. Erik rubbed at his stinging cheek, glaring back at Raider.

"That's enough with that shit," Raider spat. "I'm tired of hearin' it!"

"Get used to it," Erik growled. "I'm trying my best here!"

"Then try harder!"

"You keep smacking me around and I might not remember a damn thing at all!"

"You're wasting my time. Get the fuck outta here!"

"Not happening!"

"I told you; get the fuck outta my face, man!"

Growing irritated, Erik stood his ground, unwilling to leave his place in the room. "You apparently know more than you're letting on," he spat, "so until you tell me, I'm not leaving here!"

Raider's expression turned irate as he yanked the sword out the floor and picked up the fallen scabbard. "Don't make me change my mind!" Raider thundered. "I will cut yer ass in half!"

"Whatever; stay sore at me," Erik muttered. "I'm going home." He scooped up the stack of envelopes. "I'll see you at school, right?" Erik received no answer in return and headed for the stairs.

"Don't worry about your homework and shit," Raider called after Erik. "I got it covered."

"Thanks," Erik called over his shoulder and ascended the steps.

"Whatever…"

"What has him so cranky?" mused Erik as he entered the kitchen. *"There's more to it than me merely worrying him."* He came to a stop when he faced the man in the Defense Forces jacket sitting at the table with a bottle of beer.

"Don't mind me," the man grumbled. "Lock the door on your way out."

"Yes, Sir," Erik muttered and headed for the door. He put on the bottom lock and stepped out into the cool spring evening air, then shut the door behind him. Erik made the trek home, overwhelmed with worry.

THIRTY-SEVEN

Returning to the Greenfield residen☐ce, Erik left the letters on the end table near the staircase where the phone used to be. He entered the dining room and took a seat at the dinner table. Erik grew ill at ease once he picked up his fork, pushing around the food on his plate left for him.

John Greenfield sat across from Erik at the head of the table with a bottle of bourbon and a lowball glass. His blazer hung from the back of his chair and his dinner lay untouched.

"Don't they notice I came in with a different shirt than what I left with?" Erik mused, eating his meal in silence. *"Don't they notice I have a cut on my face?"* Shaking his head, he mulled over various methods of sneaking food to Chicago who slept in his room, only to stiffen when he realized all his ideas would fail. *"It wouldn't be long before the Greenfields find him and ask him a ton of questions!"* Erik clenched his fork, overcome by panic. *"There's no way I can keep him hidden in this house for long... What a terrible idea!"*

"Erik, dear, are you all right?" Jane Greenfield interjected, scattering his thoughts. "You're picking at your food."

"Oh!" Erik answered and laughed nervously, blushing. "I'm just thinking about some things."

"Did you complete your homework?" John Greenfield inquired. "Your friend Caelan was supposed to send you the work."

Erik glanced sharply at John Greenfield who had a pleasant expression on his face. There mere sight of him made the pit of Erik's stomach turn. *"What is with you?"* he thought in disgust. *"You're acting so fake!"* Erik cleared his throat when a lump formed. "I finished them at his house," he lied. "I'll pick them up tomorrow on my way to school."

"Continue to do good work, Son." John Greenfield finished his drink and set down his glass then left the table, heading upstairs.

Erik glanced to Jane Greenfield who had a pleasant expression on her face and glowered at her.

"What is it, honey?" Jane Greenfield asked innocently. "Why are you looking at me like that?"

"I don't feel well," Erik grumbled.

"Is the food too spicy? I decided to try something different."

"Stuffed peppers *and* grilled chicken with salsa *and* grilled vegetables?" Erik shook his head. "It's too much, Mother. Are you trying to feed an army?"

Jane Greenfield giggled. "I could feed an army, I suppose."

Erik put down his fork when the turning sensation in his stomach worsened. He rubbed at his face and studied his surroundings.

Erik looked down at the walnut table with the dark stained finish, seeing his reflection in the gloss. He turned his gaze toward the other painted white oak chair, with curved arms and a carved back fashioned into leaves. Erik frowned at the white seat cushion and swallowed hard when he noticed the white undecorated porcelain dishes they ate from.

"Is the food good?" Jane Greenfield inquired.

"It's fine, Mother," Erik replied. "Tell me again, where did you get these plates from?"

"I read about white chinaware used for special occasions in that one home décor magazine," Jane Greenfield answered. "I thought why not use nice plates for mealtime?"

Erik clutched the intricately carved table leg nearby to keep his left hand from shaking. "*Has this woman lost her mind?*" he wondered, taken aback.

"Is something bothering you, honey?"

Erik ignored her, glancing into the kitchen. He couldn't tell if the white refrigerator with chrome accents was really old or made to look that way. It contrasted against the brushed black stainless steel multi-burner stove and trash compactor. The scheme matched the checkered black and white linoleum.

"*Why hadn't I noticed all this before?*" Erik took note of the counters made of ebony with white marble tops. The cupboards, also made of ebony, had simple solid steel handles edged with pearl-accented caps. He suddenly found it hard to breathe.

"Erik, honey," Jane Greenfield pressed, "is something the matter?"

"Yes," Erik murmured and turned his attention back to her.

Jane Greenfield sat with her hands in her lap, smiling gently at Erik. She wore a simple beige dress and a small string of brown pearls about her neck. Jane Greenfield's skin appeared paler from the deep red lipstick on her lips and light rose rogue on her cheeks.

"Why are you staring at me like that?"

Erik said nothing, watching Jane Greenfield nervously tuck a strand of her bobbed light brown hair behind her ear. Her decorated bobby pins laced with tiger's eye and amber beads loosened and she adjusted them. After fixing it into place, one of her matching pearl earrings clattered on the table.

"Oh, my," she muttered. "The backing's fallen out."

"How old are the earrings?" Erik wondered aloud.

"Oh, much older than you, honey." She set the earring aside. "Why don't you tell me what's bothering you?"

"Mother, please don't worry," Erik said and cleared his throat. "Is Father all right?"

"Yes," Jane Greenfield answered warmly. "He just needs some time alone to think."

Erik tried to resume his meal in silence and coughed, almost choking on his food when he looked down at his own plate. His hands shook when he noticed the flatware was much too fine for average meal consumption, crafted from polished silver with handles intricately decorated with leaves.

Erik picked up the glass and swiftly set it down before he dropped it, noticing the tumbler was not truly glass, but blown crystal. He struggled to breathe, as everything in the room seemed to press against him.

"If you don't feel well," Jane Greenfield said gently, "why don't you lie down for awhile?"

"Is he off thinking because of someone named Jerry Schumacher?" Erik asked moments later. He heard the fork clatter against the plate and looked up as Jane Greenfield stared at him in shock and disbelief.

"How do you know Jerry?" she queried, almost breathless. "Is he somebody important?"

Jane Greenfield tried to pick up her fallen fork, only to grasp at air when her hands twitched. She quickly set her hands in her lap instead, flustered. "Erik, honey..."

Erik's appetite faded and he shut his eyes, trying to gain his bearings. *"Jerry, Jerry Schumacher, Schumacher..."* Erik ruminated. *"Who is he and why do I feel bad about it? Is he related to Justin? Is Justin Schumacher–?"*

Erik's eyes snapped open and he rose to his feet. "May I be excused?" Erik requested.

"Yes, you may."

"Mother, may I ask you something?"

"Sure, honey."

"Is Jerry Schumacher related to Justin?"

Jane Greenfield paled. "Are you sure you're sound?" she questioned instead.

"Please don't ask me again," Erik snapped.

When Jane Greenfield made no motion to respond, he promptly picked up his plate and took it into the kitchen.

Searching the cupboards, Erik came across glass containers of various sizes for the remainders stashed inside. The urge to vomit came strongly and he quickly shoved his plate into the refrigerator then raced for the bathroom upstairs.

"This is too unreal!" Erik realized, heaving into the toilet. *"Why does everything feel so fake?"*

Why is everything presented so perfectly... in black and white no less?

The light switched on and Erik turned, spotting John Greenfield standing near the door.

"What's the matter, Son?" he probed. "Did dinner disagree with you?" Erik shook his head, unable to answer. John Greenfield stepped in, towering over him. "I think I know what it is..."

"What is it?" Erik moaned, facing the toilet and waiting on the wave of nausea to end.

John Greenfield ran a gentle hand through Erik's hair, sighing heavily. Reaching over Erik, he pulled against the mirror's edge above him, revealing a medicine cabinet. Erik sat back on his knees, noticing several unmarked amber bottles two inches high filling the small shelves.

"What's all that?" Erik pressed.

You know what they are!

John Greenfield grabbed the containers and knelt beside Erik. Setting them aside, he opened one and poured its powdered contents down the toilet. Erik raised an eyebrow as John Greenfield continued with the others.

Erik took a random flask and uncapped it, then poured silvery-white powder into his hand. He dipped a finger and tasted a bit, finding it had no flavor. His tongue burned slightly and Erik spat in the toilet, grimacing.

"What kind of medicine is this?" Erik insisted and John Greenfield stayed silent as he continued emptying the powders. Growing uneasy when he received no answer, Erik brushed off his hand and emptied the ampoule. Turning to John

Greenfield, Erik grabbed him by the arms, shaking him. "Tell me," he commanded, "what's going on; what does this mean?"

"Emerald Dust, Fair Jewel, Star Ruby, Sapphire Shot, Silver Snow..." John Greenfield finally said in a dead tone.

"What does that mean?" Erik shouted. "What do they do?"

"They are all terrible things... just terrible, utterly horrible things." John Greenfield said no more and pried off Erik's grip.

That shit is poison!

Erik sat there, dumbfounded when John Greenfield pulled the handle, flushing everything down the drain.

"Why would you have that; are you telling me that it's poison?" Erik snapped. "Are you trying to kill me?" John Greenfield rose to his feet and stalked out. "I'm talking to you, Jerry Schumacher!"

John Greenfield suddenly came to a pause and whirled around, his face drained of color. "Where did you hear that name?" he demanded.

"Who is he?" Erik snapped back and picked up an amber bottle as he stood. "Is this stuff the reason why my memory's so bad?" He threw it at John Greenfield and John Greenfield caught it before it crashed out in the hall. "Is it why I'm hallucinating all the time?"

"Hallucinations?"

"Yes, Father, I'm seeing and hearing stuff!" Erik yelled. "I'm losing my mind!"

"Why didn't you say anything to me before?"

"I just did!"

"Do you want me to make a doctor's appointment?"

Erik leaned against the sink and ran his hands through his hair, moaning. "I don't know," he mewed.

"Are the voices telling you to do bad things?"

"No," Erik answered. "But if they were, it'd be easy to commit me, wouldn't it?"

"What are they saying to you?"

"They're telling me to remember."

John Greenfield clutched tightly to the bottle he held. "Anything else?" he asked weakly.

Erik lost his footing and sank to the floor. "Why is this happening to me?" he cried and held his head. "I just want to be normal!"

"You're normal, Son," John Greenfield said softly. "You're plenty normal."

"But why am I having horrible nightmares about people trying to kill me, over and over, again and again?" The bottle broke in John Greenfield's hand and Erik's eyes widened at the sight of blood running between his fingers. "Father!" he cried.

"Don't worry about me." John Greenfield gave a strained smile. "I'll worry about me." He walked away, returning to the master bedroom.

Erik stood and leaned against the sink. Turning toward the medicine cabinet, he looked at the mirror and gasped when he saw his altered reflection instead. Erik let out a frustrated scream and punched the glass, cracking it. Many other variants appeared in the cracks of the glass, smirking back at Erik.

"Stop lying to me!" Erik screamed.

Why would we lie to you?

Erik ran out the bathroom and entered the master bedroom, finding John Greenfield sitting on his bed's edge with a first-aid kit open on the nightstand. John Greenfield held a pair of tweezers between his teeth as he poked at his eye with his left hand, removing a contact lens. Perched atop his head, rest a pair of gray plastic wide-framed glasses.

"When have you worn contacts?" Erik inquired.

"For some time now," John Greenfield muttered, setting the lens in a container.

Putting his glasses on, he unbuttoned his shirtsleeve on his right arm and rolled it up to his elbow. John Greenfield then took the tweezers and concentrated on pulling out the glass from his clenched shut right hand, putting the shards aside in the kit's lid.

"Do you need any help, Father?" Erik inquired.

"I'm fine," John Greenfield spat.

"Are your eyes bothering you?"

"They burn a little."

Erik approached offside and John Greenfield looked up. "What's going to happen to me?" Erik demanded.

"Let's not discuss that right now," John Greenfield answered then returned to his task.

Erik frowned when his chest hurt at the sight of John Greenfield. He noticed several strands of hair came loose from his pompadour and hung in his eyes. Erik reached out, pushing the hair back in place. "Have you always worn your hair long?" he queried.

"I always have," John Greenfield replied.

"Have you worn it down at all?"

"I used to."

Erik sat beside John Greenfield and took his wrist, opening the stiffened curled fingers. John Greenfield blew a hard sigh through his nose and continued picking out the bloodied glass.

"Are you sick too?" Erik probed after several moments of silence between them.

"Why do you ask?"

"You suffer from what mother calls 'nervous attacks', right?"

"I guess you can say that."

"Is it hereditary? Are we both crazy?"

John Greenfield snorted. "Yes, Son, we're both crazy," he said wryly. "We're a danger to everyone around us."

"What's with that response?" Erik snapped. "This is serious!"

"I also suffer from bad dreams... Terribly awful ones."

"What is it you dream about?"

"Hurting other people.

Erik drew a shallow breath, unsure what to say.

John Greenfield smiled. "It's not what you think, Son," he answered. "I don't enjoy it at all - in fact, I feel guilty about it."

"Why would you dream about something like that?"

"Let's not talk about it anymore."

Erik sat with John Greenfield as he finished taking out the amber glass, then helped him pour on the hydrogen peroxide. Grabbing for the gauze bandage, John Greenfield shook his head.

"What?" Erik protested, raising an eyebrow.

"I want the rubbing alcohol," John Greenfield stated.

"But it'll burn like crazy!" Erik yelped, appalled. "Wasn't the peroxide enough?"

"I want to make sure it's clean," John Greenfield growled.

Erik grunted and grabbed the bottle, unscrewing it for him. He handed it to John Greenfield and held open his hand as he poured the liquid on. John Greenfield ground his teeth and shut his eyes when he broke out in cold sweat, shuddering in agony.

Erik grabbed the bottle before it fell out of John Greenfield's limp hand when he slumped forward, unconscious. Pushing him back on the bed, Erik set the alcohol aside on the nightstand and took the gauze, wrapping John Greenfield's right hand.

John Greenfield groaned, slowly coming to and Erik stiffened when John Greenfield gripped his wrist with his injured hand. Erik clenched his teeth from the crushing pressure, trying not to cry out.

"Son," John Greenfield moaned. "Will you forgive me?"

"What?" Erik tried to pull his arm free and whimpered when John Greenfield refused to let go. "What do you want me to forgive you for?"

"For all the terrible, horrible things I've caused."

"What was so terrible?" Erik strained to hear as John Greenfield muttered something inaudible. He jerked against John Greenfield's hand. "Come again?" he asked in exasperation.

"Will you come wake me when the nightmares end?"

"I don't understand... I think you're delirious."

"They're destroying your world slowly... piece by piece until there's nothing left!"

Erik yanked at his wrist and cried out when the pressure increased, forcing his arm numb. "Father!" Erik cried. "Please, let me go!"

"I don't want to dream anymore..."

Erik sagged to his knees. "Yes, I will," he moaned. "I'll try my best..." John Greenfield's grip immediately loosened and Erik snatched away his arm, cradling it close to his body.

Staggering to his feet, Erik returned to his room and shut the door behind him, slumping against the panel.

THIRTY-EIGHT

Chicago sat at the student desk with the stack of letters, pouring over them. He glanced up when he heard Erik groan in distress.

"*Algo pasa?*" Chicago asked as Erik shuffled over to his bed and sank on the edge, staring off into dead space.

"Do I look that bad?" Erik murmured.

"You look like you saw something that spooked you."

"They're trying to kill me..." Erik blew a heavy sigh and shut his eyes as he fell back on the mattress. "I don't know why..."

"What are you going on about?"

"I thought he cared too much to do that..."

"Hey, snap out of it!" Erik felt a hand on his shoulder and opened his eyes, glancing up at Chicago who looked down at him with a worried expression.

"What is it?"

"Just be cool, okay?" Chicago withdrew his hand and took a step back. "If you go *loco* on me..."

"I'm fine." Erik gave a weak smile and Chicago frowned, unbelieving.

"You sure?"

"I am."

Chicago grunted and returned to the desk. Erik sat up and glanced at his mirror, finding his counterpart standing there. He leaned against the mirror's edge, picking at his nails.

I don't believe you.

"Can I do this?" Erik complained.

Can you? The young man shrugged his shoulders. *Or will you?*

"Can I really do this?"

The question is: will you do this?

Erik clenched his hands. "If it makes Mister Greenfield stop hurting, then I will."

Then wake up, Ferdian!

"Hey," Chicago said to Erik, tossing an envelope his way and Erik caught it. "Read that back to me."

Erik removed the letter and swallowed his unease at once recognizing the handwriting written on Gen-Tech's official letterhead. Several blacked-out names and dates with permanent ink pervaded throughout the letter. *"More of Father Greenfield's letters..."* he mused. *"Why would Chico have me read this?"*

"Well, you gonna read it or what?" Chicago snapped.

Erik sighed and read its contents aloud. *"Sixteenth October ... Head Scientist received signal after word was sent about installed explosives escaping detection sent to the lab. Technical Assistant confirmed the signal placed and Secondary Scientist resumed communications with Product Number CO-191-A. The product proved defective in testing and ordered destroyed. Classified Record CO-191-A Project Data removed for creation of the altered project, CO-192-A.*

375

Samples taken were to be re-analyzed and to start project COS-100. AMASTCOMS requests needed assistance due to the War..."

"Doesn't that jog anything in that empty head of yours?" Chicago asked, cutting him off.

Erik glared up at him. "What does this mean for me?" he protested. "I don't understand, especially with all the blackouts!"

"Don't you remember?" Chicago pressed.

"If I hear that one more time...!" Erik clenched his teeth and shook his head when Chicago shot him a cross glare.

"Remember that war they fought back then?" Chicago growled. "Remember when they had all those Air Corps pilots check us out? We were sent on the ground to destroy those scientists who defected and tried to blow up the Agency's equipment!"

Erik tossed the letter back to Chicago. "No way; you're not making sense!" he yelped. "You're talking out your butt!"

"Remember, Erik! I worked with you in the same unit!"

"You got me confused with somebody else!"

"The Agency's trying to use us and program us to make us do very bad things. They tinker on us because of that C-O-one-ninety-two-A stuff!"

"Shut your face!" Erik wailed. "You're talking crazy; you're completely nuts!"

"Yeah? Then read this." Chicago handed Erik another letter and he glanced over it. Erik swallowed hard when he recognized the date despite its year marked out.

"*Eighteenth March... Dr. Fleisher and I visit PN03-CO192-A. His scores are low despite doing well in the combination tests,*" Erik read, "*The 3S-A factors are inconclusive at this time. PN03-CO192-A keeps requesting release given that he is a no-sponsor.*"

"March Eighteenth," Erik murmured and dropped the letter. "That's when I was adopted by the Greenfields..."

"Did you find these letters stashed in your father's desk somewhere?" Chicago asked, interrupting him.

"No," Erik answered faintly. "Raider gave these to me..."

"If he knows you, then he probably worked with you too."

"I've always been friends with him... I think..."

"Don't you see? This runs deeper than you think!"

"This is insane," Erik murmured and tossed the other papers aside.

"Still means nothing, huh?" Chicago asked sourly.

"Shut your face," Erik growled back. "I've got enough to deal with on my own!"

"Remember when they came to visit?"

"Who?"

"Doctor Schumacher and Doctor Schnell and Mister Petra!"

Erik shut his eyes and clutched his head when the pain returned full force. "It doesn't mean anything!" he cried. "It's just some lousy letter!"

"Your reality is *dead wrong*! Fake!" Chicago thundered. "Erik, you gotta wake up!"

"I'm not listening, Chico," Erik wailed, clamping his hands over his ears. "I think you're lying to me anyway... how can you know all of what's going on and I don't?"

377

"How can I lie when these things are written in your old man's hand?" Chicago bellowed. "Why? Because I swore to *never, ever forget!*" He stormed over and snatched Erik's hands down at his sides. "They tried to erase my mind too, but I couldn't let them get away with it! And yet *you did!*" Erik shoved him away and Chicago struck the desk. "And for what; so that you can pretend to have a nice happy life?" He snorted in disgust. "Look, even your past is totally fake! They *planted* that mess in your head, Erik!"

Erik quickly stood, glaring at Chicago. "Shut up!" he growled. "You don't know a damn thing!"

"I know *you* and you worked with me! We worked together! How can you forget me? I thought we were friends!" Erik gave Chicago a lost expression and a dark cast masked Chicago's face. He shrugged his shoulders. "Fine, don't believe me," he growled, "but I bet those dreams are making you sweat at night!"

He's right and there's no denying it!

Erik stiffened and glared at the mirror, only to face his own reflection. "*Why am I afraid?*" he thought. "*What does it mean...?*"

All those times you woke up thrashing... the white walls, the bright lights, the antiseptic, the restraints on the table...

Erik shuddered, overwhelmed as the chilling fear grew immensely.

"You have to remember before we're all dead!" Chicago screeched. "Get it through your empty head!"

"Listen, Chico," Erik said exasperatedly, "I'm virtually clueless about this whole thing! I can't help it if my memory's trashed!"

"Damn it!" Chicago roared, his face darkening in anger as he punched the desktop. "Why can't you understand any of this?"

"Because it *blows my mind*!" Erik complained and rubbed at his temples, taking in a deep breath. "I just can't get it!"

Chicago stormed to Erik and pulled him forward by the collar. Erik cringed, facing an irate Chicago whose brown eyes glowed dimly in red.

"You'd better get it together!" Chicago snarled and threw him down. Erik struck the side of the mattress and fell to the floor. "Damn this and everything!"

"Please, Chico, don't get angry again!" Erik yelped as Chicago turned away from him, balling his hands into tight fists.

"I don't want to die by their hands!" Erik quickly got up and rushed Chicago, grabbing his arm and turned him around before he struck out. Chicago pushed Erik away, wiping at his tear-stained face with the heels of his hand. "I want to live," he moaned, his voice cracking. "Before it's too late!"

"I'm sorry," Erik said softly. "I don't..."

"We have to stop it from happening..." Chicago pulled away and stomped toward the bedroom window. He leaned against the pane, looking outside.

"Why are you being so vague?" Erik complained.

"You're not listening," Chicago grumbled. "I might as well be talking to a wall!"

Erik looked toward the mirror and saw his counterpart standing there, leaning against the interior edge with arms folded across his chest.

You know what to do about it.

"I don't know if I can..."

More like if you don't know if you <u>want</u> to.

"But what if I fail?"

His double smirked. *You can always wake up!*

Erik returned to his bed and fell back, staring at the ceiling. "*I need to wake up,*" he thought. "*But how does one wake up from a dream they're already awake in?*" Erik glanced at his side, facing his own reflection instead. "*Do I go to sleep and hope to wake again in the dreamless world?*"

Can you play the same role forever?

Erik sighed heavily. "I don't know if that's possible," he murmured. "It won't be perfect..."

There's only one sure thing in this life, which is death...

"I can't stand it anymore!"

Sometimes you might have to hurt before you get better.

"There's got to be another way..."

Erik broke out in a cold sweat, disturbed when he received no answer in return.

THIRTY-NINE

Erik felt a light hand on his shoulder, shaking him firmly which brought him out of the dreamless world of sleep. He felt his back spasm and jerked as he sat up, gasping.

Weighed down by panic when he realized his vision blurred and the sounds around him were distorted and hollow within the fuzzy world, Erik clenched his hands that immediately burned.

"Erik, honey, is everything all right?" Jane Greenfield's voice called from afar. Erik felt a warm touch to his face and rapidly grabbed for the hand in a strong hold.

He heard a mild cry and Erik blinked, forcing the blurry beige mass to fade and change into a worried Jane Greenfield. She pulled away as Erik let go. "Mother, did I hurt you?" he asked.

"No..." Jane Greenfield gave a nervous smile and ran a hand through her bobbed hair. "It's just... well it's just that you never reacted so violently like this."

Erik touched his face where her hand had been and frowned when his fingertips brushed against the cut he sustained from the night before against Raider. "I guess I had a bad dream," he muttered and put his feet onto the floor as he ran a hand through his hair. "I don't remember it, though."

"Are you sure you're not worried about anything?" Erik gasped when he realized Chicago was no longer there and most likely hidden himself somewhere in the house.

"I'm fine," Erik said in false cheer and stood, clenching his hands at his sides to keep them from shaking.

"You can always come and talk to us."

"I'll tell you if I need to." Hoping his empty words would boost her confidence in him, Erik swallowed hard, uneasy when Jane Greenfield still appeared troubled.

"Your breakfast is waiting for you in the oven," she murmured and Erik nodded. "Why don't you get washed up first?"

Erik said nothing and headed toward his bureau, sifting through the drawers acting as if he were searching for something to wear. Hearing her leave the room moments later, Erik sighed, suddenly tired and gripped the dresser's edge, grimacing from the pain in his dully-aching shoulder.

"Hey, are you taking a shower or what?" Chicago asked moments later.

Erik turned, startled as he faced Chicago who padded into the room, rubbing a towel over his shaggy dark hair while wearing another towel tucked about his waist. The lotus charm necklace he wore hung dully around his neck.

"Oh, hey Chico," Erik greeted.

"The water's cold, but I highly doubt you can feel it."

"I can feel the water," Erik admitted, "though it feels like it doesn't stick to me; I'm almost like a fish."

Chicago chuckled. "Well, I'm the opposite -- I'm a complete raisin when it comes to water, but I wouldn't know if it was hot or not."

Erik nodded and gestured toward his dresser. "You can borrow my things if you want."

"Nah, I can't do that." Chicago waved a hand at Erik. "Besides, you're a stick compared to me!"

"You're about my size, Chico!" Erik protested and gave him a critical look, taking note of his short stocky frame. "How much do you weigh?"

"About one-fifty-five."

"So you're ten pounds heavier than me. How tall are you?"

"Five-six, last I checked."

Erik shrugged his shoulders. "I don't think you're that big of a guy," he replied, "besides, muscle weighs more than fat." Chicago laughed robustly in response. "What's so hilarious?"

"There's no way in Hell I can fit your clothes," Chicago protested. "I might as well go naked."

"Then go naked for all I care."

Chicago laughed even harder and Erik grabbed for his articles then trooped across the hall.

Erik grit his teeth in pain as the ache in his shoulder increased. After his shower, he stepped out and stared at himself in the mirror, sighing as he appeared satisfactory for the most part.

Touching his face, he ran his fingers over the raised scars from the cuts he received, with one down his jaw and the other across his cheek then turned partway as he examined his shoulder, noticing a reddish-black blemish resembling a second-degree burn.

"Where did this come from?" Erik murmured at his reflection and half-expected his counterpart to appear, slightly disturbed and relieved he still faced his bland self. After pulling into his jeans, he heard a shout followed by a loud crash in his bedroom.

Erik grabbed for his shirt and raced into the hall. He stopped dead in his tracks at his doorway, finding John Greenfield holding firmly onto the mast axe while standing over Chicago dressed in his clothes.

"Have you come here to hurt Erik?" John Greenfield thundered. Chicago cowered in the room's corner, frightened by the man's presence. "Why are you here?"

"Father don't hurt him," Erik called. "I invited him over..." John Greenfield glared back at Erik.

"That's right," Chicago interjected. "I'm a friend of his and I was just leaving!" He hurried for the door and John Greenfield grabbed Chicago's arm, yanking him back.

"Please, don't hurt him!" Erik pleaded as John Greenfield threw Chicago down to the floor and pointed the axe's edge at his throat.

"Who are you?" John Greenfield growled. "Tell me your name!"

Chicago wheezed for breath as the color drained from his face. "Ramone..." he rasped.

"Ramone..." John Greenfield muttered and gripped the axe tightly in hand. "You didn't bring him over last night!" he snapped at Erik. "I don't even know who he is!" Erik backed away when John Greenfield turned to him. "Why did you lie to me?"

"I didn't lie!" Erik protested and dropped his shirt as he put up his hands. "It was totally unexpected!" He backed away when John Greenfield pointed the axe in his direction. "I was just as surprised as you were!"

"You know what happened already!" John Greenfield shouted. "Don't go there with me!"

"Honestly, Father!" Erik wailed. "I'm not lying!"

"After you return home from school, you're grounded for the next two weeks!" John Greenfield hoisted the mast axe over his shoulder. "You go to school and return straight home!" Erik clenched his teeth and shoved his hands into his pockets. "This means that you can't stay at your friends' houses and they can't come visit either! Do you understand?"

"Yes, Father," murmured Erik. John Greenfield stepped over Chicago and stormed out the room. Erik grunted when pushed past.

"I've messed up," Chicago mewed, "didn't I?"

"Not much can happen in two weeks, Chico," Erik reassured and entered the room. Taking Chicago's arm, he pulled his friend to his feet.

Chicago blew a heavy sigh and shook his head. "You're wrong," he murmured. "A lot can happen…"

"Then what do you mean?"

"Remember when I told you we had to stop it from happening?" Erik nodded. "Your folks are going to get sick, *real* sick and that's just the start of it all."

"The start of what, Chico?" Chicago turned away, folding his arms across his chest. "What do you mean the Greenfields are going to get extremely sick?"

"They're going to be called away and you won't be safe here anymore..."

"But–!"

"Then they'll be told you're too sick to be cared for and you'll be sent away for testing."

"How–?"

"The treatments you get there will be *even worse* than what you experienced at General and you won't be the same once they release you, if ever!"

"Chico, what do you mean?" Erik demanded. "Be straight with me!" He grabbed Chicago's arm, shaking him. "Don't make up something so horrible!"

"You're going to go to a dark place for a while," Chicago said seriously. "They're going to hurt you..."

"The Greenfields will never hurt me!" Erik yelled, shaking him harder. "You're lying!"

"They *will* hurt you, Erik!" Chicago pulled out of his grip, glowering at him in return. "They work for them!"

"It's not true!" Erik shouted. "Stop lying to me!"

"You wouldn't know what to do if it were true, would you?" Chicago pushed Erik away. "Then you've got to learn fast, don't you?"

"Chico, stop lying to me!"

"It's scary not knowing, is it?"

Erik clenched his hands, glaring at Chicago. Unable to say anything else, he grabbed for his fallen shirt and stormed out the room.

Pulling into it as he hurried downstairs, Erik spotted Jane Greenfield standing over the stove, tense. He glanced around, finding the front door wide open and the kitchen table empty except for a cup of coffee and an open newspaper displaying the business section.

"I'll be coming straight home," Erik announced, buttoning his shirt. Jane Greenfield nodded, saying nothing in response.

Chicago came moments later with Erik's backpack slung over his shoulder. "*Hola*," he greeted softly, giving a small wave.

"Let's go," Erik ordered, taking Chicago's arm when Jane Greenfield made no motion to acknowledge him. "You're coming to school with me."

"What makes you think I want to go?" Chicago complained.

"Raider can call some people he knows well to set you up with a place to stay like he promised." Chicago grunted and let Erik pull him along out the house.

Stepping outside, they walked down the porch steps, meeting Raider coming up the walk. Raider let out a low whistle, halting at their appearance. "Hey, man," he greeted. "What's down with him?"

"Call somebody and find Chico a place to stay!" Erik snapped as he took his backpack from Chicago and slung it over his shoulder.

"What for?" Raider scoffed, rolling his eyes. "I told ya, I'm workin' on it."

"Mister Greenfield is going to murder the both of us if he hangs around," Erik explained, "and besides, Chico's parents don't care where he is, as long as he's alive." Chicago gave Erik an irate glare before stomping on his foot. Erik stiffened and doubled over, grunting in pain.

"Ay!" Raider spat and quickly grabbed Chicago's arm, roughly twisting his wrist. "I got the right to smack 'im 'round, ya dig?"

"Hey!" Erik cried and stood upright as Chicago bared his teeth at Raider while Raider glared back, his lips drawn back in a snarl.

"Hit him again," Raider growled, "and I'll fillet yer ass!"

"Go to Hell!" Chicago sneered and yanked out of his grip.

"You gonna send me?" Raider spat.

"Wanna bet?"

"Let's do this!"

"Enough!" Erik yelled and swung his backpack at Chicago, knocking him down the steps then struck Raider before he reacted, sending him to the ground. "I'm already grounded because of all this crazy mess going on!" Erik stepped over them both and stormed the path. "I don't want you two beating each other up over me; that'll make me feel even worse!"

"No one touches ya, dig it?" Raider grumbled, jumping to his feet and followed Erik. "Ya already got enough enemies as it is!"

"I'm no enemy!" Chicago screeched, scrambling to his feet and ran after them. "Shut up!"

"He's on our side, Raider," Erik snapped, "so calm down!"

"I ain't got time to weed out punks like Chico when I got tougher bags of meat to be fryin'!" Raider interjected.

Erik came to a sudden stop and whirled around, glaring at them both. Chicago came to a pause several paces away and Raider stepped back, tense. "Chico's worried about me too," Erik said sternly. "Don't you two start with me!"

"It ain't protective if he smacks ya 'round like that." Raider spat and jutted a thumb at Chicago. "I don't trust him!"

"I don't like you either!" Chicago grumbled as Raider shoved his hands in his jacket pockets.

"It's no different from when you came to visit," Erik protested.

"Ay, don't be callin' me stupid!" Raider squawked.

"I didn't mean it that way!"

"I watch your back, got it?" Raider kicked at Erik's shin and Erik grunted, glaring back. "Unlike you!"

"I said I'm sorry!" Erik retorted, shoving him back. "You want me on my knees?"

"Danae can really send you up a creek and that ain't no lie!" Raider protested. "Just watch yerself 'round that bitch, dig what I'm sayin'?"

"I'll be more careful," Erik groused and rolled his eyes.

"Look, I'll do what I can." Raider turned on his heel and stomped away, going in another direction. "I'll make some calls," he called over his shoulder, "but if he smacks yer ass 'round again, I ain't holdin' back next time!"

"We'll see about that!" Chicago yelled after him. Raider threw up an obscene gesture with his hand over his head. "You too!"

"I've never seen him this angry," Erik murmured moments later after Raider left their line of sight.

"Yeah, he's beyond pissed," replied Chicago wearily, approaching Erik's side.

"Do you know anyone named Danae?"

"I've heard of her," Chicago answered. "How long has he a vendetta on her?"

Erik sighed and shook his head. "From what I know, a long time," he replied. "A real long time, Chico..." Erik kept silent, walking onward and Chicago fell into step, keeping his distance.

FORTY

Once at school, Erik entered Home Room and Chicago lingered at the door, unwilling to go inside. Erik approached his assigned seat between Heinrich and Antony Gregg. Raider entered moments later and shoved Chicago aside, then took his usual place in the room's rear, pacing in silent fury.

Setting his backpack on his desk, Erik noticed Antony Gregg wearing an oversized dark navy tracksuit draping his thin frame. Looking at Heinrich, he wore a hooded sweatshirt with the school's mascot on the back and dark jeans. Erik peered over and frowned when he saw Heinrich sported a large bruise on the side of his face and a split bottom lip. Erik turned to Antony Gregg, noticing the dark glasses on his face and a black cap turned backwards on his head.

"What happened to you?" Erik asked gently.

"Please," Heinrich replied, "it's nothing."

Antony Gregg snorted and shook his head in response. "Hell yeah, it is!" he snapped. "He got jumped by that bitch Danae."

"Over what?" Erik demanded.

"Man, she's fucking up lots of people askin' 'bout you!" Antony Gregg said.

"Me?" Erik asked incredulously.

"Yeah, *you*," Antony Gregg spat irritably, "and I don't even *know* you!"

"Come now, I got there as fast as I could!" Heinrich said testily. "Seraphine tied up Goti and I had to go get him if we were to get you guys out!"

Erik stiffened. "Out of what?" he asked warily.

"Man... you don't wanna even know this shit!" Antony Gregg folded his arms across his chest, brewing in anger.

"Antony, seriously," Erik protested, "if someone hurt you guys to get to me, I should know!" He gripped the edge of his desk. "I hate it when people hurt someone else for no reason!"

"Heinrich got his ass beat down trying to help me kick that crazy girl's ass!" Antony Gregg growled. "You gotta watch her... She's fucking dangerous; she brought a gun to a goddamn knife fight!"

"So Vinny wasn't lying..." Erik murmured and sank into his seat.

"I don't know what the hell that bitch was thinking; I don't know you from a can of paint!"

"I'm sorry," Erik murmured.

"Sorry?" Antony Gregg snapped and whirled around in his seat. "Sorry? Is that all you can say?" He ripped off his glasses, revealing an eye patch. "That bitch took out my eye!" he shouted. "Over what? Over something you did to her!"

"Why would she target you?" Erik cried. "We never met before!"

"I ought to kick your ass!" Antony Gregg rose upright and Erik stood, hands clenched at his sides.

"If you want to, fine, go ahead, I won't fight you back," Erik said. "But I know how you feel - she put me in the hospital last week after dumping several rounds in me!"

"Bullshit!"

Gottfried entered the classroom moments later and paused at the sight of Chicago near the door, startled. After a short exchange, Chicago suddenly grew irate and grabbed Gottfried by the arm, shaking him. Gottfried yanked out of Chicago's grip and shoved him to the floor, then entered the classroom. He approached Erik offside and punched his shoulder. Erik yowled and held his arm, glaring back at him.

"What was that for?" Erik yelped.

Gottfried narrowed his eyes. "You know what for!" he snapped.

"I don't know," answered Erik, "I can't remember!"

Gottfried clenched his hands. "You're lying," he snarled through gritted teeth.

"Why would I?"

"We'll discuss this later!" Gottfried stormed away and left the classroom, pushing past Chicago who blocked his path.

"Touch me again!" Chicago screeched after him. "I'll send you to Hell!"

Antony Gregg suddenly punched Erik's chest and Erik coughed, crashing into his seat. He slumped forward and Antony Gregg cracked his knuckles then returned to his desk.

"Feel any better?" Erik groaned.

"Yeah," Antony Gregg grumbled, "whatever."

"Why did she show up at your party in the first place?"

"She thought you were invited for some reason."

"I don't know you or your friends. Where'd she get that notion?"

"She said you knew Special Kaye and Two-tone Tony."

"So it's true with what Vinny said!" Erik said is disbelief. "She got them sent to Centerville!"

"Yeah and I can't live with that." Antony Gregg struck the desk with his fist. "I couldn't do nothing about it; that bitch was just way too strong!"

"I'm sure they'll be all right!"

Antony Gregg turned his seat, glaring back at Erik. "What the fuck do *you* know?" he snapped. "Rotobot's in fucking *traction*! How's *that* for okay?"

"I'm sorry about your friend..."

"She was my girlfriend," Antony Gregg snarled. "You wouldn't understand."

Erik swallowed hard. "I don't remember Kaye or Tony," he said instead. "Were we close or anything?"

"Yeah, y'all were tight; even used to rumble together."

Erik held his head in his hands and blew a hard sigh. "Some monster I used to be," he muttered. "A damn beast..."

Gottfried returned to the door and Chicago swung at him. Gottfried immediately sidestepped his attack then grabbed Chicago's arm, flipping him over onto the floor. Chicago kicked Gottfried away, sending him crashing on the ground. Chicago immediately sprang to his feet with hands clenched, growling as Gottfried immediately stood, ready to fight.

Erik swiftly rose from his seat and slapped a hand against his desk. "Chico, stop it!" he shouted. "Don't make me come over there!"

"I swear!" Chicago screeched. "One more time, Erik, one more time -- he touches me again and he's a goner, for real!"

"Cool it!"

Chicago huffed and turned away, grumbling under his breath.

Gottfried stepped around Chicago and entered the room. He approached Heinrich, standing near him. Moments later, Raider came near Erik's desk.

"You need me for something?" Erik asked, glancing back at him.

"I can't sleep with all the noise yer ass is makin'," Raider spat irritably.

"It's not my fault Antony's heated over what Danae did to his friends," Erik retorted.

"The hell it ain't!" Antony Gregg thundered.

"Check this; we gonna trash that girl, ya dig?" Raider said. "We already got into it with her before."

"Yeah." Antony Gregg snorted. "I got it."

"I mean it!" Raider clenched his hands. "We gonna shake the bitch down and get rid of her ass."

"Sure thing," Antony Gregg mumbled.

Raider pointed to Erik. "You be comin' wit' me today; I don't care how many classes I bounce!" Erik nodded and Raider turned around, facing the class. "Ay," he called, "any of y'all better not get dirty on Danae and Seraphine without tellin' me first!"

"I ain't down with that," Antony Gregg snapped.

Raider turned to him, shaking his fist. "Leave her to me, got it?" he threatened. "This ain't your battle!"

"Fuck you, man," Antony Gregg snarled. "She took out my eye and I'm gutting her ass! I'm not letting you be the only one to fuck her up!"

"Listen to me," Raider hissed in a low tone. "Leave well enough alone!"

Antony Gregg scoffed. "You can't stop me."

"She'll fuckin' slaughter ya!"

"Then that's a risk I'm taking, you hear me?" Antony Gregg stood and poked Raider's chest hard. "She's eating lead tonight, for real!"

"Check it," Raider growled. "Yer granddaddy's Gibraltar ain't gonna do beans to that heifer, dig?"

"All I thought about when I was in the hospital was getting back at her. You're *not* gonna deny me that right!"

"Now listen close," sneered Raider, "she *ain't* in yer league, man. I'm tellin' ya; fighting her *ain't worth it*! Don't even *think* of rumblin' with them!"

"If I die, then oh well! You don't give a shit about me!"

"What makes you think I don't?"

"I better not see you," Antony Gregg hissed. "I'm turning her ass to fucking grass." He pushed past Raider and stormed out the room.

"We'd better get ready," Heinrich said to Gottfried. Gottfried nodded and both left the classroom. Chicago entered and took Heinrich's former seat.

"I guess I'm watching over you today," Chicago said softly.

"Why?" Erik demanded, glaring at him.

"It's going down today, I'm sure of it."

Stunned and utterly at a loss for words, Erik sank into his seat, realizing he had nothing else to say.

"Hey," Raider said to Erik.

"What is it?" Erik grumbled.

"You down?"

Erik nodded. "I got your back."

"Good, that's what I wanna hear."

Raider also left the classroom and Erik moaned, putting his head on the desk.

"I guess you'll need backup," Chicago murmured at his back.

"Thanks," Erik answered, "but you really don't have to."

"I want to. Besides, you owe me a favor."

Erik grunted and hid his face in his arms. "*What favor would that be?*" he wondered.

FORTY-ONE

Erik found it hard to concentrate during his classes, tense with worry about Seraphine or Danae attacking. Chicago followed him around, keeping Raider at a distance, but always on his guard. Other students paid little attention to Chicago, despite his always being near Erik.

At lunch, Raider and Chicago parted ways, leaving Erik free to grab a tray of cafeteria food. Once he took his meal of the day, Erik made his way to an empty table.

"How's the prison food, you punk?" a voice snapped at him and before Erik knew it, a swift hand flipped over his tray.

Erik stood indignantly, glaring down Seraphine who laughed cruelly at him. Other students turned in their direction, watching what they might do next.

"It was fine until you let the floor have it!" Erik yelled.

"Then why don't you lick it up?" Seraphine kicked Erik in the groin and Erik grunted, slipping to his knees. Seraphine then slugged Erik's face and he fell back stunned.

"I've had it with you!" Erik thundered and spat blood on the floor.

"You're supposed to be gone!" Seraphine shouted. "Who the hell let you out?"

"What difference does it make?" Erik scrambled to his feet and held his fists at ready. "Come on!"

Seraphine swung and Erik leaned out of the attack, then Seraphine turned, kicking him back with a jumping roundhouse. Erik struck the floor on his face from the hard blow.

"Why do you bother me like this?" Erik wheezed, struggling to get up.

"Don't tell me you changed your mind about fighting me!"

"I'm not fighting you here now!"

Seraphine stomped down on Erik's shoulder, leaning forward. "You're moving a little slow," he teased. "Are you going to cry now?" Seraphine crouched down before Erik, grabbing his hair to keep him from standing. "I dare you; go on and cry!"

"Shut your face!" Erik snapped and shouldered him back, then hurried to his feet as Seraphine reached forward again. Erik reversed him, shoving him to the floor and stood back, clenching his hands at his sides. "Why don't *you* cry already?"

Seraphine laughed darkly as he stood, brushing off his shirt. "Not in front of you," he snapped.

"You're crazy!" Erik stepped away, holding up his fists in guard. "I want you to leave me and my friends alone!"

"You think I'm crazy, huh?" Seraphine scoffed. "Aren't I?" He charged Erik, jamming his shoulder into his chest. The force slammed Erik against the wall, breathless. Erik grabbed his hand going for his throat and struggled to push him back. "The last time I checked, I was pretty normal." Erik yowled in pain when Seraphine turned out, flipping him overhead onto the floor with a crash. "Why don't you fight me back?" Seraphine spat.

"You're not worth my time!" Erik moaned.

"Yeah, I'm not worth your time?" Seraphine snapped his foot into Erik's chest and Erik immediately grabbed for Seraphine's heel, fighting to keep him back as Seraphine struggled to bear down. "Maybe you're just weak, is that it?" Erik pushed Seraphine back and Seraphine returned with a reverse snapping heel kick, jamming his foot into the side of Erik's neck. "Is that it?" Seraphine shouted.

"Get off!" Erik growled and grabbed his ankle, tripping him onto his back. Seraphine yelped in surprise once he struck the floor.

"You son of a bitch!" Seraphine bellowed. "You can't beat me at all! You never got upgraded!"

"The hell are you talking about?" Erik jumped to his feet, heaving for breath as he grew enraged. "I've had enough!" he screamed. "You attack me again and you're dead!"

"Bring it!"

Erik's vision flashed red as he grabbed Seraphine by the collar and slammed him against the wall. The air around them became charged and he drew back his fist. Seraphine returned with a swift kick in Erik's side before Erik could land a punch and Erik stumbled rearward. Seraphine advanced as Erik drew back and Erik threw a powerful uppercut, launching Seraphine to the floor with a hard thud.

"Just stay away from me!" Erik roared over Seraphine's downed form. "I don't know what I'm capable of, but if you find out, you might regret it!"

Seraphine let out a short laugh. "Oh, that isn't possible."

"Don't push me!"

Seraphine rose upright and stepped forward, delivering a swift roundabout kick. Erik grabbed his foot before it met his face, immediately flipping him down to the floor in return.

"I will break you!" Erik screeched.

Seraphine swept his free leg under Erik, tripping him back and he struck the floor, smacking his head against the tiles.

"Rather I break your ass, Punk!" Seraphine snarled, standing. Raising his foot, Erik grabbed Seraphine's heel as it came down to smash his face and struggled against him.

"What's with you?" Erik demanded.

"You already know!" Seraphine pulled back and slammed his knee into Erik's chest, forcing the air out of his lungs. "I'm warning you!" Seraphine dug in, applying more pressure as Erik's face slowly turned red. "Listen, Punk, no one threatens me and lives!"

Erik grabbed Seraphine by the collar. "I told you--!" he hissed.

"Are you threatening me?" Seraphine screeched. "You're threatening me, yeah?" He threw a sucker punch into Erik's jaw, snapping back his head. "Then it's time for your punk ass to die!"

"I am," Erik snarled, glaring back at him and grunted when grabbed by the face.

"Fight me back!" Seraphine raged. "This weak ass shit isn't your best!"

Erik struggled to stay awake as a low drone buzzed in his ears and his breath thinned when Seraphine pushed his head back at a painful angle. Taking Seraphine's wrist with his free hand, Erik yanked off his grip and threw him overhead, sending him crashing to the floor as he sprang to his feet.

Seraphine quickly gained his footing and charged. Erik turned out, grabbing him by the arm to reverse him and pitched downward, also having his body brought down by the momentum.

Seraphine screamed in pain as Erik slammed into him, also pulling his shoulder out of socket. They both struck the ground together and Erik quickly let go, hurrying to his feet.

"Stay down," Erik growled and wiped away blood from his cut lip with the back of his uninjured hand. "Just leave me alone!"

Seraphine lay dazed on the floor of the cafeteria, groaning and Erik gasped, noticing his shoulder stuck out of place and his arm below the elbow bent in the opposite direction. Glancing up, he stiffened when he spotted Danae among the crowd of gawking students and she turned around, walking away.

"Did you see that?" a student asked in bewilderment. "He totally ripped out his arm!" The other students gathered around Erik as he looked down at Seraphine who continued to moan in pain.

"I told you to leave me alone," Erik snapped, "but you just wouldn't listen!"

"Stupid son of a bitch," Seraphine grumbled. "I just wanted to fuck with your head!"

"I warned you!"

Stepping over Seraphine, Erik pushed through the crowd and took off down the hall.

"Wait!" another voice called to him.

Erik increased his speed and entered a break in the corridor. Before he could decide whether to go right or left, he sensed another presence coming from behind and turned, hurling a punch at his pursuer.

Erik grunted when grabbed by the wrist in a firm hold and pulled forward. An arm came around his shoulder and Erik tried flipping them overhead using their weight, strength and momentum against them, only to get squeezed in a headlock. Erik's hazy sight flashed red and his legs grew weak.

"I give!" Erik wheezed. His opponent let him go, releasing him as a heap on the floor. Erik grabbed at his throat, choking and gasping for breath.

"What the hell is wrong with you?" Stearne's voice snapped. Erik looked up, finding him standing over him in his usual stark white outfit underneath his dark overcoat. "You need to calm down!"

"I just want to be left alone!" Erik yelled and staggered upright. He pushed Stearne away and Stearne deflected his hand, throwing Erik back down on the floor. Erik struck his head against the tiles and the drone in his ears abruptly stopped. He held his head, groaning in pain.

"Stop," Stearne commanded.

"What do you want with me?" Erik complained, sitting up. He held his head between his knees, waiting for the dizziness to end.

"Once you've calmed down," Stearne answered, "I want you to come with me so that we may talk."

Erik sighed. "Fine, whatever," he grumbled. Stearne lent out a hand to Erik and Erik grabbed for it, getting pulled upright.

"Are you calmed down now?"

"What about Seraphine?" Erik asked instead.

"That's what we're discussing."

Stearne headed down the corridor and Erik immediately followed in step. Approaching the nurse's office, Stearne let Erik in first and Erik sank into a nearby chair while Stearne shut the door, locking it behind him. Stearne came out of his coat and set it on the desk, then started pacing.

"So, what do you have to say about Seraphine?" Erik murmured. "I know he's a total head-case, so no need to reiterate that point to me."

"No need to get fresh with me," Stearne retorted. "You shouldn't fight here in school."

"Then what else you want *me* to say?" Erik complained. "He keeps attacking me for no reason!"

"There's no such thing as attacking without cause!"

"Okay, fine, apparently we fought before, but I don't remember the guy!"

"Did he give you any reason?"

"What reason is there to give?" Erik squawked. "If you hadn't noticed, he completely wrecked my arm!"

Stearne grunted and approached Erik, grabbing him by the arm and pushed against his shoulder. Erik screamed when his shoulder popped back in place and his hazy vision flashed red once Stearne twisted his arm in the opposite direction. He fell forward into the darkness when overwhelmed by pain.

FORTY-TWO

A low drone slowly roused Erik, taking him out of the darkness. His ears rang as the thrum gave way to faint explosions.

"What the hell did you do?" a voice shouted, clearer than before. Erik gasped when shaken hard and his eyes snapped open, facing Arizeh dressed in a navy uniform, gripping his shirtfront. "If I don't like your answer, I'm kicking your ass!"

"What makes you certain--?" Another explosion followed louder than before and both ducked down to the floor when the room around them rocked.

Erik looked around his surroundings, finding they were in a moving cargo van with blackened windows, surrounded by other soldiers in navy uniforms, wearing black helmets with polarized visors.

"Hey, driver," a nearby soldier called, banging at the partition separating them from the van's front. "Watch where you're going!"

"Then get out there and kill those bastards or cut that racket!" the driver shouted back. "I was told to transport you monsters, not help you fight!"

"I'll kill you later," Arizeh snapped, letting go and bounded to his feet. "Let's get out of here; we have a battle to get to!"

"Fine by me!" Erik said and Arizeh grabbed him by the arm, pulling him up. Arizeh kicked the exit door open and jumped out onto the road behind them.

Erik followed and they rolled with the fall onto the ground as gunfire sprayed around them. The armored transport vehicle suddenly swerved to a stop as a rocket blasted near it, flipping it over on its side.

The soldiers clambered out, taking off in different directions once the van exploded, spewing fire and metal shards.

Arizeh scrambled to his feet and dodged the incinerating debris then raced away for a safer position. Erik hurried after him onto the field of battle, as more soldiers and tanks surrounded them.

"On your right!" Arizeh called, dodging a grenade and Erik turned out, diving for the ground as it exploded behind him.

"Why aren't we fighting back?" Erik shouted back and rolled to his feet then continued racing after Arizeh. A loud whirring tore through the sky and Erik looked up, spotting an armored helicopter.

"We can't; it's not time yet!"

"They must've known we were coming!" Machine gunfire ripped from above and both he and Arizeh darted around the bullets tearing into the ground, throwing up dust. "Otherwise they wouldn't be this heavy!"

"Jump!"

Erik took a leap as the helicopter exploded and crashed onto the ground, unleashing a burning fireball charring everything around them. The blast's force threw Erik back into an armored car, crashing out the windshield. He groaned and fell over onto the dirt, heaving for breath.

The door opened and Erik glanced up, looking at a female soldier who stepped out, wearing a light armored suit and helmet with a dark eyeshades. Harnessed around her waist she wore a pair of high-powered pistols.

"Didn't you see that coming?" she asked, holding out a gloved hand. Erik took her firm grip and she pulled him to his feet. "Get inside and let's punch it!"

Erik hurried around the car's other side and yanked open the door as the woman jumped in and started the engine. Slipping into the passenger side, Erik slammed the door close once she pulled away.

Racing across the battlefield where the other soldiers in navy fired at their enemies in black, around them, tanks, helicopters and other support vehicles were blasted to pieces.

"Where are we going?" Erik asked as she swerved the car, dodging missiles and grenades flying in her direction.

"To that building ahead -- the heart of the monster!" Erik looked ahead and saw the looming crystal tower come into view, with a large white antenna protruding from the top. "Once we destroy it, we can shut this whole mess down!"

A sudden bang slammed into the cruiser's roof and part of it peeled away with a sickening metallic rip. Erik looked up in horror at a white-haired navy-uniformed young man with glowing green eyes crouched above him, grinning devilishly as his left hand flared in crimson flame.

"Get out or burn!" the fighter thundered.

The female soldier slammed on the brakes and unleashed her pistol then pointed it overhead, firing once. The bullet tore between the young man's eyes, the force throwing him off.

"Let's go!" she shouted and opened the door, tumbling out. "We'll make the rest of the way on foot!" Springing to her feet, she raced ahead.

Erik opened the door and stumbled out, getting slashed across the face by a flaring long sword slicing deep into his skin. He struck the ground, stunned as the white-haired soldier stood over him with blood running down his face.

"One down," snarled his enemy and pointed his blade at Erik's throat, "then one more to go!"

"On your left!" a voice called.

"What?" The enemy soldier turned, staggering forward once riddled with bullets in the back. The female soldier raced up, kicking him down.

"Is he dead?" Erik asked as she stood over him, pointing her pistol at the back of the man's head. She fired once and dark blood pooled beneath him.

"As dead as dead gets!" the female soldier answered. Erik jumped to his feet as she yanked up the fallen sword. "Are you sure you can handle that?" she asked, tossing it to him.

"I think so," Erik replied, catching the blade.

"Then cover me!"

Erik nodded and kept pace with her, running for the glass building in the distance.

Slicing into soldiers who stepped out onto their path, Erik took off arms, heads and legs with ease, barely stopping to think as he severed through flesh and bone.

Before they reached the area surrounding the main gate, a sudden electric-blue charge tore through the air, throwing soldiers and other machines back onto the ground, causing explosions.

Erik grabbed for the woman, diving to the ground as another cyan blast discharged near her. Her helmet split open and she let out a cry once she struck the dirt.

"Here they come!" a voice bellowed. "The other units are arriving; fall back!"

"Thanks for saving me," the female soldier said as Erik got on his haunches.

Erik quickly scanned the area as more enemy soldiers scattered from their former positions. "You helped me once," he replied, "so the best I can do is return the favor..."

"It's going to get interesting..." The soldier sat up, pulling off her helmet and shook her head, revealing curly light brown hair. "Find where those force bolts are coming from and shut it down! I'll catch up!"

"Are we getting any reinforcements?" Erik asked, rising to his feet.

"What reinforcements?"

"You can't be serious!"

"Get going!"

Erik charged ahead as violet lightning rained around them.

"Get back!" Arizeh's voice called.

Reaching the gate entrance, Erik stopped dead in his tracks, watching Arizeh fire a large rifle into an enemy soldier who unleashed a strong charge of light, obliterating the gate and the ground around him.

Erik shielded his eyes as a blast of brightness blinded him and once the dust cleared, he backed away when the enemy soldier loomed over him, his uniform covered in blood. Behind him lay Arizeh's still form, badly burned.

"You killed him!" Erik screamed and raised his sword.

The soldier grabbed the blade with a swift hand, shattering it on contact. A sudden blast tore through the enemy fighter's head, blowing a large borehole through his helmet. He dropped to the ground, revealing the brown-headed woman standing behind him holding a high-powered pistol. She grinned, pushing up dark polarized glasses up on the bridge of her nose with her free hand.

"I returned the favor," she said, grinning.

"Thanks!" Erik said gratefully.

"Sure, anytime!" She lowered her gun and turned back for the building behind them. "The gate's open and those Agents are holed up in there! Let's clear them out!"

"But we don't have anything left!" Erik squawked.

"We'll steal what we can; now let's go!"

Erik ran with her as they stormed the gate and clambered up the steps. The ground beneath them suddenly trembled and fissures raced along the ground, causing the rivulets yawning open into craters as the concrete fell away.

More muffled explosions generated below and Erik dodged the cracking earth, jumping over the pits as the ground split open. The woman ahead of him also made leaps over the widening crevices, trying to climb higher before the stairs fell into the gaps below.

Hurtling over a large crack, the female soldier missed her footing and her glasses fell from her face as she grasped onto the ledge with her free hand to keep from falling into the hole. A large concrete boulder broke away from the staircase, tumbling for them.

"Take my hand!" Erik called.

The woman looked up, her brown eyes wide in fear and Erik pulled back when the boulder crashed where he stood moments before. He fell rearward on the ground, panting for breath as the staircase's remainder crumbled into the lower levels of the tower's underground parking garage. The concrete crushed the cars and the remaining steel beams underneath.

A low drone drummed in his ears and Erik sat there, dumbfounded and numb. He heard footsteps approaching from behind, crunching on the shattered concrete debris.

"I'm sorry you had to see that happen," a voice Erik didn't recognize said in a condescending tone. Erik stiffened when cold steel pressed against the back of his head. "Let me put you out of your misery then..."

Erik's world faded to black immediately.

FORTY-THREE

Erik's eyes snapped open, looking up at Stearne who stood over him with a concerned look drawn on his face.

"What happened?" Erik asked. "Why am I on the floor...?"

"Your arm..." Stearne started.

Erik gasped and grasped his arm, stunned when he found it in working order again. *"Just before it was busted,"* he thought, sitting up. *"There's no way Stearne could have fixed that!"*

"What were you thinking," Stearne reprimanded, "with combating Seraphine like that?"

"I only broke Seraphine's arm," Erik retorted. "He attacked me first, so what did you expect?"

"I didn't expect him to break *you!*" Before Erik could protest, Stearne held up a hand, shaking his head. "Listen to me, Erik. I am only saying this as a warning. You can't fight them here, or anywhere."

"Then what am I supposed to do?" Erik retorted. "Let them trash me; let them send me back to General again?"

"I don't want you to be tied up in a dark place for a long time..."

"What do you mean by that?"

"If you continue on this path, you may accidentally kill someone."

"Kill?" Erik squawked and scrambled to his feet. "You know I don't like that!" he shouted. "I'm *not* like that!"

"Have you ever wondered why you're so averse to killing?"

Erik clenched his teeth, unable to say anything in response. A knock resonated on the door, killing the tension.

"Hey, man, this kid like, so chucked on my shoes, man!" a voice called from outside. "And he, like, don't look too hot!"

"I must go," Stearne said in a flat tone and left Erik's side, heading for the door. "Remember my warning. I can't always be there for you." Erik nodded numbly as Stearne unlocked and opened the door.

"Yeah, like over there, man," said the student.

Stearne stepped out into the hall and followed the student to wherever the ill classmate may be.

Erik exited the office moments later and sagged against the wall. *"What just happened?"* he wondered. *"What's wrong with me?"*

"Hey, Erik," Chicago called. Erik nodded to Chicago as he approached. Chicago leaned against wall nearby and folded his arms across his chest. "Why didn't you finish the fight, *buey mudo?"* he cracked.

"Stop calling me that!" Erik spat. "Besides, I don't like to attack other people," he protested. "I get scary in a fight, it seems."

"Really?" Chicago gave Erik a wry smile. "So what was that all about back there?"

"We've been feuding for a while," Erik admitted. "I don't remember the origins, though."

"You should've seen your face - you looked like you were ready to kill him right then and there!"

"At this rate, maybe I should!"

Chicago snorted. "How can you with skills like that?" he retorted. "It's obvious you're only a defensive fighter and can only hit at what you see coming!"

"What would you know about fighting?" Erik spat. "You're the one to talk, you animal!"

"What?"

Chicago's clenched fist came swinging at Erik and Erik immediately stepped aside. Erik grabbed Chicago's wrist before he could throw another punch and twisted it at his back, then slammed him into the wall.

"Why are you attacking me?" Erik growled in Chicago's ear.

Chicago laughed at Erik. "See, I'm right," he crowed.

Erik let go and struck Chicago's arm in irritation. "Don't play with me like that!" he snapped. "I hate that kind of joking!"

"See, Erik?" Chicago complained. "I told you that you're *different!* Think about it; I've been trying to tell you this all along!"

"What are you talking about?" Erik grumbled and pushed him away. "I'm so tired of hearing about it, of thinking about it!" He blew an angry sigh. "And you know what? I just want to forget it and live a normal life!"

"There is *no such thing* as a 'normal' life!" Chicago snapped as Erik stormed down the hall. "A so-called normal life is nothing more than a fabricated lie used as a means of control!" he shouted after Erik.

"Maybe I like it that way!" Erik called over his shoulder.

Approaching his locker, Erik did the combination and opened it, withdrawing his backpack. Chicago blew a frustrated sigh upon approach as Erik kicked the locker shut.

"Look," Chicago grumbled, "what is your Gym Class?"

"Why are you asking me?" Erik demanded.

"I'm having whatever you have."

"Whatever." Erik left the locker and Chicago followed his stride, heading down the corridor.

Chicago blew a heavy sigh. "I wish I could forget all this too," he muttered. "I wish I could forget all the testing we're forced to take, of all the pain we have to suffer through."

"Then why don't you?"

Chicago suddenly stopped walking and socked Erik's arm. Erik winced, rubbing at his sore limb. "You *can't* forget what they've done to us," Chicago shouted. "You need to *remember* what they're trying to turn us into!"

"Monstrous beasts, right?" Erik spat sourly.

Chicago grunted. "You need to remember," he said softly. "These tests are bad, real bad, bringing out the worst in us. They treat us like a piece of nothing until we can't recall who we are and the people we love and care about become ghosts..."

Erik shook his head. "I'm still not entirely sure," he murmured. "I mean, I have a lot of questions, but I don't know whom to trust to ask and tell my concerns to."

"Then they're already halfway there!"

Erik blew a heavy sigh. "How long are you going to stay with me?" he asked instead.

"Long enough."

Approaching the locker rooms, Chicago left Erik alone while he headed for locker fourteen. Erik set his backpack aside and tensed as he unbuttoned his shirt, hearing a rattling noise in the room.

After changing into his swimming trunks and gym T-shirt, Erik made his way silently around the locker room and caught sight of Garcia Leuong huddled in the corner at a bench on the other side.

Sneaking up on Garcia, Erik glanced over his shoulder, watching him sift through a black bag he held in his lap. Erik clenched his teeth when Garcia withdrew a clear-bodied pen with an orange cap and a cartridge of dark red liquid.

"Are you skipping classes to show me up?" Erik asked.

Garcia stiffened and quickly held onto the capped needle once the bag fell out his lap and struck the floor. He scooped up the vial and whirled around, his green eyes narrowed in glacial fury as he glared at Erik.

"I see we couldn't hold our lunch," Garcia sneered, rising upright.

"Seraphine fed it to the floor," Erik replied and shrugged his shoulders. "Not a big thing."

"Oh, so he forced you to eat it, is that it?" Garcia grinned and thumbed off the cap, exposing a needle. The hard plastic top clattered to the floor. "I always knew you were weak!"

"Ask Seraphine once he gets out the nurse's office," Erik said, smirking. "I had to show him a thing or two about trying to bully me."

Garcia snorted and set the cartridge containing the red serum inside the clear pen, snapping it into place. The serum filled the pen, leaving the cartridge in the body's center clear. "You think you're so hot, huh?" he snarled. "Well, you won't win today's test; I'm making sure of it!"

"How are you going to rig it?" Erik demanded. "There's no way!"

"There is!" Erik grabbed Garcia's arm as Garcia rushed into him and grunted when slammed back against the locker walls. "This handy stuff will make sure you can never beat me!" Garcia crowed.

"Forget it!" Erik shouted and struggled against Garcia's hand holding the needle, increasing his grip on Garcia's wrist.

Garcia growled, pushing back and kneed Erik's groin. Garcia laughed sinisterly over Erik as he doubled over, stunned. "Enjoy a bit of this, Hotshot!" he sneered.

Garcia collared Erik and held him against the locker. Jamming the pen directly into Erik's chest, Erik let out a cry as Garcia pushed the plunger down, releasing the unknown serum into him.

A burning sensation chewed through Erik's chest and spread up his arms and down his back with each beat of his heart. Garcia pulled out the needle and released his hold.

Erik fell to all fours, gagging. "You--!" He gasped and clutched his throat once it became harder to breathe.

Immediately his skin grew numb, his body stiffened and his eyes watered. "I can't feel... Why can't I move?"

Garcia held the drained pen and laughed darkly, standing over Erik. "Hurts like a bitch, huh?" Garcia teased. "Feeling not so great anymore, huh?" Garcia snapped a swift kick into Erik's side, jarring him. Erik fell over, coughing and choking. "I was right; you *are* one of those freaks!"

"Have you lost your mind?" Erik wheezed and cringed when kicked again. "What is this?"

"It's called Star Ruby!" Garcia declared and kicked Erik's face. "I'll let you in on a little secret: Star Ruby don't do jack shit to regular humans, other than turn their piss green. But on freaks like you... well, you're feelin' it, huh?"

Erik's vision began to blur and his head snapped back when kicked again for good measure. "*Father Greenfield mentioned Star Ruby!*" he thought in utter horror. "*He said they were terrible...*" Erik struggled to get up, only becoming frustrated when his limbs refused to respond. "*He warned me about others trying to destroy me, trying kill me!*" He winced when Garcia stomped hard on his chest, breaking his ribs.

"Why...?" Erik moaned. "Why over some lousy competition medals?"

"Live long enough and maybe you'll find out!" Garcia spat.

"Why are you trying to kill me?" Garcia kicked Erik over onto his back and stomped hard on his hand, cracking the bones underneath his sneaker. "You're insane!" Erik wailed. "You need serious help, Garcia!"

Garcia put his foot to Erik's neck. "Well, we all have our faults, Hotshot," he said, grinning devilishly. "It's a shame really…" He raised his foot, ready to crush in Erik's face and suddenly froze when a loud noise crashed into the locker room. "Who else is down here?" Garcia shouted, stepping away.

"Leuong!" a voice roared from the other side of the room.

Garcia whirled around, dropping what he held. "You can't prove anything!" he snapped. "Whoever you are, forget it! I'll destroy you too!" When Garcia heard no response, he looked down at Erik. "You set me up, you sack of shit!"

"You did this to yourself!" Erik rasped.

"Too bad you're paralyzed for the most part," Garcia said, grinning darkly, "but at least you're numb to whatever I do to you."

"What are you going to do?" Garcia approached and knelt before Erik, grabbing him by the throat. "Garcia, please!" Erik pleaded.

"Shut up!"

Chicago stormed into the locker room, stomping toward Garcia. "Let him go!" he snarled and yanked Garcia by the collar. Throwing him against the wall, Garcia struck the floor on his back.

"Who the hell are you?" Garcia demanded and scrambled to his feet.

Chicago stood over Erik, appearing concerned. "*¿Qué está pasando?*" Chicago asked. "Will you be okay; can you talk to me?"

"Don't you dare ignore me!" Garcia thundered and clenched his hands. "I'll destroy you too!"

"Go to Hell!" Chicago snapped.

"Get out, you freak!" Garcia screamed and charged forward. Chicago leaned out of a swing and slugged Garcia's face with a swift counterattack, then grabbed his shirtfront before Garcia retaliated and threw him downward with a crash.

"Make me!" Chicago dropped over Garcia and clamped his hands around the young man's throat, throttling him.

"I'll put out your eye!" Garcia hissed, grabbing Chicago's face and pushed back.

"Do it!" Chicago growled. "Come on; you think you're so bad - do it!"

Garcia jerked and immediately stiffened, wheezing for breath as his hold loosened when Chicago squeezed harder. After struggling for several moments, Garcia's twitching body fell slack and his cool green eyes faded into blank voids, outlined in hazel.

"Don't..." Erik moaned once Chicago let go and picked up Garcia's slackened body by the arms then hurled Garcia overhead. Garcia crashed into the wall then slumped over as a heap on the floor.

Chicago turned to Erik and knelt at his side. He shook Erik by the shoulders when Erik's eyes rolled to the back of his head. "Don't fade on me!" Chicago cried. "Get up!"

"You--!" Garcia shrieked.

Chicago looked over his shoulder as Garcia hurried to stand, clutching his face with his left hand and heaved for breath. The three long dark thin scars across the Garcia's right cheek turned a darker shade of pale and his eye changed from dark green to pale yellow-green.

Chicago thrust forward a hand at Garcia. *"Djotaien!"* he screeched and a blast of force slammed into Garcia, forcing him against the wall.

Garcia fell to his knees and tensed when the air around them rapidly heated. "What the hell?" he cried, bewildered.

"Erik!" Chicago wailed and turned toward his friend, finding him unresponsive. He threw a powerful punch into Erik's chest and Erik jerked as he gasped when his eyes abruptly snapped open. "Can you hear me?" Erik nodded slowly. "Can you get up; can you move?"

"Get over here!" Garcia bellowed and rushed Chicago again. Garcia grabbed Chicago by the collar and he let out a yelp when yanked back toward the floor. Chicago turned with the fall and threw Garcia overhead, then rolled to his feet. Garcia turned out the way and charged once more.

"Al diablo con ustedes!" Chicago growled.

"I'm not scared of you!" Garcia retorted and they grappled each other, trying to force the other to the ground.

Finding his limbs able to work, Erik struggled to his feet and clenched his hands as the numbness began to fade. "What is he?" he wheezed when he noticed Garcia's left eye continued to stay cool green. Erik clutched his sides and doubled over, struggling to keep the nausea at bay.

"Leave!" Chicago roared, his light brown eyes flashing dark red.

"Chico, don't!" Erik yelled.

"You know this prick?" Garcia shrieked and shoved Chicago back, throwing him on the floor. Chicago stepped away and

422

held up his fists at ready on guard. "You're after my medals too!" Garcia smirked. "Don't worry; I'll get all of you!"

"*Kanetsuo!*" Chicago sneered and the room suddenly became encased in dry heat. Garcia gasped and staggered back, clutching his chest. Erik clenched his teeth when his skin also quickly tanned in response.

"*He has the same response as I did!*" Erik thought in horror.

Garcia shook his head, regaining his bearings. "You bastard!" he sneered through gritted teeth. "I'll get anyone that tries to show me up, even pieces of shit like you!"

"Chico, I'm begging you," Erik pleaded as Chicago advanced. "Don't hurt him!"

Garcia grabbed Chicago by the arm and flipped him down, applying pressure to his wrist. Chicago let out an agonizing scream and struggled against Garcia's ever-increasing power, clawing at his wrist when Garcia broke bones.

"He's poisoning you, Erik!" Chicago wailed. "I can't let that happen!"

"Stearne warned me if I had to fight, that it could accidentally kill someone," Erik protested. "I don't want him dead! Don't let your anger out on him!"

"Yeah, that's right," said Garcia, adjusting his grip. "Don't want to end up at that dark place for eternity, now do you?"

Giving Chicago's arm a firm yank, Garcia wrenched it out of socket and Chicago howled in anguish. An unexpected force tossed Garcia back, slamming him to the floor.

"Chicago, don't hurt him!" Erik shouted and hurried over to Chicago who stood, gearing for another blow. Erik yanked him aside and shoved Garcia back by the chest before he advanced then stood before Chicago, blocking his path as Chicago swiped back in return with his good hand.

"Back off!" Chicago screamed and Erik turned out of another swing.

"I won't let you!" Chicago rushed Erik then dropped low, slamming his shoulder into his chest. The force threw Erik back into Garcia, flooring them both with a crash.

A sudden flash of light blinded Erik and he let out a cry as unexpected pain attacked him at once, followed by the sensation of frigid numbness and searing heat burned his skin at the same time.

"Get up!" Chicago hollered and Erik staggered as dark burns appeared on his arms, chest and back. He struggled to his knees when his strength receded and Erik doubled over, wheezing in pain.

"I'm not here to fight you," Erik said weakly. "We're friends, aren't we?"

"So stay out of my way," Chicago yelled, "or I'll have to hurt you too, friend or not!" He turned back to Garcia, thrusting forward his uninjured hand. *"Shunsuo!"* A wall of flame immediately flared before Garcia.

"The fuck is this?" Garcia yelped as the fires died. "I'm gone you freaks!" He took off running. "This isn't the last of me, Hotshot!" Garcia called over his shoulder. "Don't think you're not getting the same the next time around!"

The heat in the room began to taper once Garcia departed and Erik shuddered, huddling forward on the floor as the dry heaves worsened. Chicago staggered over to Erik, slipping to his knees by Erik's side. Erik shut his eyes, concentrating on keeping whatever his body tried to give up down inside.

"The poison should be out of you by now," Chicago grumbled. "You still shouldn't be feeling that bad!"

"Well, I do!" Erik moaned.

"You should've sweat it out already!"

"Apparently it's too much for my body to handle..."

Chicago pushed against Erik's chest with a gentle hand. "Just try to relax," Chicago said benevolently, "and let me get the rest of that mess out of you that might be in there, alright?"

"Am I going to die?" Erik asked and groaned from his abruptly painful touch once forced to lie back on the floor.

"Look at me." Erik opened his eyes and looked up at Chicago whose eyes continued glowing faintly in red. "I promise to keep things in check if you help me deal with it, okay?" Erik nodded in response and Chicago smiled faintly as he ran a hand through his hair.

"*How can I help Chico with his problem?*" Erik wondered and grasped Chicago's hand. Chicago blew a short sigh as his glowing red eyes slowly faded back to light brown. "*Is it the one he told me about or the one I can't remember?*"

"Erik," Chicago called. "Can you hear me?"

"Please," moaned Erik, "don't leave."

"I'll still be here," answered Chicago gently.

Erik shut his eyes once his vision turned fuzzy and the overwhelming pain shut him down.

FORTY-FOUR

Erik awakened gasping and choking for air. He let out an agonized wail and quickly sat up, clutching his burning throat. Throbbing pressure ravaged through his chest, spreading throughout his back and arms.

"Take it slowly," a warm voice said kindly. "You're safe now." Erik ran his hands through his hair and took in ragged breaths, feeling the pain slowly recede. "Here..." Erik glanced up, finding Stearne standing over him holding a cool towel, appearing deeply concerned.

"Thanks," Erik said weakly and took the towel from him, then pressed the cold cloth against his face.

"I'm glad you're still with me," Stearne replied and pushed Erik back gently by the shoulder. "Rest some more, please?"

"But--!"

"This is the second time you've wound up here in the infirmary!" Stearne reprimanded. "It'll look suspicious..."

"Can't you write it off as a severe allergic reaction or something?" Erik complained.

"Broken ribs isn't an allergy!"

"Please don't tell Mister Greenfield about it."

Stearne blew an annoyed sigh. "I'm grateful someone dropped you off here," he continued, "because by the appearance of your condition this time, I thought you lay dying."

"Why do you say that?" Erik asked. "What do you mean?"

Stearne grabbed a nearby chair, scraping its metal feet over the floor and set it beside Erik. He sat across from Erik and took off his glasses, wiping absent-mindedly at the lenses with the edge of his shirt.

"You know what I mean," Stearne retorted, slightly annoyed.

Erik looked down at his arms and frowned when he found the skin back to its normal paleness. "I thought I was burned," he murmured.

"You don't have any burns," Stearne objected. "What are you talking about?"

Erik clenched the cold towel in his hands, sighing as he closed his eyes. "I don't know what's going on," he moaned. "Am I losing my mind?"

"You were injected with a strong poison," Stearne replied dully. "It possibly caused a hallucinatory reaction."

"If you say so..."

"You have to be careful Erik, for it can kill us. I'm just happy that whatever you were injected with didn't kill you outright."

"I was told it was Star Ruby." Stearne growled under his breath in response and Erik opened his eyes, catching sight of Stearne standing over him with hands clenched at his sides. "Where can someone find something like that...?"

"Bastards!" Stearne spat and the glasses he held cracked in his hands.

"What is it?"

"Only people affiliated with The Agency have access to the Star Ruby serum," Stearne said in a controlled voice and turned away. "You must stay away from whoever tried to poison you. They are dangerous."

"It was Garcia who had it," Erik admitted. "What's this Agency you're talking about? How would he get it?"

"Erik, I can't tell you about The Agency, you know that!" Stearne answered in an exasperated tone, ignoring his initial question. "Just be lucky that you're alive!"

"Why do you say that?" Erik murmured. "Chicago said it would poison me..."

"Yes, slowly, but they tried for your heart!" Stearne blew a heavy sigh. "Star Ruby is potent enough to shut down the central nervous system..."

"What do you mean?" Erik snapped. "How when it hardly affected Garcia? Are you saying it only has some kind of effect against Core Irons then?"

Stearne's face immediately lost color. "What are you talking about?" he said guardedly.

"Star Ruby is one of the contrabands, right? Apparently it only bothers people with Core Irons and apparently I'm not a regular person."

"You got lucky for now, to say the least, for whoever injected you probably diluted it or it was old or who knows..." Stearne shrugged his shoulders. "What matters is that you're fine for now, so please don't be idle for class any longer."

"You're lying to me!" Erik spat. "Why would Garcia own something that they used specifically, especially something

428

that deadly?" He tapped at his chest. "If you hadn't noticed, that wingnut nearly killed me!"

"I don't have any further information for you," Stearne responded mechanically.

"Isn't it impossible for Garcia to be working *with* them, unless he's got a family member that *does* work there and probably stole it, desperate to keep ahead in the game?" Erik demanded. "Then what makes him different from me? Why am I different?"

"We're no longer discussing this," Stearne snapped, growing tense.

"So if it's not as deadly as you say, then why let him poison everyone else?" Erik retorted. "Or are you telling me he's probably enhancing himself for his own twisted benefit?"

Stearne growled under his breath. "We're done talking about this," he grumbled and stalked away, clearly disturbed.

"Damn you, Stearne!" Erik spat after him. He clenched his teeth and threw the towel on the ground.

"*Why aren't you telling me everything?*" Erik thought. "*It's clear that you know something, maybe even more than what you're letting on!*" He then bit his fist as the pit of his stomach turned. "*Is that what Seraphine was looking for? Something about Core Irons?*" Erik left the cot, trooping back to his gym class. "*This is getting too serious! If Garcia is somehow working with Seraphine, I need to stop them before it gets worse!*" The disconcerting feelings bothering Erik intensified and he rushed out the room.

Entering Indoor Pool Three, Erik spotted the other students clustered around the side of the pool, far from the nearby edge. Other concerned students met him with warm greetings and Erik waved back to them in response.

"Dude, I thought you'd never show up!" a familiar voice called loudly. "We got Spring Tourneys coming up, so it's time to get cracking!"

"Well, I'm here, aren't I?" Erik answered and turned around. He faced the tall, thin student with long stringy platinum blond hair who ambled toward him. Dressed in the school's issued swimming gear, he also wore wide green-tinted swimming goggles over his eyes.

The young man gave Erik a friendly punch to the shoulder. "You okay, bro?" he inquired.

"I'm okay, really," Erik replied, nodding. "I don't go down that easily."

The student beamed, giving another friendly jab. "Awesome!"

Erik gave a nervous smile and rubbed at his aching hurt shoulder. "*I wonder how he knows me,*" he thought, slightly at a loss.

"Cheer up, man," the goggled student said. "You worry too much!"

Erik brightened slightly and grinned. "You look like a bug," he teased.

The tall thin student chuckled and gave Erik another light-hearted punch. "Buzz!"

Erik laughed in return.

Moments later, the instructor Lachlan entered the room, clipboard in hand. "Okay, boys, listen up!" he called as the class assembled near the pool and sat on the edge, hardly listening to whatever Lachlan had to say. Some of the other students pushed each other on the shoulders in friendly jostling while some kicked lazily at the water.

Erik heard a low growl and looked around. His gaze then fell on Garcia who bore his teeth at him, clearly enraged with his hands and face twitching in tempestuous fury. Erik tensed and swallowed hard, unsure if Garcia were about to hit the water and swim over to drown him.

"Mister Hart, I'd like for you to listen!" Lachlan snapped and rapped Erik on the back with his clipboard. Instant dull pain ripped through Erik when the piece of plastic struck the raw area he had on his shoulder. He let out a stunned cry and hunched forward. "Oh my!" Lachlan yelped and suddenly pulled away. "What's wrong?"

"It's nothing," Erik said, smiling weakly. "Really!"

"You can't swim in that condition, Mister Hart," Lachlan said smartly. "I suggest you refrain until that heals."

"I'm not worried about getting poor marks in class," Erik replied. "I'm just here to keep that wingnut in check!"

"What did you say?" Garcia shouted.

Before the instructor could reply, a sudden bang killed the silence as the double doors to the pool area swung open from a heavy kick. In stomped Chicago, clearly in a foul mood.

"Who might you be young man?" Lachlan asked, turning to him. "Are you another new student?"

"Yeah, I'm Chicago Ramone," he spat. His face reddened as some laughter followed. "Yeah, I said it!" Chicago shouted. "It's Chico to you sap-heads!"

"Chico," Erik called, "calm down, please!"

Chicago turned to Erik. "Yeah, sorry," he grumbled and sighed, brushing his shaggy dark brown hair out of his eyes. "I promised…"

"Can you swim?" Lachlan asked and tensed when Chicago suddenly laughed, clutching his sides.

"Like hell I can!" Chicago crowed.

"I just want a yes or no."

"You can't!" Garcia screeched, getting to his feet.

Chicago bared his teeth, clenching his hands as he let out a low growl. "Like hell, damn it!" he sneered.

"Listen, Mister Ramone, either you can swim or not."

Chicago turned to Erik and Erik shook his head. Chicago's brown eyes flashed red in deep hatred for both Garcia and Erik. "I know just enough to float," Chicago said evenly through gritted teeth. "It's easy, right?"

"We'll see if you can actually tread water." Lachlan wrote a note in his clipboard. "Okay class, we have another test. Line up to where I am standing when I call your name."

Erik sighed, drawing up his knees and wrapped his arms around them, waiting for Lachlan's calls to be over.

FORTY-FIVE

After the attendance check, the students had formed four lines. Erik's queue consisted of competitive swimmers, across from the line of average swimmers who swam casually and next to the other group of competitive swimmers who needed more practice.

Cold sweat broke out on Erik's forehead after noting Garcia stood in the same line with him, pacing and cursing under his breath. Chicago stood with the poor swimmers and he paced in agitation, shuddering in rage with fists clenched at his sides, trying to keep his anger under control.

"Chico, please," Erik said gently as Chicago passed by him, only to be met with an ugly glare in return.

"Class," Lachlan called over them. "I want to make two teams out of this group. Everyone pick a team leader."

"Hey, you wanna be team leader?" asked the lanky student with the bug-eyed goggles. He gave Erik a friendly jab on the arm. "I bet you'll be awesome once that sore heals!"

Erik shrugged his shoulders in response. "Why don't you do it?" he said. "You seem to be a decent swimmer to be in this line."

"You know with team leader, there's the responsibility of showing us the various moves and junk when it comes to swimming," interjected another classmate nearby before the tall thin student could answer.

"I guess I could," Erik murmured, "but I haven't been doing this long." He ran a hand through his hair nervously.

"Well, most of you guys spin right," complained the student in the bug-eyed goggles. "You can't do this stuff in a mirror."

"What are you saying?" Erik asked, glancing at him.

"He tends to move to the left," another classmate fill in. "Are you right-handed?"

"No, ambidextrous."

"Awesome!" The tall thin student whooped and punched Erik's arm again in response.

"Now, don't get too excited," protested Erik, wincing. "I *write* ambidextrously but I tend to favor my..." Erik swallowed hard when he drew a blank. "*Do I favor my left side,*" he mused, "*or my right?*" Erik glanced down at his faintly burning hands. "*That should be a simple one to answer...!*"

"Hey, let's make Erik team leader!" another student piped up. "Leuong pushes us too much, trying to make us perfect, like he thinks of himself!"

"Yeah, dude," replied the lanky student, "that was like, so cool how you kept your fancy steps on the down-low, bro!"

"Yeah, that was righteous the other day with the reverse dive on the board!" The others gave their forms of agreement. "Dude, I'm so jealous!"

Erik laughed nervously. "Okay," he answered, "if you all agree."

"Yeah! Pump it up!"

434

Garcia fumed, glaring intently at Erik as the others gave Erik friendly jostles and cheered him. Erik immediately felt isolated between the other boys who paid no attention to them and instructor Lachlan, who busied himself with getting the various tests sorted.

Garcia closed the gap between them and stepped up to Erik, sneering. Erik grunted when shoved back by the chest.

"You'll pay for making me look bad, Hotshot!" Garcia snarled, leaning in. Erik stepped back, swallowing hard as a knot formed in his guts. "You'll pay for ever showing your face here!"

"I won't fight you," Erik snapped back, "no matter what you do to me!"

"You think you got what it takes to show those losers how to do some of the maneuvers that Lachlan commands?" Garcia said and scoffed. "Keep dreaming!"

"I'll find out how you got that stuff from The Agency!" Erik spat. "If you think I'll let you get away with enhancing yourself to get ahead, you're wrong!"

"Good luck!" Garcia hissed. "You'll be dead first!"

Sensing movement from behind, Erik turned and spotted Chicago standing near them, glaring at them both.

"You'll regret ever thinking those thoughts," Chicago growled.

"I can think whatever the hell I want!" Garcia said haughtily.

"Really?" Chicago clenched his right hand tightly, forcing corded veins straining against his skin.

"What, now you can read my mind or something, you freak?"

"I'll crush your soul and send you straight to Hell myself," Chicago snarled in a controlled tone.

"My soul?" Garcia broke out laughing. "You're crazy!"

Chicago's clutched right hand tightened, fleshing out the veins and muscles beneath the skin and his light brown eyes flashed red. He immediately grasped Garcia's chin with his free hand, lifting him off his feet from the floor. The other students nearby gave pause and quickly backed away.

"Don't force me to break that face!" Chicago screamed and threw Garcia overhead before he had a chance to react, sending him crashing into the water. Erik pulled out of his T-shirt and raced ahead, diving in after him.

Encountering the true-blue waters, Erik spotted Garcia's form sinking into the bottom depths. He grabbed Garcia and pulled him close then surfaced, facing many watery forms of people clustered near the edge. When Erik broke through, he saw a familiar smiling face.

"Take my hand," the middle-aged man said gently, reaching out a hand to Erik. "Come on." Erik took his hand, getting pulled up to the edge.

"Why is Mahjin here?" Erik wondered, climbing out. *"Has he come here looking for me?"* He frowned, noticing Mahjin wore a tan work shirt with the name of the school on the chest, slim fitting blue jeans, dark-blue cowboy boots and a lime green baseball cap over his frizzy dark blond hair. "Mahjin..." Erik started and Mahjin shook his head. Erik tightened his grip around Garcia's chest, towing him along with him.

Garcia gripped at Erik's arms, gasping. "Let go!" he wheezed. "You're killing me!"

Erik let go, letting Garcia slip and took him by the wrist, pulling hard as he perched back on the poolside's edge. Garcia slipped out of Erik's grasp and held onto the edge, coughing and spitting, then abruptly vomited water at Erik's feet. Erik kicked off his wet sneakers, letting them sink at the bottom of the pool.

"Where's Chico?" Erik asked.

"He's been taken to the school principal's office," Mahjin replied.

"Don't let him get taken away!" Erik cried. "He's got no other place to stay!"

"Don't worry." Mahjin smiled faintly and ran a heavy hand through Erik's wet strands.

"Wait, Melvin!" Erik called after Mahjin as he walked away. He immediately stood, only to get his arm abruptly grabbed. Turning around, Erik faced the bug-goggled student and several of the others who clustered near him.

"Man, what got into Chico?" one of the boys asked and Erik shook his head in response.

"There isn't really much to say," he muttered and folded his arms across his chest. "I don't have anything to say about him."

"Dude, you know him and stuff!" complained the tall lanky student with the wide goggles. "What's *wrong* with that guy?"

"Yeah," another classmate chimed in, "is he like whoo-whoo-crazy or something?"

"I hate to admit it," said a student behind Erik, "but he scares the hell out of me!"

Erik sighed, knowing they refused to refrain about the matter until he said something to placate them. "He doesn't know how to keep his anger under control," Erik answered and then quickly changed the subject. "Where's Mister Lachlan?"

"He's talking to that janitor guy," the bug-goggled student replied, "the one who fished you out."

Erik ran a hand through his wet hair, vexed by the same fears he grew to hate biting at him again full force. "*Why do I get the feeling this is going to turn out badly?*" he thought, looking back at Lachlan and Mahjin who stood outside the poolroom's doors.

Mahjin made argumentative gestures while Lachlan kept shaking his head, unresponsive. Offside near them, a man in a dark turtleneck and chinos wearing smoky glasses and wool skullcap held down Chicago who struggled to get free.

Erik ran for the door and opened it wide.

"What are you doing here?" Mahjin snapped, glaring at Erik. "Get away!"

"Chico," Erik cried, "I'm so sorry for this to happen!"

"It's not your fault, Erik," Chicago said as he slackened. "Don't worry, be cool. Where I'm going-- it's just the same song and dance to them."

"Hey man, let's dip from over here," a voice called to Erik.

Erik whirled around, finding the lanky student with the bug-eyed goggles standing nearby. "Why are you following me?" he demanded.

"Come on, Dude. They're like totally creeping me out."

Erik sighed and followed him back into the poolroom. "I just can't leave him!" Erik complained and turned back, watching the man hauling Chicago away elsewhere. "Hey!" He sprinted for the door and Mahjin quickly blocked his path.

"Get back!" Mahjin commanded and pushed Erik away by the shoulder, throwing him back into the room. Erik struck the floor dazed from the sudden show of force.

"Hey!" the lanky student shouted after him. "Not cool, man!" He lent a hand to Erik and Erik took it, getting pulled to his feet.

Suddenly, the poolroom's doors abruptly burst open and Raider rushed in with Seraphine chasing him in close pursuit.

"Yo, Erik!" Raider called, clearly troubled.

"Raider, watch out!" Erik called back as Seraphine advanced.

Raider let out a yell in surprise and staggered forward when tackled from behind. He threw Seraphine over his head, tossing him down to the floor.

The tall thin student grabbed Erik's arm, pulling him away as Seraphine rolled with the fall and sprung to his feet.

Seraphine charged forward, rushing into Raider and Raider quickly sidestepped him. Reversing the attack, Raider grabbed Seraphine's arm and flipped the young man over onto the floor with a crash.

Erik broke away from the lanky classmate's side, approaching Raider who gave Seraphine a swift kick in the face, knocking him back.

"Don't make me cut yer ass up!" Raider shouted over him with clenched hands. "Get up ya piece of shit and I'll make ya French-style, or ya want it done a different way?"

Seraphine chuckled, wholly undaunted as he rose to his feet. "Yeah," he spat, "you think you can, huh?" Seraphine grabbed at Raider's sleeve and Erik grasped Raider's arm, pulling him back as Seraphine leaned in. "You're too weak to do anything, Caelan -- we already got that new friend of yours!"

"Hands off the threads," Raider growled and pried off his fingers. "You better not touch my fresh gear again!" He kicked Seraphine's groin, forcing him to his knees.

Seraphine paled, staggering back to his feet. "Whatever," he hissed. "Once I finally get you, you'll only end up the same way like your cousin: six feet underground!"

"Touch me and my friends," Raider snarled, "and you'll die a thousand ways from Sunday, you crazy son of a bitch!"

"Oh, don't forget," sneered Seraphine, "we'll torture you just as slowly!"

Raider's face grew red in rage and he yanked out of Erik's grip. He let off a swift boot into Seraphine's side before he could react and Seraphine groaned, crumpling over onto the floor, gagging.

"Die already!" Raider screeched and stomped down, only to have his ankle caught. Erik grabbed Raider's arm before Seraphine flipped him and pulled him away. Raider ground his teeth, shaking in visible fury.

"Raider, don't," Erik said in his ear as he wrapped his arms around Raider's own. "Leave it alone!"

"Get the fuck out of here!" Raider snarled and shook Erik off. Erik took a step aside as Seraphine clamored again to his feet, clutching his side.

"You can't keep him safe for long!" Seraphine crowed. "Your ass is ours, Punk!" He glared at the bug-goggled student. "You too!" The young man gulped hard and the color drained from his face in response.

Erik stepped forward, standing between Raider and Seraphine. "Get out of here, you piece of trash," he snapped, glaring back. "I don't know how you recovered, but I'll tear you apart again!"

"You got lucky the last time," Seraphine retorted. "I'll get rid of you next time!"

"We'll see about that, Shorty!"

Seraphine bared his teeth and Erik pushed him back. "Whatever, Punk," Seraphine retorted. "I got you!"

"Don't push me!" Erik spat. Seraphine stormed away and Erik turned to Raider. "What was that all about?" he demanded and pointed behind him with his thumb. "I want an explanation!"

"Yeah, Dude," said the lanky classmate apprehensively.

"Mind yer business," Raider grumbled, shoving past Erik.

The bug-goggled young man put up his hands as Raider advanced, staring him down. "I totally get it!" he yelped and backed away.

Raider said nothing as Erik returned to the group of other students who watched anxiously. Erik paid them no attention when he picked up his T-shirt and pulled into it.

"Ay," Raider called, "why ya soaked?"

"Chico turned livid and threw him in," Erik answered simply.

"Hey, that serves the shit-faced punk right!" Raider smiled wryly and folded his arms across his chest. "Ain't gotta save jerks like him!"

"You know I can't do that, Raider!" Erik protested. "That's not right!"

"What the hell, Erik," Raider complained.

"What is it?" Erik said in exasperation.

"Damn it, I ain't stupid!" Raider grumbled and turned away, sighing in frustration as he ran a hand through his hair.

"What's your deal?"

"Come on, you goin' home early."

"Why?" Erik fussed. "I still have an hour!"

"Lemme watch your back." Raider walked away, no longer waiting to listen.

"Damn it, Raider!" Erik snapped and clenched his teeth once Raider exited the room. "You're really working my nerves!" he called after him.

"You gonna be okay, Dude?" the lanky student asked.

"I'm fine," Erik said and waved the others off. "I'll catch you next time." He hurried for the door.

"Hey, Erik!"

Erik turned and caught a pair of cheap plastic sandals sailing his way. He quickly stepped into them and kept on.

Exiting into the corridor, Erik noticed Raider standing outside the door, waiting for him.

"Where are we going?" Erik asked as he looked around, finding Mahjin and the man who held Chicago captive were now gone. Lachlan wrote notes in his notepad and said nothing to Erik as he walked past, entering back into the poolroom.

"Gettin' some pizza and a shake," Raider replied as they headed for the locker rooms. "What's your flavor?"

"Italian sausage and cherry," Erik replied and Raider suddenly laughed. "What is it?"

"Man," Raider exclaimed, "if you knew the dirty shit that went on in my mind!" He laughed harder and Erik's face flushed scarlet in response.

"Well?" Erik asked as Raider gave him a goofy grin.

"Well what?" Raider drawled and draped an arm around Erik's shoulders.

"Aren't you going to tell me?"

"Tell what?" Raider's facade broke and he snorted, turning away. He continued to laugh and shook his head.

Erik grunted and rolled his eyes. "Maybe not..." he muttered in annoyance.

FORTY-SIX

Sitting at a booth in the local drugstore, Erik and Raider huddled near the soda fountain, conversing.

"This isn't going to work," Erik complained. "Given Chico's anger problems, all he needs is just one small trigger for everything to happen and for everyone to find out!"

"Ay, I can do so much for Chico," Raider groused. "He's wearin' my ass out, dig it?" Erik held his chin in his hand, watching some students he saw frequently in the school foyer across the street at a pizzeria. Raider snapped his fingers in Erik's face. "Yo, ain't ya even payin' attention?"

"I can't control his anger," Erik protested and pulled away, looking down at his cherry-vanilla milkshake resting on the counter they sat at. "I'm not his conscience!"

"But he hears ya!" Raider struck the countertop with the flat of his hand. "Ya gotta keep using that special touch of yers!"

"My jawing isn't much of an asset," Erik objected. "Most of the time, it gets my butt handed to me!"

Raider blew a sigh and shook his head. "Look, I'm thin on my people. They're sick of me callin' 'em, man..."

"I'll keep talking to him," Erik muttered, stirring his shake with the straw. "But I doubt it'll make much difference!" He blew a sigh. "Despite my promising him *something*..."

"Look, Gottfried and Heinrich can't do it. They already got their hands full."

"I already know about that. After what Danae did to them, they're busy making sure Antony Gregg doesn't get sent to the grave."

"Then get to it." After several moments of silence, Raider nudged Erik with his foot. "Ay," he murmured, "the shake's no good or somethin'?"

"It's fine."

"What's shakin'?" Raider cracked a grin. "'Sides the shake of course!"

"Who is this 'Agency' I keep hearing about?" Erik demanded and Raider rolled his eyes. "It's always 'The Agency' this and 'The Agency' that… I mean, if they're that bad, why isn't anyone doing anything about them?"

Raider suddenly tensed and looked away. "Man, beats me," he replied in a non-committal tone.

Erik glowered back at his friend. "You're lying," he sneered.

"Do you wanna take this outside, 'cause we can," Raider said, glancing back. "Whenever you want it Erik, I got it!"

"Stop resisting me," Erik spat, slapping the counter, "and answer my question!"

"Fuck you and no," Raider shouted, "I ain't tellin'!" He banged his fist against the melamine, rattling the glasses.

"I will find out the truth, no matter what it takes," Erik growled. "If I have to directly confront someone or probe harder to get the answers I want, I won't stop!"

"It'll only get yer ass killed!"

"Thanks, but I can handle myself okay."

"Bullshit and you know it!"

"Then tell me!"

Erik's head whipped back from a firm backhanded slap. He grunted and stared angrily at Raider who glowered back, cracking his knuckles.

"I'll tell ya one last time: fuck no," Raider said flatly. "We're done."

"So you know something about those Core Irons too?"

Raider raised an eyebrow. "The fuck you talkin' 'bout?" he spat.

"Why else would Seraphine chase you down?" Erik pressed instead. "What about Chico? He was taken away for some reason!"

"Man, don't act like ya stupid under the hood!" Raider rapped Erik's forehead lightly with his knuckles. "I ain't no easy mark; they gotta shoot my ass dead with a homing rocket to drag me back there."

Erik narrowed his eyes. "You're avoiding the question!" he snarled.

"You already know the answer!" Raider spat.

"Is there a way to help him then?"

Raider waved a dismissive hand. "What ya wanna do 'bout it?"

Erik stiffened as pain suddenly flashed behind his eyes. He groaned and shut them, rubbing at his eyelids with his fingertips. "I don't understand what the fighting is about over these Core Irons," he griped. "They can't be that special."

"All I know they're somehow related to Corite. That's the best I got fer ya."

"Corite, is that so?" Erik snorted. "You mean to tell me we're mixed up in something over some damn rocks?" Erik opened his eyes, giving Raider a wary glance. "What's the deal? I'm nobody, you're nobody, Chico's nobody, so why all the pressure?"

"Because we *are* somebody," Raider answered and folded his arms across his chest, brooding. "We can do shit they only wish they could, 'cause we was made that way."

Erik pushed away from the table. "Stuff like what?" he asked. "Is it something like Chico can do?"

Raider shrugged. "I dunno what he does."

"What can *you* do?"

"What makes you think I can?"

"You and Chico know about this stuff. So that's the best I can put together!"

Raider narrowed his eyes and struck the counter with his fist, bristling. "What the fuck matters?" he spat. "This ain't 'bout me!"

"Then what is it about?"

Raider sighed, pinching the bridge of his nose as he grimaced. "Ay," he grumbled, "if ya gonna help, then make it yer care! I ain't free in the handouts department!"

"Give me more time to think about it!" Erik grumbled.

"Yeah, do that."

"I don't understand how you and these people you know well have more authority than Chico's adoptive parents," Erik complained.

Raider let out a heavy sigh and rose to his feet, digging through his back pocket. He tossed a five-dollar bill on the counter and stalked out.

Watching him storm away, Erik rubbed at his temples. "*I wonder if the people he knows have any information related to the Core Irons,*" he mused. "*If he'll help Chico this easily, then without a doubt he'll help me if I simply ask.*"

"Ay!" Raider shouted and Erik suddenly received a thump upside the head. He came out of his thoughts, noticing Raider glaring down at him with an irate scowl. "I got halfway down the block," he ranted, "lookin' like a complete jackass, talkin' to myself!"

Erik put up his hands in surrender. "I'm sorry, Raider!" he apologized.

"You comin' home, right, 'cause I ain't carryin' ya."

Erik sighed and left his milkshake behind.

Erik felt unconfident as Raider trooped ahead down the sidewalk, ready to take on anyone who seemingly gave them a menacing front. Erik groaned and grew more uptight as they headed further out of town. "Raider," he protested, "things don't feel right."

"Get off it, Erik!" Raider fussed and turned to Erik, poking him hard in the chest with his fingers. "Don't tell me ya lost yer damn nerve!"

"I'm concerned!" Erik argued. "Seraphine attacked me at school and I'm probably expelled for breaking his arm!"

"And that's a problem, how?"

"With that out the way, they'll have an easier time to try and trap me!"

"Then kick their ass when they show up again," Raider spat. "It's as simple as that!"

Erik sighed. "Fine," he muttered and they continued on, eventually nearing the mile marker where the street became gravel, also where Keely's boundary ended and the Aynslea's boundary began. The unease Erik felt worsened and he stopped walking when his hands suddenly burned.

Raider heard Erik stop and turned about face. "What's wrong with ya now?" he demanded.

"I don't know," Erik murmured and shoved his hands into his jeans pockets. "I'm sick..."

"So the fuck what?" Raider retorted. "Suck it up!"

"I'm tired of fighting," Erik objected. "I'm tired of seeing what it's doing to my friends."

"Then put a stop to those bastards for good," Raider said coldly. "Show 'em they got another thing comin' if they think they can just roll up on us like that."

Erik blew a hard sigh. "So what's the plan?"

"If we gonna rumble, make sure ya don't get yer ass busted up!"

Erik glared at Raider. "What makes you think I won't help you fight?" he squawked.

"Lately the smackdown department's been slackin' off on yer end."

Erik withdrew his hands and ran them through his hair. "I don't know what you want from me," he groaned. "I'm so *sick* of hearing you put me down!"

"Then get yer shit together!"

"Damn it, Raider!" Erik yelled, flaring in anger. He kicked at Raider and Raider sidestepped the attack, slugging his face with a swift right hook.

"Come on, Erik and quit bein' stupid!" Raider shouted as Erik staggered back and struck the ground on his rear, stunned. "Move yer ass 'fore I kick it again!"

Erik spat blood aside on the ground and glared up at Raider in return. Raider held out a hand and Erik took it, getting yanked to his feet.

"Do you mind telling me what issue Danae has with me?" Erik muttered. "Since you're Mister Know-It-All..."

Raider snorted and turned away. "Not my issue to tell ya," he answered.

Erik grunted and kept pace with his stride. "Obviously I can't remember!" he snapped. "So stop keeping me in the dark and tell me!" Erik clenched his hands. "You keep putting me off and it's only going to get worse!"

"I ain't got nothin' to tell."

"She's a threat to my family, my friends, even people I don't know!" Erik grabbed Raider by the arm and jerked him around. "Damn it, Raider! Tell me or so help me, I will kick you into next week!"

Raider glared back at Erik and slapped his hand away. "Hell, with that attitude, I ain't tellin' ya shit!"

"Then why keep fighting her if she's not a major problem?" Erik snorted. "What if it's just better for me to give up?"

Raider tensed and clutched his hands at his sides. "Shut up," he growled.

"Fine, I'll do that," Erik threatened. "I'll give up; let them do whatever they want to me. If it keeps the peace, then I've made up my mind."

Raider clenched his teeth and Erik stiffened when he heard bones cracking. Raider turned away and stormed ahead. Erik fell back several paces, keeping behind him.

FORTY-SEVEN

After walking for some time, Raider glanced back at Erik, checking on him and Erik waved back halfheartedly, letting Raider know there were no changes to his safety.

Once they reached the perimeter outside town, Raider paused dead in his tracks as Danae came down the path from the opposite end, dressed in a dark overcoat, hooded sweatshirt, jeans and boots. Raider held out an arm, holding Erik back.

"You come to party?" Raider called and pushed up his sleeves. He held his fists at ready in his fighting stance. "I'll dance wit' ya anytime, ugly ass heifer!"

"I'm not worried about you, shit stain," Danae snapped and withdrew a pair of dark glasses from her pocket. "It's Blondie back there I want."

"He ain't got no beef with ya," Raider spat, "so drop it."

"Sure he does," Danae said as she slipped the glasses on her face and grinned darkly. "I'm sure he hasn't forgiven us for ripping him a new one the last time we met."

"I can handle myself fine," Erik said coolly. "Ask Seraphine what I did to him earlier at school and you'll see I'm not in a good mood today."

"You really don't know what you're up against, do you?" Danae unbuttoned her overcoat and pushed it back, withdrawing a high-powered semi-automatic pistol she had holstered to her thigh. "So just accept that you can't stop the inevitable from happening and hurry up and die."

"Stop *what* from happening?"

Danae pointed the handgun in Erik's direction. "You're not going to live long enough to stop it anyway."

"One step, you bitch!" Raider shouted.

"Or what?" Danae replied, smirking. "Choose: either your life or his!"

Raider shoved Erik away. "You can't handle this shit," he said. "Just run like hell, Erik!"

"You don't think I can?" Erik angrily replied, pushing him back. "We're in this together, whether you like it or not!"

"C'mon, then, stay hip and don't punk out!"

"I'm tired of messing around," Danae grumbled. "You either come with me and get it over with or fight!"

"I'm fighting you!" Erik growled and picked up a rock. "So, bring it!" He chucked it at Danae and the stone struck her across the face.

Danae bared her teeth and wiped away the blood off her cheek with the back of her free hand. "You don't stand a chance."

"I'll keep being a thorn in your side then to slow you down," Erik declared. "So are you going to fight or keep jawing?"

"I don't think you can keep up!" Danae snarled and fired.

"Holy shit!" Raider screeched.

Erik staggered back, stunned when searing agony burned through his shoulder. "If you were going for my heart," he said, clutching his bleeding shoulder, "you missed."

"Shut up!" Danae screamed and fired again, striking Erik's arm and chest.

Raider pushed Erik to the ground and raced forward as Danae squeezed the trigger. Erik watched in horror as Danae emptied her round, riddling Raider with bullets.

Raider collapsed to the ground, bleeding severely and Erik staggered to his feet after Danae reached into her pocket, withdrawing another cartridge.

"You jerk!" Erik yelled. "What was that for; why are you doing this?"

"Now you've gone on and lost your damn mind," Danae snapped as she dropped her empty magazine and reloaded her gun. "You know why I'm doing this - I'm trying to kill you if you hadn't noticed!"

"Oh, really," Erik snarled. "It's not like you hadn't tried it before!"

Danae scoffed and reset the safety. "I swear; you're nuts today." She pointed the pistol at him again. "Now that your hero's out the way, die quickly."

"Damn you," Erik shouted. "You'll pay for this!"

"Shut up!"

Erik's vision flashed red and his ears rang when more burning pain tore into him. "*Why are you so intent on getting rid of me?*" he thought, falling to his knees as his labored breathing gurgled in his throat. "*Is it because you can't win against me in a fair fight...?*"

Danae stepped up to Erik, kicking him rearward by the chest. Erik grunted when he struck the ground on his back with a hard thud.

"What a joke," she said faintly, her voice distorted from the loud drone threatening to drown out all sound.

"I don't have this Core Iron that you're looking for..." Erik hissed. "No weapons, no schematics, nothing..."

"You *have* to have it; otherwise you still wouldn't be fighting this hard."

"I have a will to live."

"Live for what?" Danae loomed over Erik as he looked skyward with blank eyes. "I don't see why they think you're so special. You're nothing but trash -- always were and nothing but!"

"Trash, huh?" Erik rasped and spat at her. He let out a weak laugh as she frowned, wiping away the bloody spittle from her cheek.

Danae pointed the handgun at his forehead. "What's so fucking funny?" she snarled.

"If that's the case, then obviously I'm better than you... Better than anyone you know..."

"What makes you think that?"

"Because I'm different... and I just know."

"Just let go of this world, it's nothing but a dream to you anyway, right?" Danae grinned. "Don't worry; you'll forget everything this time..."

"That's the way it's always been, right?"

The red tinted world faded to black and the ringing immediately grew silent.

"Are you awake?" a voice called to Erik in the darkness. "Come on, get up! What's the matter with you?"

Erik's eyes snapped open and he sat up, facing Arizeh who wore a navy uniform standing over him, holding a blue steel saber in hand. Strapped to his waist he wore a high-powered revolver.

"What is it?" Erik asked breathlessly and looked around his surroundings, finding himself in a dimly lit room. "Where are we?"

"You got knocked out from the last battle," Arizeh answered. "We didn't reach our target and had to retreat."

"I'm sorry I'm so weak," Erik murmured. "I'm not made of tough stuff like you are." He snorted. "You got burned and you're acting as if it was nothing more than a mere scratch!"

"Ah, the wonders of science, eh?" Arizeh said and smirked. "Besides, you need to trust yourself more," he reprimanded. "Work with me and we'll survive anything they throw at us."

"I'll do my best and try to protect you."

Arizeh smirked. "Protect me?" he spat. "*I'm* always the one saving *your* ass!" Erik's face burned as Arizeh slapped him upside the head. "Try staying two steps ahead or you'll get yourself killed next time!"

"Alright, you proved your point..."

"While you're out dozing, I got us some new assignments," Arizeh replied. "But before we go out and kick ass, try and stay awake while the commander chews us out for whatever we've supposedly done wrong today."

"What's going on?"

Arizeh turned on his heel. "You didn't get hit too hard on the head, did you?" he called over his shoulder. "We're at war!"

Erik scrambled out of the cot he lay in and ran after Arizeh once he opened the door. "Who are we fighting against?" Erik asked, following him down a brightly lit corridor.

"Whoever the bad guys are..." Arizeh shrugged his shoulders. "They change all the time. We're not here to ask questions, we're here to kill."

"What if we're being manipulated? What if we're the bad guys?"

Arizeh stopped and turned to Erik, jabbing his chest with his elbow. "When did you suddenly start thinking?"

Erik grunted and pushed him away. "What are we," he spat, "machines?"

"No, we're being paid not to think."

Erik held back, watching Arizeh walk ahead and open the door at the end of the corridor. "Sometimes you scare me," he said.

Arizeh glanced back, holding the door open. "You know, if things were going to get real bad, you'll be there to back me up, right?" Erik nodded. "So it doesn't make any sense to worry when we got each other."

"I guess you're right."

Stepping through the door, Erik entered a new room, happening on an assembly of other young men and women in navy uniforms.

The soldiers, armed with various weapons, also wore black helmets with smoky eyeguards. An older soldier wearing a blue helmet with green eyeshield paced in front of them, armed with a crimson long sword slung low around her hips.

"Alright ladies," the older soldier barked, "let me make this crystal clear: you are the defenders of the people in this city; that means your flesh is expensive! More than that, you must take the threats you come across seriously and you gotta be ready for anything, so that means you do as I say; got that?"

"Yes, Commander," the other soldiers said in unison.

"You two," the commander snapped as Erik and Arizeh stepped in, "you wouldn't have the sense to come in out the rain if I didn't tell you to!"

"I think we can pretty much kick the rain's ass at our level," Arizeh cracked and Erik stifled a laugh.

"You think standin' 'round, like you run this shit, jawin' like some idjit is supposed to be funny, huh?" the commander retorted.

"I blame your poor attitude, Ma'am," Arizeh replied and Erik bit his fist as the commander clenched her hands in fury.

"You two brain buckets are supposed to report to Central Command!" she thundered.

"That's news to me," Erik grumbled.

"Fall in and report, do I make myself clear?"

"Yes, Ma'am," Arizeh said and jabbed Erik's chest. Erik nodded in response.

The commander turned toward the other soldiers as Erik and Arizeh crossed the floor for the exit. "Listen up," she spat, "if you think the last battle was hard, wait until you hear these new orders..."

The floor suddenly rumbled beneath them and a blast rocked the building, throwing debris into the room. Arizeh pushed Erik down toward the floor as part of it gave way and a section of the wall caved in. The other soldiers scattered and several enemy troopers stormed in, firing machine guns.

"Who are they?" Erik cried.

Arizeh withdrew his pistol. "Take this," he ordered, handing him his saber. "On my order, run!"

"Do they have any weaknesses?"

"Their body armor is bulletproof."

"Fair enough."

"On your right!" Arizeh broke left as Erik sprinted to the right. Erik jumped over a dead soldier and slashed into the back of an enemy combatant, felling him instantly before he turned around. "Behind you!"

Erik ducked as Arizeh fired his revolver into another soldier, striking him squarely in the visor. Blood splattered from inside the helmet and part of it cracked as the fighter crumpled.

Grabbing for the machine gun from the dead soldier's hands, Erik tossed it to Arizeh and he caught it once he ran past him. "Cover me!" he called and Arizeh let loose a rain of gunfire.

Erik dodged a hail of bullets, racing ahead toward more soldiers who fired into their remaining unit. He beheaded one soldier and turned, taking off the arm and leg of another.

"Move!" Arizeh screamed and Erik sidestepped a shot when gunfire blasted behind him. "Watch out!"

Erik whirled around, stepping aside from enemy soldier's gunfire and slammed his saber down into their flesh, cutting them in half by the shoulder. He beheaded another advancing soldier and pierced a third in the chest, slicing through the torso.

While dispatching the remaining gunmen, turning, Erik watched in shock when Arizeh shot the commander in the face. Arizeh withdrew the crimson long sword and kicked the woman aside.

Before Erik could process what he just saw, another enemy soldier approached. Erik immediately ran him through with the saber, striking his guts and yanking upwards before kicking him off.

Erik stiffened once stabbed in the chest through the back by the crimson long sword and dropped his saber, coughing up blood. The blade wrenched itself out of his chest cavity and Erik slipped to his knees, stunned as he faced Arizeh standing over him, holding the bloodied blade.

Why?" Erik wheezed.

"It's not your fault," Arizeh said simply. "But I don't want them to use you... not like this." He brought the sword across and Erik's world immediately grew dark.

FORTY-EIGHT

When Erik opened his eyes again, he recognized the familiar yellow wallpaper with blue sky and fluffy white clouds, realizing he lay in his bed at the Greenfield residence.

Erik tried to sit up, only to have the room drop and spin violently. He laid back and closed his eyes, hearing someone open his bedroom door and enter. Moments later, Erik felt a warm touch on his face.

"I wish I can stop you from hurting like this," John Greenfield whispered. "You're my son... I'm supposed to protect you from things like this."

Erik's eyes snapped open and he looked up, facing John Greenfield standing over him with a distant expression in his eyes. Erik sat up and John Greenfield took a seat beside him on the bed, smiling sadly at him.

"What happened to me?" Erik asked. "I thought..." He drew a blank and his voice trailed off, unable to recall what happened.

"You were having a bad dream," John Greenfield replied. "These nightmares of yours are quite dangerous; you tend to sleepwalk sometimes."

"I'm sleepwalking?" John Greenfield nodded. "How bad is it?"

"It's not too bad." John Greenfield took Erik's hand in his and gave a gentle squeeze. "When I do find you wandering around, I lead you back to bed. Sometimes you stay there, and sometimes you're up again."

"Do you know what I'm dreaming about?"

John Greenfield shook his head. "I wish I knew..."

"What do you think is wrong with me?"

"Well, if you want to see a sleep specialist, we can arrange for that." John Greenfield blew a short sigh and looked toward the floor. "I just want you well, Son..."

"What about you?" Erik asked.

John Greenfield glanced at Erik. "What about me?"

"You're having bad dreams too." Erik gently squeezed his hand and John Greenfield winced. "They're connected to your right hand somehow."

John Greenfield paled as an expressionless mask shadowed his face. "I just want you awake," he murmured and slipped out of Erik's grip. "Fully awake..."

"What do you mean?" Erik asked, growing disturbed.

"Please remember..."

"Remember what?" John Greenfield grunted and stood. "Are you all right, Father?"

"I'll be fine," John Greenfield muttered. "Just get some rest, Son. Your mother will bring up some soup later." Erik grabbed his sleeve before he left. "What is it?"

"When I sleepwalk, do bad things happen?"

"It depends." John Greenfield pried off his fingers and left the room, shutting the door after him.

Erik slipped out of bed and faced his mirror with the broken base hanging over the door. He traced his fingers along the jagged edge, then down the deep crack starting from the bottom and followed it to the mirror's center where it ended partway.

Looking at his reflection, a young man with messy blond hair, tired blue eyes and freckles across his nose and cheeks wearing a white T-shirt and flannel pants stared back. Erik gave a wide smile, revealing even white teeth.

"I look so normal," he muttered.

You're so far from normal, you monster, you beast...

Erik ran his fingers over the scars on his cheek and jaw, unable to recall how he gained it. He then turned away, opening the door and paused when he heard other voices he didn't recognize downstairs.

"How long will this take?" said one unfamiliar voice, belonging to a woman. "Hurry this up. We're to be leaving soon."

"Yeah?" John Greenfield muttered. "Where to?"

"Some recon work behind enemy lines," said the woman. "It'll be deep undercover."

"Well, the other one should be fixed up as soon as Gerald here finally gets it together," answered a second, belonging to a man. "He got the first one in working order pretty quickly."

"That's not fair," said a third voice, also belonging to a man. "He's playing favorites with us here!"

"I'm not playing favorites!" John Greenfield snapped. "Don't start that with me again!"

"I've seen it in your file, Gerald," said the woman. "Is that all you ever think about?"

"I don't want to discuss it," John Greenfield growled.

"You know it wasn't your fault," she continued. "It was that meddling woman."

"I don't blame her," John Greenfield spat. "Now please, let's drop it!"

"You ought to relax, Gerald," said a fourth voice, belonging to a man. "The Agency will always take care of you. They can give you anyone or anything you want."

"Please, shut up," John Greenfield snarled.

Erik padded out into the hall, moving stealthily for the banister at the top of the staircase. He paused when he spotted John Greenfield on the parlor floor with a bag of tools at his side, surrounded by various mechanical parts. John Greenfield knelt over a prone body beneath him and beside him rest a pile of discarded clothing.

Erik studied the mysterious visitors, noting the man dressed in a black suit standing near the front door, smoking a cigarette while a second in a gray suit reclined on the couch. Another man in a dark navy suit sat with a woman in a pale brown overcoat near the bar. He clenched his hands when they burned again and pain thudded behind his eyes.

"I've seen them before!" Erik thought, growing increasingly frightened when he couldn't recall exactly where.

They're nothing but serious trouble...

"Now stop teasing him," said the man close to the bar. "You know if Gerald screws up, we'll have to punish him accordingly."

464

The woman next to him giggled. "Don't make us punish you Gerald," she teased. "We don't like that."

"But you love punishing," said the man near the door. "It turns you on."

"And I love watching," replied the man on the couch as the woman laughed harder.

"Come on, Gerald, back to work!" she crowed and clapped her hands. "Or I'll force you to make a mistake!"

"Your taste in entertainment is pretty interesting," said the doorman.

"You're too gentle with him," the woman snapped. "He needs to be bullied a little more!"

"His strength is pretty amazing," said the barman. "I'm surprised he's gentle-natured at all."

"Why'd you have to fuck it up, Gerald?" the woman groused. "You're a bad boy, changing parameters without permission!" A beer can bounced off John Greenfield's head and John Greenfield growled, picking up a wrench in retaliation.

The man on the couch kicked John Greenfield's side before he could throw it. "Hey, cut it out," the man chastised. "Don't break him."

"Now you're ruining the fun!" the woman complained. "I don't break toys - I play with them."

"Then you won't mind the warning," said the doorman. "Remember, we need him alive - he's the key to our project."

"You're not interested in what he can do, are you Gerald?" asked the barman. John Greenfield grunted, saying nothing. "Then what is it that you *are* interested in?"

"I can't get closer to see who they are," Erik mused as cold sweat broke out on his forehead and neck. *"If I get to the edge, they would be able to see me and they might hurt Father Greenfield and me too!"*

Erik swallowed hard and slowly backed away, taking careful steps from the banister. Holding his breath until he reached the bathroom, Erik slipped in and silently shut the door behind him. Leaning against it, he groaned and slipped to the floor as his legs gave out beneath him.

It will only get worse...

"What am I supposed to remember?" Erik moaned. "What doesn't he want me to forget?" He leaned back and tapped his head against the glass. "If I'm sleepwalking, I must be repressing something..."

If you remember, it will kill you...

After gaining his bearings, Erik stood and stripped out of his clothes then got into the shower, turning on the water. He shuddered as cold water ran over his head and down his back.

"Why am I trying to forget so badly?" Erik mused, watching the water run down the drain. *"What is it that's disturbing me so?"* He pressed his forehead against the tiles, blowing a hard sigh. *"If I'm acting out my dreams, then what am I doing?"*

The bathroom door opened, letting in a cold draft and Erik stiffened.

"Erik," John Greenfield said from his place at the door. "Son, I'm sorry..."

"What are you sorry about?" Erik asked. When he heard no answer, he retreated into the stall's other end as the air turned almost near freezing. "Please answer me!"

"I'm right here," John Greenfield faintly replied. Erik shut off the water, listening as John Greenfield stepped in and opened the bathroom closet.

"What are you looking for?" Erik tried following him by the noise he made, trying to see in his mind's eye behind the shower curtain what items he manipulated. "Do you need something?"

"I..." John Greenfield blew a heavy sigh and suddenly grew silent.

"Well?"

Erik drew back the curtain, finding John Greenfield sitting on the toilet with the seat down, holding a dark crimson terry bathrobe draped across his lap. John Greenfield stared blankly at the floor and said nothing as he passed Erik the robe.

Erik took it, slipping his arms through the sleeves and wrapped the soft terry about his body. Tying the belt close about his waist, Erik stepped out the shower and knelt before John Greenfield, looking up at him. Erik poked John Greenfield's leg and he grunted.

"What do you want?" John Greenfield muttered.

"Father, please tell me, what's the matter?" Getting no response, Erik stood. "I can't help you if you're just going to ignore me."

Turning away, Erik headed for the door and paused when he heard John Greenfield call his name.

"Don't leave," John Greenfield mewed.

Erik looked at John Greenfield's reflection in the mirror. "What is it?" he asked.

"What happens in your dreams?"

"I told you... People are trying to kill me."

"Do you ever fight them back?"

"Well..." Erik blew a short sigh and stared down at his feet. "Sometimes..."

"Do you *want* to fight them back?"

"I find it hard sometimes. I don't always feel confident."

"Remember you're a very strong person."

"What about you? You said you dream about hurting other people."

John Greenfield nodded. "I thought I could get over it... But War is never a simple thing to get over."

"You mean to say you fought in the Defense Forces?" Erik whirled around. "How–? I don't see any uniforms or medals or anything around!"

"It's something I'd rather forget," John Greenfield said softly. "I sold everything relating to it. I don't like fighting and killing and bloodshed... It's a nasty horrible thing." He blew a short sigh. "So this issue you have... I completely understand what you're going through."

"Would I have to enlist?"

"Maybe..."

Erik swallowed hard. "Is there other things you dream about?" he hedged.

"A lot of things, though mainly concerning a woman..."

"Is it about Mother?"

John Greenfield sighed heavily and leaned forward, holding his head in his hands as he rested his elbows on his knees. "Yes," he mumbled, "somewhat..."

Erik stiffened and suddenly found it hard to breathe. "What about Mother?" he asked. "What do you mean, 'somewhat'?"

"She was..." John Greenfield shook his head and suddenly sat up, giving a faint smile as he rest his hands on his knees. "How's that shoulder?" he said instead.

"What are you talking about?"

John Greenfield stood and approached Erik, touching his shoulder. Erik stiffened when deep pain traveled up his arm and down his back. He grunted and pushed John Greenfield away, clutching his abruptly burning shoulder.

Erik slipped to his knees, yanking off the robe from his shoulder. Turning, Erik glanced back at his reflection, finding a deeply charred blemish resembling a third degree burn. "What *is* that thing...?" he cried. "How did that get there?"

"You have a skin infection of some kind, it seems," John Greenfield replied.

"Why didn't you tell me anything about it?" Erik spat.

John Greenfield gave a nervous smile. "I guess it didn't look that bad to me," he protested.

"It's okay," mumbled Erik, "I guess."

John Greenfield ran a gentle hand through Erik's damp hair. "I can't be too sure about it however, so it needs to get professionally checked out."

"Father...!" Erik tensed as John Greenfield's expression flattened completely.

It's a defect. Erik turned back and gasped when he saw his counterpart standing there in the mirror with a towel wrapped around his waist. He scowled at Erik as he readjusted the golden earrings in his left ear. *They're going to take you out to get you fixed... or worse, so don't be surprised if men in suits show up, looking for you!*

"What are you saying?" Erik cried.

You know what I'm saying!

"Son... I have to send you somewhere," John Greenfield said in a mildly mechanical tone and crouched next to Erik. "You're really sick and need to go to the hospital."

"No!" Erik yelled and shoved him back. John Greenfield struck hard against the closet's edge and staggered upright, appearing slightly disoriented. Erik rose as he straightened his stance and pulled back when grabbed for. "I'm not sick, really!"

"Son, don't worry!" John Greenfield pressed and firmly grasped Erik's arm. "You'll be taken in great care!"

"What's the cure, medicine to make me more like them?" Erik yanked out of John Greenfield's grip. "That's not going to happen!"

Erik looked into the mirror at his side and held his breath, watching his altered reflection standing behind John Greenfield. Instead of wearing a bathrobe, his counterpart wore a black sleeveless shirt, dark blue jeans, leather boots with buckles and silver arm bracers. He clenched his hands at his sides, shaking in rage.

"I've got some medicine to treat you," John Greenfield murmured. "It should make you feel better."

"What kind of medicine?" Erik demanded.

John Greenfield looked away, hesitant. "Let me go get it," he said faintly. "You know I want you well, Son."

"Please don't worry about me so much."

"I care about you very much; it can't be helped."

"I know you do."

John Greenfield stepped out the bathroom and once the door closed, Erik's double let out a shout and struck the panel of glass from the inside with a fist, cracking it. Erik backed away when the lights above began flickering wildly.

Liar! All lies! All of it! Everything!

Erik threw open the door and rushed for his bedroom.

Don't think you can escape!

Erik whirled around as the door banged shut and he let out a yell when he saw his altered reflection glaring at him from inside the broken mirror.

"What are you doing here?" Erik wailed. "You're not real!"

You...!

"No!" Erik cried as his counterpart formed a blue and gold sword sheath and withdrew a silver-blue saber. Erik raced toward the mirror when his double tossed the scabbard aside and it vanished. Slashing down, a sudden force flung Erik rearward and the mirror shattered. Erik struck the floor, moaning in pain when silvered glass pierced his skin.

The door opened moments later and John Greenfield entered, holding an amber vial. "Please don't fight me," John Greenfield said upon approach. "I do this to help you..."

Erik gasped and sat up, then immediately crawled back. "What are you planning to do to me?" he cried.

"I'm just trying to keep you alive..." John Greenfield objected and gave a strained sad smile.

"Don't touch me!"

"Just... please, let me do this... I have to..."

"No!" Erik's back met the wall and John Greenfield stood over him, blocking his only means of escape. He gasped when his counterpart faintly appeared behind John Greenfield, wielding his flaring green cutlass.

What are you going to do, Jerry?

"What do you mean?" Erik yelled.

What are you planning to do to me, to us? The reflection raised the blade high over his head. *You only want to destroy--!*

"If you die now," John Greenfield uttered, "then I won't see you again..."

Erik's vision flashed red and his counterpart vanished. Erik clutched his head as it thundered in pain and he screamed.

Wake up!

Erik shoved John Greenfield back onto the floor then sprang to his feet, standing over him. "Don't you realize the damage you're causing?" he shouted and snatched the amber bottle out of John Greenfield's hand. Erik hurled it at the wall, shattering it to pieces.

John Greenfield staggered upright and backed away as Erik advanced. "Please," John Greenfield pleaded. "Why do you keep tormenting me like this?"

"Because!" Erik grabbed John Greenfield by the collar. "I'm no feverish nightmare; I'm not some demon from your past!"

"Why won't you leave me be?"

"I want you to wake up, Jerry!"

"Please, stop!"

Erik reversed John Greenfield and threw him back violently, hurtling him hard into the chest of drawers. John Greenfield slipped to the floor and slumped forward, gasping weakly for breath.

"You'll regret doing this to me!" Erik thundered.

"I already do!" John Greenfield moaned.

"Liar!" Erik stomped forward and grabbed John Greenfield by the shirtfront, yanking him up.

"Please, calm down," John Greenfield said gently. "There's no need to be enraged!"

"I have every reason to be!"

"Let me help you... Please, trust me."

"I don't know if I can."

"I'm not the one you should be fighting."

John Greenfield grabbed Erik by the wrist and Erik grunted as the firm force caused pain shooting up his arm. Erik let go and John Greenfield continued to apply pressure, forcing Erik to his knees in agony. John Greenfield then released his grip and Erik cradled his wrist, stunned. His red-tinted vision turned hazy and he suddenly found it hard to breathe.

"What are you going to do to me?" Erik mewed.

"I won't punish you," John Greenfield said. "It's not your fault that you can't sleep... It's making you irritable and have angry outbursts."

John Greenfield withdrew a small clear-bodied pen holding a cartridge containing dark green liquid. Erik grew nervous when John Greenfield knelt toward him, gently taking his arm.

"What's that for?" Erik wondered aloud.

"It's for the infection, Son." John Greenfield answered flatly. Erik clenched his teeth when John Greenfield thumbed off the protective cap and stabbed him in the crook of his arm. He pushed the plunger, draining the contents into the vein. "This will help you, don't worry."

Erik struggled to see through the cloudy world, his eyes meeting John Greenfield's vacant stare. "That's good to know," he said faintly, wincing as his skin burned from the injection site.

John Greenfield withdrew the needle and pet Erik's head. "You have school tomorrow," he said cheerfully, "would you feel up to going?"

"I don't know if I'm able to," answered Erik. "I think I got suspended."

"Are you hungry at all?" John Greenfield inquired. "Do you want anything?"

"Some soup is fine." John Greenfield nodded and rose upright. Erik moaned and clutched his head when his world tilted violently. "What did you give me?" he cried. "You're trying to turn my brains to gravy..." Erik huddled close to the floor, sobbing. "I swear it's going to drain out of my ears!"

"The dizzy feeling will fade after awhile," John Greenfield retorted. "If you don't rest, you'll get sick."

"Please don't leave me like this."

"I'll stay with you."

"I'm afraid..."

"What are you afraid of?"

"What will happen if I don't wake up?"

"You have to stop dreaming in order to wake up," John Greenfield muttered. "Otherwise, those monsters will keep coming for you, out of nowhere and everywhere...."

"I can't give it to them... I don't know what they want from me."

"They're looking for something from you?"

"Something about weapons and Core Irons and schematics..."

"Wasn't that what you were dreaming about?"

"What is it they want from me?" Erik begged. "You know, don't you?"

Loud ringing in Erik's ears drowned out John Greenfield's answer, and then his world dissolved away into darkness.

FORTY-NINE

Loud ringing brought Erik out of the realm of darkness. He groaned and turned over, reaching out. His hands touched cold metal and he knocked it over, forcing the ringing to stop.

"Hello?" a tinny voice called. "Hello, are you up yet?"

"What?" Erik groaned.

"Get up!"

Erik gasped and sat up with a start, fighting off the sheets tangled around his limbs. He fell out of bed, striking his head against the nightstand and let out a yelp.

"Aren't you going to answer me?" the strident voice squawked. "You'd better not ignore me!"

Erik grunted as he clutched his head and looked over, noticing the blue-green receiver hanging off his nightstand. Picking it up, he heard other voices in the background and sounds of machinery grinding.

"What is it?" Erik complained. "What time is it?"

"It's time for you wake up!" said a cheerful female voice over the line.

"I'm up!" Erik snapped. "Now what?"

"Get going!"

"And do what?" The line cut off and Erik glared at the receiver. "What kind of prank is that?" he grumbled. After rubbing at his head, he looked down, noticing a small smattering of blood on the heel of his hand. Blowing a heavy sigh, Erik stood and dropped the handset back in the cradle. Turning away, he paused, realizing he didn't know where he was.

Looking about the room, Erik took note of the beige wallpaper on his walls with a blue sky and white cloud border near the top edge. He looked back at his nightstand containing his blue-green princess model telephone and large wood-bodied alarm clock with a split-flap display.

Erik approached his chest of drawers and opened them, finding pastel dress shirts and dark high-waist jeans with different styles of over-stitching on the pockets.

"This doesn't seem right," he thought and returned to his nightstand. Opening the drawer, Erik found photograph books stashed inside, a faded bottle of painkillers and a dented cigarette tin. He took out one book at random and opened it, revealing several pictures of an indigo-eyed raven-haired woman. Erik clenched his teeth as pain throbbed in his chest while he flipped through the pages.

"They're all about her," he murmured. "Who is she?" Tossing the book aside, Erik took out the others and found more photographs.

Growing frustrated, Erik threw them on the floor and turned back for the door, giving pause at the cracked mirror hanging there. IIe approached and traced the large fissure starting from the bottom and ended at the center.

Erik then focused his attention to his reflection, staring blankly back at a young man with freckled skin, blue-green

477

eyes, and strawberry blond hair. He touched his face, tracing the scars on his jaw and across his cheek, then the crookedness of the bridge of his nose.

"Who are you?" Erik asked his reflection.

Lately I've been having weird dreams...

Erik made his way across the hall to the bathroom and stripped off his clothes. He studied his nude reflection behind the door, noticing the numerous scars on his body.

In my dreams, I'm somebody else... I become him, I am him and I have no will of my own...

Erik grunted and stepped into the stall, switching on the cold water. He stood under the icy stream, trying to ignore the increasing pain traveling from his chest and down his arms.

"Damn it," he muttered. "The water heater must be out again..."

In my dreams, I can only feel what he feels... All he feels are sadness, pain, rage...

"Are you ever happy?" Erik murmured.

In my dreams, someone's always trying to kill me...

Erik blew a short sigh and ignored the pain radiating in his hands as washed. Shutting off the water, he returned to his room and changed into clean clothing.

Cuffing up his sleeves, Erik's phone rang and he approached the nightstand, picking it up. He held the receiver away from his ear when a string of explosive expletives filled the line.

"Damn it, Raider!" Erik yelled into the mouthpiece. "What's your problem?"

"The hell you been?" Raider's voice squawked from the earpiece. "Get yer ass down here or I'm gonna kill ya!"

"For what?" Erik spat back. He heard the phone change hands and a calmer voice speak over the line.

"Erik," said Hanalei. "That headache of ours is getting worse... She's going around causing more trouble."

Erik snorted. "I see," he murmured.

"We can't let her get away with this. She's hurting innocent people!"

"Let's just finally kill that bitch!" Raider's voice shouted in the background. "Let's rumble!"

"Where are you guys?" Erik asked.

"Franny's sitting on him at my house," Hanalei answered. "Please come quickly."

"I'm on my way."

Erik hung up the line and searched for his shoes. Kicking aside the photo albums, he dropped to the floor and looked under his bed, finding a pair of loafers tucked in the corner.

"What happened to my slip-on sneakers?" Erik wondered as he pulled them out and slipped into his shoes, then made his way downstairs. He slowed his walk when he entered the parlor, a large room with yellow carpet and a large stuffed couch upholstered in brown and yellow flowered cloth. Before the couch rest a cherry and glass cocktail table and on the opposite end of the room rest a large oak wide-screened floor-model television. *"I thought the carpet was white! Wasn't the couch black leather...?"*

Hearing the back door open, Erik raced into the kitchen and paused when he saw a violet-eyed red-haired woman enter with several shopping bags in her arms.

"Oh!" she said brightly. "Help me bring in the rest of the groceries, will you honey?"

"Er, sure," Erik murmured. Walking past her, he exited on the back porch and paused when he saw a blue coupe parked in the rear driveway.

"Didn't the house have a carport," Erik mused as he approached the car and opened the door. He withdrew the remaining bags of groceries from the passenger seat and returned to the house.

Erik came to a dead stop at the door, noticing the kitchen counters were different - made of heavy oak and white tiled counters instead of ebony and marble. Yet the plain white walls, the checkered linoleum floor and the steel appliances stayed the same.

"Are you all right?" the woman called to Erik behind the refrigerator. She shut the door and gestured toward the kitchen table. "Just set it there and I'll handle the rest."

"I'm fine, I think..."

"Is something the matter?"

"The water heater's out again."

"Oh, possibly a loose connection." The woman raised an eyebrow at Erik. "Weren't you going out today?"

Erik nodded. "My friends invited me to hang out," he answered.

"Why are you looking at me like that?" the woman asked. "Are you running a fever?"

"I suppose..."

The woman cracked a wry grin and took a seat at the kitchen table. "For a moment there, it looked like you didn't recognize your own mother." She smirked. "I wouldn't blame you..."

"What?"

"Never mind, honey."

Erik approached the table and set the bags there. "Will you be all right?" he asked gently.

"Sure, as always." The woman smiled sadly at Erik. "Don't worry about me."

Erik nodded and left for the front door. He noticed a red cap on the end table near the door and picked it up, fixing it on his head. Erik made his way outdoors, heading for Hanalei's house.

He later approached the row of apartments and hurried up the steps. Knocking on the door, it opened immediately, revealing Hanalei wearing a brown and yellow-checkered dress with small side pockets and yellow slippers.

"Hey," Erik said and embraced her. Hanalei giggled and blushed as Erik held her back by the shoulders, admiring her outfit. "You're always so cute!"

"Thank you," Hanalei said shyly.

"Stop drooling," Francisca spat.

Erik looked behind Hanalei, finding Francisca sitting on the floor atop Raider's back in the parlor. Francisca wore black jeans, red calf-high boots matching her crimson blouse and her long sandy hair in two braids.

"Don't kill him," Erik said and let Hanalei go. She stepped aside and he entered, approaching Raider. Erik crouched down at his side, grinning. "Can you do a push up with her on your back?" he asked.

"Damn it!" Francisca yowled and punched Erik's shoulder. Raider broke out laughing when Erik landed on his rear and Erik smiled brightly.

"Let's get going," Hanalei called as she changed into her shoes near the door. "We need put a stop to her antics."

"Yeah, you can sit on Danae while I kick her face in," Raider grumbled. Francisca stood and held out a hand to both Erik and Raider, pulling them to their feet.

"She said she's waiting for us at the park," Hanalei said as she stepped outside, "and that you'd better arrive before noon!"

Erik scoffed, following after her. "Why before noon?" he demanded. "What, she's got some kind of lunch date planned?"

Francisca chortled in response. "Yeah," she jeered, "a lunch date with a can of whoop ass!"

"Hurry up!" Raider whooped and bounded outdoors. He took off down the road and Erik ran after him.

FIFTY

Erik glanced around the building's corner he hid behind, looking across the street. He spotted Vicente pacing before the library steps, hands in his jacket pockets. Erik glanced to Francisca who hid behind a large tree near the park's entrance and she signaled back that things were clear on her end.

Erik then looked to Hanalei across the way who held several books in her arms. She approached Vicente and dropped her books at her feet. Vicente paused in his pacing and offered to help Hanalei grab her books. Hanalei signaled to Erik that she didn't see Danae while Vicente picked up the fallen hardbacks.

"Where is that bitch?" Raider grumbled and Erik leaned against the wall, blowing a heavy sigh.

"Maybe she set us up," Erik replied. "She's no idiot, you know."

"That bitch better not waste my time!" Raider spat. "I'm gonna rain hell on her ass so hard...!"

The church bells down the street rang when noon approached and Erik left his place at the wall. "Let's go," he groused. "It's obvious she wanted to make a fool of us."

"Fuck this," Raider growled. "I'm gonna find out where she lives and knock her punk ass out!"

"Don't do that!"

Rounding the corner, Erik suddenly received a swift blow in the face, knocking him back into Raider.

"Hey, boys," Danae crowed, slinging a baseball bat over her shoulder. "Glad you could make it." She wore a black trenchcoat over a navy blouse, mini-skirt and black tights with short boots. On her face, she wore a pair of reflective glasses.

Raider pushed Erik forward and Erik held up an arm against Raider, holding him back.

"Let me handle this," Erik said. "Go find her brother."

"Yeah, that chicken shit can't be too far behind."

"Oh, so letting your guard dog loose, huh?" Danae teased.

"Say that again!" Raider screamed and lurched after Danae. Erik immediately jumped on Raider's back and held him by the arms, pulling him away.

"Ha," Danae smirked and put a hand to her hip as she rest the bat's edge on the ground. "What's wrong with calling you for what you are, dog?"

"That's a low thing to say," Erik retorted.

"What ya know 'bout dogs, bitch!" Raider shouted.

Danae chuckled. "Oh, so you actually read some books, you greasy loser!"

"Don't start with me!" Raider shrilled.

"I got somewhere else I need to be, so let's settle this. It'll be short, I know, since I can beat both of your asses with my eyes closed."

"Don't talk down to us," Erik snapped.

"You know what I want, so just give it up."

"What you want is undeniable proof that I'll totally kick your ass," Erik spat. "So, bring it!"

Danae laughed. "You mean it this time!" she vaunted. "Okay, let's do this!"

Erik let Raider go and Raider spat at Danae.

"Fuck her up good," Raider commanded and stormed away.

Danae growled and wiped away the spittle with the back of her hand, glaring at him.

"This is the last time you bother us," Erik snarled and put up his fists. "You got me alone, so do your worst!"

"Now you're talking!" Danae focused on Erik and tossed him the baseball bat. He captured it as she reached under her coat, withdrawing a pair of long daggers. "Now, if you get on your knees and beg, I'll maybe go easy on you."

Erik advanced with the bat held high, making a swing at Danae. She ducked and turned out the way, slashing at Erik with a return thrust. Erik stepped out of her lunging attack, blocking her furious swipes as she came at him, swinging wildly.

"Come on," Erik egged, "quit playing around and fight me! Land a solid hit on me if you can!"

Danae let out a scream of frustration and lashed at Erik, cutting his cheek. He slammed the bat into her wrist, knocking away the first dagger, and then bashed the weapon into her arm, forcing it lame. Erik kicked her to the ground and pointed the bat at her throat, panting hard for breath as she glared back at Erik, heaving for breath.

"I won," Erik said and wiped away the blood on the back of his hand. "Now back off and leave me and my friends alone!"

"Hey!" Francisca's voice cried.

Erik tensed when a gunshot cut through the afternoon air.

"Shit!" Raider shouted.

Hearing a scream, Erik ran for the sound and approached the library's steps, where he found Raider clutching his side. Francisca knelt beside him, holding his wound as a pool of dark blood slowly stained his shirt.

"What was that about?" Erik demanded.

"That punk Seraphine shot at Raider," Francisca explained. "Hana took off after him."

"Which way'd they go?"

"Behind the library!"

Erik raced around the building and when he found no one around, he hurried for the park across the street.

Emerging onto a clearing, Erik came to a pause when he saw a young man with curly blond hair and vibrant blue eyes, wearing a black jacket and dark jeans. Erik swallowed hard and backed away when the young man held up a golden rapier in his left hand, pointing it in Erik's direction. The burning pain in Erik's hands came on strongly, traveling up his arms.

"I've come for you," the young man said. "You're near your end."

"What?" Erik yelped. "What do you want with me?"

The young man charged and Erik swiftly dodged his attacks, swinging back with the bat.

"*Damn it*," Erik thought in frustration when his attacks missed. "*It's like hitting nothing but air!*"

"Having a hard time, Ferdian?" the young man crowed. "It's like I can see your moves before you can make them!"

"If you did anything to Hanalei–!"

"I'd never hurt her, you *know* that!"

"Then where is she?"

"Defeat me first to find out!"

Erik yowled when stabbed in the shoulder and he staggered back, dropping to the ground on one knee as he wheezed for breath. Several more young men and women appeared, wearing navy jumpsuits with silver buttons, dark helmets with reflective eyeguards and armed with a variety of bladed weapons.

"Come on, Ferdian," the young man called. "Don't insult me. Draw your blade and show me who's boss!"

"What are you talking about?" Erik spat. "Why are you calling me Ferdian?"

"Because that's your name!" The young man tapped at his cheek. "Come now, be a good boy and land a solid blow on me."

"Why do you want me to hit you?"

"Because if you don't, then both of us are going into the scrap yard!"

Erik let out a terrified cry when the other young men attacked. He sprang to his feet, swinging with all his strength and ignoring the gnawing fiery pain in his left shoulder as he fought back. Erik found himself slowing down when he received a gash to the side and kicked one young man back, sending him barreling into another.

Finding his chance, Erik took off running through an opening and raced for the park's other side.

"*I need to find Hana,*" Erik thought as he outpaced his pursuers. "*If that creep Seraphine does anything to her, I'll kill him!*"

Suddenly tripping over his steps, Erik dropped his clubbing weapon and bowled head over heels. Landing on his face, Erik grunted and struggled to get up. The others caught up and surrounded Erik as he staggered to his feet, hands up in guard.

"I don't have time for this," Erik growled.

"Then let's make this quick!" one young woman retorted. "Get him out the way!"

Erik dodged out of a swift lunge and threw a powerful punch into one swordfighter's chest then kicked him aside. He received a stab in the side in return and staggered back, stunned.

"Hey!" a voice called. Erik held his side, searching for the sound's source. "Let him go, you monsters!"

"Hana!" Erik cried when Hanalei approached, rushing toward the group. She came to a stop as the others turned to her and she backed away, surprised. "Get away or they'll shred you to bits!"

"We don't want her," a swordfighter snarled across from Erik, glaring back at him. "We're here to destroy you!"

"Don't touch him!" Hanalei pushed through the group and cried out when one fighter slashed at her.

"Hana!" Erik yelped, watching in stunned silence when she fell and slumped against a nearby tree.

"Now that she's out the way," said the group's leader, "you can focus."

"You beast!" Erik screamed and kicked up the bat from the ground. Capturing it, he fought back in rage, smashing and kicking at the other fighters ganging up on him. He ignored the pain and the injuries he sustained, going ahead with a single-minded objective: to destroy.

After shattering the bat when he grounded the last sword-wielding opponent with a forcible knockout, Erik ran up toward Hanalei's downed form and knelt at her side.

"Hana!" Erik cried, taking her hand. "Hana, wake up!"

Hanalei slowly roused and moaned softly in pain, clutching her deeply gashed side. "What's with that look?" she murmured.

"What look?" Erik spat, incredulous. "You could at least be a little panicked!"

"Don't worry about me." Hanalei dug through her pocket with her free hand, handing Erik a translucent blue pen with a crimson nib. "You can use this better than I can..."

"What's this?" Erik took the pen from her.

"It's the only way..."

"I don't understand!"

"Even if something bad happens, they'll never find it."

"What...?"

"Don't tell me you did all this bare-handed!" Seraphine's voice called.

Erik stood as Seraphine approached, wielding a high-powered revolver. Seraphine twirled the gun on his finger and grinned when other young men and women in black jumpsuits flanked him, armed with swords of various sizes.

"They were weak and I defeated them," Erik snapped. "The same will happen to you if you cross me!"

"You're barely able to stand, Punk!" Seraphine retorted. "You're done!"

"I'll wreck you once I get done pulverizing these guys, Shorty!" Erik spat back. "Don't push me!"

"Get rid of him!" Seraphine commanded.

The pain in Erik's arms and hands lessened as the pen he held cackled in crimson light and transformed into a golden saber. Erik slashed down into the first fighter storming him, hacking her in half. He parried another blow from a fighter to his left and kicked him aside, taking off his arm, then riposted with an over the shoulder stab against another behind him, turning and followed with a diagonal cut, cutting down his next opponent on his right.

After clearing the blade-wielding attackers, Erik panted hard for breath, surrounded by bloodied bodies at his feet. Across from him stood Seraphine with his gun, smirking in response.

"Is that all you got?" Erik snarled.

Seraphine pointed his revolver at Erik. "You didn't fight at full power at all!" he complained. "But that's fine. You're on your way out."

"I was holding back for a reason," Erik hissed. "I'm saving my strength to destroy you for good!"

"Don't give me that shit. Good luck trying!"

"Bring it!"

Erik dove at Seraphine, dodging shots fired and swung, missing completely as Seraphine easily sidestepped the attack. A sudden fiery blast tore into Erik's back and he staggered forward, clutching his chest with his free hand as blood sprayed from the wound.

"How…?" Erik gasped and slipped to his knees, coughing up blood. "You never…"

"I landed a solid on you," Danae's voice said over Erik.

Erik pitched his saber into the ground and let out a weak hacking laugh. "You still can't do anything without your sister's help, Shorty!" he rasped. "Just go kill yourself!"

Seraphine's face turned red in rage. "Fuck you!" Seraphine thundered and unloaded his round into Erik.

Erik jerked back from the impact and collapsed on his face when his world grew dark.

FIFTY-ONE

Erik heard faint chains rattling behind him in the darkness and stiffened when he felt cold metal press against the back of his neck.

Get up!

Erik opened his eyes and sat up with a start, finding his counterpart standing over him, wielding a blue steel saber. The young man directed the blade at Erik's throat, sneering.

"What are you doing here?" Erik groaned. "You can't hurt me; you're not real!"

I'm as real as it gets!

"You're just my imagination!"

I'm going to destroy you... You refuse to listen to me! The young man withdrew the steel blue blade and hoisted it over his shoulder. *I don't care how many times I have to do this; I'm not letting those demons ruin us!*

"Leave me alone!" Erik cried. "I can't help you!"

Do as I say!

The young man pulled Erik up forcefully by the robe's collar and threw him out the door. Erik sailed across the hall and crashed through the bathroom door, striking his head against the sink. He scrambled to his feet as his counterpart stormed in.

"What are you going to do to me?" Erik wailed. His double whacked him across the chin with sword's pommel and Erik turned out, slipping to his knees as his vision flashed crimson. He cringed when his reflection raised his blade. "Please, don't kill me; I can do better!"

This is the end for you, Dreamer; you lost your right to exist!
"No!"

Erik tensed as the crushing blow drove through him once his reflection thrust the sword down, shattering the blade across his back. Erik let out an agonized scream when his senses were flooded with rushing pain.

Shut up!

"Please!" Erik begged. "I've done all I could... Don't punish me!"

The phantom made a gesture and a green steel saber appeared in his hand. He delivered a snapping roundhouse and his foot smashed into Erik's ribs, with the resulting force sending him flying back into the shower stall. Erik cracked his head against the porcelain tub and he slipped onto his face, struggling for breath.

If you don't want to die, then remember!

"Have mercy!" Erik whimpered. "I give!"

The young man kicked at Erik and flipped him over onto his back. He held up his sword that cackled in golden energy and paused when John Greenfield called for Erik from out in the corridor.

"Are you okay?" John Greenfield called and Erik's counterpart vanished immediately.

493

Erik caught his breath and slowly rose unsteadily, only losing his footing instead and sank to the floor, shuddering in fear. *"Why is he trying to kill me?"* he wondered. *"Why did he flip out like that...?"* Erik held his hands to his head as the thunderclap of pain followed stronger than before, making his muddy world that much fainter. *"What does he want me to remember?"*

They're trying to control you... destroy you...

"You're lying!" Erik mewed. He heard a snap and felt warmth draining down on the side of his face. Gingerly touching his face when pain radiated from his skin, Erik looked down at his fingers, gasping when he noticed his blue blood stained them. "What's happening to me?" He wiped at his eyes and suppressed a scream when he found more azure staining them.

You are starting to truly see... truly understand!

Erik rose and faced the cracked medicine cabinet mirror, heaving for breath. Staring back glared a pale-skinned young man with blue blood running from the corners of his eyes. "This is your fault!" Erik screamed at his fractured reflection. "This started with you!"

It started with you... this is all your fault!

Erik turned away and wiped at his face with his sleeve, then left the bathroom, bumping into John Greenfield who stood outside the door.

"Who is Ferdian?" Erik demanded and John Greenfield raised an eyebrow.

"You tell me," John Greenfield said carefully, "and I'll tell you what I know, if anything."

"I have no idea who he is," Erik complained. "Since I started dreaming about him, all sorts of weird stuff has been happening to me."

"What kind of weird stuff?"

"You obviously know something about him!" Erik snapped. "You don't look the least bit surprised!" Erik grabbed John Greenfield by the shirtfront. "I want to know what's going on! It's driving me crazy!"

"There isn't much to say about him," John Greenfield answered sullenly and pulled Erik's hands away. "He's just…"

"But why do people keep calling me by that name?" John Greenfield sighed and left down the corridor. Erik stomped after him, growing incensed. "Answer me!" Erik shouted at him. "Or I'll ask your weird friends downstairs!"

John Greenfield came to a stop and clenched his hands. "They're no friends of mine," he snarled. "Now get dressed so we can go."

"Where are we going?"

"I'll tell you when we get there."

Erik grunted and returned for his room, quickly changing clothes. He later stepped out into the hall and growled when he saw his counterpart standing there, wielding his blue-steeled saber.

"Not you again!" Erik snapped. "Get out of my way!"

If you go with him, you're not coming back!

"I don't have time for this!" Erik shoved past him and headed for the master bedroom door.

Don't you ignore me!

Erik knocked on the door. "Father," he called. "I'm ready to go."

The door opened, revealing John Greenfield wearing a dark brown suit and his long brown hair pulled back into a short queue. "You don't have to come with me," he said softly, "and I really don't want you to."

"Are you saying those people downstairs are putting you up to this?"

"I'll tell you what you want to know."

"So stop stalling and just say it!"

"Erik, do you remember your true name?"

Erik gave John Greenfield a blank look in return. "What kind of question is that?" he protested. "Are you saying these dreams I'm having aren't really dreams?"

"What are you saying?"

"Those crazy people in my dreams keep calling me Ferdian. Are you trying to say that's my name?"

"That's not your name."

"Then what is it?"

"Don't overstep your bounds, Gerald," called the woman at the staircase. "You say one more word and he's gone."

John Greenfield glared back at the staircase. "But if he doesn't know–!" he started.

"It's best he doesn't know the truth," the woman replied. "Besides, it'll hurt less that way, true?"

"It's not like that," John Greenfield protested. "He just happened to ask me..."

"You have somewhere to be, remember?"

Erik clenched his hands when John Greenfield blew a heavy sigh and appeared dejected.

"You're right," John Greenfield muttered. He glanced to Erik and smiled faintly. "Don't worry, Ace, it'll be over with and it'll be nothing but another bad dream." John Greenfield tousled Erik's hair.

"*He didn't get a chance to really tell me,*" Erik thought, glaring at John Greenfield as he walked past for the stairs. "*It's those people threatening him somehow.*"

John Greenfield came to a pause at the staircase and turned to Erik. "Aren't you coming?" he asked.

Erik shook his head. "I don't want to," he replied. "I don't trust them; I just have this bad feeling about it."

"What about them you dislike so much?"

Erik shrugged his shoulders. "Please don't make me go. I don't think I can handle it."

"I'm sorry... It's my fault."

"What's going to happen?"

John Greenfield approached and put his hands on Erik's shoulders. "Listen, Ace, it won't matter after tomorrow. We don't have any further to run. Whatever befalls us..."

"What's wrong with me?" Erik groaned. He leaned forward, pressing his forehead against John Greenfield's chest. "My head hurts..."

"You'll be good as new tomorrow," murmured John Greenfield, patting Erik's back. "Don't worry anymore."

"If you say so..."

Erik pulled away and headed down the stairs. He blew a sigh of relief when he noticed the parlor empty of the mysterious men and the woman. Turning for the door, Erik let out a yowl in pain when punched in the side. He staggered back in shock, facing an irate Raider standing before him in ripped jeans and denim jacket.

"What was that for?" Erik spat. "What's wrong with you?"

"Put up your dukes, yo!" Raider snapped and took on his fighting stance.

"I'm not fighting you!" Erik retorted.

"Then stand still and let me beat ya!"

Erik sidestepped another body blow and grunted when clipped in the chin by a fast jab. "Not until you tell me why you're attacking me!" Erik yelped and held his busted lip.

"I don't have shit to say to ya anymore!" Raider shouted and threw another punch.

Erik jumped out of the attack and shoved Raider aside. "It's because I still can't remember, is that it?"

"That ain't it at all!"

Raider charged and Erik reversed him, shoving him against the wall. "Then why are you ticked off at me?" Erik demanded.

"It's 'cause you won't say nothin'!" Raider ranted. "You keep puttin' up with their shit and flippin' out when it gets too bad!" Raider grabbed Erik by the arm and flipped him over onto the floor. Tripping backwards, Erik banged his head against the cocktail table and struck the floor hard, jarring his vision into a distorted fog. "We been worried about yer stupid ass, Erik!" Raider spat and stomped on his chest, barring movement. "Don'cha even *trust* us?"

Erik arched back as the sharp ache shot across his shoulder blades and down his back. A hollow warped drone rushed in his ears and the drumming beat of his heart became amplified. He panted hard for breath, hearing many disembodied voices speak to him at once.

Insanity, pain... that's all they give us...

They want us to become one of them...

The pain will stop once we join their side...

We can't defeat them, no matter what we do...

There is no compromise for the demons...

They either destroy us and break us down or make us anew, more corrupted than before!

Erik shut his eyes and drew a weak breath. "Something serious happened for me to flip out, as you say," he murmured.

"Yeah, and you keep acting like everything's cool when it ain't!"

"To tell you the truth, I'm scared," Erik retorted. "If I let go, it might push me off the edge!"

"Then jump!"

"*I can't be losing my mind,*" Erik mused, opening his eyes. He pushed Raider's foot away, and then rose unsteadily upright. "*I am losing my mind... But I'm normal!*"

Shoving past Raider, Erik staggered into the kitchen and came to a stop at once he saw his counterpart standing near the table.

Look who's awake! His counterpart gave Erik a derisive glower and Erik swallowed hard, wincing when the hissing droned louder in his ears.

"Normal people don't flip out like this," Erik said to him and frowned when the standing reflection appeared to take on a more adulterated countenance.

Do they talk to themselves and see and hear things that aren't supposed to be there?

"I see them!" Erik bellowed. "Yes, they're real!"

You are not real!

"You're the one to talk!" Erik shouted back. "You're not real!" He ran for the drain board and grabbed a butcher knife. "I'll cut you open! If you bleed, then I'll believe it!"

The young man grinned and beckoned to Erik.

Bring it!

"Don't push me!" Erik whirled around. "I'll make you disappear for good!"

That's never going to happen!

"Shut up!"

Erik lunched forward, making wild slashes at his counterpart who easily evaded his strikes. He swung back, blocking with his saber and cut into Erik repeatedly.

Yes, give into it! The pain makes us stronger!

"Stop talking!"

Would you rather the pain kill us instead?

"I'll kill you if you keep pestering me!"

Sanity left us and the agony is all that remains...

Erik let out a cry when stabbed in the chest and kicked back, sending him crashing into the kitchen table. He struck the floor and looked up at the young man standing over him, whose skin resembled sticky latex plastered together.

"I'm not letting you get rid of me!"

Stop pretending to hesitate then, Brother!

Erik felt weaker as the rushing ache continued to penetrate and overload his senses. He grabbed for the saber as his reflection brought it down, struggling against his strength.

"Do you really want me to kill you?" Erik snarled.

If you don't then I will kill you!

Erik clenched his teeth, trying hard to ignore the inundating agony coursing through him as blood ran down his arm. He let out a shout and shoved the young man back, sending him hurtling across the room. The blade clattered to the floor and Erik kicked it up, grasping it tightly in his uninjured hand.

Erik held the saber at ready, heaving for breath as his hands shook. "You want to kill me, then come on!" he shrilled. "At this point I don't care anymore!"

That's right! He'll only revive you again like before!

Erik gasped when he noticed how the skin around his knuckles started to split; forming small jagged seams and his wrist had the same sticky appearance.

"*It's spreading!*" Erik thought in full shattering horror. He backed away when his counterpart shook off his stun and jumped to his feet then formed another golden saber in his hands.

Is this real or am I dreaming?

The young man stepped in with a forward pierce and Erik blocked the attack with a diagonal thrust, and then pushed away. His counterpart fought back with almost superhuman strength, unleashing a ferocious barrage pushing Erik back on the defensive.

Finding an opening, Erik countered with an overhead swing and his reflection countered with a flash cut, slicing open Erik's arm. Erik grunted and kicked him away. He staggered rewards, stunned when part of his skin ripped like paper and fell away, revealing metallic sheen.

Erik's hard gasps turned to weakening pants for breath as he struggled to control his terrified shaking. He clenched his teeth when his hands warped and dug in his heels as he held up the saber.

"*Why is it worsening?*" Erik wondered, panicked at the sight of the tendons straining tightly against his skin. The green veins underneath became threaded lines, bulging intensely and the bones cracked from pressure, forcing his fingers to become disjointed and locked out of place. Erik's reflection recovered to his feet, standing unbalanced as he held his cutlass at ready.

They deemed how long we live and how soon we die...

"I really don't want to die," Erik pleaded, "but why do they keep killing me?"

They want you to forget...

"What are they trying to make me forget? That this isn't real? That I'm not real?"

Yes! You're getting warmer...

"But why? Why can't I be real?"

Because I'm the real one and you're the fake!

"I can't be fake! I feel pain, I hear and see everything!"

Then why can't you remember?

"They trashed my memory to make me forget–!"

Erik's breath thinned and he slipped to his knees as faint came on strongly. He let out a wail when the first violent jerk wracked his body and he thrust the saber into the floor, cracking the tiled surface as he firmly held on. Erik clutched his head when another booming crack of pain rushed into his mind stronger than the last and another seizure wracked his body.

If we're not perfect enough, we're wiped out, never to exist!

I want to exist... They never gave me a choice...

Erik struck the floor as the intense tremors rattled him and after the violent tic stopped, Erik lurched forward, biting his hand to keep from breaking his teeth. He moaned when blood seeped on his tongue and swallowed hard to keep down the acrid taste from welling in his throat.

They did this on purpose because we are destined to be greater than anything ever imagined!

They did this to protect what was lost... We'll never regain it, never replace it...

Erik's stomach turned and he got up on his knees, fighting dry heaves. Pressing his forehead against the floor when the hissing drone in his ears turned into a monotonous noise, Erik started sobbing as it becoming louder with each breath, threatening to bleed out his ears.

Maybe there is nothing more we can do...

Our backs are against the wall...

This is the end... I can feel it!

I don't want to do this again!

Erik screamed and clamped his hands over his ears. "Get out of my head!" he wailed. "Please, stop!"

There is no god...

They all abandoned us!

Maybe we are meant to be this way... to be used and discarded at will...

"*I don't understand,*" Erik thought, struggling to breathe and stand on stable footing. He stumbled backwards, pressing his back against the counter for support. "*Why do I hear all this in my head? Why do I feel this pain?*"

You can try to forget... But it'll only corrupt you...

Conflicted when his skin became tighter, splitting slowly open and the fear deepened, squashing his remaining, yet already wavering confidence, Erik reeled, struggling against sensations from various sources that assaulted him.

Because you are to never forget... always remember...

Erik cried out, pushing away his apparition-like aggressors his mind kept telling him, insisting were there and his body responded with cuts appearing from phantom knives, burns from non-existent flames and bruises from invisible punches.

"Father, help me!" Erik screamed and clawed at his neck with his free hand as deep threaded marks appeared around his throat on his skin, resembling corded rope. "They're trying to kill me!"

Erik sank to his knees, choking and gasping when his throat tightened, trying to pull free of the invisible rope strangling him. He grew weaker as dizziness overcame him and his world turned spotty and red. Above him stood his reflection, holding the saber at his side.

Erik received a phantom punch to the chest cracking his ribs under pressure, releasing the chokehold. He coughed up blood and gulped for air, struggling for breath. Sinking forward onto his face, Erik's weakened body fell still as he wheezed in pain and fierce agony struck him hard and fast between the eyes, completely silencing all auditory sensation.

Erik sensed a warm touch on his head and pushed against his shoulder, turning over onto his back. He looked up at John Greenfield who had a concerned expression on his face. Standing behind him was the faint apparition with Erik's likeness and Raider.

Don't disregard me. Don't resist me.

"*I can't move,*" Erik thought, watching John Greenfield reach out to him with a gentle hand, stroking his face. John Greenfield spoke soundlessly and Erik grew frustrated when he couldn't understand. "*I can't hear him... Have I finally broken?*"

Just let me take over. I'll catch you if you fall too hard.

"*If you really cared,*" Erik wondered, "*why let them do this to me?*"

He had no choice...

Erik's counterpart vanished and his vision blurred, then faded to white. After several moments of whiteout, everything slowly fizzled out and he fell into the darkness.

FIFTY-TWO

"Hey," a voice called. "Hey, wake up!" Erik groaned when jarred by the shoulder. "I had one hell of a time trying to find you! Don't act like you wanna ignore me and sleep the day away!"

Erik yowled when bat upside the head. He sat up with a start, facing a young man wearing dark jeans, a navy t-shirt, and white slip-on sneakers. Erik frowned when he noticed the young man had his likeness, with freckled skin, shaggy light brown hair and bright green eyes.

"Who are you?" he demanded.

"What a mean thing to say!" the brown-haired man said and chortled. Erik gave him a blank stare and his counterpart snorted. "So it's true you don't remember..."

"I've been trying to tell everyone that all along!" Erik grumbled and looked around his surroundings, noticing he lay in a hospital bed in a lone room with plain beige walls. "What am I doing here?"

"What does it matter? I'm springing you."

"First tell me who you are and I'll consider it."

The young man frowned and stepped away from the bed. "If you're resisting, then it must mean they put in some new programming." He blew a heavy sigh. "Well then, I guess it can't be helped..."

Erik's eyes widened when the brown-haired stranger formed a pair of sabers, one made of blue steel and the other crafted of green.

"What do you think you're doing?" Erik screeched and kicked the young man back, sending him bowling head over heels. He jumped on the bed, holding his hands up in guard as the green-eyed stranger scrambled to his feet.

"You're going to need more than that to defeat me!" the young man shouted and charged.

"Damn it!"

Erik jumped out of a wild slash then ducked under the swordfighter's guard, grabbing him by the arm. Throwing him overhead on the floor, Erik twisted the young man's wrist, wrenching one saber free and blocked a slice aimed at his side.

"Let's have some fun!" the young man crowed and kicked Erik away as he jumped to his feet. "Just like old times!"

Erik staggered rearwards and immediately held up his sword in guard, facing the swordfighter who copied his stance.

"Why is everyone trying to kill me?" Erik shouted. "I don't remember anything, so what difference does it make?"

"It makes a big difference that you're alive."

"So you've been sent here to kill me as well?"

"I never meant to hurt you like this! I want you to live, I really do..." The young man lowered his blade and extended his hand to Erik. "I came here to jog your memory. So come with me. We're going back."

"Back where?"

"To The Agency."

Erik shook his head. "I can't," he said. "They're the bad guys."

"Maybe you're the bad guy being used by them."

"What?" Erik lowered his saber, stunned. "What are you talking about?"

"What's that in your hand?"

Erik looked down at the dimly glowing blade in his hand. "I'm not sure," he murmured.

"Have you always wondered why you're a decent fencer?"

"Like I know!" Erik snapped and threw the blade aside. It clattered on the floor and vanished in gold light.

"So you agree there's no need for us to stick around here then."

The door opened and Erik turned, facing John Greenfield who wore a white lab coat over his dark brown suit. On his face, he wore his gray plastic wide-framed glasses.

"What are you doing up?" John Greenfield asked, appearing mildly surprised.

"What are you doing wearing that getup?" Erik spat back.

"I'm a weapons engineer, remember?"

Erik gasped when the pain flashed behind his eyes. He moaned and held his hands to his head, doubling over. "Not again!" he mewed.

"Please awaken from this awful dream," John Greenfield pleaded. "Hurry and open your eyes!"

"Shut up, toymaker!" the sandy-haired swordfighter thundered and pointed his saber at John Greenfield. "Don't believe him, Erik! Come with me and I'll help you."

"Both of you stop it!" Erik cried. "You're killing me here!" He slipped to his knees as the agony worsened.

"Weren't you resting?" John Greenfield pressed. "You had a severe migraine and wanted to sleep it off."

"Don't listen to him!" shouted the fighter.

"Why would I ever lie to you?" John Greenfield retorted.

"Then tell me who I am!" Erik wailed. "Tell me everything you know about me!"

"You're one half of a whole that was never supposed to exist..."

"What did you say?" the brown-haired swordsman screamed.

"You're no mistake, please don't think that," John Greenfield murmured. He stepped forward and frowned when the green-eyed stranger advanced, barring movement. "Oh, you want a piece of me?" he spat and put up his hands as the swordfighter pressed the edge of the blade against John Greenfield's chest.

Erik scrambled to his feet and clutched his hands at his sides. "Leave him alone!" he shouted. "He's not a part of this!"

"Weren't you trying to remember who you were?" John Greenfield inquired.

"I know who I am!" Erik responded. "I think..."

"Oh? Then tell us!" snapped the brown-haired swordfighter. "You give me the wrong answer and this toymaker loses his head!"

"So don't go and keep your promise," John Greenfield threatened. "The choice is yours."

"What promise did I make?" Erik asked. "I made a lot of promises, apparently..."

"You promised to keep yourself alive so that we can meet again..."

Erik cried out when his vision flashed red and he clamped his hands over his ears when a loud drone buzzed in his head. The burning pain returned with full force in his hands and traveled up his arms.

"That's enough!" the green-eyed stranger growled and slashed at John Greenfield. John Greenfield stepped out of the attack and kicked the young man back, sending him bowling over on the floor.

"Remember who you really are!" John Greenfield called as he entered the room and pushed up his sleeves. The young man jumped to his feet and John Greenfield turned out a swift pierce then followed with a hard jab into the man's side, forcing him staggering back. "Prevail! Fight! Destroy!"

"This is a dream, I'm sure of it," Erik thought when the young man blocked John Greenfield's next attack and jammed his sword into the older man, hacking him in half by the torso with a flick of the wrist. *"I'm just dreaming again, about people I never met, about places I've never been..."*

Erik stood as the pool of blood spread near him and a translucent blue pen with a golden nib clattered on the floor beneath John Greenfield's fallen form.

"Accept it," his counterpart snarled. "Just lie down and die, just like your maker!"

"Why did you have to kill him?" Erik shrilled and picked up the pen, glaring back at the young man with his likeness.

"Because his job was complete and he's no longer needed, as are you."

In my dreams, I become another person in a world that has nothing to do with me...

The searing agony in Erik's hands dissipated and the pen cackled in cyan energy as it transformed into a golden rapier. He held up his sword in guard as the sandy-haired swordfighter approached.

"Any last words?" Erik's counterpart sneered as he approached.

I don't know why I've been having these dreams...

Erik narrowed his eyes. "Why are you trying to destroy me?" he growled. "At least give a dying man an answer!"

"Since you forgotten everything, I can't bring you back," the young man replied, "so I have no choice but to dispose of you."

I don't know why I can't remember...

"I need more time!" Erik protested.

The swordfighter scoffed. "Time is something you don't have!" he exclaimed.

I don't know why they want to destroy me...

"I have every right to live!" Erik screeched.

"There's only room for one contender at the top." The green-eyed fighter grinned darkly and raised his blade. "My life or yours... It's time to ante up!"

I don't know which parts are the dream and which parts are real!

Erik stepped out of the attack and whirled around, slashing at his counterpart's back. The swordfighter made an over the shoulder block and turned, striking back with an underhanded pierce. Erik deflected the strike and kicked back, sending his opponent tripping rearwards.

"Aren't you ready to die?" Erik jeered and kicked the brown-haired fighter down to the floor.

"You get rid of me and more will keep coming," Erik's counterpart snapped. "Wasn't it better not remembering and staying in that dream?"

"If only I could dream forever, is that it?" Erik snarled and raised his blade. "You're not erasing me!"

"I don't like the idea either, but only one of us can leave and it'll be me."

"You're not important! You're not supposed to exist because you're nobody!"

"Oh, now you remember!" The green-eyed swordfighter grinned. "I was worried there for a second."

Erik raised an eyebrow and lowered his blade, slightly perplexed at the sudden reaction. "Worried about what?" he asked.

Erik's counterpart laughed. "You almost damn near fooled me... Pretending that you remember when you really did lose all your memory."

"Stop messing with my head!" Erik shrilled and brought down his blade with a savage swipe. The swordfighter blocked and pushed Erik back then sprang to his feet.

"I actually envy you," sneered Erik's counterpart. "I wish I could easily forget, but no, it's in there, all there, over and over again! When I sleep, when I wake... It never ends!"

"Then let me put you out your misery!"

"Forget it!"

"Don't push me!"

Erik charged and made wild slashes at his brown-haired duplicate, who easily blocked and deflected his blows, twisting and turning out the way. He stomped on Erik, sending him sailing across the room and crashing against the wall.

"Come on!" roared the swordfighter. "Try to remember! Try! Remember!"

"Remember what?" Erik grumbled as he staggered to his feet.

"Everything you thought you knew, your friends, your family... They're fake! All of it's fake!" Erik's counterpart pointed his saber at Erik. "The Agency created it to control you!"

"Nobody controls me," Erik spat bitterly. "You're just a figment of my imagination too! You're just as fake!"

"You idiot!" the brown-headed fighter roared. "You'll regret this forever!"

"My only regret is meeting you!" Erik bellowed.

"That one you thought you knew is long gone! Accept it!"

"Stop lying to me!"

"Fine, I see how it is..."

Erik rushed forward as the swordfighter also raised his blade to attack. "Get out of my way!" Erik shrieked.

"You first!"

Your reality is dead wrong! Fake!

Burn out and die... before you destroy everything you're trying to save!

You're becoming too dangerous to keep alive!

You're no longer Erik Hart; he does not exist...

Ferdian is dead as well...

Erik jammed his blade into his opponent's chest and grunted when a sharp blow aside his head forced his vision dark. Pain flooded Erik's senses completely and he lost his connection to his world.

FIFTY-THREE

"Hey," a voice called from afar. "Hey, pull yourself together!"

Are you dreaming or something?

"What?" Erik moaned. "What is it?"

"Don't scare me like that!" called the voice.

Please let me see her one last time... Before I forget...

"I'm up..." Erik muttered, "I think."

"Come on, get up!"

I have something to tell her... I need to tell her something important!

"Why are you bothering me?" Erik groaned.

"Because I can! Now open your eyes!"

Erik's eyes snapped open and he found himself in bed with the sheets over his head. In his hands, he held a telephone receiver where he heard a woman's voice calling for him on the other end.

"Are you awake now?" she asked. "Are you up now?"

"Don't hang up," Erik pleaded. "Please, come see about me. I need to see you."

"You know I can't do that."

"I don't know how much longer I can put up with this."

"I'm sorry..."

"You keep calling me!" Erik shouted into the mouthpiece. "Come over, or so help me, I'll burn this place to the ground!"

"I will come over, I will!" the woman yelped. "Please don't get upset."

"You know I'm serious!" Erik snarled. "Don't go there with me!"

"I'll be over."

"You got an hour! One minute late and this place is burnt to the foundation!"

"Then hang up so I can get going!"

Erik tossed off the sheets and reached over the nightstand, throwing the handset on the cradle. He sat up and yawned, rubbing at his face. Planting his feet on the floor, Erik opened his nightstand and sifted through the items inside.

Erik withdrew a bottle of painkillers and unscrewed the top, pouring several pills into his palm. He cupped them as he took out his cigarette tin and flipped it open with his thumb, then took out a cigarette.

Erik gulped down the pills as he got up and kicked up a pair of flannel pants. After pulling into them, he headed across the hall to the bathroom. Turning on the water, Erik cupped water in his hand and swallowed, choking down the pills. Grabbing the lighter set aside on the bathroom counter, he lit his cigarette and blew smoke over his head.

Erik glared back at the young man staring at him, with dark red hair and sunken violet eyes. Three prominent scars covered his face: one down his jaw, across his cheek and over his left eye. The bridge of his nose was crooked and Erik frowned at the numerous scars and old burns on his chest and arms.

"You monster, you beast," he grumbled. "Why do you even bother?" Erik blew a heavy sigh and set down the toilet seat, plopping down. He smoked in silence, tapping his ashes in the sink. After his cigarette burned out, Erik moaned and held his painfully throbbing head.

The phone began ringing and Erik grunted as he rose reluctantly to his feet. Heading downstairs, he entered the kitchen and picked up the phone there.

"You sure took your time to answer," the woman's voice said on the other end of the line before Erik could say anything. "So, did you decide yet?"

"I don't feel well," Erik grumbled. "The headaches are starting again."

"Well, that's too bad. So, are you going to turn against them?"

"Why did you choose me?" Erik demanded, growing annoyed. "Why did it have to be me?"

"Did you just remember something?"

"I'm not sure... What am I supposed to do again?"

"You need to wake up."

"Why aren't you here? I need to talk to you!"

"I'm on my way. I'll answer any questions that you have, okay?"

"Please hurry up."

Erik hung up the line and turned on the percolator. Taking a seat at the kitchen table, Erik groaned and rubbed at his temples.

"These headaches are getting worse," he muttered. "The painkillers should've kicked in by now..."

The telephone rang again and Erik growled under his breath. He leaned back in his chair and yanked the phone's cord, unhooking the handset from the cradle. Capturing the receiver, he ground his teeth in irritation when he heard the haunting melody he grew to hate in the background.

"Stop messing with me!" he screamed and rose to his feet. "Why? Why me? Why are you trying to destroy me? What do you want me for?"

"What a pity, your fate..." said a voice Erik hardly recognized.

Erik gasped when the pain in his head worsened. "Doctor!" he cried and staggered back against the counter. "My head's killing me... The painkillers aren't working anymore."

"Please just wait a little while longer," said the doctor. "I'll need more time to restore you if you're going through with it."

"I'm waiting on her."

"I'm sorry, she can't come."

"But she promised me!" Erik shouted.

"Just do as you're told."

"I'm tired of being used!"

"If you rebel, then you'll be disposed of."

"So be it!"

"You should've been grateful that you were left to live in a dream."

"Stop lying to me!"

"You had nothing to begin with! You've always been nobody, always have been an existence that's not supposed to exist. You were never supposed to feel, to reason, to experience. You were only to watch and eventually destroy."

"Why are you treating me like I'm some blank slate?" Erik shrilled. "I think, I feel, I care, I love, I hate! I am somebody! I have a purpose, a name, wants and desires! How dare you treat me like a machine!"

"Because you are one."

Erik screamed in frustration and tore the phone out the wall. He threw it on the floor, shattering the plastic body. Growing enraged, Erik let loose, punching and breaking anything he could get his hands on in the kitchen, smashing and shattering everything breakable.

Hearing the back door open, Erik picked up a pair of butcher knives and tossed one out the door. A woman yelped in response and a young man wearing a dark navy uniform, gray tinted glasses and black cap on his head entered. Erik threw the other knife and the young man caught it, grinning darkly.

"What are you doing here?" Erik snarled as the young man tossed the knife in his hand.

"Damn, you really trashed this place," he replied, glancing around.

"What do you want with me?"

"How much longer are you going to keep acting out like this?" the young man snapped.

"What does it matter?" Erik spat back. "It's nothing but a horrible dream anyway."

"Do you remember me this time?" the young man suddenly asked. "Just tell me my name and we can forget this whole thing. It'll be over soon and you won't have to keep hurting like this."

"Why should I bother trying?" Erik growled. "Nobody would miss me, right? I'm nobody, a machine." Erik snorted. "A machine doesn't feel happy or sad, jealousy or love or hatred... It just follows orders until its use runs out and is sent to the scrap heap!"

The young man guffawed. "What a load of shit!" he crowed. "Who told you that?"

"That doctor..."

"He's a liar, like all of those toymakers." The young man caught the knife he tossed and passed the handle to Erik. "Look, if you want to kill yourself, go ahead. I'm not gonna stop you. But know that I'll miss you if you did that."

"I'm flattered, but you're too late. I made up my mind." Erik slapped the blade away, forcing it clattering aside on the floor. "There's no sense in warning me. I know what's going to happen."

"Don't go."

"But if I let you save me again, you'll be a dead man."

"So what, I choose to save you."

"Maybe I don't want to be saved." Erik turned on his heel and froze when he heard the hammer of a revolver pull back.

"I'm not letting you go!" the young man spat. "So help me, you're going to Hell with me, whether you like it or not!"

"Then go to Hell!" Erik dove for the knife on the floor, barely missing the shot aimed at his back. He turned and kicked the young man away as he aimed again and slashed at his wrist.

"That's it!" the young man whooped. "That's more like it!"

"I'm not going with you!"

"Then show me how badass you are! Fight me!"

"Forget it!" Erik dropped the blade and walked away, heading for the parlor.

"I'm not going down without a fight!" the young man bellowed at his back. "Don't think I'll spare your stupid ass!"

Erik heard a shot fire off and staggered back in shock. He gripped his burning chest and looked up at the woman standing in his parlor, armed with a rifle. She wore a matching uniform with dark cap and reflective glasses covered her eyes.

"That was a good shot..." Erik moaned. "That... That really hurt!"

The woman paled and appeared uncomfortable. "How is that?" she cried. "You're not supposed to feel anything...!"

"But why do I have to disappear...?"

"I'm sorry... But it's for your own good. Your heart wasn't in it and we can't afford to fail."

"Is it because I'm nobody?" Erik let out a weak laugh and coughed up blood. "What do you want from me?"

"I'm sorry."

Tears ran down Erik's face. "I hate you!" he cried. "I don't deserve this!"

"Good," said the woman. "Hold on to that hate. Pass it on to them and show them!"

"My heart belongs to me!" Erik shrilled. "It's my life; I should choose how I want to live!"

"You were supposed to follow orders."

"No one orders me around!"

The woman adjusted her aim at Erik. "Let's meet again in the next life."

"There's no changing your mind, huh?" Erik said weakly.

"It can't be helped."

"Yeah, I'll be waiting..."

The woman gave a faint smile. "I know you will," she said softly. "I'll be waiting too."

"If only we could achieve peace," the young man said behind Erik, "then we could live without fear and don't have to use weapons anymore."

"Peace is a long way off," the woman murmured. "A long, long way." She fired again and Erik's world darkened immediately.

FIFTY-FOUR

"Erik!" called John Greenfield from afar. "Erik!"

Erik slowly came to as pain saturated his body and mind, forcing him disoriented and unable to understand what went on around him. He sensed he traveled without moving, his limbs jerking around on their own volition while still rooted firmly into place.

Aware he ran with a purpose, despite the darkness clouding his vision and filling the world around him with alternating shadows, his body continued onward; putting one bruised and bleeding foot in front other, though the ground did not move beneath his feet, turned when he did not, nor inclined steeply upward on a slope that did not exist before him.

The cool evening air waft against him as he raced on what felt to be familiar ground, though his legs did not move and the air around him seemed still, almost suffocating.

Erik felt the tall grass and rush and field stalks brush against him with his groping arms pulling him forward, conflicting against the sensation of his arms tied down to the cold hard table he grew to despise.

He screamed, only to hear the frenzied heartbeat thumping in his ears. Erik opened his eyes to see nothing but darkness, yet when he closed them, he saw himself hurrying through the fields across from the Greenfield residence. His frantically searching mind tried to settle on either going to or from something wanting him, in which he understood clearly.

The pathway became an edge and Erik tumbled headlong, falling through space before splashing into frigid cold filling his lungs as he sank ever downwards.

His breath thinned as all sound turned distorted, hollow, submerged in the shifting and aqueous world. Erik's body snapped to and his uncertain arms began propelling him upwards toward freedom before his lungs protested and burst, breaking through to sweet fresh air.

He scrambled across hot dry sand, the sky above glaring down at him with a blazing sun beating at his back, then a chilly stiff rain fell, tearing icy daggers at his skin, slowing him as the frigid grip of bitter frost and snow lashed out against him, numbing his hands and freezing his feet.

"Erik, wait," John Greenfield continued. "Please, come back! You need to return..."

You need to wake up! Wake up and live, Ferdian!

"*What's real?*" Erik thought as he kept running. "*I don't know what's real and what's fake anymore!*"

You know deep down that if you stopped now, you will no longer survive!

Erik tripped and stumbled forward, only to regain footing and continued to run. "*I bet it's that medicine that's messing with my head!*"

That's a lie and you know it!

"*What should I do?*"

Just wake up and truly see!

"What if it's one of those dreams where you wake up within the dream?"

Erik slammed into a hard surface, it gave way unnaturally, crumpling forward without sound and he fell, striking a cold hard surface. The earth's grass and stones felt comforting, finally motionless underneath his exhausted body, with the night cold's dew soaking through.

Get up! Get going!

"I need to keep moving forward," Erik told himself, though his body did not immediately respond. *"Keep going..."*

The earth's reassuring calm soon gave way to a metal door closing behind him, its hinges groaning. Erik swiftly jumped to his feet and kicked at it, bursting through then ran away once more.

The hollow dark world released a supersonic drone, crashing against his panting breath and his thudding heart filling his ears. The many voices talking at him became louder.

The dream is reality and reality is nothing but a complex illusion.

There are no days, no hours, no moments, nothing in induced madness...

There is no place, no particular time here. No way to know, no way to be...

"Then what's the illusion created by?"

Erik grew frustrated when he saw nothing but the dark, unaware of the branches tearing at his arms, legs, back and face, the limbs shred what clothing he had left.

His feet hit the ground unevenly and the assorted stones and sticks on the forest floor ripped into his skin. Erik's heart pound furiously in his chest and his breath thinned as he gasped for air, driven by the only directive his body commanded, by what his mind ordered: to run away and survive another day of freedom quickly slipping from his grasp. The many voices continued around him.

The illusion...

The dream...

Within, without, outside, under, over...

They are everywhere and nowhere, here nor there, yet gone and back again...

There are near and far, inside and out, in our dreams, in our waking hours...

All of it, built up and created, broken down and destroyed...

All of it, by no one and yet by all...

All of it, by us and also by them...

Resurrected by the flames of purity, also corrupted by the flames of destruction...

We are all to blame!

Erik screamed when he felt a stabbing pain in the back of his neck, throwing him forward. He clawed at his neck, feeling a steel dart there and yanked it out as his shadowed vision slowly tinted in red. Scrambling forward, Erik continued racing away when he heard heavier footsteps closer in pace following after him.

"Erik," John Greenfield pleaded, his wailing voice echoing in the distance. "Erik, please, stop! They'll punish you for running away again!"

Keep going!

Many emotions surrounded and besieged Erik: fear, guilt, pain, sadness, hurt, regret, and the searing pain starting in his head and neck moved down into his chest, spreading to his arms and legs, followed by deep lacerations slowly slitting open the skin on his arms and legs, burning as the wind that was there, yet not there, blew into them.

All sound became a rushing howl in Erik's ears and the disembodied voices continued calling for him warped and taking on an almost alien sound.

"Stop him!" a commanding voice shouted clearly over all else.

"Erik!" John Greenfield's voice shrilled. "I'm telling you now!"

We've had enough of your lies!

The red quickly became blinding white once Erik felt the sharpness stab at him in his temples, ripping forcefully through the center of his forehead. The sound around him turned diffused, isolating only his drumming heartbeat and his ever-weakening gasps.

Tackled from behind, Erik let out a yelp and struggled against the person who dragged him down to the ground. Erik's vision suddenly cleared and he looked up at John Greenfield who straddled him, holding him down by the shoulders. John Greenfield's face appeared painfully drawn and his eyes distant behind cracked plastic-framed eyeglasses.

"What–?" Erik started.

"Listen, Ace," John Greenfield said quickly. "Trust no one. They only want to use you."

"What about you?"

"Eventually they'll use me too."

"Then who can I trust?"

"Your judgement."

"But what about–?"

"Forget it all. Forget everything. Just destroy them!"

"But I can't kill..."

"If you don't, then they'll kill me!"

Several men and women in uniform appeared behind John Greenfield, running up to the scene.

"That's enough, Gerald," called one woman.

"Let him go," barked one of the men. "He's done!"

"No," John Greenfield wailed and scrambled to his feet. Erik also stood as John Greenfield withdrew a pistol from his blazer. "You'll have to stop me before you lay a hand on him!"

Join me... together we can defeat them!

"I don't know if I can..." Erik moaned.

"Run!" John Greenfield ordered and aimed his gun, firing off a shot.

"Shit!" one of the uniformed members screeched. "That son of a bitch shot me!"

"Shut him up and take him down!"

Erik took off and a dull muffled shot ran out, cutting through the air, followed by a scream. He stiffened when he heard a body slumping onto the ground with a sick crack under pressure.

Erik felt pain splitting through his back after another shot followed, forcing him slamming onto the ground on his face. Invisible forces tapped Erik of energy, suddenly overcoming him with weakness.

Erik gagged and struggled to his knees, tasting liquid copper in his mouth. Dark outlines approached Erik's side as he coughed up blood, his body turning numb when their threads came from nowhere, grabbing him by the arms and legs, snapping him back and holding him suspended.

Erik fought out of their grip, struggling to breathe as the heaviness in his chest threatened to choke him to death and the holds binding him strengthened, threatening to break his limbs.

"Let him go!" another faraway voice screamed Erik faintly recognized. "Please, don't hurt him, I beg of you!"

"We've got orders, Doctor Fleisher!" came back the reply. "Tend to Doctor Schumacher..."

"*Gerald Schumacher!*" Erik thought and the memories came flooding back at once. Before he could focus on one memory, shocking warmth assaulted his being and Erik cried out as it coursed through his back, sending him crashing into the earth.

His world abruptly dropped beneath him, erased by a blinding red-out. The bindings became heavier, turning metallic as more darkness whipped forward, winding tightly around his waist, chest and neck. Vertigo struck Erik hard, leaving him floating in his skull, unable to touch the ground.

The surrounding reddened world began filling with a faint blue light as brushed titanium and buzzing blue-plate lights slowly came into view. Erik strained to see the environment's full view, hurting his neck while looking about with limitation, trying to figure out where he was.

Seeing what supported him, Erik realized he stood suspended with wrists and ankles locked in cold steel harnesses holding him over darkness with no clear bottom.

He looked up at the murkiness overhead reflecting a soft orange light off the interior and heard a low hum penetrating the room. Erik let out a piercing scream when a frigid iron probe jammed into the back of his neck.

"What are you doing?" he wailed.

Not again...!

Erik received no reply as a high whine filled the room and the bright blue-white lights changed intensity, reflecting heat back at him when they turned fierce reddish-orange. He screamed louder when he felt more steel needles jam through his ears, dispersing the echoing sound of his anguished shriek.

Another probe touched the base of his skull while six more slowly went through his head, barely touching bone. Erik suddenly lost his sight; everything quickly switched to excruciating darkness as all seven shoved through at the same time.

CONTINUED IN BOOK TWO:

DANGEROUS METHODS

Erik Hart thought he knew who he was, but everything – his name, his family, his school, his life... It becomes nothing, as if his whole world had been erased!

After confronting someone who seems to know him and his past at the research hospital, Erik's life takes a deviant turn that may break his world altogether.

At what price would he pay for peace of mind?

Will he be able to overcome his penchant for trouble?

Will he uncover the facts before it's too late?

Searching for the truth nearly pushes Erik off the edge of sanity, as every answer only leads to more questions...